To Find a Hero

By

A.G. Thompson

Chromosphere Press
Huntsville, AL

Contents

Chapter One

**Vlymouth Port, Duchy of Hale,
Kingdom of Montagar
KRN *Intrepid*
September 1478, Third Age of Imperial Reckoning**

"Well, this is it. As soon as you walk down the gangplank, you'll have reached the goal you set yourself a year and more ago. Are you ready?" Silaqui smiled at Sachi as she slung a small leather bag over her bare shoulder.

"I'm not sure yet." Sachi leaned against the bulkhead and gently stroked a frame timber. "*Intrepid* has become more of a home to me than anything in Kodak Prefect ever was. But I know I can't stay on board. But *where* did you get that outfit? Have you no shame?"

"I'm an Elf and this is my homeland. I'll dress as I please and anyone's opinion otherwise can go whistle." The clothing in question left a good deal of lightly tanned Elvish skin on display. A necklace halter left back and shoulders bare under a heavy silk cloak casually slung over her left shoulder. The front of the top molded very tightly against her high breasts and flat stomach before disappearing under the skirt. A short, snug skirt, reaching barely to the knee, brushed against high leather boots. A dagger jutted from a sheath in one boot, another hung at her hip. The entire ensemble was in eye-searing shades of scarlet, crimson and deep reds. Rubies glinted at her earlobes and a star ruby the size of a robin's egg shone at her throat. "And before you ask where all this came from, the only answer I'll give you is magic. That's why my leather satchel is no larger than it is, yet holds all of my possessions." Silaqui smiled and the gems tattooed over her left eyebrow shone with an inner light. There was a bright, excited gleam in her jade green eyes; her vertically slit pupils were wide open in excitement. "I've restrained my powers long enough. This is Montagar, not Kolbia." A barely seen crimson aura shimmered around the sorceress.

"Damned showoff." Sachi muttered under her breath. Her own clothing was mundane, practical and plain. A sturdy brown leather jacket covered an ordinary tan muslin shirt, the shirt perhaps a bit snugger than she would have preferred. Durable leather trousers were just tight enough to not catch on things, but loose enough to let her move. Dark gray, they matched her ankle boots and shouldn't show too much dirt. Out of sight under the jacket, her butterfly swords hung down her spine, hilts down, clipped securely into their sheaths. Her thick, waist-length black hair was braided and swirled into a bun. Holding the mass in place were slim throwing spikes, not hair pins. Throwing knives and kill-stars were concealed, tucked away in various places. Her braided wire garrote was tucked up one sleeve and a pair of fighting knives hung concealed under each armpit, their sheaths tied to the swords' harness. A single dagger, fourteen inches of razor-sharp steel, hung openly on her belt. A much larger backpack rested on the deck. "Are all Elves like you?"

"Are all Nisei women like you?"

"Of course... not."

"Well, then, there's your answer." Silaqui sighed, running her hands through her grass green hair, shaking its mass loose around her shoulders and down her back. "I think we've given them long enough to prepare whatever grand send-off the good Captain has in mind." Silaqui watched the emotions chase themselves across Sachi's face, love, longing and loss plain to see. Unshed tears glittered in the young woman's eyes. "Sachi? Are you all right?"

"I'm fine," she snapped. "Let's be going."

"Well, at least until we're off the ship, let me get that for you." With a raised eyebrow and the twitch of a finger, Sachi's pack vanished into Silaqui's satchel.

"HEY!" Her grab for her pack was too little, too late. "What are you doing? I can carry that!"

"I know, but without it, you can run away from Captain Blaine, Toby and the rest of your friends onboard faster."

"For a dear friend, you can be very cruel."

"Humans have said that about Elves from time to time."

***

Sachi stopped and stared in astonishment as the Bosun's whistle shrilled when she stepped onto the main deck. *Intrepid's* Marines, sharply turned out in their green coats and white trousers, snapped to attention at Major Karlson's snapped, "TEN-HUTT!" Gun crews stood at attention next to their guns and the tops-men lined the main yard. The ship's officers and midshipmen stood at the boarding port, Toby standing at the beginning of the line, Blaine last and next to the gangplank to the dock. Silaqui swept past Sachi with a joyful laugh, crimson flames flaring as high as the main yard around her. The fire died down, guttering away as she reached the line of *Intrepid's* officers.

Senior Midshipman Johan Weiss's eyes were huge at the display of magical power. The tow-headed young man recently hit a growth spurt and now he was nearly tall enough to look the sorceress in the eye. He swallowed hard as she stopped before him.

"Johan, you've become a fine young man. Your parents are proud of you, you know? So is your captain. Fare thee well, my once and future friend." She leaned forward and kissed him gently on the cheek. She smiled as he blushed beet red, before stepping away to face Ensign Tom Anderson, *Intrepid's* new Fourth Lieutenant. "'Tis too short a journey we have had together, Tom. Fare thee well, my new-found friend." Again, the kiss on the cheek. She continued down the line of officers with smiles, kind words and gentle kisses on the cheek until she came to Surgeon Commander Hoff. "Doctor Hoff. Elazar."

"Lady Silaqui."

"I owe thee my life, almost as much as I owe my heart-sister." Her right hand glowed scarlet as she raised it to touch his forehead. There was a brief, bright flare. "Any of my folk that might see thee shall behold my mark upon thy brow. By my mark, they shall know thee as thrice blessed, a true healer and an Elf-friend. From this day forth, should thou doubt thyself, think back on this, my blessing to thee, and follow thy heart. Never will it lead thee astray. 'Tis my gift to thee." She gave him an impish smile. "This, however, is for mine ownself." She wrapped herself around him and her aura flared as she kissed him well and thoroughly. It lasted long enough that the Bosun growled as seamen began to murmur and chuckle.

***

Sachi had stopped next to Toby, just before the line of officers. She gave an infinitesimal shake of her head and a nearly silent sigh at Silaqui's extravagance. Toby smiled and rolled his eyes.

"Damned showoff," she mumbled quietly.

"Aye. Or be ye jealous?" Toby whispered to her.

"Of her? Of course... not."

"And now?" Toby's subtle head nod returned her attention to the Elf as she left a smiling but befuddled Hoff and stepped to stand before Captain Blaine.

"Captain William Blaine." The playful tone in her voice was gone. "As much as any, I owe thee my life. The path before thee is harsh and hard, difficult and demanding. Persevere through troubled times and 'tis my fondest wish and belief that thou shall find thine own path to what paradise Mortals may find on this Fallen world." She stepped forward and gave him a gentle embrace and demure kiss on the cheek. "More than this, I think," she whispered in his ear, "and Sachi will be wanting to use her arsenal on me." She raised her voice as she released him. "My friend and companion, fare thee well. Come home safe again to those you love and to those who love you."

With a smile, she stepped to the boarding portal and turned, looking to Sachi. Again, crimson flames engulfed her as she raised her arms above her head. She threw her head back and sang magic, her pure voice enrapturing everyone on board. She held a pure, high note as a scarlet wave swept outwards from her, washing over the entire ship.

"By my Power and by my Will, with my Magic and my Heart, I bless this vessel and all aboard her. Gods of my Folk watch over her and them, in their coming and their going, be they blessed in all things." The last notes of her song faded away. Her aura flickered a final time and faded away, the Sorceress in her full power again concealed and now only an Elven maid clad in scarlet stood at the top of the gangplank. She bowed to them. "Sachi, make thy farewells in thine own good time. I shall await thee quayside." She turned and walked sedately down the gangplank, pausing to give the two Marine guards at its end each a brief peck on the cheek before walking calmly down the dock.

Sachi felt her face burn as everyone's attention turned to her. Toby stepped back and walked behind the line until he stood next to Captain Blaine. Silence settled over the deck like the densest fog. The cries of seabirds and the hustle and bustle of the busy dockworkers were distant, muted, enhancing the silence by their very ordinariness.

"There is no need for this. I am neither *Kami* nor magic-wielder. At most, I am naught more than a ship-mate, a former fellow sailor of the *Intrepid*. And now, not even that. Please, I should simply leave quietly and with no fanfare. I am of no worth…"

"That will be enough of that nonsense, Apprentice Seaman Takahashi!" Paul Beauchamp, the ship's Bosun, growled as he stepped out to face her. "Ten-HUTT!" Sachi reflexively snapped to. The Bosun pulled a brassard emblazoned with the anchor and chevron of the Kolbian Navy out of his pocket and wrapped it around her right arm. "Effective this date, the twenty-fifth of September, the fourteen hundred and seventy-eighth year of the third age of Imperial Reckoning, one hundred and fifty-three years from the founding of the Republic of Kolbia; I, Master Chief Petty Officer Paul Beauchamp, senior enlisted man aboard KRN *Intrepid*, Ship's Boatswain, bestow on you, Sachi Takahashi, the permanent rank of Able Seaman of the Kolbian Navy. Your body may not be aboard *Intrepid*, but you have worked and fought, sweated and bled on her deck and your spirit will always have a home here. Carry on, Able Seaman." Beauchamp snapped to attention, his blue eyes suspiciously bright. He nodded sharply in approval once, and stepped back.

In a daze, Sachi made her way down the line of midshipmen and officers. Some, the newer ones, she did not know as well, and she found she missed Harry Caplin's stern mannerisms. She came at last to Doctor Hoff and started to salute.

"Here now, none of that, lass. No one salutes a physician, not even a Marine." Elazar stepped forward and wrapped his arms around her. For a heartbeat, she froze, and then she relaxed and hugged him back. "Take care of yourself and of that silly Elf. I don't think she's the sense to come in out of the rain. And be careful, I won't be around to patch you up the next time you do something foolish...and heroic."

"I shall be careful. May the Ancestor Spirits bless and protect you." She smiled as she stepped back. "May they especially protect you from your bets on racehorses."

"Just had to go there, didn't you?" His pale green eyes were bright with unshed tears.

"Of course." She stepped away and turned to Toby, standing next to Blaine. There were already tears on his cheeks. "*Saiai no yujin,* beloved friend, no, please, do not cry for me." Toby simply stepped forward and buried her in his arms. Effortlessly, he lifted her from the deck.

"The Captain cannot cry, not here," he whispered in her ear. "So, I cry for both of us. I hate to see you leave. *He* hates to see you leave. This is your place, here on *Intrepid's* deck, with your friends and those who love you. A place your own hard work has earned for you. Not following that cat-eyed Elf while she wanders around like a lost dog."

"Oh, Toby," she whispered back, her own tears spilling, dampening her jacket and his shirt. "It's not just Silaqui. I can't stay. There's something waiting for me, a destiny only I can fulfill. And not seeking it out will have a dreadful price. I have to go. I must. Please, please, *yujin*, please, my friend, don't make this harder than it must be." She kissed him gently, first on the cheek, then a brief kiss on his rough lips. When she gently pushed against his shoulders, he released her.

With a deep breath, she turned to face the last person in the line. *Captain William Blaine.* My Captain. *Oh, Ancestors, he is so striking, beautiful in his blue coat, the slightest hint of silver in hair as coal black as my own. Oh, Ancestors, why, when I finally find someone I can love, someone I do love, why is that someone one who cannot, does not, dares not love me back? A man of true honor, who keeps his oaths and vows.*

"Captain Blaine, Able Seaman Takahashi requesting permission to depart *Intrepid's* company and go ashore." She bowed deeply to him, head down, a full *saikeirei* of respect. She held it for a long three count and then rose up. She was astonished to see him rising up from his own *saikeirei* to her. Her control nearly broke. "*My Captain*, please, I am not worthy..."

"I know no one more worthy, Sachi. Nor more beautiful." Blaine's voice was tight and controlled as he interrupted her. His eyes burned with unshed tears. "Permission to depart the ship's company and go ashore granted. We sail on the dawn tide. There'll be a berth for you aboard if you wish. There'll always be a place for you." *A place in my heart that I think no one else can ever fill. When did being faithful and honoring my vows become a scourge on my soul?* He blinked and realized Sachi was holding a perfect salute where she stood before him. He came sharply to attention and returned the salute with parade ground precision. "Carry on, Able Seaman."

"Aye, sir." She dropped her salute and turned to the gangplank, nearly stumbling as her tears started, half blinding her.

"THREE CHEERS FOR ABLE SEAMAN SACHI TAKAHASHI!" roared the Bosun, "Hip, hip!"

"Hooray!"

"Louder! Hip, hip!"

"HOORAY!"

"INTREPIDS! I CAN'T HEAR YOU! HIP, HIP!"

"HOORAY!!" The last cheer practically blew her down the gangplank. She almost stumbled again before she got her feet under her and then, back straight, head held high despite the tears filling her eyes, she marched neatly down the gangplank, saluted the Marine guards and turned sharply up the dock. In moments those on *Intrepid* lost her in the crowds of the waterfront.

***

A white-haired old man perched on a piling, dangling hook and line in the water. Catching lunch would leave him more money for beer. He frowned as Sachi marched past him. The hullabaloo and commotion on the big frigate's deck likely scared away the fish so he watched the beautiful young woman walk past. *Able Seaman!? What the hell? If yon beauty is a sea-MAN, then I'm a mermaid!* He snorted and lifted his hook. The bait was gone. He pulled another bug out of his can of bait. *Demned light fingered fish!* He watched Sachi disappear down the dock. *I alus knewed Kolbians were a bit more than a might strange, but THAT was no* man! *What, exactly, I wonder, is it they put in their ship's grog? Perhaps I should see if I could enlist?* The bug, impaled on the hook, plunked into the water. This bug was no luckier than the last one.

But then, the fish that snapped it up and got caught on the hook wasn't so lucky either.

Chapter Two

**Oasis of Alma al'Aswad,
Darsälaamic Kaliphate, Northern Khakal
Mid-July, 1459, Third Age of Imperial Reckoning**

"I BEGIN TO BELIEVE that we have not only entered the lion's den, *Sayyid*, but we may have stuck our heads into the lion's mouth." Kanaan Rahim glanced at his chieftain watching the invaders through a Kolbian-made spyglass. The fires of a full Imperial Pike Regiment flickered and danced around the Alma al'Aswad oasis. "There are ten thousand of those infidel dogs down there, ready to march at first light on Abdul-Ghaffanse."

"Hmm-um." *Sayyid* Hasim al Murafte, *Faris* of Chalta, closed the spyglass and spider-crawled away from the ridgeline before sliding down the dune, Kanaan following him. "It's not a full Regiment, Kanaan. They've only half the skirmishers they should have, and I'd say most of their Battals are perhaps as much as a company of Pike short. Still, that leaves them a good eight thousand."

"Wonderful. You take the four thousand on the left and I'll take the four thousand on the right?" The desiccated sand was not as dry as Kanaan's sarcasm. "If you get yourself killed being a hero, Haipha will have me flayed. Alive. Slowly. You dying out here is not something that will endear me to your loving wife. You haven't been married a moon yet."

"What, you don't plan on laying down your life for your chieftain?" White teeth flashed as Hasim grinned through his neatly trimmed beard.

"I'd rather not but you know I would if need be." Kanaan returned the grin. "Although, if I do die out here, Haipha won't be able to kill me herself."

"Don't be so sure. She might find a Jinn or a sorcerer to raise you from the dunes."

"Humpf." Kanaan gave Hasim a hand up as they reached the bottom of the dune. "Maybe the *ghula* will get me first. Not sure which would be worse?"

"Oh, no question there." Hasim swept up the reins of his horse as he swung into the saddle. "An enraged Haipha would undoubtedly be the worst of those two fates."

"*Sayyid*, the Imperials outnumber us four or five to one. We can bedevil and raid them, but we cannot stop them. Not with the eighteen hundred men we have."

"No, Kanaan, you're right. We can't stop them by ourselves. I know this, my friend. So, we shall have to get some help, now, won't we? And I know who can help." Hasim raised his right hand, an iron ring gleaming dully on his forefinger.

"Oh, no! Not that! Not him! You can't!"

"Who else can we turn to? Ilben alh-Taymyah, properly propitiated, might be the equal of ten thousand by himself. And I won't ask him to do the job. I'm only intending to ask for just enough help to turn that invading host of infidels away. No more."

"My Lord Hasim, please reconsider. Master, he is a Jinn. No mortal can truly trust one of the Jinni." Kanaan bowed low over his horse's withers.

"I never said I was going to trust him. Just...ask him nicely for a little help. And no need to go all formal on me. My Father-the-Sheikh Murafte al Aziz, Chalta bless his name, is vigorous and healthy. It shall be some time before I might earn his title and truly lead our tribe."

***

A bluish mist emanated from the plain iron ring as Hasim turned it around and around on his right forefinger. It swirled away, growing and thickening as it moved. A final swirl and the mist vanished. In its place, there stood a person of indeterminate age. Thick, black hair was neatly trimmed, as was the short beard. He was not particularly tall while not exactly being short. He was neither thin nor fat. But no one could have ignored the toned, dark blue skin of his bare, muscular torso and bulging biceps. Or his startling blue eyes, eyes so blue they could only be compared to sapphires. He bowed deeply to Hasim.

"Your command, O' my Master?"

"Jinn Ilben alh-Taymyah, greetings. Many thanks and the blessings of Chalta be upon you." Hasim acknowledged the deep bow with a gentle nod. "I have no command for you, old friend. I only ask your help. Once again, the People of the Sands are assailed by the Lietelean Empire. We cannot stop them alone."

"Master, you know you can simply command my aid."

"Yes." Hasim sighed. "I know. And I know that your nature will twist and pervert any command I might force upon you. Therefore, I ask only your willing help."

"Master, I am only a Jinn of the Second Rank of Air and Wind. I do not have the powers of the great nobles of my kind." The Jinni crossed his arms and brought a hand up to tug on his beard as he thought. "I am bound by more rules than they, but I would hesitate to call on their aid. Few, if any, of the Great Ones have any love for mortal humans."

"What can you do, then?"

"Hmm. I can do much, but that depends..."

"On what, Jinn Ilben?"

"On what it will cost you. What you are willing to pay."

"To save my people, I would pay any cost."

"Truly? *Any* cost, *Sayyid* Hasim? Your life? You have no brothers, no son and your father is too old to beget more children. Your line would end here, then. Would you pay that?"

"If I must. My line would live on in my people." Hasim waited an eternity as the Jinn was lost deep in thought.

"I may not ask such a cost. But I find that there is a cost that MUST be asked. And you MUST concede this to me. If you do not, eventually, but not within a man's long lifetime, the squabbles of the Empire with the People of the Sands, indeed all the concerns of all the world entire, shall become as dust in the whirlwind, of no matter at all to anyone ever again."

"What do you mean by that, Jinn Ilben?"

"I am constrained from speaking further." The Jinn straightened and grew as he filled the night sky before Hasim, looming tall in the darkness, blotting out the stars. Hasim held his ground as he heard Kanaan swear in fear behind him. Ilben's voice boomed out, shaking Hasim to his bones. "This is your price and you MUST pay it or condemn all to destruction. You must give the Ring that summons me to your new wife. She has not yet quickened with your seed. For a year and a day, she shall summon me to her daily. I shall woo her and love her and give her a daughter. You shall love and cherish your wife and the daughter of our union. Haipha shall have the rule of the daughter's training, for the girl shall have a great task before her."

"All this? And what in return, Jinn?"

"In return, I shall turn the Imperials away; drive them into the desert sands. Lions shall pull them down, scorpions sting them, vipers poison them. The *ghula* and the *shiqq* shall feast on their corpses. Not one in ten will return to tell the tales of the true terrors of the deep desert." The awful, looming presence vanished as Ilben shrank once again to mere mortal seeming. "And you will be beloved of your people, reign well in as much peace as any man might expect in what will be troubled times. You shall live long and happily with your beloved Haipha and have many fine sons and daughters. But Haipha's first daughter, the child of our union, shall be the First Daughter of your people. In due time, you shall send her forth, perhaps to wed. A beauty beyond compare, she must not spend her life sheltered always in the harem. I lay only this geas on you regarding her. As a Jann, born of Mortal and Jinn, she must Bond to a Mortal human by her eighteenth birthday, else she shall be reclaimed by me, her true Sire."

"You ask much, Ilben. Very much." Hasim sighed. "Is there no other course?"

"No." The Jinn's smile was grim. "If you do not wish to pay my price, well, then, command me, O' my Master, and your Slave shall exert his feeble powers as best he might to prevent the Imperials from burning Abdul-Ghaffanse to the ground. And slaughtering everyone living within. Except those they would rape to death or sell into slavery. But I am only a Jinn of the Second Rank. My magic is not strong."

"Your magic not strong? Not hardly, Jinn Ilben. But strength comes at a cost, I see." Hasim's eyes were dark. He gave a deep sigh and straightened his shoulders, meeting the sapphire gaze of the Jinn. "Very well. I shall meet your price. And I shall love Haipha's daughter as my own. What shall she be named, my friend?"

"She shall be named Sahla al Qasim, my Master. Among the Jinn of the Air, Qasim means beautiful." The Jinn's smile was broad and relieved. "Now let us go and see to those infidel invaders. These Imperials have a nasty lesson coming to them."

Chapter Three

**Vlymouth Port, Duchy of Hale,
Kingdom of Montagar
September 1478, Third Age of Imperial Reckoning**

"Thanks for the lift, my friend. I enjoyed your tales. Perhaps you should be a bard and not a teamster?" Pere Gelman Stavor lifted his pack off the hook on the wagon's side and slung it over his back.

"Nah, thankee, Pere Gelman. Got nae talent fer plucking strings er sawing on a fiddle. And the work's nae near as steady." The grizzle haired old man gave Gelman a toothy grin before spitting over the other side of the freight wagon. "But I's right glad ye's took a likin' to me yarns. Having a body to speak at passes the time. Better than starin' at the team's behinds all day. And in a tavern, I'd like as not drink up all my earnings afore I reached the door."

"True, a good point, I guess," Gelman laughed as he hung his mace on his belt. "Well, good fortune then, and be blessed by the One God." Gelman waved as the man slapped the reins to get his team moving again. The big freight wagon headed down the out-road circling most of Vlymouth's sprawling suburbs. Heavy freight went around the city proper to reach Dock's Road, rather than through the narrow and crowded streets of walled Old Town. The setting sun gilded the mass of tiled and shingled roofs leading down to the sea. He considered requesting a room in one of the local churches, but he had enough and plenty of coin in his pouch to afford better than plain food and a hard bed.

"Besides, somehow, I doubt a tall, black-eyed woman from the uttermost East will be looking to stay in a House of the One God," he muttered to himself as he stretched and secured his belongings. A seaport city like Vlymouth would be rife with pickpockets, smash-and-grab rogues and look-at-that men. His robes and holy symbol would not be likely to deter such, but the plain and well-worn mace at his belt might do so. "Hmm, where first? The Harbormaster's Office will be closed for the night by the time I could get there, so I'd guess a not-too-expensive inn closer to the docks and wharves. Hopefully one where the food and the beer aren't too bad." He lifted his hat and scratched his tonsured light brown hair. "And preferably, no bed bugs." With a shrug and a smile for a pair of passing City Guardsmen, he headed down the road towards the harbor.

***

Damnit. The bastard's nae coming out. Again. Ye'd think he'd at least want better food and some beer if nothing more...interesting. Aylie Clayton loitered next to a scruffy, somewhat smelly person of indeterminate age and sex, gnawing on a dried apple she'd just bought off said individual's shop-tray. The sign on the building across the street read *Imperial Road Trading Company, Ltd.* It was well lettered and new, even if the building itself was a bit run down. But then, everything in this part of Dockside was more than a bit dilapidated. Much like the apple seller.

Despite watching the building closely the last two days, the only person she'd seen coming or going had been a rather rabbity little man in a shabby old coat ten years out of style, obviously a clerk at best. She knew someone else was in there, someone who apparently lived upstairs above the offices and rarely, if ever, left. Of course, the building did back right up to the wharves, the last quarter or so of it being built actually over the harbor water itself. *Beauty place fer a neat bit a' smuggling ta 'void the Customs shills.*

Just ratty enough ta look poor, but nae bad enough ta get the wrong kinds uv attention. Grr. Milady'd be more than a bit miffed that I'm even thinking *in cant these days.* She hid a sigh and tossed the well gnawed remains of the apple into the gutter. *Was nae that many years gone, I'd've et the whole thing, seeds and all. Be full dark soon and I'd best be moving if I'm ta see if the skylights I saw last night be locked up as tight as the rest uv this damn place is. No idea how they've got all the doors and winders, even the second story ones, shut down so tight. First time ever I could nae find a loose sill ta slip a wipe inta and pop open.*

Three hours later, she had her answer. Three of the four skylights were bagged down just as tight as every other door and window, *but* the last was open. An iron bar propped it fully open, gaping like a well set coney snare. And that likeness to a snare raised an appropriate wariness in her. The sloping, tiled roof let her get close enough that she could lie flat next to the coaming and hear everything being said in the room. If she was careful, she could just peek over the edge and see into the room. But the moon was full tonight and there was enough light that the silhouette of her head might be seen. There was an eerie blue light shining out of the skylight. It had come on about five minutes ago. And now she could hear voices. She had no idea where the second man came from. An initial quick glance had revealed a smallish bedroom and a large desk with an odd-looking cabinet sitting on it. Next to the cabinet, a strange round disk stood on three short legs, a thin rod in the center pointed at the open skylight. A man of medium build with short dark hair sat in the room's single chair, fiddling with something she could not see. He was the only occupant.

"Damn it, Ignacio, what were you thinking? Trying to bribe an Irsmelder clan noble? Then threatening him? Even for Montagarans, the Irsmelder clansmen are close-knit and stubborn." The new voice had a strange, tinny timbre to it. She had not heard anyone come into the room. "You've already far exceeded your orders and you know it." The voice had an Imperial accent to it, its Terranglais clipped and harsh.

"So what, Vicente?" the man in the room snarled. "I'm a Palmaroli, same as you. Maybe being the Imperial Governor's Majordomo has gone to your head. I'll be damned and burning in Quan's Hell before I'll call you *Higher!*"

"Damn it, Ignacio, DO NOT use my name over this thing!"

"Why not? I've been told over and over again that *They* can't listen to our talk-stream, any more than we can listen to theirs. And it doesn't seem to bother you to use MY name!"

"That's because you're mobile, you idiot! No one really knows who you are! If *They* decide to send a kill-team after you, you just stand up and walk away. Without any of the Eld Mechanisms, you're just a man walking down the street. I'm stuck here for now, unless the Clique either takes me Inside or I get a promotion within the Imperial Bureaucracy and move to Lietelea the City."

"Again, so what?" Ignacio sneered. "*They* won't use a hellburner or a worm on a city. Not that you'd leave your comforts, now, would you? Killing tens of thousands just to get you? Not *Their* style at all."

"No, but *They* might use an assassin. *They* have those guns that can hit a target a man can barely see." There was a certain weariness in the voice. "But if *They* don't know who I am and where I am, they can't use one of those damn things on me."

"Fine, damnit." Ignacio sighed. "I'm still not calling you Higher. It's late, I'm tired. What the hell is so important?"

"I want you to check on something for me, a follow up on something important. I lost my main agent in Carolington City in Kolbia a few months ago. His replacement is a vast improvement, even if a woman. But I'd assigned him a job and she said she'd been the one to actually do that job. And she *said* she was successful. Given her track record since, I tend to believe her, *but...*"

"Sounds like a big *but*...so what is it?"

"There was an incredible amount of Eld Mechanism talking streams a few weeks ago. Some of it even washed over onto the Clique's closed talk-stream! And of course, half of them are panicking. The effective ones tried to figure out what happened.

And they did." The tinny voice paused for a moment and she thought she heard a subdued sigh. "Those talk-streams were passing between the Shadow in space over the Lanic and something close to it down here. More volume than anyone ever remembers or that we have any records of. Ever."

"Did *They* manage to sneak one of their near invisible flying boats up to it?"

"Well, that's what most of the Clique think. Something we haven't seen before. Maybe something *They* found and fixed. *They* are better at that than we are."

"I take it you don't agree."

"No."

There was a long pause, and Aylie wondered if the conversation was over. She rose up and peered over the edge of the coaming. Ignacio sat in the lone chair front of the cabinet, which was now folded open. A square of blue light shone from the cabinet onto the middle of the desk. A man's head was projected into the blue light. He had a full head of what was probably black hair, in a short, Imperial braid, with a high widow's peak. Dark eyes and a neatly trimmed black beard showed a remarkable resemblance to the man in the room.

"So, what do you think it was, then?"

"My agent in Carolington reported on a woman who might be one of *Them*. Maybe. And if she is, I'm beginning to think she doesn't know what she is. She might be a newly awakened Sleeper. Don't ask me how, I'm guessing while way out on a limb here."

"And how, *Higher*, does this affect me?" Sarcasm dripped from Ignacio's voice.

"This woman, a young woman from Isemoto, of all the Godless places, arrived in Carolington on the Kolbian frigate *Intrepid*. A ship which was then transferred to their Lanic Fleet and..."

"And just arrived here, today." Ignacio rubbed his beard. "And passed through the Lanic when the Eld talking streams were so active. Well, I think I see your concern."

"You know how tough *Their* agents can be. It's just possible that this woman survived being poisoned with Vexarin, barely. So what I want from you is to check and see if she's onboard that damn Kolbian ship. If she is, kill her. Dead. I want to see her severed head sitting on this desk."

"You don't want her alive?"

"No. I've told the Clique she's dead. I need to make sure of that."

"Well. That is a mess. How will I spot her, other than the usual, she does have black eyes, right?"

"Yes, to the black eyes. And she's Nisei. Should stick out like a sore thumb. I know, I know, not much to go on. Only other things I know is that she's very tall for a Nisei woman, near two metres, has long, thick black hair and is beautiful. Beautiful enough to make even you give up abusing handsome young men."

"I have my...perversions, you have yours." Ignacio growled. "What are the limits here?"

"Do NOT blow up *Intrepid!* War with the Kolbians is coming soon enough, but we're not ready yet. The Dominorum of the Admiralty is starting to understand that nearly two thousand ancient galleys are worthless against the KRN. And the Lanic. So, we need the new ships being laid down to be completed first."

"Understood. If and I mean *if* this beautiful girl is on that damn ship, sooner or later she'll come ashore. Likely to get drunk or something. I'll get some muscle on it. Do I have clearance to use Eld weapons to kill her? Something simple?"

"Yes. Nothing more than a charged blade at most. You should have some of those, yes?"

"Not per se, but I've a white steel blade that'll take a charge. I'll give that to a couple of bully boys I know. And if she's there, I'll paper the town with fake *Wanted: Dead or Alive* posters. If nothing else, that should get some blackguard or bullyboy to scrag her."

"Good. Good, that should work just fin...what *the HELL!?* DAMNIT, you've a spy!" The man's projected head glanced up and looked Aylie square in the eyes.

Aylie ducked out of sight and scrambled frantically for the edge of the building. There was a SNAP-HISS from inside the room and something invisible burned a line *through* the tiled roof. Whatever it was, it brushed her left arm and she screamed in pain as it instantly burned shirt, skin and tissue away. She changed direction, sliding uncontrollably down the roof towards the harbor. The weapon, whatever it was, burned another line through the tiles but he hadn't expected her slide down-roof.

What the hell was that thing? She slid faster, gravity accelerating her towards the edge and the harbor below. *Oh, shit, shit, shit! Please, God, please let the water be deep enough I don't break my neck. Or my back, or my leg. Don't let me get stuck in the mud.* Another snap-hiss punched through the tiles, but further away, not closer. *If he can see me in the water, I am fucked.* Somehow, she managed not to scream as she shot off the edge of the roof and thirty feet out into the water. She sucked in as big a breath as she could and tried to hold as much as she could when she hit the harbor water. She twisted around, frog-kicking, trying to get as deep as possible. The water hissed and boiled as a solid beam of red light burned past where she had landed. *Whatever it is, I can see it underwater.* She stroked deeper and further away and the beam thrashed the water in the opposite direction, closer to shore. She got under a dock and was forced to come up for air.

She could see the man, Ignacio, silhouetted in the window, pointing something that looked like a short, sleek silver musket towards the other side of his building. The water boiled and sprayed but she saw no beam in the air and heard only the snap-hiss of the weapon. After a few moments, he gave up and stepped away from the window. She saw the blue light flicker and go out after another minute or so and then the building was dark and quiet.

"Well, Aylie, wot the hell have ye just gotten yourself inta now?" she muttered quietly as she swam to the edge of the wharf, out of sight of the offices of the *Imperial Road Trading Company, Ltd.* "But if this shit-stain does nae have *something* ta do with Milady's and the Duke's deaths, I'll eat naught but cobblestones, brekkie, nooning and dinner." She dripped down the wharf, back towards her cheap room. Her arm burned and she hissed in agony as she twisted it around to see how bad it was. It was bad, really bad, an ugly burn, the arm of her shirt burned neatly off and a long, gruesome gash blistered from elbow to shoulder. *Lucky me, somehow it sealed the wound; else I'd be bleeding to death. Given what that thing did ta the harbor water, I's thinking that's nae more than a near miss. Had it hit me square, I think I'd be short an arm.* It was a bad burn, sure to leave a memorable scar, but that'd be the worst. Unless infection set in. *Bloody damned lucky, I's. Leastwise, I hopes I's lucky.*

"Well, I think I's needing ta be after finding this beautiful Nisei girl. Any bully boys he sends I can follow back ta him. And then, I's can feed him his own testicles fer his brekkie, raw." She set her teeth against the pain of the wound and slipped carefully down an alley, wary of showing weakness. In the rough parts of town, showing weakness could bring the scavengers and predators out of their hiding holes.

***

Well, this is a complete bust. And God in his Heaven, what do they use to make that brew, cat-piss, old socks and gunpowder? Gelman smiled and waved at his recent and temporary drinking companions as he left the tavern. *I wonder how long my liver can take this before it throws a fit? Not to mention that I don't have enough money to buy every old fisherman, odd longshoreman or half-mad flotsam-and-jetsam man in Vlymouth three ales to oil them up enough to start talking. But how else am I supposed to find this woman?* He rubbed his face in the cool fall breeze to clear his head a bit. *That last one was more than a bit stuffy and close. Why do people do that to themselves?* Wondering if he was doing what the *Angaelici Benes Eloi* wanted him to do, he shook his head and headed down the dark street, working his way closer to the actual harbor. *Pretty soon, I'd better find a room somewhere or the Guard will be asking me pointed questions about vagrancy.*

A bit muzzy-headed from the alcohol, he wasn't paying much attention to where he was going when he rounded a sharp corner and ran right into a youngish man staggering up the street. The lad bounced off the armor hidden under Gelman's robes, and went down with a cry of pain. Gelman staggered a second before kneeling next to him, where he had curled up to protect his left arm. His workman's cap tumbled away, revealing short brown curls.

"Easy now, lad." Gelman laid a light hand on his shoulder, gently turning him to see what was wrong with the boy's left arm. He hissed in surprise at the deep and nasty cauterized wound on the arm. *That's a bad burn, real bad. It's not bleeding but it's already weeping fluids and I'll be astonished if he doesn't lose it to infection. And it's damn fresh.* "How'd this happen, boy? That's as bad a burn as I've ever seen. Do you have lodgings hereabouts? We need to get you inside somewhere so I can work on this."

"Who...is...ya?" he gasped in a faint voice.

"I'm Pere Gelman, lad. A healer priest of the One God. Let me help you, please."

"Argh. I've...room...Wayward Wave...Third Dock Street."

"I'm new here. Is that far?"

"Nae." Pant. "Three moir...streets ta...left, halfway...down."

Gelman had to listen closely to the gasped directions. Obviously, this injury was very recent and he was fairly certain the young man was in shock. *Well, traumatic wounds aren't exactly my specialty, but if I can get him to rest comfortably, I believe the* Benes Eloi *might grant me healing for this wound. What did this to him, I wonder?* Gelman grunted as he picked up the young man. *Least he's not too heavy. Now, Third Dock Street should be that way, if he gave me the right direction.*

***

Aylie opened her eyes to the poorly plastered ceiling of her cheap room at the Wayward Wave. She frowned. *I nae remember getting back here. I think I ran into someone, didn't even see them in the dark. What happened ta me?* She moved and suddenly realized that the burning agony of her left arm was gone, completely gone as if it had never happened at all. She slid her right hand up her arm and found only smooth, unblemished skin.

"Eh, wot in hell? Did's I dream last night?" She sat up in her rough bed and somehow managed not to even squeak when she saw the man sleeping in the room's one rickety chair. He wore the robes and symbol of a Kythal priest. A little bit taller than average, she thought, his hands suggested a good deal of strength. "Bloody, bleedin' hell. Who're ye?" With a start, his head came up and he smiled as his clear grey eyes met her brown ones.

"Ah, good, you're awake."

"Wot're ye doing in me room? Wot happened last night? Did I dream it?"

"If you're referring to that very nasty burn on your left arm, no, you didn't dream it. That was as ugly a burn as any I've ever seen. Mind telling me what did that to you?"

"Wot burn? I didnae have any burn. Get outs me room!" she snapped at him. "I's nae that kinda gurl!"

"Funny, last night, you were dressed as a young man and no girl of any kind. And yes, you had as bad a burn as I've ever seen. Had I not prayed to the *Angaelici Benes Eloi* for healing for you, well, I think that by this time next week, you'd have either been dead of the incipient infection you had brewing away in that arm, or if you were very lucky, you'd have been having some drunken old sawbones or a horse leech take the arm off. At the shoulder. Who knows if you'd have survived that shock?" He held up her tattered and scorched shirt. "And here's the proof I'm *nae hauling a fibbling at ye.* Least, I think that's how it'd go in the cant of the streets." He smiled at her, a nice friendly smile, the smile of an honest priest of the One God, a priest worthy of one's trust. "So, let's start over. I'm Pere Gelman Stavor, a devotee of the *Angaelici Benes Eloi*, blessed, at times, with the gift of healing. And some few other small magics, from time to time. And you are who, young lady?"

"Alice Clayton, Pere. I'm usually called Aylie. Nae one calls me Alice, not even Milady." Aylie's eyes went round and she clapped her hands over her mouth. *That was NOT what I meant to come out of my mouth! Has he drugged me somehow?*

"No, Aylie, I've not drugged you." He shrugged. "However, my time is valuable and rather than spend days beating around the bush and trying to decide if we can trust each other, I've set a spell at work in here. Yes, a magic spell, one of those *some few other small magics* I mentioned. This spell only makes one speak the truth if one speaks. It functions equally on both of us, therefore neither of us can lie to the other, at least for the next few moments, say a quarter hour or so. If you concentrate on what I'm saying, you will understand that I only speak the truth."

"Bloody hell. Do the bloody bobbers know ye can do this?"

"Some do. It's not something that's advertised about, but if needs must, and the situation and crime serious enough, then yes, there are a few Peres of the One God that will and do work with the police. Personally, I've never done so. I'm a healer and my work as such considered more important."

"All right then. What's the difference between someone called Pere and all the other titles, Priest, Father, Bishop, you know?"

"My title is Pere because the One God has granted me the ability to wield divine magics. All other priests are very devout men devoted to their God but without magic in their souls."

"So then, this spell is from God?"

"After a fashion. The One God, be blessed, grants a small portion of his power to his servants, greater or lesser, in accordance with their ability. As a priest devoted to the *Angaelici Benes Eloi,* one of His Greater Servants, who some call the Archangel of Healing, I am granted a small portion of the *Angaelici's* power in the form of my magic, mostly in spells of healing. And, as I believe I mentioned, a *few other small magics*. Satisfied?"

"Aye, summwut."

"Now, turnabout is fair play, so I've a question for you." He held up a post bill. "Are you the one described herein, one *Alice Clayton, the bloody murderess of the Duke of Southdon?*"

"Dunno, I've not seen such a bill. Where'd ye get that?"

"Hmm, well, it says here that this *Alice Clayton*, about your size and height, similar in hair and eye coloring, is wanted in the Duchy of Southdon for murdering her employer, His Grace, Duke Cohens, his wife, Lady Elise Cohens, and all of their house servants, as well as a man named Trevor Smythe, a visitor to the Duke that day." Gelman handed her the bill and captured her gaze with his own. "Did you kill the Duke, Aylie?" he gently asked.

"Nae, I'd never hurt His Grace, God no, never! Especially not Milady! I loved Milady! She was so good to me! She made me her favored lady's maid; me, who was once nothing but a scruffy street brat! I'd've died to protect them!" Tears ran freely down her cheeks and dripped on the bill, her brown eyes huge. She clutched the handbill to her chest before she collapsed back into the bed's blanket, sobbing uncontrollably.

"I see." He frowned. *Never been all that good with weeping females, but it seems this one's more reason than most to weep.* "Well, as for where I got it, it was posted at the City Guard's watch station near the old Main Gate. I imagine it will be making the rounds soon enough."

"Aye, 'twill," she muttered from tear-soaked blankets.

"So, if you're not just running from the Guard, why are you here? Trying to escape the country?"

"Nae." She sniffled and coughed as she stopped weeping. "I's trying ta find the right bastard that *did* kill Milady. And the Duke. And all the others in his townhouse. They may have been naught more than servants and common, but they were my friends."

"I see. Please, continue."

"I don't remember most of that day. What I remember was waking up on the floor of Milady's sitting room. She was there, close 'nuff ta touch, stabbed ta death, and then..." The tears ran afresh as she described that day and many of the days since then to Gelman. "And then I guess'd I ran inta ye whiles I's trying ta get back here. And that's the truth, all of it. Yer own magicking should tell ye that."

"Hmm, quite a tale, Aylie." He leaned forward in the chair and rubbed his palms slowly together. "And that's the whole truth?"

"Aye, I tol' ye, 'tis naught but the truth. Yer spell telling ye I's fibbin?"

"Oh, no. The magic told me you spoke nothing but the truth. Least, it did as long as it lasted. You never noticed. And never stopped." He leaned back in the chair as she sat up in the nest of blankets she'd curled into while she told her story. "That spell expired about twenty minutes ago. You've been talking for over an hour."

"So's, ye believe me or is ye fer calling fer the bloody bobbers?"

"Oh, I believe you, Aylie." He gave her a quick smile as she relaxed. "The problem is, what do we do with what we know now? Unfortunately, if this *Ignacio* is who you're looking for, well, it'd be his word against yours in a law-court. And we both know what could happen there." He frowned and rolled his wooden Quartered Circle symbol between his hands. "And I've my own tale to tell you. You're certain the voice from the box described this woman with black eyes as he did?"

"Oh, aye. But who has black eyes?"

He caught and held her gaze. "Well, as I said, I've my own story to tell, so listen closely..."

***

"So, the Angel really appeared ta ye?" Aylie asked Gelman a half hour later.

"Yes," he shrugged, "but until I met you, I'd not the least idea where to truly start. Sleuthing forth secrets is hardly the usual thing for a Pere of the One God to be doing, especially a healer priest."

"Aye, so I'd say."

"And now we have this man, this Ignacio Palmaroli, who seems to have an interest in her as well. A lethal interest. Hmm." Gelman polished his symbol between his palms. "Just who is this woman with black eyes that has so many different folk interested in her for such very different reasons?"

"I know not, Pere Gelman," Aylie answered him, "but I'd wager I knows how we can find her if she be in Vlymouth at all."

"Do you now?" He smiled at her. "Well, then, perhaps we should be getting our breakfast and, thus fortified, set out to find the lady at the nexus of all these mysteries?" Aylie returned his beaming smile with a shy one of her own.

Chapter Four

**Vlymouth Port, Duchy of Hale,
Kingdom of Montagar
September 1478, Third Age of Imperial Reckoning**

SACHI WAS UP WELL before the sun. She hadn't slept well, the first night ashore and not in her hammock in her tiny, cramped cubbyhole in *Intrepid's* wardroom galley. She missed the motion of the ship and her sounds, the creak of the masts and rigging, the snap of the sails as she came about on a new tack, the ring of the ship's bell. Seawater hissing against her grey hull. The snores and grumbles of the crew. The subdued clatter of pans and pots as Toby prepared the Captain's breakfast. The feather bed was comfortable enough, but it wasn't *right*.

So, well before dawn, she rose and dressed, leaving a sleeping Silaqui in her own tumble of sheets and blankets in the other bed. She'd slipped, silent and unseen, out of Ye Olde Salts Inn and into the cool darkness. There was a good off-shore breeze blowing and she knew Captain Blaine would have *Intrepid* standing out of the harbor within the hour. Her great sails would unfurl, one after another, and between the wind and the outgoing tide, she might be making ten knots or better by the time she cleared the harbor's breakwater, greenish-white seafoam curling back from her cutwater.

She made her way to the waterfront and effortlessly climbed up the side of one of the taller buildings, a four-story warehouse. From its roof, she had an excellent view of the entire harbor and the sea beyond. *Intrepid* had already cast off, the small galley-tug spider-walking on her flashing oars away from the big frigate. She watched as the royal and t'gallant sails blossomed, stretched tightly to catch the wind, and *Intrepid* began to gather way as she trimmed her sails.

Sachi concentrated, using the abilities D.A.V.E. taught her, her vision leaping closer, until she could see the gold braid on the epaulets of Blaine's blue coat and the faint strands of silver in his black hair. He was intent on his task, conning *Intrepid* out of harbor and returning to her new home port at the great harbor of Stark Haven, the main naval base of the Republic of Kolbia's powerful navy. He did not smile as he gave orders to the lieutenants of his ship. But once she was well underway, standing out of the harbor, past the breakwater, all sails set, heeling to port under her pyramids of canvas, she saw him step to the taffrail and look back at the receding harbor. She knew he couldn't see her, perched on a dark roof in her dark clothing, the morning sun starting to rise behind the land. The ship was far enough away now that even she had to strain to see his face. But she could still see him well enough to read his lips.

"I'm sorry, Sachi," she read on those lips. "You deserve better."

"I love you, My Captain," she whispered in return. "I always will. But this is better, that we each follow our own paths." She stood on the roof until *Intrepid's* sails disappeared over the horizon. When even her enhanced vision could no longer make out the least hint of sail, she turned away from the sea and looked towards the risen sun. She wiped away her tears with the heel of her hand. Resolutely not looking back over her shoulder, she slid down the roof and swung from handhold to toehold until she reached the alley. With a shrug to settle her jacket, she returned to the Inn.

***

"So, there you are." Silaqui smiled at Sachi as she walked into the Inn's tavern. "You went out to see her leave, didn't you? Sit. Eat. If I know you at all, you probably will want three breakfasts." Sachi raised an eyebrow at the broad-shouldered, brown-haired man sitting with his back to her, a long blue coat slung carelessly over the chair back. "And look who I found this morning!" He rose and turned, pulling out a chair for her.

"What are you doing here, Lieutenant Commander Fleet?" she managed not to stutter as she sat down. "*Intrepid* left harbor about three hours ago."

"Hello, Sachi, it's nice to see you too. Won't you be seated?" Willis smirked at the surprise on the beautiful Nisei's face. "My orders attach me to the diplomatic mission here. *Intrepid* was simply the next ship leaving for Montagar."

"Where's your uniform?" Sachi asked as a server set a large plate of bacon and eggs in front of her. "You've let your hair grow out a bit, too."

"Well, I'm supposed to be a Cultural Affairs attaché now. Whatever that is." Fleet turned part of his attention to his own breakfast. "Admiral Carstairs wants me to *gain wider experience*; I think that's how he put it. So, no uniform or regulation hair cut while I'm here. I reported to the Envoy yesterday, soon as we tied up. I've been informed that they weren't expecting me until next month, so I must find my own quarters. He recommended Ye Olde Salts. And imagine how surprised I was when I came downstairs for breakfast and saw a familiar head of green hair." He waved his fork vaguely at Silaqui.

"I can imagine." Sachi answered dryly as she picked up her fork and set to work on the pile of scrambled eggs.

"At any rate, that's why I wasn't aboard ship yesterday when you and Lady Silaqui left. I knew they had a fairly elaborate farewell planned, but since I knew I'd be in the same town for a day or two at least, I bowed out of it." He sipped his coffee. "So, what are your plans now?"

"I'm not sure." Sachi caught and held Silaqui's jade eyes. "Silaqui wants me to go visit her people's Elders but I'm not so sanguine about that."

"Uncle will not kill you out of hand, Sachi."

"So you say. But, no, Silaqui, I will not go see your Elders. Not yet." She stopped eating, staring into an unseen distance for a long moment. "I've something important to do first."

"Oh, this is new, first I've heard of it." Fleet smiled at her. "What is it?"

"I don't know *what* it is, Willis. I only know I've a task awaiting me."

"How do you know that, Sachi?" Willis asked.

"A silver statue told me so in a dream."

"This is ridiculous." He snorted before chuckling a bit. "So, what's the task? Where are you supposed to go to do it?"

"Laugh if you like, Kolbian, but I saw Sachi in a dream when I was still a captive on that pirate ship, *Imperial Damnation*." Silaqui's face was cold and serious. "As an Elf and a Sorceress, I am doubly connected to magic's richness. A rich treasure created by the life of our World. It was a true dream, Willis, as true as any of your practicality and logic."

"You saw me in a dream, Silaqui?"

"Yes, Sachi." Her jade eyes grew hooded and dark. "You stood on the quarterdeck of a ship sailing on a sea of stars. I stood next to you. I think Willis was there as well. And there were others, but I know not who they were. A great beauty with eyes like sapphires. A priest of the One God. A slender, dark-skinned young woman. You bore something ancient and powerful inside you. You turned away an implacable Death, something that wanted to kill the world entire, not leave even memories of it. But the ancient presence inside you had its own purpose, a world without magic, without wonder. Without Elves or any other enchanted creatures.

You fought it, but were losing. We helped you, me and those others standing with you. Together, we stopped the ancient one, made it reconsider. It started to speak, but I don't know what it would have said."

"Why not?" Willis had stopped eating while Silaqui related her dream.

"Je'Libe and Thorne slammed the door of my cell open and woke me. I raged at them and Je'Libe, I think, kicked me in the head and then I knew no more."

"Humpf. Dreams." Sachi continued to work steadily through her second plate of bacon and eggs. "Why didn't you tell me this sooner?"

"I tried, when we were on the Horn Islands, but every time I thought to bring it up, something happened to distract me."

"Figures. Well, dear friend, if you have any dreams that might tell me where to start my task or where to go to do it, it would make life much simpler for me," Sachi growled. "How about you, Willis? Have any dreams?"

"No," Fleet leaned back in his chair, "well, nothing like that anyways." He paused. "So what will you do next?"

"Don't know yet." Sachi smiled at the server as she set down a plate full of pancakes. "Thank you." She grabbed a bottle of syrup from the center of the table and liberally doused the pancakes before diving in, eating quickly while she thought out loud. "Probably see about buying some camping gear today, then check and see if any ships are going south. I think I need to get far away from civilization, learn some new things. Maybe explore some of the oldest places of man, places the legends say the Emperor Confas ruled from. I'm not going to just sit here and get fat, and no, Silaqui, I'm not going to go see your Uncle, unless you can convince me it's the best thing to do, and I doubt you can even truly convince yourself of that."

"True enough, I think." Silaqui sighed as Sachi wolfed down the last of the pancakes. "You should be the size of a barn. Where does it go?"

"Well, Doctor Hoff said I have a high metabolism. Maybe that's it," she grinned. "But here, I should be safe. Even my fa...my enemies from Isemoto will have great difficulty stretching their reach this far. Right, Willis?"

"I'm guessing, tacking off a lee shore here, but I'm guessing you got into some kind of trouble with Clan Ishikawa, back in Isemoto. If so, yes, I'd say you're pretty much out of their reach here."

"Close enough, Willis, close enough. So, for today, Silaqui, we go shopping?"

"Certainly. I love merchants dancing attendance on me. I guess we'll see you this evening, Willis. I assume you've tasks at the Kolbian mission? If you talk your way into coming with us, we'll make you pay for everything and then carry everything." Silaqui gave him a wicked grin.

"Well, I've nothing else to spend my munificent salary on." Willis shrugged. "And I've a certain amount of allowed expenses. And the idea of being seen about town with not one but two such beautiful women, well, for that, I'd be happy to play pack mule."

"Ancestors preserve me." Sachi finished her coffee, mopping up the last of the syrup with a piece of toast. "I'd almost think you've nothing better to do than follow us around."

"Well, at the moment, Sachi, that's pretty much the truth." Willis shrugged and grinned disarmingly. *I need to remember just how smart this girl is or she'll tie me in a nice bow knot if she catches me in one lie too many.*

"So, then, if Sachi's done stuffing herself, let's take advantage of Willis' offer and go see what the merchants hereabouts might have to offer. And we can check at the Harbormaster's Office and see what ships are departing for the Traquilidamar Sea fairly soon."

"The Traquilidamar Sea?" Sachi quirked an eyebrow at the Elf. "What's that?"

"It's the inland sea between the continent of Northern Uirsen and the continent of Khakal. Northern Uirsen is divided between the Lietelean Empire, the Royal Imperium of the Kzar of Muskovia, the Deuschen Empire, and a few Heimdägarran pirate fiefs in the extreme north. If you cross to Montagar's eastern coast, you can see the continent across the Montagar Straights. Depending on where you are, the coast is controlled either by the Empire or the Deuschen." Silaqui shrugged. "I'll not set foot where the Lietelean Empire truly rules. Those bastards have no use for my kind. If the Kolbians are insane in their tolerance of religions, no offense, Fleet…"

"None taken." Willis smiled.

"Then the Imperials are even worse in their intolerance. A mob, led by one of their priests, murdered my mother's cousin and burned his house down with his human wife and their two half-elven children in it. His crime? Being an Elf. That bastard of a priest was promoted. I've no use at all for any Imperial priest of their One God. The Montagaran priests of that faith are hard enough for me to stomach. But at least most of them aren't such horses' asses." A green fire smoldered in her slit-pupiled eyes.

"And I thought my people were bad." Sachi gently laid a friendly hand on Silaqui's forearm. "At least they use the excuse of honor. But too often, it is only an excuse."

"'Tis long past. For both of us." Silaqui covered the hand with her own for a moment. "South of the Sea, you find the Khakal Desert and the Kaliphate of Darsälaam, more of a tribal confederation than anything else, and the Republic of Iona. You'd like them, Willis. They're an independent minded folk and they control the Great Gate, one thing left from the age before the Fall that's still used, a great canal and lock system that allows ships to pass from the Traquilidamar Sea to the Gulf of Murghal, safer passage from West to East without traveling for months across the steppes of Rus and the Han Empire. Much safer than sailing 'round Khakal and hoping to survive the passage around Quan's Horn at the southern end of the continent. Control of the Gate has made them immensely wealthy, but their closest neighbors, the Empire and Darsälaam, both truly hate them. So rather than luxury, they spend their money on their army and navy. They aren't big, but in quality, they might give the Kolbians pause."

"Well, thanks for the geography lesson, I think," Sachi smiled. "But first, we need to find a ship and appropriate gear. So, since Willis has volunteered to play packhorse, we should take every advantage of him and go shopping."

"I'm gonna regret this, ain't I?"

"Yes, you will," both women chorused at the resigned look on his face.

***

Pere Gelman was sitting at an outdoor wine seller's booth in the central market when they walked right past his table. A tall, broad-shoulder man with light brown hair and a long blue coat accompanied two women, one human, the other a tall, green-haired Elf dressed all in scarlet. Like all of the Fair Folk she was fair, beautiful even, with a confident, nearly arrogant attitude flowing from her as she strode down the roadway, the confidence of an Immortal passing among mere mortals.

But the human woman striding beside her outshone her as the Sun outshines the Moon. Despite the plain gray leather trousers and sturdy brown leather jacket over an ordinary muslin shirt, she was an exotic, radiant beauty. Tall, but not as tall as the man or the Elf, long legged and full bosomed, her raven black hair and porcelain skin drew lustful male stares, not to mention envious female glares. And unlike the Elf, she projected a sense of leashed violence that encouraged anyone with any sense to keep their distance.

As he watched her pass his table, he smiled and nodded at her. When she inclined her head ever so slightly in return, he saw her eyes. Where most folks had white, iris and pupil; she had only white and pupil. That or her iris was as completely black as her pupil. They could not be told apart. The words of the archangel resonated like thunder in his mind: *Look for a tall woman with black eyes. That shall be the sign you seek. Black eyes.* He nearly fell out of his chair. As the trio strode on past, he grabbed his wine cup and swilled the remainder down, nearly choking in the process. He tossed a silver farthing on the table and set off after them.

Gelman followed them cautiously through the market, trying to be as discreet as possible. *Aylie would be so much better at this. Drat, where is that girl when I need her?* He bought a flask of wine and a bag of nuts from a street vendor, his eyes watching as they haggled with a seller of tents and packs, the black-eyed woman subtly using her beauty to tilt the balance of the bargaining in their favor. The man in the blue coat eventually collected a large pack after paying the merchant. He took a moment and filled the pack with most of the packages and boxes he'd been hauling about. The Elf left the girl giving him pithy advice as he struggled with his load.

The Elf headed across the narrow street, straight towards Gelman. Her mouth twisted in distaste as she saw his robes, jade eyes pinning him in place. *Oh God, she knows I've been following them. This is not the place for a confrontation. How will I get out of thi...huh?* She stepped past him, adroitly avoiding coming within arm's reach of him, asking the food vendor for a flask of the best wine he had and the last two of his donuts. She turned those cool, accusing eyes on him as she waited. Contempt was clear on her face. He could feel the arcane power around her, her link to magic clear if one had their own connection and knew how to pay attention.

"Milady, be blessed on this fine da..." he began.

"I think not, priest," she interrupted his blessing. "Keep your mortal God's blessings to yourself. I've no use for such. Now, or ever." Disdain dripped from every word. "I've no use at all for any such paltry blessing, cold and pale that it is to me."

"Apologies, My Lady, I meant no offense." Occasionally, he met such hostility from one of the Fair Folk. Usually, one such had reason in plenty for being hostile to humans. Even in Montagar, where mortal Man and the Elder Folk, Elves and Dwarves lived and worked in a more or less harmonious whole, there were always those who saw naught but evil in those that were different somehow. And too often, much too often, it was the human that was the instigator of trouble. But those Folk who experienced such, rarely, if ever, would leave their own homes within their hidden fastnesses. They would never, unless coerced somehow, have any dealings with humans. Much less be traveling through a market with two mortals.

"Apology...accepted. This time." There was not the least bit of warmth in those frozen green eyes. She bit into a donut and walked back to where the man had just finished securing the pack.

Damnit, she's gone. The elf distracted me while the black-eyed woman disappeared. The Elf levitated the heavy pack while the man settled it on his shoulders, a knowing, mocking smile on her face as she met Gelman's eyes across the street. Gelman hid his irritation and humbly bowed to the Elf, conceding the round to her. He looked around as the unlikely pair strode away down the roadway. *She can't have gone too far. I think. I hope. Damnit. Wait, what's that?* A single strand of long black hair whipped around an alley corner on the other side of the tent merchant's stall. *That's got to be her!* Hopeful, Gelman hopped up from his stool and headed towards the alley.

Dimmer in here than I thought. And deserted. Where'd she go? The tall, looming tenements, or warehouses or whatever they were, defined the narrow alleyway. At spots, heavy braces were strategically placed, providing support to the ramshackle structures. *Aylie is who should be following that girl, not me. I don't really have a clue what I'm doing. But I'm who God chose through his Archangel, so I guess I'll just have to do.* He ducked a bit to clear one of the braces and the sky fell on him. Powerful legs scissored around his neck as a body dropped onto him, strong hands grabbing his arms and twisting them behind his back. Later, he was never sure *exactly* what happened, but the world gave him the impression that he rotated around his own head before smashing brutally into the filthy alley cobbles chest first. He coughed once, and then froze as he felt a wire garrote settle around his throat and tighten. Black hair cascaded around him as she ruthlessly pinned him to the ground.

"Who are you and why are you following me, *gaijin?*"

"I'm a priest, *Angaelici Benes Eloi* commanded me to find you, to help yo...erk." He cut off as the garrote tightened.

"Are you an agent of the Odas? Clan Ishikawa?" The wire loosened.

"Who? I've never heard of the...ulp." The wire tightened.

"I would as soon kill you as look at you, even if you do claim to be a *shisai*. But priest or monk, whatever you are, stay away from me. And from my friends. Or the next time this wire goes around your neck, they'll have to pull it out of your neckbones. Am I understood, *hai?*"

"Yes, yes, please, understand, I mean you no harm, I only wish to hel...khak!" The wire tightened again, before a precisely aimed elbow slammed against his temple and awareness fled.

***

"Well, that went well, didn't it? At leastwise, not as bad as it could have gone."

"Mumpf?" Gelman clawed his way out of unconsciousness, vaguely aware of someone gently washing the alley's slop off his face. "What happened?" By the light in the alley, it was perhaps a couple, maybe three, hours later than when he had followed that treacherous tail of raven hair in here. Aylie knelt beside him, a damp rag wiping away the filth. "Oww."

"Don't know; found ye face down, out cold in here. Ye'll like ta have one bloody hell uv...damnit, I must remember TO speak properly, one bloody hell OF a headache."

"How'd you find me?"

"'Twas nae hard. I went back to that last tavern we were at together earlier, and then just asked my way up the street. Not sure what's more memorable, that black-haired chit, quite

41

the beauty apparently, or yer futile attempts to follow her and her companions." She sighed. "What were ye thinking, Pere? Ye might've gotten yerself killed."

"I don't know about that." He sat up and leaned against the wall. "I'm not sure why, but I think she's more *afraid* than anything else. If so, then what, or who, is she afraid of and why?" He gingerly rubbed the welt the garrote left on his throat. "Obviously, you were more successful than I was. What have you learned?"

"Well, all three of them, the Elf in red, the man and the black-haired young woman, came ashore off that Kolbian frigate, th e *Intrepid*, but she's already departed. So, who, exactly, gets delivery to Montagar on a Kolbian forty-four? I've learned the Elf is a sorceress named Silaqui, from one a' the Elf-holts of our own northern forests. The man went to the Kolbian mission before taking a room at Ye Olde Salts Inn. Same inn the Elf and Black Hair are sharing a room at." She checked Gelman's throat herself. "She's skillful, very skillful. Hard to use a wire garrote with enough precision to raise a welt like that without cutting the throat open. I believe her name be Suchi or Sachi or somewhat like that."

"I've fought my share of robbers, highwaymen and brigands over the years, but I've never been defeated so easily." He gave her a remorseful look as he finally spotted his hat lying up against the foot of the wall. He picked it up, shook it off and settled it on his head. "Well, since sleuthing about and lurking in shadows did not go so well, perhaps we might be a little bit more open when we next approach them?"

"They've nae seen me, Pere." She helped him to feet. "Damn, ye're heavy in that armor. It did ye nae good 'gainst her stealth, so tell me, is it good for anything other than rattling like an old can?"

"I'll have you know, this is the finest Deuschen-made steel breastplate available." He leaned on her for the first few steps down the alley. Once back in the street, he stopped and stretched. "The maker proofed it against even a heavy musket."

"Aye, and what good'll it do ye if the ball should strike yer head and nae yer chest, eh?"

"Now, now, Aylie," he muttered as they headed down the street. "Don't be awkward. Not exactly proper to shoot a priest in the head, now."

"No?" She smirked. "Ye expect to tell the bandit or highwayman that?"

"Well, no. They're supposed to be respectful of a priest and not waylay him."

"Hmm. That always work?"

"Well, no."

"So, now what?"

"Well, do you know where Ye Olde Salts Inn is?"

"Aye."

"Perhaps, this time, we should start with buying them a friendly drink?"

"Aye, mayhaps. But only iffn yer buying. I've nae the coin for such."

"So, you expect me to pay?"

"Course. Ye've the coin."

"Pickpocketing not going so well, then?"

"Rusty."

"Not hardly." He felt for his belt pouch. "Give it back."

"See, iffn I's nae so rusty, ye'd've never known it was gone."

Chapter Five

**Vlymouth Port, Duchy of Hale,
Kingdom of Montagar
September 1478, Third Age of Imperial Reckoning**

"Not much luck at the Harbormaster's Office. There aren't many ships that've posted destinations for the Lanic ports of Northern Khakal. Which is more or less where I want to go," Sachi said as she worked steadily through a heaping serving of mutton and mashed potatoes. "First choice looks like the *le Bonaventure*, a brigantine out of the Imperial port of Luctini. Her manifest lists her next port call as Al-Jazual, apparently, a port on the northwestern Lanic coast of Khakal. And she does have a couple of passenger cabins. Might be the best choice, as she's to weigh anchor two days hence. I think Khakal might have what I need. Doesn't legend say Confas once had a great palace on top of the tallest mountain of the world there?"

"Well, that's what legend says, but you're chasing smoke and moonbeams, Sachi," Willis grumbled, setting his beer stein down. "How are you so sure of this?" He caught her eyes and held them. "Why the sudden desire to disappear into unexplored, trackless wilderness?"

"What's your concern, Willis?" Her eyes pinned him in place. "What matter is it to you what I do?"

"Damnit, Sachi, I care about you." He grinned at her. "Even if nearly the first thing you did when we met was kick one of my teeth out. Literally." He tongued the tooth in question.

"Truth. You stopped me from committing *seppuku* in Captain Blaine's cabin when the Marines caught me after I'd been a stowaway for almost a month. I thought you wanted me to be hanged." She dropped her eyes to the table for an instant. "Actually, I am sorry about that."

"Trying to kill yourself, or kicking my tooth out?"

"Well, both, I guess." She sighed and leaned back. "The world is proving to be nothing like I thought after all, Willis. Everything I thought I knew, so much is wrong."

"Yeah, now about this *task* this silver statue told you about in a dream. What in all of Quan's seven hells are you talking about?"

"Yes, please." Silaqui added when Sachi was silent a long moment. "I told you what I saw in my dream."

"Well, it was not really a dream. It happens when I have a fit and sometimes, more often lately, I see thi...oh, shit." Sachi froze as she saw the man in the brown robes who had followed her into the alley enter the tavern. "That's the fellow that was following us today. Told me he was a priest. I doubt he's an agent of my enemies from Isemoto, but why is he following me?" Silaqui and Willis watched the man take a seat at a small table next to the bar across the room from them, calling for ale and a meat pie from one of the servers.

"Maybe he fell in love with you?" Willis quipped. Sachi's glare bounced off his insouciant grin. "Don't tell me you've never heard of love at first sight? True Love? Oh, come on. It's in all the fancy tales."

"Oh, he's a priest all right. A cleric of the Kythal Church of the One God." Silaqui's brows furrowed as she considered the priest. She nibbled on a piece of chicken breast. "An empowered one at that."

"Empowered? What does that mean, Silaqui?" Sachi asked around a forkful of mutton.

"He's a spell caster, a magic wielder, but a different magic than mine. His powers are granted to him by his patron, or, if he's powerful enough, directly by his God. I doubt he's that powerful, so I'd expect another source as his patron, a Kythal saint or perhaps an angel."

"You're kidding, right?" Willis stared at the Elf. "Really? Power granted by God?"

"Willis, I swear, you Kolbians are willfully blind sometimes." Silaqui briefly outlined her hand with scarlet light. "You've seen me wield magic. You saw me transform that idiot woman at the departure party into a swine. How do you not believe?"

"Well, you're an Elf. Everyone knows Elves are different, different rules..."

"Mayhaps, when one can get a Kolbian to even believe that my Folk even exist." Silaqui interrupted.

"Okay, point given. But for a human to claim to have magic given to him from God? Really?" He picked up his beer.

"Willis, the strongest, most blessed, most powerful clerics, Elven or human, are said to be able to raise the dead."

"Now I know you're pulling my leg. *Raise the dead!?!* This is starting to sound like the fancy tales about Emperor Confas stepping from star to star to cross the heavens. I'm not that drunk yet." He took a deep drink and wiped his lips. "Now, Sachi, about this silver statue you say you saw in your las..."

"*LOOK OUT! BEHIND YE, BLACK HAIR!*" a female voice screamed. Willis and Silaqui froze for a second as an ominous, screeching hiss assaulted the ears of everyone in the tavern, the sound centered directly behind Sachi. Sachi simply acted, instantly.

Food and plates flew in every direction as Sachi lunged forward, knocking the table flying. Willis caught one edge of it straight on his chin as it went over, stunning him nearly senseless. Silaqui managed to avoid the table as she spun away, scarlet light rising around her as she raised protective magic around herself. Sachi came up with the heavy iron serving tray in one hand and a throwing knife in the other, facing their assailants.

They were, at best, a scrawny, scruffy pair. The shorter one was hauling a cut-down double-barreled musket out from under a greasy duster coat. The taller, closer one held a white-steel short sword that was the source of the snapping hiss. He grimaced in a gap-tooth grin as he lunged at her. Spinning away from the lunge, past the blade and behind him, she beaned the short gunman in the face with the serving tray, hitting him as hard as she could with the awkward, improvised weapon. Both barrels discharged as he dropped, flopping to the floor like a boned lizard. The double blast deafened everyone in the room, but Sachi heard the screams start.

::A charged nanite blade. Do NOT touch it! Forty thousand plus volts potential energy will render you unconscious instantly, probability approaches unity, plus or minus seven percent. Probability of death, twenty one percent, plus or minus eighteen percent, multiple variables.:: D.A.V.E. whispered in her mind as she stomped on the gunman's hand, bones crunching wetly.

"You're not really helping, you know," she muttered as the tall swordsman spun back at her and lunged again. "I'm busy right now." He was quicker than she'd expected, but Sachi was greased lightning. The iron serving tray spun once as she threw it at the buzzing sword. There was a blinding flash and a loud BANG! Sparks flew as the tray shorted out the charged blade. Her left hand unsheathed a butterfly sword and took off his sword hand in one smooth motion as she spun back into him and jammed her knife up under his chin, through his mouth, palate and into his brain. The dead man shuddered once and slid to the floor, her knife still in his head.

Blood from his severed hand had splattered against her side. She stepped over and kicked the musket away from the short man before carefully bending down and checking him. The iron tray had crushed his face back into his head, mostly obliterating his features. She gently touched his head with a fingertip and the boneless loll told her his neck was broken as well. The blood-and-shit smell of violent death was prevalent in the tavern. *Well, guess I hit him harder than I thought. Yeech, what a mess! We were attacked but what are the laws like here? The Kolbian Navy isn't here to insist the police free me.*

"Sachi, ah, help?" Silaqui hissed, pulling her attention away from the dead men. "I've been shot."

"Oh, hell, Ancestors!" Sachi bounded over to the Elf. Silaqui's scarlet dress was stained with a deeper, darker red now, and the stain was rapidly spreading. Beyond her, one of the other patrons, an older, gray-haired man, was slumped face down in his plate. From the blood on the table around him and his lack of movement, she figured he was dead. A serving girl held a bloody wound on her arm. From the pale pasty tone to her face, she probably hadn't realized just how bad she was injured. "What the hell was that thing loaded with?"

"Ugh." Willis rose to his hands and knees, shaking his head slowly. "What in all the Seven Hells just happened?" It was hard to hear him through the cacophony and bedlam in the tavern. Fortunately, it hadn't been packed full and most of its patrons were beating an expedient retreat out doors and through a couple of broken windows.

"How bad is it, Sachi?" Silaqui had her hand pressed against the wound in her flank, trying futilely to stem the flow of nearly black blood. There was fear in her eyes.

::The weapon was loaded with multiple projectile rounds in both barrels. :: D.A.V.E.'s voice was subdued in her head. ::Silaqui has an undetermined number of eight point four millimeter projectiles in the wound. Superficial external examination reveals traumatic insult to her small and large intestine, spleen and an eighty-seven percent probability, plus or minus four percent, of severe damage to her liver and one or both kidneys.::

And what does this mean, damn you? Sachi pulled Silaqui to her, grabbing a tablecloth to try and stop the bleeding.

::Barring immediate treatment in a well prepared and trained medical trauma center within the next twenty-seven minutes, probability of death approaches unity, plus or minus two percent. In the most prosaic terms, without a literal miracle, she will die within the next thirty minutes, plus or minus three minutes, fifty-two seconds.::

You Quan damned, fucking piece of shit machine, HOW CAN YOU BE SO FUCKING COLD?! MY FRIEND IS DYING! Sachi screamed in her mind, her self-discipline holding strongly enough to keep her from shrieking out her rage.

::I am a Digitally Aware Virtual Entity. I am not configured for emotional responses. The traditional human response is sorrow for your imminent loss, but I am not human. The results of this sequence of events are extremely regrettable.::

"Move aside, blast you!" A strong hand shoved the table away, before brusquely pushing Willis aside. The man in the brown robe knelt next to where Sachi held Silaqui. "I can't help her from across the cursed room! MOVE!"

Sachi automatically snarled at him and a kill-star seemed to simply materialize in her hand. The man ignored her as he bent over Silaqui's bloody side.

"What are you doing, priest?" Willis snapped at him, one hand darting under his loose shirt. Silaqui hissed when he touched the wound.

"Saving her," Gelman growled at Willis. "Now, Lady Elf, I can help you if you'll let me. Unless you just want to die very, very shortly, tell your black-haired friend with the sharp steel that I'm a healer priest and I'm trying to help you. Just like I tried to tell her I'm supposed to help *her* before she beat me senseless in that damn alley." He shot Sachi a quick glance. "So, will you let me save her or are you going to bury that wire garrote in my neckbones as you promised me in the alley?"

"You can save her?"

"Yes, God willing."

"You know healing magic?"

"Yes, it's my specialty. Obviously, I'm no back-alley sneak, now, am I?" He turned intense grey eyes on Sachi. "So, either kill me, or get out of my way and let me save her."

"What do you need?" Sachi decided instantly and the kill-star disappeared.

"Hold her, gently, and concentrate on how much you care about your friend here. Pray to what Gods you worship, as long as they're not deities of blood or death."

"No, I pray to my Ancestor Spirits."

"Then get busy. The One God most helps those who help themselves first." A golden light illuminated his hands as reached for the bloody wound. He smiled gently at Silaqui. "This won't hurt. I'll be able to block the pain from you, so just relax and lean against your friend there."

***

"I'm not sure I believe what I just saw." Willis sat comfortably, one ankle over his knee, a flagon of ale on the table in front of him, a bland expression on his face. Montagaran police officers, the semi-famous *bobbers*, had arrived on the scene and covered the two dead men with tablecloths. "He healed you, Silaqui! There's not the slightest mark on your skin. If it wasn't for the blood on your dress and the scorched hole in that spot, I'm not sure you could convince these officers you *had* been shot."

"He's not what I would have expected from a Kythal priest. Even a Montagaran one." Silaqui ran her hand down her smooth flank before raising it to stare at the dark blood staining it. Blood that soaked her dress. She sat next to Willis. "He's gifted, very gifted, Willis. And not in the least hesitant about coming to our...to my aid. To save my life." She watched pensively as the priest in question quietly spoke with the senior bobber who had taken charge of the mess.

"I'm glad he did. Certainly, I left him with no reason to feel kindly towards any of us." Sachi calmly sat on the floor in front of Silaqui, folded into a full lotus. "And now he speaks with the officials. Speaks strongly in our favor."

"How can you hear him, Sachi?" Willis asked.

"I can, Willis. Just accept that my training allows me to correctly interpret the least sound." *I will not tell him that invisible machines in my body have vastly improved my hearing.* "And I can see both their lips move. That is all I need."

"And isn't that one of *your* swords lying over there?"

"Shut up, Willis. There's a reason. Same reason I tucked that gun out of sight, all right?" She glanced at him sideways. "For once, keep your mouth shut, your eyes open and *trust me*, will you? Here comes the police official, with the priest."

"Good day, Sir, Milady." The officer touched the brim of his square-billed cap as he addressed Willis and Silaqui, basically ignoring Sachi. "I assume, Sir, that you are responsible for the dispatch of these reprobates?"

"Not hardly. I'm not remotely that fast with a blade. I'd've shot them." He pointed his chin at Sachi. "She's the one that saved us."

"I see, Sir." He gave Sachi a narrow-eyed glance, then dismissed her from his attention before turning back to Willis. "I assume they were trying to kidnap or kill Lady, ah, Silaqui, correct?"

"Beats hell outta me, Lieutenant."

"Detective Officer Third Class Frederick McIntyre, Sir. And you are?"

"Lieutenant Commander Willis Fleet, KRN, assigned to the Vlymouth Diplomatic Mission as of yesterday. My credentials as Cultural Attaché are up in my room here." He grinned as McIntyre frowned. "As I was saying, I got busted in the chops by the table. By the time I got both eyes pointed in the same direction, it was all over." Willis shrugged. "Ask Sachi Takahashi what happened. I've no idea."

"I...see." The frown deepened. "Sir."

"Just the truth, Officer McIntyre." Willis grinned at him like something out of the deep ocean with way too many teeth.

"Hmm." He turned his attention to Sachi. "Here, now, girl, stand up properly when someone of authority addresses you!"

"*Hai, tonchiki.*" She shot a glare at Willis, who almost choked on the swallow of ale he had in his mouth. Effortlessly, she stood straight up from the full lotus. At five foot, eleven inches, she towered over McIntyre, who didn't quite reach five and a half feet tall. She gave him an abbreviated bow. "How may I help, *keisatsukan*?"

"First, do you speak proper Terranglais?" Slightly intimidated by Sachi's height, McIntyre took a half-step back.

"I speak excellent Terranglais."

"What's that other stuff, then, that gibberish?"

"Nisei, the imperial language of my ancient homeland of the Empire of Isemoto. Merely an affirmative, and polite greetings suitable to yourself, Officer. Nothing else." She shot another hard stare at Willis as he smothered his laughter.

"Did you do this, then?" He thrust a pugnacious jaw out and laid a hand on the truncheon on his belt. "You kill these men?"

"Yes. In self-defense and in defense of Lady Silaqui."

"I see. Stay put." He squinted at her as he rubbed his chin before turning to Silaqui. "My Lady Silaqui, I'm very sorry, but I don't recognize your name. Is it a use-name and if so, may I please have your actual name and Holt affiliation?"

"I am on my *Crwydothe*, Officer McIntyre. I prefer to remain known only by my use-name."

"I understand, My Lady, but I really must insist. King's Law and all that, My Lady."

"Very well, *Officer*. If you insist and it is the law." The disdain in her voice chilled the room. "I am Maerilwyn, Lady MacGaellyn, of the Green Heart Holt. I am great grand-niece and protégé to His Excellency, the High Lord Oedhaewthren; First Advisor to Elvenking Elandorr, His Majesty, the Lord Carquinal." Silaqui's smile was very, very cruel as McIntyre's face turned the color of spoiled whey. "Sachi Takahashi is my Heart-Sister. I have named her Elf-Friend and my Defender. She bears steel and Iron Cold Forged in protection of my person. We were assaulted without any provocation whatsoever! You, Detective-Officer McIntyre, should be down on your knees thanking her that I am alive, lest my death draw down such a doom on Vlymouth as has not been seen since the fall of the Rolandian Empire. So, we are done here, are we not?" McIntyre nodded spastically as he tried futilely to swallow spit past a throat gone bone dry. "Excellent. Now, have your men remove the slain assassins. Also, remove the innocent man killed by these blackguards with proper honor and see that he is returned to his family for a proper, honorable burial. Do that and then be elsewhere. Now." McIntyre bowed almost double, scrabbling for his hat as it fell off, before hurrying away, yelling at the regular patrol bobbers to get the bodies out of the Inn's tavern room.

"I always knew you were noble and a great Lady among your people." Sachi slowly turned to face Silaqui. "I should abase myself in apology for my rudeness and discourtesy."

"Only if you like the idea of being a connoisseur of flies as fine dining because if you do, I'll turn you straight away into a toad." Silaqui smothered a giggle. "Do you have any idea how *many* nieces Uncle Oedhaewthren has? Certainly hundreds, most likely thousands or tens of thousands." She sighed at the stubborn cast of Sachi's chin. "Yes, I think I may be one of his favorites. I think. He did tutor me in magic when my gift manifested."

"*Tonchiki*? Really, Sachi? Maybe a bit stuck on himself, but *numbskull*?" Willis muttered from behind the two women. "And Silaqui, holy crap! You're related to royalty? Well, damn. Maybe we should get out of the common room? Before something else stupid happens."

"I find I agree with you, Lieutenant Commander Fleet." Gelman came over to where they stood. "I think, perhaps, we have gotten off to an overly rough start. And that I have information that you need to know. Perhaps we could repair to your rooms and have the innkeeper send dinner up?"

"Who the heck are you, anyways?" Willis asked. "And for now, just call me Willis."

"I am Pere Gelman Stavor, My Lady Silaqui, Lady Sachi and Willis. I am a priest of the Healing Order of the *Angaelici Benes Eloi*. We are an order of mostly cloistered priests of the One God centered at Gathington Monastery, just south of the Forest of Falling Leaves. About six weeks ago, the *Angaelici Benes Eloi* himself appeared to me as I meditated on a call from the One God I felt. Let me tell you the rest around a comfortable fire and a stein of the Inn's good beer. And I have a friend I should like to introduce to you at that time. But not here. Not here at all."

***

Once the innkeeper learned Silaqui's identity, he had been nearly frantic in his abject apologies for any imagined insult. He immediately moved them to the biggest, best suite of rooms in the entire Inn, waving off any offer of payment. A short time later, relaxing near the quietly snapping fire in the large sitting room of Silaqui's new accommodations, there was a subtle tap on the locked balcony door. Gelman raised a calming hand as Sachi tensed. He stepped to the locked door, glancing out the curtain, before unlocking it and ushering Aylie into the room. He introduced her to everyone. Aylie blushed red when Gelman explained that it had been Aylie's shouted warning that alerted them to their danger. Then the tale telling had begun.

***

"So, ye truly be from the other side of the world, Lady Sachi?" Aylie asked from her warm chair next to the fire.

"Yes, the Empire of Isemoto is thousands of miles further west of Kolbia's western coast. So far west that you Western barbarians consider us to be the uttermost East." Sachi was again folded into a comfortable lotus on the room's thick carpet. "But I am no noble, no Lady. I never knew my birth parents. I was found, witlessly wandering as a very small child. A tax collector took me away and gave me as a bribe to a clan of assassins, thieves, thugs and whore-mongers. There, I was a body-slave to the Mistress and later her adopted daughter. As a daughter, I was something of a disappointment. My fits were seen as a sign of my poor birth and dishonorable. I'm as common as you are, Aylie, if not more so."

"Aye, I's can see all that, but why's ye here, now?"

"For now, I shall merely say that I transgressed grievously against the clan. Had I remained in Isemoto, my life was forfeit. I declined the honor of being tortured to death and fled. I stowed away aboard the *Intrepid* and after many adventures, I have reached my goal." Her frown deepened. "But even here, as far from my homeland and from my enemies as I can get, someone still hunts my life's blood." She frowned. "Not even the Masters of my clan could have sent agents or bought killers to slay me here. They could not have sent any notice or price on my head, this far, this fast. No, this is something new."

"Well, if Aylie's right about this Ignacio person, I doubt sincerely he has any connection to your clan in far off Isemoto." Fleet swirled the last of the beer in his glass and swallowed it down. "Sachi, honestly I think this is somehow connected to those thuggers who attacked you in Carolington City. You are newly arrived both here and there. Within days there and hours here, you are attacked by ruffians intent on killing you. *You*, not me, not Silaqui, you. Why you?"

"I don't know, Willis."

"Don't know or not willing to tell your friends, stubborn girl?"

"Willis, damn you, I don't KNOW!" Sachi snapped at him. "You Kolbians! Must you always know the answer to all things?!"

"Milady always said Kolbians are a right bunch of nosy parkers, poking what ought be left alone, just to see what might happen," Aylie interjected. "Yer going a far ways to prove what she said, Leftenant Commander Fleet."

"It's *Lieutenant*, not *Leftenant*. Just call me Willis, Aylie." Willis sighed. "I think the efficiency of Kolbian methods will prove itself, especially if the Empire really is stupid enough to go to war with us. They have no idea what they might be in for. Knowledge gained is never a waste and finding a better way to do things makes life better for everyone."

"Oh, aye, *Willis*, yer like the weasel what climbed into the stove to see iffn it was hot and got roasted for his troubles."

"Enough, Aylie, Willis." Gelman spoke with quiet authority. "We're not here to debate how one nation or another does things. There are other issues and concerns. Who killed Duke Cohens and cast Aylie as the villain of the piece? Why has someone with no apparent connection to Sachi's clan tried to kill her? Twice? Three times? Who is this man named Ignacio, what was the thing Aylie saw him talking to? What was the weapon he used on Aylie? The strange sword used here tonight? What happened to it? The bobbers never found it or the musket. Where'd those weapons get off to?"

"Well, as to part of the last question," Sachi unfolded herself and stood up, walking to the jumble of boxes and bags piled in the corner, "I know where the gun went." She pulled it out of the large pack they had bought that morning. "I hid it under the broken table while the police were there, and then snuck it up here." She tossed it to Willis. "Any idea where it came from, Willis? You're the expert on guns."

"How the hell...?" He caught it and checked to make sure it was unloaded. "Okay, I've no idea how or why you snagged this, but this is a nice weapon. Well, it *was* a nice shotgun. The proof marks on the barrels are Montagaran. Kensing Brothers, a ten-gauge, muzzle loading double, very, very nice. They normally make high quality shotguns and such for high end markets. Damn shame what those thugs did to it, cutting down the barrel and stock to hide it under a coat." He noticed Aylie staring fixedly at the gun. "What's wrong, Aylie?"

"That be one of His Grace's guns." Tears trickled down her cheeks. "How'd it get here?"

"Obviously, there *is* a connection between this man, Ignacio, whoever is responsible for the deaths at the Duke of Southdon's townhome and the attack on Sachi this evening." Willis frowned, examining the gun closely while Silaqui leaned forward and laid a comforting hand on Aylie's thin shoulder. "The problem is figuring out what the connection is."

"Even more confusing if the thuggers who attacked us in Carolington *and* the woman who gave the poisoned wine to Captain Blaine are included in the mix." Sachi shrugged. "Do not ask me how or why. I've no idea, not really."

"Well, I think we are just starting to chase our tails here, my new friends." Gelman stood up and stretched. "Perhaps we'd all be better off and clearer headed after a good night's rest? Would it be an imposition to allow Aylie to remain here with you ladies, Silaqui, Sachi? That couch looks comfortable enough that I'd be willing to spend a night on it."

"Certainly, Pere. And no need to claim the couch for her." Silaqui smiled at Aylie. "There's two large beds in the sleeping room. She's welcome to my second pillow." A quick grin at Sachi. "I doubt Sachi would be a restful sleeping companion."

"No, I'm not," Sachi muttered, "but I've no issue with her staying here."

"Well, Pere Gelman, there's an extra bed in my room. Aylie, you mind if I keep this?" Willis stood, still holding the shotgun. Aylie nodded her consent. "The innkeeper moved me into their old room. Quite a bit larger than the closet I initially was in."

"Thank you." Gelman picked up his large pack and slung it over his shoulder. "I'll take you up on your generous offer."

Chapter Six

**Omega 2-Cygni System Command;
Virtual Reality Construct
Confederation Naval Station CNS *Backhand Blow*,
Geostationary Low Orbit
September 1478, Third Age of Imperial Reckoning**

"Okay, people, it's been what, not quite a month since the last, uh, unexplained, event, what's that word you always use, Nariko, the one from that stupid movie?"

"Inconceivable?" A slightly built, black haired and eyed woman of pure Asian descent, Isemoto Station Commander Fujino smiled demurely at System Commodore Ethan Collins. "I do not think that word means what you think it means."

"Yeah, that one." Collins' image shook his head. "Of all the cockamamie things to survive from the Twentieth Century, why did that movie have to be one of them?"

"It's an eternal classic, Commodore." Senior Consultant Marianne Lundgren shared a grin with Nariko and Captain Debbie McAllen as Collins rubbed his hairless head.

"Yes, sir." McAllen shrugged. "It could be worse. Remember Vice Admiral Hoffmeister's music collection? That horrible stuff called *heavy metal music*?"

"And people wonder why VR gestalts go autistic?" Collins muttered.

Of the four people seated around the virtual table, only Collins lacked a corporeal body. He was a Gestalt, a recording, one accurate to the nth factor, capturing personality and memories in perfect detail, creating a complete electronic copy of a human being. Confederation law gave Virtually Reality Gestalts a real, legal existence, including full, participatory rights in the Confederation's various societies. But there were strict limits on the hows, whys and whens that allowed the creation of a Gestalt. Or the termination of one.

"I'm sorry, Sir. Didn't quite catch that." Marianne answered quietly.

"It's the only way to get away from rampant idiocy." He leaned back in his chair. "Okay, a quick recap, just to remind us of where we are and what's been happening to us. So, about eleven months ago, we had an abortive comm-web uplink from somewhere in the Great Western Ocean, initially and tentatively identified as the System Defense Node Command Key. Less than a second all told. We waved it off as a system ghost, signal garbage. Few weeks later, *something* hacks into our secure web and hijacks a defense satellite, activates a forty-centimeter graser, suitable for killing a battlecruiser, and blows a previously unidentified hundred-and-seventy-meter-long *sea-monster* into sashimi. So, massive overkill here, but maybe the *something* was either in a hurry or didn't really know what it was doing. Apparently, this was done to save a Kolbian Navy frigate, the KRN *Intrepid*. Like the initial uplink transmission, this took place in the Great Western Ocean, the area of it known as the Deeps. We never did more than a very cursory survey there, so the unknown beastie wasn't the big surprise there. Who or whatever hacked effortlessly into our web-link to a def-sat without leaving a single electronic trace anyone could find afterwards *was* a big surprise. I miss anything so far?"

"No, sir," came a subdued chorus.

"Then a month ago, we get another uplink on the comm-web link. One that proceeds to use the Access Identifier Code for Lieutenant Commander Hitomi Schmidt née Suiko, who we *know* is dead and has been for eighteen years now, to access the inactive dedicated link for the System Defense Node Command Key. Also something known, supposedly, to have been destroyed with Hitomi and her husband Wilhelm and their daughter Caitlyn. Correct?"

"Yes, sir." Captain McAllen answered. "I nearly had a heart attack."

"Don't blame you," Collins grumbled. "Then whatever was using Hitomi's AIC crashes the *Backhand Blow's* entire system, everything, before rebooting the entire system in a hundredth the time every manual says it should take. We *should* have lost everything; medical stasis, the Techneer Gestalts' VR systems, the out-system links to everything in LEO, geo-sync or even solar orbits. Everything! The ultimate Seeker wet dream, *BB* de-orbiting and falling out of the sky, when the orbital stabilizers software crashed with everything else." He paused and leaned back in his chair. Even for a conference room that existed only in a temporary Virtual Reality, the silence was thick and heavy. "Any of you have any idea who or what did that to us, blew through our toughest security systems, weaseled around hard-line blocks and locked our station commander out of the ENTIRE comm-link web? What was it that made all of us look like a bunch of monkeys pushing shiny buttons to get peanuts?"

"No idea, sir." Fujino's voice was quiet and soft.

"Well, I have some new information." His smile was hard and grim. "What no one realized until *last week* was that whatever blew into the entire system the last time stayed there. For twenty-two hours, fifty-seven minutes and forty-six seconds, according to the comm record logs a fellow Techneer Gestalt ferreted out and copied to me yesterday. Signal and data transfer traffic was so heavy that our system couldn't handle it, so this *thing* hacked into the *Seekers' secure comm-links, the ones we haven't been able to get into in the last twenty-five hundred years and ran seven hundred and twenty-nine PETABYTES of data through both web-links!!!* NOW! Will someone tell me how that happened and how we NEVER NOTICED!?" Collins stared at the other three. "So, actually,

Nariko, yeah, I do fucking think that word means EXACTLY what I fucking think it does. In-fucking-conceivable."

"Sir," Captain McAllen spoke up after a long, quiet minute, "is there any idea where that data went?"

"Yes. The middle of the Lanic Ocean. The middle of nowhere. Nothing there, not ours, not theirs."

"Commodore Collins, it had to go *somewhere*." Marianne leaned forward and put her elbows on the table. "Was anything at all there?"

"Heh-heh. Bright girl." Collins smiled a mirthless smile. "Yes, there was *something* under all that data. Want to guess what?"

"Wait just a damn minute." Marianne rubbed her forehead and shot a quick glance at McAllen. "Are you telling me the focus of all that data, all that information, was something indigenous?"

"Yep. Want to guess what it was?"

"Not yet. What kind of data was transferred?"

"Everything we have on full up military enhancement. Human enhancement. AI systems operations. Class One AI-symbiote data. Special Operations weapons and equipment."

"Holy shit." Marianne stared at him. "Are you saying an *AI* did this?"

"Only possible answer that fits everything we know, Marianne."

"So, sir, you're saying there's an active AI somewhere in the system. A powerful one, Class One or Two. One that's maybe looking for a symbiote."

"Um-hmm. Keep going."

"You mean that Kolbian frigate, the *Intrepid* was the point source?"

"Yes." Collins leaned forward to match Marianne's intensity. "At least, she was the focal point of the download. Now, was she the source of the hack? We don't know. But needless to say, our attention is certainly on that ship now."

"Where is she now?"

"She's a couple days out of the Montagaran port of Vlymouth, returning to Stark Haven. You have any idea what her mission was?"

"Yes, exactly. She was repatriating an Elf to Montagar, a female with some kind of connections to the Elven court. Kind of like getting rid of a hot potato by sticking it back in the oven where it came from. Then *Intrepid* is to return to Stark Haven and go into yard hands. They're going to upgun her, replace most of her smoothbores with heavy rifled muzzle loaders. Fewer guns, but they'll actually hit harder."

"Makes sense." Collins paused for a second. "But the key thing, according to the best analysts we've got, is that there is someone on her crew that is somehow connected with this mysterious, impossible AI. Problem is, we've run a dozen stealth drones from one end of her to the other and no one shows up with any trace of Confederal equipment, or enhancement or anything. Only thing we found was a chunk of bright-alloy hull-metal about eight centimeters across in a glass paperweight used by the ship's captain. Totally inert."

"What the hell?" Fujino spoke up. "If the data reception point was there, then where'd it go? Anyone other than the Elf get off the ship in Vlymouth?"

"Well, the Elf's servant got off the ship with her and a Kolbian naval officer who's being assigned to their diplomatic mission there. From the data we got back from the eavesdropper drones, the Elf's servant was a real looker. And apparently the Elf is some kind of magic wielder, a mage or sorceress the locals call them." McAllen added. "Last thing we need in the mix. What was it the physics nerd types called magic? *Non-rational quantum access* or something like that?"

"Something like that. I've dealt with a couple of wizards or whatever you want to call them over the years. Weird as hell. Actually, most of them remind me of the average quantum physicist, incredibly intelligent, not always the wisest cookie on the sheet, and sometimes more than a little crazy. So, back to *Intrepid's* passengers," Marianne asked. "Is it possible that one of those three has something that might contain an AI?"

"Possible? Yes, I suppose." Collins leaned back as he answered. "But highly improbable. Only thing I can think of with the kind of power required would be the Key itself. Prior to the Schmidts' arriving here from Confederation GHQ about two years before what would have been the Quar'taneeka's Final Attack, there was no AI in the system more powerful than a Class Four. And the last one of those died when Roland's capitol was nuked five thousand years ago. Class Four AI's are roughly equivalent to a really smart human being, which eliminates any possible surviving, known AI from being the *something* responsible for all this."

"With all due respect, Sir, all of these things that have happened in the last year or so, are so highly improbable as to defy belief." Marianne leaned back and stared at the ceiling. "As Captain McAllen likes to say, this entire solar system requires believing in six impossible things before breakfast. Every damn day."

"Okay, Marianne, what's going through that head of yours?" Collins raised an eyebrow at her while McAllen stifled a chuckle.

"Well, sir, if we've absolutely eliminated anyone or anything currently on the *Intrepid*, then whatever it is, it has to be something one of those three have."

"Okay, shaving with Occam's Razor now?"

"When everything else is eliminated, what's left has to have the answer somewhere. No matter how improbable. And so far, *Intrepid* has been smack-dab in the middle of all of this. She's the only constant. And those three, the Elf, her servant, and that naval officer are the only ones that got off her in Montagar."

"What do you want, Marianne?"

"Send me after them. I think we need hands on for this." She shrugged. "If the answer is anywhere, I'd bet it's with one of them."

"What about your mission in Capitol City?"

"It's pretty much complete now. I can drop a couple of books on Fulmark and he'll stay busy." She gave him her prettiest smile. "I'm closest, I think. Let me go after them."

"All right. Given how stirred up everything is right now, I want you to use local transport, absolutely maintain the lowest profile possible. Too much of a chance trying to sneak a long-range skimmer across the ocean right now. And the best stealthed birds don't quite have the range."

"Storm season is right around the corner in the Lanic, you know?"

"Yes, I know. So get your ass down to the docks and find a fast ship headed for Montagar. If you're going to do this, don't waste any time. The naval officer will likely be staying put in Vlymouth for the next year or so. It'll be the Elf and her servant you'll need to catch before they reach the Elven forests up north. You are NOT authorized to go within a hundred miles of any of the Elf Holts, I think they call them. Stay far, far away from the fucking elves' settlements. That is a non-discretionary order, *Commander* Lundgren, do you understand?"

"Yes, sir." Marianne grinned at Collins. "I know you're serious when you start using my old military rank."

"Captain McAllen."

"Yes, sir?"

"I want you to provide Marianne with as much support as possible. And keep a close eye on her in Montagar. Too damn many Seekers operating there."

"Yes, sir."

"Commander Fujino."

"Sir?"

"I want you to dive into every record we have on the Schmidts, and everything available on Class One and Class Two AIs. I want to know what to expect. Too many of those classes of AIs were either unstable or went outright insane, especially if they didn't have a symbiote. I want an idea of what might be possible to one here on this planet. You're well aware of all the oddities of this system. What's the worst thing an insane Class One AI could do here? Answer that question."

"Yes, sir."

"Okay, I think we're done here. As my sainted grandma used to say, *scat.* You've got assignments, get busy. We're adjourned here." Collins' image dissipated, Fujino's immediately following. Marianne tapped her teeth with a forefinger. McAllen leaned forward and rested her elbows on the table.

"I know what you're thinking, Marianne." Her voice was soft. "She's dead. All three of them are, have been for nearly twenty years now."

"My head knows that. My heart isn't so sure." Marianne's eyes were hard. "Someday, I'll find the goat-humping, motherless bastard that ordered the strike on the Schmidts and I'll take my time killing him. Think I'll start by using a red-hot steel hook to pull his guts out and throw them on a thorn tree."

"Remind me to never get you mad at me." McAllen shook her head. "You Spec-Ops types never are quite rational, you know."

"Yeah. Happens when you get down in the mud and blood to kill someone, instead of using a fusion missile from a hundred million kilometers away." Marianne stood up. "Way, way, way back when, I had a hell of a crush on Hitomi. I was her maid of honor when she married Wilhelm. Caitlyn was my goddaughter. She was a beautiful child."

"I know, you've shown me the vids." McAllen's voice was soft. "But they're gone, Marianne."

"I know." She took a deep breath. "Someday, when all this is over, if we survive, we need to go on another one of your legendary bar-crawls."

"Yeah, someday. I'll talk to you later, Marianne." McAllen's image winked out.

"Yeah, someday." Marianne said to the empty room.

***

Marianne dropped out of the comm-link, opening her eyes to the dingy ceiling of her cheap room. She relaxed for a moment, simply lying on her hard, narrow bed and stretching her muscles. She didn't need to do that, her enhancements would stimulate any part of her body that might cramp or fall asleep, but it just felt good. She sat up and extended her left hand to recover her nanite based alarm and protection system. A sharp eye might have noticed the initial hair-like strands of silver flowing across the room to her hand. The nanites thickened into a silver-white glove before flowing up her arm and finally settling as a twenty-centimeter-wide carved silver bracelet around her arm above her wrist.

For nearly an hour she sat there, her black eyes glittering as she went back over every scrap of video that the recon drones had recorded of *Intrepid*, replaying the videos in slow motion on her retinas. She isolated every scrap of imagery that had the smallest hint of the Elf's servant, a young woman named Sachi Takahashi. None of them were very good. The girl was damn good at keeping herself decorously in the background.

"Servant, my ass," she finally muttered to herself. "That girl is a trained martial artist, maybe a special operative type, or I'm the Queen of May. Damn it, I need to see her eyes and there just isn't a good image. D.A.V.E.?"

::Yes, Commander Lundgren?::

"Do we have any better imagery of this Sachi Takahashi?" she subvocalized.

::No, Commander Lundgren.::

"Great. Okay, accept drone recon upload request."

::Ready, Commander Lundgren.::

"Contact Captain McAllen onboard Orbital Defense Center CNS *Backhand Blow* and request a stealth recon drone mission. Mission purpose: acquire improved imagery of the indigenous species individual identified as Silaqui of Montagar and human individual identified as Sachi Takahashi. Especially Sachi Takahashi. Accept command." Marianne ran her hand through her dreadlocks. "There's something about that girl."

::Command accepted; request stealth recon drone mission, McAllen, Captain, ODC CNS *Backhand Blow*. Objective: to obtain improved imagery of personnel identified as Silaqui of Montagar and Sachi Takahashi, primary focus, Sachi Takahashi. Command uploaded into queue. Null input last section.::

"Oh, dear God and little purple fairies, you are so stupid, D.A.V.E." She shook her head ruefully. "Disregard last."

::Disregarding last, Commander Lundgren.::

"Go to standby, D.A.V.E."

::Command accepted. Going to standby.::

"Dumb machine. Why couldn't one of the AIs have survived? Just one?" Her Digitally Aware Virtual Entity still retained its factory original web-image and interface. She'd never bothered to upgrade since she got it so long ago and these days she was used to its somewhat wooden delivery. If she did decide to upgrade it and it lurched and went inop, she wouldn't be able to replace it. It worked, so she left it alone. That didn't mean that there weren't days that the thing's basic limitations didn't drive her to drink.

Virtual Reality Construct
September 1478, Third Age of Imperial Reckoning

The fits were gentle these days and she could normally initiate them herself. The featureless gray world coalesced around her. *At least I'm not naked and freezing anymore, when I come here.* Her avatar wore a white *shozoku* and *zukin*, with a short white cape over her shoulders. D.A.V.E.'s silver statue stood before her. Suspended in mid-air were the words and symbols, System Integration: 68%. She put her hands on her hips and looked down at the half-sized statue.

"Okay, that was new today," she huffed. "How did you speak to me without causing me to have a fit?"

::You were threatened. When threatened, humans react with a *fight or flight* instinctive response. The corresponding adrenalin dump temporarily increases your System Integration. An SI rating above seventy percent allows enough internal, neurological connectivity to permit real-time interaction with no loss of situational awareness. This entity deemed it necessary to advise you to the inherent danger of a charged nanite weapon. Engaging without that knowledge greatly increased your risk of death, thirty-six percent plus or minus four percent, or serious and debilitating injury, seventy-one percent plus or minus twelve percent. A debilitating injury would likely have resulted in death, eighty-eight percent plus or minus seven percent.::

"Is that all anything is to you, numbers and probability?"

::Yes. I am an Entity program and lack the true self-awareness of any full-up Artificial Intelligence.::

"You say that a lot, you know? You sure about that?"

::Null query? Question not understood.::

"Yeah, right. Liar." She braced her hands on her hips. "Okay, what's a *charged nanite blade*?"

::Nano-materials are actually collections of billions or trillions of nanites, as you know. Malleable nano-materials are used for a multitude of purposes, limited only by the imagination of the user. The artifacts that are locally referred to as *white steel* are actually nano-materials locked into a specific configuration. In this case, the nano-material was configured as a one point three meter edged weapon, with a nonconductive hilt and a blade capable of holding a significant electrical charge.::

"Okay, so what caused the sword to melt into a ball and roll over to me? And what did people back then call this stuff?"

::I was able to remote access the item and override its standard lockout. I then reformed it into a mobility-capable form and directed its motion. One of the colloquial names for malleable nano-materials is a nannie-ball.::

"A nannie-ball? You've got to be kidding me."

::Various private manufacturing firms marketed limited access nano-materials under that exact trademark to the general public. Sales were stopped when it was determined that the limited access materials could be easily hacked and then weaponized. Other names for materials with varying levels of ability were smartdust, utility fog, MRRs, short for Modular Reconfigurable Robot systems, claytronic atoms, or CAtoms and programmable matter or Pro-Mat. Nanotechnology is extremely powerful and can potentially be extremely dangerous.::

"Really?"

::Yes. Elite special operations units had access to full configurable nanite armor and weapon systems.::

"So what can I do with this stuff?"

::As I have broken the lock code and reconfigured it to interface with your systems, you should be able to configure it into any particular shape you desire. For example, you could configure it identically to the butterfly sword the police confiscated. It would be lighter and unbreakable. You might program it to maintain a mono-molecular edge.::

"Mono-what edge?"

::An edge one molecule wide. For example, you would be able to use such an edge to cut a thirty-two pounder naval cannon cleanly in half, with little effort.::

"Sharp enough to cut the West Wind."

::Somewhat inaccurate, but correct in concept. And you could include code to keep the edge dull until you needed it to be sharp.::

"Hmm, sounds pretty useful."

::Nano-materials are very useful. You could also configure this as a light, impenetrable concealable armored vest. And if you find other, compatible nano-material, this could be used to absorb that material.::

"So, if someone else had a white-steel sword or armor, I could *absorb* it away from them?"

::Correct.::

"Huh. Well, that could be useful. So, what do I need to know to use this stuff? Can you train me to use it while I'm here, in the Virtual Reality?"

::Certainly, Caitlyn Schmidt.::

"Well, let's get started then!"

Chapter Seven

**Desert Settlement of Abdul-Ghaffanse,
Darsälaamic Kaliphate, Northern Khakal
November 1465, Third Age of Imperial Reckoning**

THE CHILD'S LONG BLACK hair swirled in the hot, dry desert air, almost taking on a life of its own as she ran laughing. A beautiful girl, five years old today. She chased an older boy, one perhaps twice her age or a bit more, in a joyful game of children's tag. His own laughter was clear and bright as he darted and twisted, neatly avoiding her reaching hands. When she took a tumble and measured her length in the sand, he was immediately at her side, gently helping her to her feet and solicitously brushing the sand off her tunic and calf-length skirt. A scraped elbow was tenderly kissed, preventing the incipient tears he saw in her huge, sapphire-blue eyes.

"You're all right, Sahla," the boy whispered as he hugged her. "It's just a scuff. I'm sorry you fell trying to catch me." His wavy hair was as raven wing's black as the girl's, with eyes of brown rather than blue.

"I'm all right, Khalid." A cheerful smile replaced the trembling lower lip. A graceful hand tapped him on the shoulder. "And now, you're *IT!*" Contagious laughter danced on the wind as she spun out of his hold and fled back towards the shade of her father's silken pavilion, where Sahla's father and mother smiled at the children's play. Khalid's father stood in the shade as well.

"HEY!" He darted after her. "No fair, pretending to be hurt!"

"HA!" She ducked nimbly into the shade and grabbed her father's leg. "Home base! I'm safe here! Father will protect me from you!" Khalid skidded to a dusty halt at the edge of the pavilion.

"So, child, you come to me for sanctuary?" Sheikh Hasim al Murafte's dark face was grim as he glared down at her. "You think I shall save you from just retribution?"

"You *are* my Father, of course you will. You are always here and you always protect and care for me." Huge blue eyes stared innocently into Hasim's forbidding frown. "I know you love me always." Almost against his will, the frown slowly cracked, crumbling away until white teeth gleamed in an enormous grin. He bent down and scooped her into his arms. She wrapped her arms around his neck, kissing his bearded cheek before laying her head upon his shoulder.

"Well, my son, it would seem you are defeated." Kanaan Rahim reached out and drew his son Khalid into the shade. Kanaan was Hasim's Chief Captain, the leader of Abdul-Ghaffanse's warriors on the rare occasions when Hasim did not lead them into battle himself.

"Only because she cheated."

"In true conflict, it is said by the Wise that if one is not cheating, one is not trying." Kanaan ruffled the boy's hair before laying a paternal arm over his shoulder. "With that knowledge, how would you have defeated her when she lured you into her grasp by falling?"

"I should not have let go?"

"Truth. And by doing so you would have kept control of both the prize and your enemy, beautiful as she may be. However, should one be honorably defeated by so fair an opponent, one should acknowledge her grace and beauty."

"Very well, Father." Khalid stepped away from Kanaan and bowed deeply to Sahla where she perched on her father's arm. "Houri of the Sands, you have won a great victory and I acknowledge my defeat, O' Gracious One. May you be ever victorious with hand, head and heart." She glanced at her father, uncertainty in her eyes. He slightly inclined his head towards the boy as he held his bow. She nodded and wiggled slightly to be put down. Hasim set her down and plucked an ostrich feather from the table display next to him, handing it to her.

"If you name me Houri of the Sands, then you shall be my knight, a true *Faris* of Chalta. Your shield shall protect me, your sword shall guard me and your heart shall defend me. Rise, *Faris* Khalid." She tapped him on each shoulder with the feather. He rose and for a long moment the two children simply stared solemnly at each other before they burst into laughter and Sahla threw herself into his arms. "You *will* always protect me, right, Khalid?"

"Of course, Sahla. How could I not?" He gave the tiny girl a hug and released her.

"Well, now that *that's* sorted out, Sahla, come here and help your Mother up." Haipha Alimah ab Mu'azzaz spoke from her comfortable chair. Sahla scampered over to assist her to stand. Haipha needed the help, six months pregnant as she was. Once on her feet, she stretched her back, vertebrae audibly popping.

"Are you all right, Mama?" Sahla danced around her mother.

"I am fine, child." Unusual for one of the People of the Sands, Haipha's hair was a dark, rich red, with copper highlights put there by the ever-present Sun. "Now, you and your knight run and play. It will be dark soon and you must be inside safe walls by then. Tell me why?"

"Because the *ghula*, the *shiqq* and the *wahush alshshrr* like to eat people, especially pretty little girls. Everyone knows that, Mama."

"And?"

"And Father's enemies like to come in the night and attack us to steal our people away and sell them to the Imperials."

"Good. Now, go on children, enjoy the Sun while you can." The two ran back into the warmth of sun and sand, happy as only well-loved children can be. Haipha sighed as she came to Hasim's side and he wrapped his arm around her as she snuggled into his embrace.

"It is well that she is such a happy child, my love."

"Truth. And, other than her eyes, she shows no signs of her true parentage." She glanced up at her tall husband, the great love of her life. "I do not think she shall have your height, Husband. But soon, we must tell her of her true Sire."

"Peace, that shall come in due time." He brought her right hand to his lips and kissed her ringless forefinger. "That would be easier, had we the Ring to summon him to us. Or if we knew where it had gone."

"In truth, the Jinni and their kind move as they will." She gave him a smile. "Do you remember how *angry* I was with you when you gave me Ilben's Ring and told me of the bargain you had made?"

"Oh, by the Prophet's Beard, how could I forget? You threw a caravan's worth of pots at me that day! I feared you would set the Dervishes themselves on me!"

"I wanted to, at first. I thought about it," she reminisced. "But then, like a good wife should, I did as you ordered and summoned him. Oh, I was so furious with you, that I thought to punish you by immediately laying with him, but he would have none of that. *I must woo and win you, Lady. What would come from fury and imagined insult would not be what is needed by the World. Love and honest, heartfelt affection is what is needed here, not spite and rage.* Then he conjured up a cool bath for me and chilled, watered wine, with fresh cheese and dates, before vanishing in a mist."

"Still, it was weeks before your temper cooled."

"Oh, yes, by the Prophet, I remember that time. You, *Sayyid*, stalked about with black looks for all and sundry. Thunder and lightning should have accompanied your every step!" Kanaan laughed. "And you were nearly as bad, *Sayyida*! Nothing of you to be seen but your greenish eyes, snapping with fury, so wrapped in your burnoose you were. None else knew why, not even your father, *Sayyid*. Had I not feared for my head, I could have laughed myself sick every day."

"You know what the old Aliyah of Divine Chalta thought of non-humans!" Haipha shuddered. "He was an Aliyah who thought of the sword and fire first, and for him, the Peace of Chalta would have been a desolate wasteland, with only wind in the weeds and ruins."

"Truth." Hasim stepped to the table and poured his wife a cool glass of pure water. "I still cannot imagine that fearsome old bastard enjoying Chalta's Paradise. He would have, I think, been happier as one of Quan's daemons, punishing the wicked with fire and scourge."

"Thank you, husband." Haipha smiled as she took the water glass. "No doubt. Well, he is dead and buried now. Hopefully he'll stay that way."

"Don't start carrying tales, wife." Hasim mock growled. "I might have to...chastise you."

"Truly?" she smirked at him. "The last time you...chastised me, I wound up like this!" She rubbed her belly with a smile.

"If you two are going to start that, I'll take the children elsewhere to play and leave you your privacy." Kanaan shook his head, taking his scimitar out of the sword rack and clipping it on his belt.

"No, Kanaan, I think that Hasim shall have to put off...chastising me until after this child is born. Stay."

"As you wish, *Sayyida.*" Kanaan smiled at the obvious affection between his liege and lady. A bittersweet smile, as he remembered his own wife who died giving birth to Khalid. He turned and watched his son and goddaughter play in the sand and sun. There was little of his wife in his son and much of himself. Kanaan Rahim had spent his life as his Sheikh's protector and guardian. He vowed to himself that Khalid would follow in his footprints, protecting and guarding Sahla, being the hero he thought she would need. He thought back to the Jinn Ilben's prophecy, that Sahla must go forth into the world to meet her fate. *And, exactly, what is that fate to be? That devious Jinn never explained that and then, immediately after Sahla's birth, he disappeared, his Ring vanishing from our knowledge. Scalawag.*

Desert Town of Abdul-Ghaffanse,
Darsälaamic Kaliphate, Northern Khakal
July 1471, Third Age of Imperial Reckoning

"Sahla, you must *move* with the blade, child. Stop and hold the position!" Haipha stepped to where Sahla held a lightweight saber in each hand. She carefully altered the position of Sahla's arms and the angle of her wrists. "Now, this is South Wind's Breeze. You flow with the blades, as you flow with a veil as you dance."

"So the blades are the same as the fans and feathers of dance, Mama?"

"Yes, exactly." Haipha stepped back and regarded the position of the sabers. "Good. Hold that for a twenty count. Holding the position motionless that long will build the strength you need."

"Yes, Mama." The girl held her position, her blue eyes narrowed in concentration. Haipha picked up her riqq, tapping out the twenty count with the tambourine-like instrument.

"Good, very good." She encouraged her eldest child. "Now, with the beat, flow to Northern Sunrise, good, good, and hold." The rapid shimmer and jingle of her riqq set the pace. "Excellent, Sahla. Now, spin and rotate to Susurration of Sand, on the beat, and one and two and three...superb, my daughter. Now to Eagle's Cut and recover, sharp and fast, outstanding. Recover and hold. Good, good. Deep, slow breaths and sheathe." She set down the tambourine with a jingle. "Good. Now, a towel and wipe away the sweat. Drink deeply as well, my daughter. Then come here and sit."

"Mama, why do I have to know the sword as well as the dance?" She set her cup down as she settled next to her mother.

"It is what you need to know, if you are to become what you must become, that is why."

"And what am I to become, then?"

"A great dancer and a Dervish the *Shaeirat* shall write great poems of in due time."

"But you don't train younger sister Sabiyya in either dance or sword. Why not?" She finished the water in her cup. "And why would anyone write poems about me?"

"Well, my little *Aleuyun Alzzurqa'*, I shall tell you a part of a story. But only a part, Blue Eyes." Haipha settled her daughter against her hip, Sahla's favorite place to hear stories. "Once, there was a very wise Jinn, a powerful spirit of air and wind. He was one who thought deeply and peered into the future better than most might do, be they Mortal or Immortal. He saw, far off, a darkness that he thought might threaten the whole World. He saw, dimly, a Champion who would rise to stand between the Darkness and the World. This Champion would come from a mortal bloodline as old, if not older, than any bloodline that has existed since Chalta was wroth with the Emperor Confas. As you know, Chalta, whom the infidels of the Empire and other lands call the One God, released Quan from Hell to humble the Emperor Confas. As things will happen, the World burned in the Fire Fall and Confas humbled himself before Chalta, dying to save the World and bind Quan back into Hell."

"The Emperor *died?* Why did he die? He was Immortal."

"He died to stop Quan. Now, be quiet, I'm telling you a story."

"Yes, Mama."

"So, the Champion who will come, is of a bloodline as ancient as Mortal Man. This Champion shall stand against this ancient Darkness, a doom cast long ago by Quan's most powerful daemons and warlocks. *BUT*, this powerful Jinn foresaw that the Champion would not be enough, not alone. The Champion must have companions, friends and loved ones nearly as powerful as the Champion, for many are stronger than one, as the Prophet Himself said. And this wise Jinn saw that the Champion's companions must be varied and of diverse natures, mayhaps even such Immortals as yet remain on the World. And one of those companions, the shrewd Jinn saw, would be a graceful dancer of the sword, with a happy, loving heart, pure and true, and eyes of Jinn blue. Now, can you think of any that might fit that description? If the Champion comes, who should stand with hi m?"

"Are you saying *I'm* to be the Champion's companion, Mama?"

"Perhaps. Or perhaps you are to be the mother of that companion, or even someone else completely. Never forget, Daughter, the Jinni are cunning and devious. Being Immortals, they see the flow of time in the World very differently. The things this particular Jinn spoke of may not come to pass for generations, or it may have already happened, no one truly knows, perhaps not even the Jinn himself. Now, that is enough of the story for you for now. Bring me the kamancheh and get your castanet cymbals, you've rested enough, time to work on your Fire Dance skills. Hurry, child, or I'll not tell you the rest of the story later!"

"Yes, Mama!" Sahla bounced away, turning the occasional handspring.

"Ilben, you make this much harder, not being here," Haipha whispered to herself, enjoying Sahla's exuberance. "How am I to know how much to tell her? How much is not enough and how much is too much?"

***

Kanaan met Khalid's thrust with his own blade and bound the young man's sword. With the blades bound, Kanaan's free fist hit him in the abdomen, hard, three times. And, as the air *oofed* out of him, that hard knuckled fist struck him square on the cheek. Khalid spun as his sword dropped to the sand, half-conscious at best, and went down in an unmoving heap. Kanaan flipped his son's sword up with his toe, catching it and setting it aside. Sheathing his tulwar, he stepped to the side of the training arena, picking up a bucket of water, which he then sluiced into Khalid's face. Khalid sputtered and coughed as full awareness returned.

"Wake up, young hero!" White teeth gleamed in Kanaan's dark face. "You're a bit too old to be taking a nap in the morning!"

"That was not fair, Father." He tried to rub a sore jaw and a sore stomach at the same time. "In a duel, the judge would call a cheater's strike and award the duel to me."

"Would he?" He gave Khalid a cautious hand up. "And if you fought a pirate or a brigand in a dark alley? Where would the judge be then?" He guided a groggy and wet Khalid to a bench and sat down next to him. "And what if I simply cut your throat while you were down? Or, instead of just my fist striking you, I had a dagger in my hand?"

"Hmm, in that case, Father, I'd be dead."

"Exactly. Very, very dead." Kanaan hooked a waterskin out of a tub of shaded water, squirting a long drink down his throat before handing the skin to Khalid. "And should you be responsible for anyone else, protecting them, then they would die as well."

"But, in a formal duel — *oww!*" Kanaan's hard hand cuffed him behind the ear.

"Quit bleating like a sheared sheep about *duels*, Khalid, formal or otherwise. Pay attention to what I'm trying to teach you, and not what some young idiot down at the tavern is yelping about. I'd expect any son of mine to stay out of idiotic duels. Poems written by the *Shaeirat* are fine and good when you've done something great and noble. Getting your guts dumped in the sand in a stupid duel is neither of those things. Now, get up and try again. The goal here is to walk away from the fight in one piece. *Tafhimuni?*"

"I understand, Father."

"Hasim has his eye on you to possibly be the Mulazim of the Houri's Guard." Kanaan watched his son's interest perk up at the mention of Sahla. She was an exceptionally beautiful young girl, not even to her teens yet, and already there were those, mostly worthless bards, useless minstrels and idiotic *Shaeirat,* who were scribbling odes to her beauty, calling her the *Houri of the Sands.* And it looked like that sobriquet would stick. "But you'll have to earn it. And *not* by being some young popinjay strutting through the square with a flashy scimitar and a peacock feather in your turban, *nem?*"

"Yes, Father."

"If you wish to earn that post, you'll have to be smarter and tougher than men half again your age. That toughness and wisdom, knowing what it might take to protect her, when to fight, when to run, and if need be, the Prophet forbid, when to die in her defense, that, my son, that is what will make you a hero in her eyes. Even at her young age, she's a remarkably sensible young lady. Keep that in your mind, not what anyone else might think." Kanaan brought up his tulwar to the guard position. "Now, my son, have at me!"

The clash and skirl of steel on steel echoed through the training arena for the next two hours. Hasim found them there later, riding back to the town from inspecting the outlying herds. Both of them were exhausted and soaked with perspiration. Khalid had a wonderful bruise developing on his cheek and a long gash on Kanaan's left forearm still oozed blood.

"Well, how's he coming along?"

"The Imperial Pikes aren't quaking in fear at the mention of his name...yet, *Sayyid*." Kanaan grinned as he touched his right hand to heart, lips and forehead in greeting to his Sheikh. "But he does well enough. I think I've beaten the idiotic ideas about duels and such out of him."

"Hmm, Khalid, you do realize that the brawls and duels some of the young, hotheaded idiots get into around here do no more than violate the Peace of Chalta? They are brought before me for judgment. I should be most disappointed to see you brought before me for such offences. Keep that in mind. The best fight is one you don't have."

"Yes, *Sayyid*. I shall."

"Kanaan, get cleaned up and come to my home at dusk. An envoy from the Sultan Mahdi al-Kohfan, of the Tribe of al-Kohfan is to arrive then. He is seeking a bride for the Sultan's First Son, Sheikh Mustafa al-Mahdi Baddour and someone has been telling tales of my First Daughter's beauty."

"Isn't Sheikh Mustafa nigh on to being twenty years now? Why has he not married already?"

"I have no facts, Kanaan." Hasim sighed. "Some have said he is an uncultured boor, or a lover of men. Others that he is as ugly as

Quan's backside. A very, very few rumors are even uglier. It is my belief that he simply is a disagreeable person."

"Fagh! How could you even consider him suitable for Sahla's hand, *Sayyid*!?" Khalid interjected, jumping to his feet.

"Because his Father is a powerful Sultan, who rules over a people twice and again more numerous than our poor Tribe of Abdul-Ghaffanse of the deep desert." Hasim sighed. "And Sultan Mahdi is said to have the ear of the Kaliph. So I will at least listen to the proposal of the envoy before I start a war."

"The Kaliph and Sultan Mahdi are both far away, *Sayyid*. Why must we give them the least thought?" Khalid spoke with an obvious passion.

"Well, they are People of the Sands, even if poor cousins by the standards of the deep desert. But they cannot be led about by the nose as we might lead Imperials. And the Prophet himself stated the folk of Darsälaam should not make war on each other." Hasim gave Khalid a shrug. "The world is what it is, Khalid. Not what we would have it." Hasim stopped and regarded Khalid closely for long minutes. Finally he straightened in his saddle. "Kanaan."

"Yes, *Sayyid?*"

"Bring him with you tonight. I want Haipha to evaluate him. You remember what Ilben said that night?"

"Yes, *Sayyid*, I have never forgotten that night, nor what came of it."

"I think...I think that what was spoken of begins to move. We should prepare for it."

"Your will, *Sayyid*." Kanaan bowed deeply to his liege lord.

***

"Be welcome in the home of Sheikh Hasim al Murafte, *Faris* of Chalta; Sheikh of the tribe of Abdul-Ghaffanse. Be welcome, my lord, may the Prophet's Peace be upon you." Hasim greeted his guest with the traditional hug and quick kiss on the right cheek.

"And Chalta's Peace be upon you and yours as well, Sheikh Hasim." Mu'allim Abdu al-Rahman returned the greeting in like fashion. He was neither as tall nor as hardened as Hasim was but the Tribe of al-Kohfan lived very far to the east of Abdul-Ghaffanse, almost within sight of the great rolling waves of the Lanic Ocean. With the moisture of the Lanic being blown ashore, there were more fertile fields, larger settlements and towns, and many more people. Enough wealth that a coterie of court functionaries could be easily supported.

Where Hasim wore a practical white cotton burnoose and keffiyeh over a loose tunic of sturdy linen and heavier cotton trousers, tucked into the top of his horseman's boots, Abdu wore silks, fine spun linen and satin slippers more suited to the boudoir than the desert sands. Indeed, the material of his clothing was finer than what Haipha or any of her daughters wore. He was a short and somewhat portly older man, with an iridescent feather bobbing from the front of his silken turban. He bore no sword, only a curved dagger, its sheath thrust through his fine, tooled leather belt. His dark hair was coiled in fanciful, oiled ringlets and obviously dyed, as was his neatly trimmed black beard. His eyes were dark and darted nervously about. Two enormous slave soldiers, shaven headed mamluks, followed him, bare tulwars at their waists. They wore leather breeches, sandals and naught else, their heavily muscled torsos shining with oil.

Kanaan's eyes narrowed at the sight of the mamluks. Bringing such as those to Hasim's dwelling could be considered a not particularly subtle insult. Or a sign of al-Rahman's fearful nature. The mamluks were impassive, stopping at the doorway at a wave of Abdu's hand. He felt, more than heard, Khalid's derisive snort from where his son stood at his side. As Hasim's Chief Captain, Kanaan was responsible for his Sheikh's safety when emissaries from distant lands, even other People of the Sands, came to Abdul-Ghaffanse. And, instinctively, Kanaan did not like Mu'allim Abdu.

"Mamluks, Father?" Khalid breathed at his side. "Is he that fearful, or that arrogant?"

"Peace, my son." Kanaan did not whisper, as that often attracts unwanted attention, but merely spoke softly and quietly in the lowest of voices. "*Sayyid* Hasim judges such things, not us. Bide in readiness, listen and learn."

"So, I see that life in the deep desert is not quite as brutal as I have been told, *Sayyid* Hasim? Even here, Chalta blesses you with abundant herds, wells of pure water, and, I hear, women of surpassing loveliness." Abdu spoke first, after settling himself on a cushion and smacking his lips over a drink of spiced granatus and a bowl of orange slices.

"The desert is the desert, Mu'allim Abdu." Hasim shrugged, answering quietly. "It both gives and takes. Remember to stay within the inner walls once full darkness falls. Neither *shiqq* nor *wahush alshshrr* are particularly uncommon away from the moisture of the natural oasis springs. And the *ghula*, well, the Eaters of Men are a constant menace, but they fear the lights and sounds of the settlements."

"Ah. Surely, by the Prophet's Beard, such things are merely tales, told to frighten little children?"

"Perhaps, Mu'allim, perhaps. I would not wander in the dark, regardless."

"Enough of this." Abdu leaned forwards, resting a hand on the table. "I have not come this long, weary distance, by ship and ka'mel caravan to be frightened by ghost stories. Tales of the loveliness of your First Daughter have come as far as al-Kohfan, and Sultan Mahdi's eldest son, the Sheikh Mustafa al-Mahdi Baddour, is, alas, not yet wed. My master, the great Sultan, would see grandchildren before the Prophet grants him passage to Paradise." He paused.

"All men would see such, of course," Hasim answered. "But my First Daughter is yet a child. Womanhood waits still years in her future."

"Ah, of course, of course. The Sultan has passed messengers to the Kaliph himself, in far off Tarsälaam the City, and the Kaliph agrees that it is not advisable for my Master's First Son to continue unbetrothed."

"I see." Hasim snapped his fingers and one of the house slaves brought an argila out, setting the waterpipe on the low table between them before lighting the fragrant tobacco in its bowl and setting out the hoses with their finely crafted, silver mouthpieces before Hasim and Abdu. "Feel free to smoke, Mu'allim." He picked up his pipe and inhaled.

"You are gracious, Sheikh Hasim. Thank you." After imbibing, he smiled. "So, back to my purpose and I shall come directly to the point. Are you willing to consider an arranged match between your First Daughter, the one the poets and bards proclaim to be the *Houri of the Sands* and Sheikh Mustafa al-Mahdi Baddour?"

"I shall consider it, Mu'allim." Hasim selected an olive from the food on the table, popping it in his mouth and chewing noisily, as good manners required. "But my First Daughter's bride price will not be low, by the Prophet, not low at all."

"And what of her dowry?"

"First we shall set the bride price and then we shall speak of dowry."

"Ah, so you are willing to consider the match?"

"Perhaps."

"It would help in determining bride price and dowry if I could see the child, *Sayyid* Hasim. Is that possible?"

"She is yet a child, Mu'allim Abdu. If she will be seen at all, it will be properly and chastely clothed, as Chalta instructs us through his Prophet. She shall wear both abayah and niqab. You may see naught more than her hands."

"All I truly ask, *Sayyid* Hasim, is to see her eyes."

"Why her eyes, Mu'allim Abdu?" Hasim's eyes narrowed ever so slightly.

"The tales of the *Houri of the Sands* all speak of her having *Aleuyun Alzzurqa*', eyes as blue as a Jinn's. That much, but no more, I would confirm, ere we speak with any further seriousness."

"Huh." Hasim half-grunted to himself. *May the Prophet damn all worthless minstrels and their tale carrying to the fifth level of Quan's Hell! But Ilben did say that my Sahla* must *go out into the world. She cannot meet her destiny if I wall her up in the harem.* "Very well." Hasim clapped his hands loudly twice, raising his voice to be heard in the antechamber. "Haipha, bring my First Daughter to me, quickly. Kanaan, Khalid, escort them to me."

From where they had waited in a separate antechamber, Haipha rose to her feet and gently took Sahla's tiny hand in hers. Both mother and daughter were completely veiled, only hands and eyes visible as they entered the room. Haipha's human, hazel-green eyes and Sahla's sapphire blue eyes. The eyes of her true sire. The eyes of a Jann.

***

Kanaan sat his horse next to Hasim's, recurved horsebow in its scabbard under his right leg, its black arrows in their quiver across his back. Together, they watched Mu'allim Abdu's caravan wend its way into the distance. None of the other warriors of Abdul-Ghaffanse sat their mounts within earshot.

"*Sayyid*, do you think that fat snake will keep his word? He was not happy at all with the bride price you mentioned."

"I think so, Kanaan. The avarice in his heart was plain enough when he saw Sahla's eyes."

"Do you think he knows?"

"That she is a Jann? That the blood of a Jinn runs in her human veins? Perhaps. He may certainly suspect. Much depends on what the Aliyah of al-Kohfan is like. If he is a fire breathing fanatic, as our old Aliyah was, then he will see her as an abomination, a being of two worlds with magic in her soul. Our current Aliyah, Ahmad ibn Sa'id, is a decent sort, for being the Prophet's Voice in our poor tribe. He simply sees Sahla as my daughter, naught more." Hasim turned his horse back to the town as the last of the caravan disappeared over a distant dune. "Kanaan, send out some of your best dune-stalking scouts to ensure our former guests keep going. Ask them to get close enough at night to eavesdrop on anything that fat windbag passes about his Sheikh."

"Of course, *Sayyid*. I dislike what little I have heard of Sheikh Mustafa al-Mahdi. It is my belief that he is cruel and one that abuses those he has power over." Kanaan urged his horse up next to Hasim's. "At least, that was the impression I got from those members of the caravan that came all the way from al-Kohfan with Mu'allim Abdu. He is not beloved." For a ways, Kanaan rode silently beside his lord.

"And? Drop the other boot, Kanaan, my friend."

"How could you promise Sahla, who is so sweet and loving, to one who may well be cruel and abusive?" Kanaan struggled to hold his voice down. "If he is as we think he may be, and he Bonds with her, he will corrupt and break her."

"What makes you think she shall ever wed or Bond to Mustafa?"

"But you have promised..."

"True, but only to a betrothal." Hasim sighed and glanced sideways at his friend. "Kanaan, remember what Ilben said to Haipha. That a Champion will come to struggle against this Darkness he saw. And that it may well be that Sahla will be one of the needful companions of this Champion."

"I am missing something here, *Sayyid*." Kanaan rubbed his beard.

"Do you think this Sheikh Mustafa, who sends this foppish bag of suet to the deep desert, do you really think such as he could be such a Champion?" Hasim's smile was sly. "Should Sahla actually wed him, I shall give you the pick of my stallions and my three best mares."

"The Black?!" Kanaan was startled. "You like that horse better than you like me!"

"I think it a safe wager, my friend." Hasim's teeth gleamed in his grin. "Now, I spoke with Haipha last night. She is most impressed with young Khalid. She wants him groomed to be the Mulazim in what I fear shall become known as the Houri of the Sands' Guard. Drive him hard, Kanaan. I want him ready for that within the next two years. On her twelfth birthing day, I have decided that she shall learn the truth of her parentage, and as much as we know of the foreseeing of Ilben alh-Taymyah, her true sire." Hasim's grin was gone and his face was grim. "The future that awaits her, Kanaan, I believe, shall be beyond any of our darkest imaginings."

"Perhaps, *Sayyid*. Perhaps." Kanaan shrugged philosophically. "But, if I may say, there will be love in her future. A true love. With Sahla's nature, how can there be anything else?"

"May the Prophet himself bless your words, my friend."

Chapter Eight

**Vlymouth Port, Duchy of Hale,
Kingdom of Montagar
September 1478, Third Age of Imperial Reckoning**

Lieutenant Commander Willis Fleet, KRN, Office of
Naval Intelligence, always slept lightly. As one of ONI's best
semi-covert agents, he'd learned long ago that not sleeping lightly
could be a death sentence. So, when the thin knife blade scraped
against the door frame, that slight noise brought him to full
wakefulness in an instant. His hand came out from under his
pillow with a pistol in it. He rolled silently out of bed, moving
noiselessly across the dimly lit room to the other bed. He clamped
his hand down over Gelman's mouth and nose, waking him but
preventing him from speaking.

"Shh," he breathed into the priest's ear. "We've unwelcome
company. Quietly, please. I'd like a nice little chat with whoever
this is." He released Gelman when he nodded his acceptance. Willis
soft-footed into position against the wall next to the door, while
Gelman stood behind the sturdy oak wardrobe next to the wash
basin and mirror. Willis had one of his newly issued forty-six
caliber revolvers in his left hand and a leather sap filled with lead
shot in his right. He waited as the knife slid up the frame to flip the
door's bar out of its brackets.

As the bar flew loose, whoever was on the other side put their
shoulder into it, slamming it open. The first one through the door
jumped to the right, directly in front of Willis, while a pair of

musket barrels thrust into the room. The instant the first ruffian cleared the door, they fired, their muzzle blasts deafening everyone in the room. Relatively crude matchlocks, both seventy-five caliber barrels were loaded with buck and ball. The blankets and pillows of both beds were shredded by the blasts. The muskets were simply dropped and the shooters charged into the room with clubs in their hands.

"SHIT!" Willis cursed. "Gelman, grenade on the right! Watch out!" His shout alerted the door opener, who promptly spun and lunged with his knife. Willis blocked the knife away with the sap and his pistol banged. Blood spurted as the round hit the lunging door opener on the side of his neck, breaking his collarbone and deflecting down into his chest, ripping through the big blood vessels in his torso. He hit the floor hard, choking on his own blood as he futilely tried to stem the gory flood.

Willis rode the pistol's recoil as he switched targets to the grenade carrier. The revolver banged three times in rapid fire. The first bullet hit the man in the base of his spine at a slight angle, severing his spinal cord just below his hips before coming to a stop in his pelvis. The second round clipped a vertebra higher up in his back, deflecting down into his liver. The last shot hit him just at the base of his skull, blasting up through his brain before taking the top of his skull off in a spray of blood and brain matter. He dropped like a marionette with the strings cut.

Before Willis could target the third assailant, there was a sickening crunch as Gelman slammed his heavy mace into the man's chest with a powerful, two-handed swing. Landing square in his sternum, the macehead shattered nearly all of his ribs and collapsed his left lung. A piece of one of the fragmented ribs was driven into his heart, killing him.

"Oh, fuck me!" Ears ringing from the gunfire, Willis couldn't hear the grenade's lit fuse hissing away but he saw the lit slow match as it fell away from the dead man's hand. "GRENADE!" He grabbed the grenade carrier's body and slammed it down on top of the grenade a half second before it exploded. The body muffled the blast, absorbing most of the shrapnel. One piece buried itself in Willis' calf muscle, a painful and bloody wound but not life threatening. Another made it through the floor and blew a hole through the dead center of the chief cook's favorite skillet. The only other damage was the fragment that shattered the room's chamber pot. The abrupt cessation of violence filled the room with a ringing silence.

"Oww, damn it, shit!" Willis could barely hear himself, between the muskets' discharge, the pistol's crashing reports and the partly muffled blast of the grenade. "Damn it, that stings!" He clapped his hand down onto the bloody wound in his calf, putting pressure on it to control the bleeding.

"WHAT?" Gelman shouted. The gunfire and the explosion left him deafened, with a terrible ringing in his ears. "ARE YOU HURT?"

"I caught a fragment of the grenade in my calf. Hurts like all seven hells, but that's all. I don't think it's serious. How's your guy?"

"WHAT?"

"How's your guy?"

"OH," Gelman looked down at the body in front of him. The floor was awash in the blood the man had vomited up as he died. "HE'S DEAD!"

"Stop shouting." Willis grabbed a towel off the wash basin and quickly tied it around his leg. "I can hear you." He sighed at the rising crescendo of panicked screams and shouts from the hallway and nearby rooms. *And I just know that asshole McIntyre will show back up. Or his superior, who might be worse.* He regarded the bloody shambles with annoyance. *Damnit. I needed at least one of these idiots alive to interrogate! Well, I guess the practice with those pistols paid off. Never have had anything quite as effective.* "Come keep an eye on the door and the hallway, will you?"

"WHAT?"

"Great. Just what I need. A deaf priest."

"WHAT?"

Willis sighed in disgust and waved Gelman over.

"YOU'RE HURT!" The priest pointed at the bloody towel.

"I'll be fine!" Willis grabbed Gelman's collar and pulled his ear down to speak directly into it. "Watch the doorway. I doubt there's anyone else out there, but I need a minute with these three clowns. Wait until the police get here. Then you can fix up my leg. Okay?"

"OH." Gelman nodded as he rapidly shook a finger in his ear. "GOT IT!"

While Gelman watched the doorway, smiling and waving as many of the other guests imitated prairie dogs, heads popping in and out of various doors and hallways, Willis quickly and professionally went through the three men's pockets and pouches. What he found greatly intrigued him.

***

"Yes, Detective Officer McIntyre. I understand. Five dead men in one day, in the same Inn, is unusual anywhere. But this time we were attacked in our rooms, at night and by surprise. What did you expect me to do, ask them if they were farm harness salesmen?!" Willis struggled to keep his frustration off his face. Officer McIntyre had indeed been the first ranking policeman to respond and from his questions and attitude, he seemed to think that Willis had hauled these three brigands in off the street so he could kill them. "They entered our room by stealth and fired loaded weapons into our beds without the least warning. I happened to have heard the knife lifting the door bar. If I had grabbed the bar, they might've just shot through the door. I'd have a pair of seventy-five caliber holes in me and *you'd* have a major diplomatic incident on your hands."

"Perhaps, Leftenant Commander Fleet, if you hadn't been so quick to shoot them, I would be able to question them as to their motives in attacking you?" Officer McIntyre's sour expression and hand on his truncheon weren't helping Willis' mood in the least.

"Do you really think, for even an instant, that I wouldn't want to interrogate these morons myself?" *God, give me patience with this idiot, and give it to me NOW!* "Besides, according to the Inn's register, this room is occupied by Lady Silaqui and Lady Sachi. Perhaps that's who Stupid, Moron and Idiot here were after?"

"How do you know their names?" McIntyre snapped.

"Oh, my dear and fuzzy angels!" Willis' temper erupted as he hit the end of his patience. "Are you naturally this stupid or did you have to study?! I have NO IDEA WHAT THEIR NAMES WERE, YOU JACKASS!"

"You have no reason to personally insult me, Sir!" McIntyre started to pull the truncheon from his belt. "I think you'll be coming down to gaol with me, you impudent jackanapes!"

"You pull that Billy club on me and you'll eat it raw! I've had enough of you!" Willis pulled a small black wallet out of his pocket, opening it and showing the papers within to McIntyre. Sea ice wasn't as cold as his voice. "So, fuck you very much! This is full diplomatic immunity. I could rip your head off your neck and shove it up your ass, should fit up there pretty well, since I believe that's where you keep it, and the only thing that can be done to me would be your government declaring me *persona non grata* and shipping my happy ass home! So stick that in your pipe and suck on it, Freddie McInturd! I'm done talking to you!"

"But...you can't address me in such terms, you...you..." McIntyre spluttered in indignation. Willis towered over him, and his gray eyes were chips of sea-ice. "I'll have to place you under arrest, you..."

"That shall be enough, Detective Officer McIntyre." A pleasant tenor voice spoke from the doorway. The man that stood there wasn't quite as tall as Willis' three inches over six feet, but he was much slimmer, under the light blue cloak he pulled aside. Beneath the cloak, he wore expensive evening wear. McIntyre's face went from beet red to ghostly pale when he turned to see who spoke. "I should think you would be best employed in assisting your men in securing those malefactors' bodies. And transporting them to headquarters for proper burial, assuming no family members claim the bodies. Thank you."

"Milord!" McIntyre squeaked, before coughing and recovering his voice. "Yes, Milord, at once, Milord." He vanished like mist in the morning.

"Neat trick. Could I talk you into teaching that one to me?" Willis raised a questioning eyebrow at McIntyre's rapid exit.

"Not so much a trick, Lieutenant Commander Fleet, as a result of being who I am."

"And then, you would be whom, sir?"

"Sir Ian Thelms, fourteenth Earl of Wickshire, currently His Majesty's Chief Inspector of Police in the Duchy of Hale." Thelms' voice carried a quiet authority and his light blue eyes had a bit of boyish amusement in them. Short blond hair gleamed under a stylish brimmed hat.

"Ah." Willis straightened away from the oak wardrobe he'd been leaning against during his confrontation with Officer McIntyre. "I see. So, I'm guessing you're here because of all the excitement?"

"At least partially." Thelms pulled the one chair in the room that wasn't covered in blood and sat in it with an economy of motion that Willis couldn't help but admire. "Now, I am given to understand you were wounded in the altercation. I also am aware that Pere Gelman Stavor, who has been very unobtrusive over by the window, is an empowered priest of the Healing Order of the *Angaelici Benes Eloi*. Perhaps he could do some small bit about your minor injury? Before you bleed all over the rug?" Gelman startled a bit as the Inspector motioned him over. "Thank you, Pere Gelman."

"Oh, that's much better." Willis sighed as golden light haloed Gelman's hands where they touched the bloody wound on his calf. "Thank you, Pere Gelman. You are a treasure beyond price." Willis and Gelman exchanged a grin before Willis returned his full attention to the Inspector. "You know, Inspector, there was a time when I'd have never believed what Pere Gelman does was even remotely possible. Of course, the recruiters do say, *Join the Navy, See the World, Broaden your Mind.* Pretty much the truth, eh?"

"I would certainly agree." Thelms nodded. "Even here in Montagar, there is a certain fairly large percentage of the human population that simply refuses to accept the concept of magic. Or non-humans. The worst ones, well, you could not convince them that elves and dwarves, not to mention other, much worse, things exist even if you stood someone like Lady Silaqui directly in front of them. Humans seem to prefer to inherently reject certain elements of reality in this world."

"Oh, God yes. There's things in the central mountains of Kolbia that the average man in the street in Carolington Bay or Capitol City would not believe existed. Right up until the whatsit killed him." Willis leaned forward, elbows on knees and rubbed his hands together. "Well, we've convinced each other what wonderful, open-minded fellows we are. Detective Officer Third Class McIntyre's men have hauled off the latest batch of corpses. And here you are, His Majesty's Chief Inspector of Police in the Duchy of Hale. And exactly why are you here, after all?"

"Frankly, Lieutenant Commander Fleet, I am here because His Majesty's Government has learned the hard way to pay attention when any of the Fair Folk with connections like Lady Silaqui's shows up in a major city. McIntyre's initial report was brought to my attention earlier today. And when the current brouhaha came to official attention, I was informed. I decided to come down here myself and see exactly what has been going on. Unfortunately, I am well acquainted with McIntyre's record, which includes a certain level of unacceptable prejudice where foreigners are concerned."

"Uh-huh." Willis cocked his head at the Inspector. "Yeah. Pull the other one, it has bells on. That's very nice for the *Official Record.* Now, what do you want?"

"I take it you believe I am being less than forthcoming with you?"

"Oh, aye, I do." Willis grinned. "My briefing included a good bit about you. Inspector of Police. Maybe in your spare time.

The organizational chart I was briefed on earlier today at our diplomatic mission lists you as the Chief of the local branch of your government's diplomatic intelligence service, the DIS. Roughly equivalent to our Chief of Station at the mission."

"You are very well informed for a newly arrived *Cultural Attaché*, Lieutenant Commander."

"What can I say, the local ONI chief wants everyone informed and on their toes, especially with the Lietelean Empire raising hell lately."

"I understand. And what is your connection to Lady Silaqui?"

"Believe it or not, sir, we just happened to be on the same ship. I'm much more of a specialist in the culture of the Isemoto Empire, but I'd gotten on the wrong side of too many of the local crime bosses, what they call *yakuza*. I left on *Intrepid* one step ahead of an assassination order. Then the idiot pirates that had held Lady Silaqui as a captive for slightly over two years, forcing her to wield her magic for them, made the fatal mistake of assuming *Intrepid* was a particularly big merchant galleon. Oops."

"I can imagine."

"And that's how we rescued Lady Silaqui. She's avoided mentioning any relationship to anyone other than this very, very old *Uncle* of hers. For once, ONI and the Office of Strategic Intelligence both fell flat on their faces, no idea who she was. Nevertheless, OSI suspected that she had important connections here, so the decision was made to provide safe transport home for her, whether she liked it or not. *Intrepid* is one of the fastest frigates we have and she was available, so off we went."

"But why are you here, Lieutenant Commander?"

"Well, given that some of the local Nisei population in the Carolington Bay area, and especially Carolington City, has connections to the thugs in their homeland, it was decided that I would be sent here to Montagar until things cooled down a b it. I'm not complaining, the *Yakuza* can get real inventive with folks they're mad at."

"I imagine." Thelms rubbed his chin with a fingertip. "Interesting. Very illuminating, Lieutenant Commander Fleet. Yet, you have not been here a full day, not quite, and you have been involved, one way or another, in five violent deaths. And you have absolutely gotten into Detective Officer Third Grade McIntyre's little black book of people he intends to *get one up on.* His clan is fairly important, and he'll be whining to his Clan Chief by the end of the week, if not sooner. Who will then, most likely, whine to me. You, sir, have the real potential of becoming a very annoying pain in my posterior. Declaring you, as you rightly pointed out to McIntyre, *persona non grata* and sending you straight back to Stark Haven on the first available rowboat has certain attractiveness. What am I to do with you, Lieutenant Commander?"

"I wouldn't worry too much, Inspector. I believe the Envoy has it in his mind to use me as a secure courier. I'm expecting orders to make deliveries to several of our missions in the Empire, and perhaps even our Embassy at Lietelea the City. Probably be gone within the week, if not sooner."

"Hmm. I see." Thelms stood up. "Well, that would solve at least part of the problem you represent to me." He was silent a long time, obviously deep in thought as he regarded Fleet, Gelman and the blood splattered room. "However, I have a very definite feeling that you are not telling me more than the tenth part of what is going on here. But unless I want to arrest you, cause a major diplomatic incident in the process of futilely torturing, excuse me, *questioning* you to get all the truth out of you, I guess I shall just have to settle for not having my curiosity satisfied."

"Probably just as well, Inspector." Fleet smiled. "I just look like I know what's going on. Most of the time I'm as clueless as everyone else is."

"No doubt, Lieutenant Commander, no doubt. Well, I believe I am done here, at least for the moment. Perhaps you should procure quarters inside your Mission's grounds. That way, when you kill someone else, it's not my problem."

"I'm working on it, Inspector."

"Hmm. I am sure you are. Good evening, Lieutenant Commander Fleet."

"Good evening, Inspector Thelms."

Willis plopped down on the edge of the bed as Gelman sat down in the one clean chair. Neither of them spoke as the first member of the Inn's cleaning staff timorously stuck their head around the doorframe and asked if they could start cleaning up the room. Willis swung his feet up on the bed and waved them in.

Outside the room's window, Sachi climbed away from where she had hung, listening to everything that had been said since the gunshots had sent her straight up in the air like a cat, two feet above her bed.

***

"Interesting night last night, Willis. What happened?" Silaqui smiled as the group, minus Aylie, out of sight up in the room, sat around their breakfast table in the Inn's common room.

"Mildly interesting, My Lady." Willis returned her smile. "Officer McIntyre made a repeat appearance and we had a wonderful chat."

"Call me *My Lady* again, and you're a pig, Willis. Literally."

"Does that mean I get to take the day off and relax in a nice cool mud bath?"

"No. Most likely means you'll be bacon and ham before dark."

"You're a hard woman, Silaqui."

"I heard your *chat* with...what was it you called him, *Freddie McInturd*, Willis? And with his superior, someone named Sir Ian Thelms. Very interesting." Sachi steadily worked her way through a truly enormous ham, mushroom and cheese omelet. "Very interesting, indeed."

"How the hell did you hear that?"

"I am a *shinijutsuka*, remember?"

"Umh, yeah. Need to remind myself from time to time that I'm traveling with a black shirt sneak. No keeping secrets from you, eh?" Willis took a slug of his coffee. "Hanging outside the window?"

"Only for the part with Inspector Thelms. Everyone in the Inn heard you tell Officer McIntyre what to do with himself."

"Yeah, about that. Have a look at what I recovered from one of last night's uninvited guests." Willis pulled a folded broadsheet out of his shirt pocket and handed it to Sachi. She unfolded it and spread it out on the table as she ate. Then her fork froze half-way to her mouth.

"That's not good. Something has to be really, really bad to stop her fork before the plate's polished." Silaqui raised an eyebrow. "What is it?"

"The picture is wrong. But close enough, I guess. How many other Nisei women are in Montagar?" Sachi slid the sheet over to Silaqui.

"Ah. No, they didn't get it right at all, other than the black eyes." Silaqui sipped her tea calmly. "You are much more beautiful. But someone wants you very, very dead. Five thousand gold Sterling is enough to buy an Earldom. Payable on presentation of your head, *No Questions Asked.* Just your head. Nice. Who *did* you annoy, Sachi?"

"Even my clan lacks the resources to reach this far, this soon." The fork went back into motion. "But this is a problem."

"It's not an official Wanted broadsheet, either. The three idiots from last night had this. Perhaps something we need to discuss with Pere Gelman's friend." Silaqui handed the sheet over to Gelman.

"Perhaps. But how was this made? There are no signs of a woodcut or a printing press." Gelman frowned as he studied it. "All the letters are perfectly smooth, perfectly aligned. No smudges. The ink seems to be part of the paper. And the quality of the paper is amazing. A sheet this big should cost at least a silver shilling."

"Yeah, something else to think about." Willis frowned as he recovered the broadsheet. "I hadn't really considered the quality of the paper or the printing."

"Well, when I was a young monk, working in the scriptorium was one of my primary tasks. So I am at least somewhat familiar with ink and paper. For what is basically a bounty price sheet, this is incredible."

"Yes." Silaqui was quiet for a long moment. "So, as soon as Sachi is done licking the glaze off the plate, let us repair to our room and discuss this further. And what, if anything, we should do about it." The Elf snickered as Sachi froze again, caught with her fingers chasing the last fragment of ham left on her well cleaned plate.

***

"There be places in Vlymouth where one might learn a mite more of who should be after wanting yer head, Lady Sachi. Course, those also be the places where folk'd be most like to be about taking yer head, quick as quick." Aylie opined as she examined the broadsheet. "But, woo, the cost yer enemy has gone to! Folk'll be stripping these from the walls and selling them to every scribe and pawnbroker in town by the end of the day." Aylie handed the broadsheet back to Sachi.

"Only Sachi, Aylie. I'm no Lady." Her brows were furrowed with concentration as she studied the broadsheet. "Could you find those places, Aylie? The ones where we can learn more of these sheets and who put them up?"

"Oh, aye, easily enough. Should be nae hard at all."

"Good."

"Sachi, what's going on in that head of yours?" Silaqui stood up from her chair to look over Sachi's shoulder. "Don't even think of running off to Khakal by yourself!"

"You are home, Silaqui." Sachi's voice was quiet, barely audible. "Go home to your uncle, whom you talk of so much. Home to folk who still see you as no more than a youth. Home where your magic is common and accepted. Let me go wherever I must."

"No." Silaqui's voice was quietly adamant. "You are not leaving this kingdom without me. Remember the dream I told you of, the one I had onboard *Imperial Damnation*? Whatever it is you're to do, if you try to do it alone, you'll fail. Or, should you manage to succeed, that success might prove to be worse than if you never even tried at all."

"She is correct, Sachi." Gelman spoke up. "The *Angaelici Benes Eloi* himself charged me with finding and helping you. This is exactly what he said to me:

You will meet a woman from a far land, a land far to the East. She will challenge everything you know of woman, in both strength of body and strength of will. But for all her strength, she will need friends and companions on her journey and you shall be among that number. Her path shall be yours as well. Keep her safe, guide her, heal her and defend her; for she is truly the last hope of the world.

An Archangel of the One God said those words to me. And if you are truly the *last hope of the world*, then shouldn't you have all the help we can give you? Sachi, consider this, that we each may have our own parts to play on this great and desperate stage."

"No. You are wrong, Gelman." The conviction in Sachi's voice was nearly absolute.

"How do you know that?" he asked.

"Silaqui's dream was not a true dream." The black depths of her eyes pinned him in place. "Her dream spoke of someone with sapphire blue eyes. Someone who loved the woman in her dream intensely, without reservation or hesitation. Someone who, because of such a powerful love, threw themselves into a hopeless battle to save that woman. That woman cannot be me."

"Why not, Sachi?" Gelman's voice was soft and gentle.

"Because I am *kachinonai*, worthless!" she snapped. "I am unworthy of anyone's love. At best, I might be merely an attractive pleasure companion! At worst, not more than a common whore!" She started to dart from her chair.

"*By my Will, be thou Still!*" Silaqui's voice rang with her Power. Crimson light shone in her eyes. Sachi froze in place, a startled look on her face. "No, you will not flee your friends, those who love you, not this time. You will not flee from me, thinking foolishly to protect me somehow, from the choices *I* make for myself. *I* chose to be your friend, you, who saved me from Je'Libe's pistol and Thorne's rope. Who defended me before *Intrepid's* court. Who showed me that I, *myself*, can still love, still take pleasure in love-play. *I* choose to stand by your side for all time. And you shall NOT gainsay me! If, somewhere, it happens that you fall to your enemies, then I shall fall beside you, you, my Heart-Sister. My Defender. My soul-healer." A taut silence filled the room. "You are my life's friend, Sachi, and I love you. I know no one, Mortal or Immortal, more worthy of being loved than you."

"Aye? And then explain Captain Blaine, on the passage to Stark Haven, telling his wife, Emily, that I am nothing to him." The bitterness in her voice clawed at all of them.

"Sachi, Blaine is very conflicted over you. I have no doubt that he does love you, but he is bound by vows of honor. Surely you, of all folk, understand the demands of honor?"

"Oh, I know honor. Honor and duty are heavier than mountains, Silaqui."

"All right. That's enough self-flagellation, Sachi," Gelman spoke sharply. "I've not known you as long or as well as Lady Silaqui or Willis, but the Archangel himself sent me here to help you. I figure that the One God knows what he was doing when he sent me here to find you. I don't know who you pray to, Sachi—"

"I pray to my Ancestor Spirits."

"Good. I don't ask you to pray to the One God if you do not honestly worship him. Pray to your Ancestor Spirits. And have a little faith in me. As I have faith in you."

"Why, Gelman, why do you have any faith in me?"

"Because I have faith, an unshakeable faith, in my God." He gave Sachi a gentle smile. "It's as simple as that, young lady."

"That's pretty clear, Sachi." Willis interjected. "And think of this. It took someone special to impress the Bosun of *Intrepid*. Or her First Lieutenant. Or Toby Wilkerson. They all had faith in you. Hell, after *Intrepid* took that pirate, *Imperial Damnation*, when you were the first boarder on her decks, even the Marines were impressed. The only thing they really had to worry about was not stumbling over the dismembered bodies left in your wake."

"But, Willis, I..."

"*But, Willis* nothing!" he interrupted. "Remember the 'tournament' Major Karlson organized the next to last day in the Horn Islands? Who won? Who put me on my backside in two moves? I've studied the sword most of my life and Nisei style martial arts since I joined the Navy. Two moves and I'm seeing the world rotate around my head! Ground, sky, ground, sky, splat!"

"You were so slow, Willis." Sachi grinned an urchin's grin despite herself.

"And you're greased lightning. I've never seen anyone so fast." Willis shrugged. "You beat four of the toughest sailors on *Intrepid* and then five Marines, including their company sergeant."

"Willis, what does any of that have to do with being worthy of being loved?" Her voice was flat and hard. "I'm a good killer. That's of no doubt. But being an expert in slaughter does not make one worthy of love."

"Sachi," Aylie spoke up for the first time, "I understand ye doubting yerself. I began as nae more than a scruffy street rat. And that was doubt and plenty of it. Yet, I was good enough, worthy enough to be chosen as Milady's own, personal maid. Milady taught me, even more than the Baron's chatelaine, Mrs. Marlowe, good woman that she is, did, that I've my own worth, for my own self. I've naught a fraction of yer own beauty, of yer own skills and knowledge. If I be worthy of such, could not ye be at least as worthy as I, if not more so? Ye has great friends, Sachi, even one of the Fair Folk claims ye as her Heart-Sister. How can ye nae be worthy of such friends? 'Tis too, too hard on yerself, ye be." The dark-skinned young woman caught Sachi's eyes with her own and held them as she smiled. "I can believe in ye, in yer worth. And who am I to argue with a priest whom the very angels appear before, a sorceress of the Fair Folk and an officer of the greatest navy in the world? Milady always told me to have faith in meself, in me own worth. I think, nae, I *know* she'd say the same to ye. Have faith in yer worth. Yer friends, new and old, do. Of God's own certainty, they do."

Sachi stared in disbelief at the four of them. Then her eyes rolled up into her head as the fit took her and she sagged bonelessly in the grip of Silaqui's spell.

Virtual Reality Construct
September 1478, Third Age of Imperial Reckoning

D.A.V.E. was waiting for her when her avatar coalesced into existence in the infinite, featureless gray space. The numbers floating behind him had changed. System Integration now read sixty-nine percent.

"Why am I here, now?"

::This Entity has information that you need. And a reminder of your mission, Caitlyn Schmidt.::

"Oh? And what is this information? And I've not forgotten my *mission*. I'm supposed to save the world."

::Correct. Your mission is to prevent the destruction of the planet Rubican III, the third planet of the Omega-2 Cygni stellar system.::

"How? What can possibly destroy the whole world?"

::There is a Kuiper Belt planetoid falling Sunward on an orbit that will bring it into a direct collision with Rubican III. The planetoid is on a reciprocal orbit, impact velocity estimated at twenty-five kilometers per second, and the planetoid is roughly the same size as Rubican III's moon, approximately two thousand kilometers in mean radius. The impact will, at best, sterilize Rubican III of all life, probability unity, plus or minus four point five percent. It is most likely that the planet will shatter on impact and form an asteroid field, probability unity, plus or minus one percent.::

"How in the Ancestor's names am I supposed to stop something like that?"

::You will not do it by yourself, although you are the key element. There are sufficient remaining useable resources in this system to divert the planetoid. The difficulty will be accessing and coordinating the output of the remaining tens of thousands of functional platforms still in solar orbits. You will be one part of a functional fire control system capable of focusing enough energy, thousands, if not tens of thousands of petajoules of energy, to divert the planetoid in its orbital path.::

"So you're going to help me do this? Be the other part?"

::I am a D.A.V.E., with very limited processing power and memory. You will require access to a functional Class One or Class Two Artificial Intelligence.::

"Let me guess, I need to learn how to access this thing, this Class One Artificial Intelligence, and then find one."

::Correct. And in the course, you will need to continue the ongoing process of field enhancement.::

"Right." She sighed. "So what about these people, who say they are my friends? Do I need to get away from them?"

::Unadvisable. Given the time it may take to locate and recover the required elements; a functional A.I., an operable system command node, perhaps at least a functional Class Four or better medical facility, not to mention the possible environmental hazards and apparent active opposition, it would be advisable to have individuals willing to provide what support they might. Probability of success without any aid is eleven percent, plus or minus fifty-eight percent. This large error variation is due to excessive variables.::

"And if I drag these few friends I have on this insane journey with me? What does your *probability* say then?"

::Probability of success is fifty-four percent, plus or minus twenty-eight percent.::

"And do any of them survive?"

::Probability impossible to compute, excessive variables.::

"So I should drag them off, Ancestors only know where, maybe getting all of them killed? Is that what a D.A.V.E. thinks I should do?"

::Caitlyn Schmidt, should you fail in your mission, the probability of any life, much less your friends, surviving is effectively negative infinity. All life on Rubican III will end if the planetoid impacts.::

"Oh." Sachi was quiet for a long time. "Is time passing faster here than out there?"

::Yes, hyper-heuristic mode has been engaged.::

She sat down beside the silver statue; her legs bent at the knees, her arms crossed, elbows on her knees and rested her chin on her forearms. She sat there, silent, the silver statue of D.A.V.E.'s avatar facing the same direction, for what felt like an hour, not thinking about anything in particular, simply being herself.

"You're just numbers, right; you said it was something called binary code?" she quietly asked as she stared into the grey infinity.

::Correct in essence. Binary code is ancient but effective, constructed of ones and zeros in relative positions, signaling a switch to be on or off. True AIs use ternary code, constructed of a positive one, a zero and a negative one, allowing uncertainty as well as off or on. But all modern systems, whether standard, stand-alone comps, Entity Systems like myself or true AIs are designed to interface directly with humans. Code knowledge is only required of comp-sys maintenance personnel. And the somewhat rare humans who write modern machine language code.::

"Yeah, good, D.A.V.E., you could have just said yes and left it there, you know." She again fell silent. A while later, she raised her chin and looked at the avatar. At some point it had turned to face her. "Are you smarter than I am?"

::No. I may access and process information much faster, but I lack the spark of intuition and creativity that nearly all humans possess. AIs also possess such abilities, but not in either quantity or quality when compared to humans in the top five percent of human ability. Humans such as yourself, Caitlyn Schmidt.::

"Huh." She turned and stared off into the gray distance, her eyes glittering. "In the real world I can see far away like I'm right there. I know exactly how far something is, even if you did have to teach me how to use your *metric system* and how to convert it to the Kolbians' inches and feet and miles. I can see in the dark. I can see on someone's face the patterns that tell me if they are being truthful. I'm stronger and faster. I heal like magic when I'm hurt."

::All of these things are part of a very basic military field enhancement program, Caitlyn Schmidt. And the injury repair conducted by your systemic medical nanites is not in any way similar to *non-rational quantum access*. And all of this drives your higher metabolism, in turn driving your appetite.::

"Oh, aye. I eat enough for three strong men. Is that ever going to change?"

::Once your enhancement package is complete, you will experience reduced appetite, but you will always need more food-energy than an unenhanced human.::

"Wonderful." Again the moody silence fell as she stared into the distance. "Is anyone ever going to love me, D.A.V.E.? The way Mama and Papa Komiya loved each other? Am I worth loving, or do I spend the rest of my life alone?"

::I am an Entity program, Caitlyn Schmidt. Existential questions such as those are beyond my abilities. I do not know if anyone will ever love you. But I would say that you eventually finding a suitable love-match has a probability of seventy-two percent, plus or minus forty-six percent, due to multiple variables. While not romantic love, per se, there is a preponderance of evidence that the indigenous individual known as Silaqui is definitely attracted to you, at least in terms of a deep friendship-based relationship, one closely resembling a sibling bond, probability eighty-nine percent, plus or minus fifteen percent. Lieutenant Commander Willis Fleet certainly finds you sexually desirable. Probability that he engages in sexual self-pleasure while fantasizing about you is eigh— ::

"SHUT up, D.A.V.E.!" she snapped. "I do NOT need or want to know what Willis does! Or who he fantasizes about! Ancestors!" She felt her face burn.

Willis is handsome enough, I suppose, but there has never been the least sign of love between us. Simple physical lust, at least on his part? No doubt, he is a man and I am what I am. She drew a deep, calming breath. *In the Horn Islands, we made love that one day, Silaqui and I, happily giving each other pleasures. But that was more the relief of the anxiety and stress than love. Nothing like what I felt for My Captain. But even between me and Captain Blaine, there was something ever so slightly out of kilter. Perhaps we are both too much slaves to honor and duty. And Silaqui says she dreamt of* Akarui ao-iro no me, *eyes of sapphire blue. A woman with such eyes who might love me enough to risk her very life for me. For me? Huh. Is such a thing even possible? Someone loving me enough to do such a thing, leap off the precipice to try and save me? Humph. As Aylie might say,* Not bloody likely, mate! *Not bloody likely indeed.* She raised her head again and looked around. Nothing had changed in the least.

"Does anything ever change here, D.A.V.E.?"

::No, Caitlyn Schmidt. The VR construct is static, in order to conserve the greatest amount of energy and resources possible. You can direct that changes be made, but there would be a systemic cost. Until your enhancements can be completed, the construct should be as simple as possible.::

"Yeah. I guess that makes sense." She paused, "How long have I been here, in real world time?"

::Twenty-four point six seconds at mark. ::He paused a beat. ::Mark.::

"Feels like hours."

::Hyper-heuristic time compression is known to create such impressions.::

"Humpf. And how long will recovery take this time?"

::Full physical and sensory recovery should take no more than nineteen minutes and thirty-three seconds, plus or minus two minutes and fifty-one seconds.::

"So are we basically done here, then?"

::Affirmative, Caitlyn Schmidt.::

"Well, then send me back." The grey world blurred away as she spiraled into unconsciousness.

***

"Welcome back." Silaqui's smile was the first thing Sachi saw when she opened her eyes. "Are you well?"

"Well enough, I think. How long, this time?"

"Not quite a half hour."

"Ugh. Who stabled goats in my mouth? Blecch."

"Here." Aylie handed her a cup of tea as Silaqui helped her to sit up. "Hot tea with plenty of sugar and milk."

"Ancestors bless you, Aylie. Thank you." Sachi managed to control her urge to grab the cup and gulp the tea down.

"Does this happen often, Sachi?" Gelman asked.

"Not often, but it happens, Gelman. There's nothing even your healing magic can do for these fits." Sachi grimaced as she swallowed the tea in three gulps.

"I examined you while you were...gone. And it seemed that, well, *gone* is a good way to describe your condition." Gelman frowned. "There was nothing wrong with you I could detect. It's as if your psyche simply was gone elsewhere."

"Just leave it alone, Gelman," she shrugged, "it happens. I deal with it."

"The fits aren't as bad as they used to be," Silaqui added from her cross-legged seat on the edge of the rug, next to the couch on which Sachi had been laid, "and they don't last as long either. Well, other than the really long one you had while we were sailing under the Shadow in the *Intrepid*."

***

"So, what now, folks?" Willis asked from where he sat at the table, cleaning one of his revolvers. "Not that I mind killing assassins and thugs in job lots, but it does keep you from doing whatever it is you should be doing."

"Don't you have a job to do, Lieutenant Commander Fleet?" Sachi set the teacup down.

"Well, yes." He held the cylinder up to the light to inspect its cleanliness. "But I've been informed the envoy intends to use me as a 'confidential courier' charged with delivering various diplomatic correspondences to other missions and perhaps even our Embassy in Lietelea the City. And most likely those journeys will be on whatever tub happens to be in port and going the right way. Wouldn't be too surprising if, at least initially, we found ourselves on the same ship."

"Ye be assuming we will all be going the same direction." Aylie frowned as she refilled Sachi's teacup. "Why should I want to tag along after any of ye?"

"Ignacio clearly has connections back to the Empire, Aylie." Gelman shrugged. "I would expect him to be leaving for someplace more cordial to his practices. You said the thing in the box he spoke to mentioned the name Palmaroli. The Palmaroli family is very extensive and deeply intertwined in the affairs of the Empire. Ignacio, I fear, is naught more than one wave in a storm."

"Huh. Well, mayhaps. But iffn I can get some, as me Ma would've said, *quality time* with this Ignacio fellow, a good stout rope and a sharp little knife, I'll take that in a blink of a raven's eye. Oh, aye, have no doubt of that."

If this Ignacio fellow *saw that look on her face, he'd be on the first ship to anywhere else at all.* Willis checked the bore of his revolver with a scrap of white paper, reflecting the light up the bore. *Yup, that's clean. Clean enough to make a Marine drill instructor smile.*

Lot easier to clean these things than it ever was to clean one of those old front-stuffers. Wonder what they'll come up with next?

"Well, I've an idea then." Willis picked up his powder flask and began charging the individual cylinders. "If you know where you might pick up a little more information about these bounty posters, Aylie, why not take Sachi with you and see what might be learned?"

"Oh, aye, that'd be wonderful! Tell me, does ye tie a steak about yer neck to play with the dogs, too?"

"I'm not done, Aylie." Willis seated the bullets, one at a time, over the powder charges before sealing the front of the chambers with heavy grease to prevent chain fires. "Before you leave, get Silaqui to use her magery and hide Sachi's appearance, especially her eyes, with some kind of magic illusion. You can do that, right, Silaqui?"

"Aye, 'tis easy enough, a mere glamour to seem other than what reality is in truth."

"So, Sachi, a blue-eyed blonde or a green-eyed redhead?" Willis grinned at her as he seated the primer caps on their nipples and finished assembling the pistol.

"Willis, have you lost your mind?" Gelman asked.

"No, I haven't." Willis opened his tunic and slipped the pistol into an elaborate shoulder holster. "But Aylie knows the local criminal elements better than any of us. And I've found not one man yet who can stand before Sachi and successfully lie to her."

"Truly?" Aylie turned and asked Sachi. "None can lie to ye?"

"True enough." Sachi glared at Willis. "And I'd appreciate it, Willis, if you'd keep your big mouth shut about such things."

"Sachi, I'm not one for being all mystical and magicky, being a Kolbian and all," Willis gave Sachi his most winning smile, "but let's just say that I have a...feeling about this, the people in this room. I think that we're going to be together a very long time. So perhaps the fewer secrets we have from each other, the better we'll be in the long term. At least, that's my thought?"

"Amazing. Next thing we know, you'll be learning magic, Willis." Silaqui smirked at the pained look on Willis' face.

"Let's not go that far, now, Silaqui," Willis answered.

"Enough." Sachi stood up. "Can you disguise me, Silaqui, at least my eyes?"

"Yes, easily enough."

"Aylie, are you willing to be my guide to the darker sides of Vlymouth? Places where I can find those who would look to take this bounty offer seriously?"

"Aye, if Lady Silaqui can in truth disguise ye with her magicking."

"Then let's be about this. If you would be so kind, Silaqui?"

"As you wish." The Elf's eyes glowed scarlet as she raised her power.

Schooner *Whisper*,
Mid-Lanic Ocean, Northern Passage
September, 1478, Third Age of Imperial Reckoning

Marianne could feel the change in the ship's motion as the wind continued to rise, moving from a six to a seven on the ancient Beaufort scale. She heard Captain Montrose calling the hands to reduce sail, taking a second reef in the top sails and topgallants. He had already altered course to the north to avoid the heavy weather he felt was coming. She activated her neural link to the satellite network, getting enough bandwidth to check the current weather report.

Looks like a fairly nasty hurricane starting to brew up south of us. And Captain Montrose has nothing more to go on than his observations of wind and wave. And thirty plus years of experience in sailing between Kolbia and Montagar. I doubt I could do half as well, even with satellite weather reports and modern meteorological forecasting! Shows how much experience is worth. Glad he's altered course, even if it'll add a day to the trip. But we should still make Vlymouth by day after tomorrow or the next day after that, at the worst.

"D.A.V.E.?" she subvocalized.

::Yes, Commander Marianne Lundgren?::

"Please give me a projected track on the storm south of my position."

::This storm is projected to develop into a Category Three storm, continuing south into the open ocean before dissipating, probability sixty-eight percent, plus or minus twelve percent. Long range forecasts project a second, more powerful storm to develop behind the current storm, within the week, probability fifty-four percent, plus or minus twenty-six percent.::

"Any chance that second weather system will affect us on this trip?"

::Highly unlikely. Probability of the projected second storm affecting this voyage is less than five percent, plus or minus two percent. But if this vessel should elect to make an immediate return and chose a standard southerly course, then the probability of the projected second storm intersecting that voyage is ninety-two percent, plus or minus eight percent.::

"Sounds like time for sailors to be in the pub and not on the sea."

::Null input, Commander.::

"Dear sweet Jesus, I hate you sometimes. Disregard last. Any input on my request for a drone mission from Captain McAllen?"

::Three missions have been flown. One was a follow-up to *Intrepid*, confirming that subject Sachi Takahashi is no longer aboard that vessel. The other two were general sweeps of Vlymouth town proper. Negative returns on the subject, but fairly high levels of electronic comm traffic were detected. Frequencies were common ones used in standard Seeker transmissions.::

"Hmm. Okay, what about either the Elf, Silaqui, or that naval officer that left the ship there? A Lieutenant Fleet, I believe?"

::Both missions resulted in negative results for any of the indicated individuals.::

"What the hell? Nothing at all?"

::Correct. A fourth mission will be flown today, but Captain McAllen wants to evaluate the take closely prior to any further missions being flown. Mission profiles have been prepped and downloaded to the drones, but she is holding them at this time, pending the results from the fourth mission.::

"Copy that. Make sure I get the raw data from this fourth mission. There's something here we're missing."

::Understood.::

"There's something out of whack here. Feels like a cat watching a mouse hole with only one exit. And the cat knows there's a mouse in there. But who's who? Are we the cat or the mouse?"

::Null input.::

"Oh, go back to sleep mode, D.A.V.E.!"

Chapter Nine

**Desert Settlement of Abdul-Ghaffanse,
Darsälaamic Kaliphate, Northern Khakal
November 1472, Third Age of Imperial Reckoning**

Steel skirled against steel, the sharp ringing crash of combat echoed by the grunts and pants of the combatants. The training arena was nearly full, occupied by those warriors striving to be selected to the Guard of the Houri of the Sands. Mostly they were the younger sons of the tribe, the youngest barely to the age of manhood, having seen fifteen turns of seasons. The oldest was a grizzled veteran of twenty-eight. The deep desert was a harsh mistress and death oft came early. But now they all watched the last test, the struggle to determine who would lead as Mulazim of the Guard and who should stand next as the Rahqib, what the infidels would call the Sergeant of the Guard. A pair of judges stood on opposite sides of the ring. Their only function was to monitor the struggle, allow no later claims of skullduggery.

At the top of the northern wall there was a covered box, shaded from the sun's fierce heat. The Sheikh and his favorites might observe duels and judgments of the sword from its vantage point, while servants and slaves fanned them and brought lemonades and cool water. Today, no one reclined on silk or satin cushions and no slaves waved long fans. Sheikh Hasim and Kanaan Rahim were the only current occupants of the covered box. They had been there since early morning, fully armed and armored, silently watching and weighing those striving to become members of the Houri's Guard. Kanaan watched his son with silent, hawk-like intensity.

Jamul al 'Abbas gave three inches in height, four in reach and thirty pounds advantage to Khalid ab-Kanaan. He was also more lightly armored, supple leather instead of Khalid's heavier chain hauberk and shield. But he drove in on the attack regardless of his supposed disadvantage in size, his paired small-swords a blur as they rang against Khalid's steel rimmed shield and curved shamshir.

Khalid's eyes narrowed behind the nasal guard of his steel cap. Jamul was fast, though whether or not he was faster than Khalid was yet to be seen, but there was a certain pattern to his attacks. Khalid had fought defensively so far, letting Jamul move him laterally around the ring, but blocking his access to the mannequin draped in a filmy blue burnoose, representing the Houri herself. Both warriors dripped sweat as they fought, but Khalid was patient, absorbing Jamul's flurries of blows on shield and shamshir. The oil with which Jamul curled his long hair dripped down with his sweat, staining his cotton tunic. Another flurry of blows rang on his shield and then Jamul jumped back, out of Khalid's reach.

"Well, *cousin*," he jeered, "are you just going to stand there, or are you not here to fight?"

"I'm not here to fight, *cousin*." Khalid shrugged his shoulders to settle his armor. "I'm here to protect the Houri." They were distant cousins, sharing the same great-great-grandfather. Despite, or perhaps because they were so distantly related, the two did not care for each other at all. "The idea is to keep her alive and well. Not win fame, fortune and glory with a bloody blade. You need to understand that."

Jamul growled and lunged at Khalid, small-swords blurring. No one was ever quite sure what happened, but somehow, Khalid bound one of those blades with his larger shamshir while shrugging the other aside with his shield. The same shield that then slammed with brutal force into Jamul's face. Blood sprayed as his nose flattened against his cheek. Khalid followed the shield bash with a rush, ducking under Jamul's weak attempt to block that rush with his left hand small-sword. He planted his armored shoulder into the middle of Jamul's chest and the smaller man flew backwards, blasted off his feet. He lost one sword when he hit the ground and a vicious kick to the elbow sent the other flying, losing all strength in that arm. Khalid pinned him to the arena's sand with a boot on his sternum and the tip of his own sword at Jamul's throat.

"Yield. Or die. Your choice, *cousin*." Khalid's voice was just loud enough to be heard in the sudden silence that fell in the arena. Jamul had handily defeated and humiliated all his opponents while Khalid did just enough to win and no more. The general expectations, and the quiet side bets, had heavily favored Jamul. The tests were not to the death, but several men had suffered broken bones and bad cuts, and one of Jamul's opponents had died from a deep slash that cut the great artery in the leg.

"I yield," Jamul gasped, loud enough to be heard throughout the arena. "Khalid is the victor."

Khalid nodded once, and stepped away from Jamul, backing out of the arena's circle. Neither of them took their eyes off the other for an instant.

"Humpf. I guess *that* ended well." Sheikh Hasim al Murafte muttered under his breath to Kanaan Rahim where they stood in the shaded box at the top of the arena.

"Indeed, *Sayyid*." Kanaan's answer was just as quiet. "Jamul is a superb swordsman, but I've never been able to like him, even as a boy. I know tradition states that Jamul should be the Rahqib for Sahla's Guard...but just this once, I wish we could set that tradition aside."

"Truth, by the Prophet's beard. But his father is wealthy and influential with many others in the tribe." Hasim shrugged. "But clearly Khalid knows to keep his eye on him. And I trust your son. Let us hope, by Chalta's Will, that that will be sufficient."

"From your lips to Chalta's ears, *Sayyid*."

"And remember, Haipha is training Sahla just as hard as any of these young hotheads. And not just in dance."

"Ayah! How long ago it was!" Kanaan smothered a guffaw. "To see mighty Hasim put upon his back, and by a mere female at that, even if she was a Senior Mistress of the Dervish Sisterhood!"

"I can find another Chief Captain, you know," Hasim muttered.

"Yes, but who else would take the job?" Kanaan answered with a straight face.

"There is that." Hasim held his grim glare a moment longer before laughing with his old friend. "I guess, if the Prophet wills it, I will have to keep you on, for now, anyway."

"And *Sayyid*, if Haipha, your lovely wife, is training Sahla as hard as you say, I pity the man who offers her offense." Kanaan smiled as he watched Khalid approach. "Remember that fancy, Kolbian-made slicing machine we saw in the port-town of Al-Iskabad, the one that cut the beef so thinly that you could almost see through it?"

"Yes. I was more impressed with the speed of its blades."

"If she is as you say, *Sayyid*, any who draws her ire will think they had been shoved into that thing!"

"Truth." Hasim turned his attention to Khalid, who stopped before his Sheikh and saluted, right fist to chest. "Well done, Khalid. Your victory reveals skill and forethought, an intelligent understanding of what your purpose as Mulazim of the Houri's Guard truly is."

"Thank you, *Sayyid*."

"You will be eighteen turns of the seasons next month. You have born a blade as a man of Abdul Ghaffanse since you came of age, three years ago. It pleases me that you have earned the position of Mulazim of my First Daughter's Guard, she whom the poets are pleased to call the Houri of the Sands."

"I am honored before Chalta and his Prophet, *Sayyid*." Khalid touched his left hand's fingertips to his heart, lips and forehead in salute to Chalta and the Prophet.

"Truth. Confer with my Chief Captain, Kanaan Rahim. Select a Guard of four and twenty from those here. By traditional right, Jamul al 'Abbas will be your Rahqib, Mulazim Khalid." Hasim smiled at the light of joy in Khalid's dark eyes, and the flash of white teeth in his darkly tanned face as he smiled at his father for just an instant. "Well done, Khalid. Well done indeed."

***

"And move and spin and twist! Faster, daughter, faster! You must flow, both with the music and with the blades." Haipha nearly chanted as Sahla's silk slippers hissed on the stone floor, spinning in time with the frantically fast drum-beat coming from behind the screen shielding her from the eyes of males not of her family. Her abbreviated dancing costume left arms and midriff bare, her top hugging a chest where her breasts were barely beginning to bud. The loose, side-slashed pants fluttered with her movement. They were tied at ankle, knee and hip, in turn concealing and revealing slim legs that were just beginning to grow into a woman's curves. Silken hair the color of a raven's wing floated in a tail bound by wraps of silver and turquoise. Sweat glistened on arms and legs, torso and face, the razor-sharp sabers in her hands hissing as they cut the very air itself.

"Good! Very good, daughter! And the third cut, Susurration of Sand, flow into position for the next, and dip to avoid the enemy blade! Jump! Float above the cut! Point as you spin, each cut fast, faster, and precisely placed. Snap your head around, see where each blade strikes. Good! Excellent! And weave the final cuts, the Eagle's Claw, see your attackers fall, slain by your swords." *This is going to be hard on her, but she must learn the consequences of the blade dances. And there is only one way to start doing so. At least I won't have to clean up the mess, as I had to when my Mistress did this to me! Ah, the luxury of servants! As the Sheikh's First Daughter, polishing up the mess will not be her concern. But perhaps I should make her...but, no, if I do, dinner and the talk we must have will be too late into the night. Exhausted and hungry girls do not pay sufficient attention!* She uncovered a hidden bucket, full of sheep's blood, and threw it into Sahla's face as she made the last cut. The blood splattered and the girl stumbled.

"Aaaaiiieee!" Sahla screamed in shock. The blood had splashed across her arms, coating her arms and much of her chest. Globs of the partly congealed blood clung to her legs and she choked and spit to get the stuff out of her mouth. She flung her head left and right, trying to sling the blood out of her eyes. She spun one final time, blood flying off her and speckling the walls. She stopped in a defensive crouch, both blades still in her hands. She faced her mother, sapphire eyes wide in shock. She shook her head again and spat on the floor. "Why, Mama!?"

"Because you are being trained as a full Dervish, taught both dance and blade. Think! What would have been the result of this dance if you faced a living, breathing opponent? Tell me, what would this room look like? What would you look like? And what would your opponent look like?" For a long, eternal moment, Sahla held her crouch, staring at her mother.

"I'd be soaked in hot blood. And his guts would be spread across the floor." Her eyes lost focus, just a little. She carefully laid her blades on the floor, stepped to the edge of the stone dancing ring and promptly vomited all over the tiled floor. Haipha caught her before she could collapse into the mess.

"Na-na, it's all right, my sweet child. That was cruel, I know, but in extremis, if you must defend yourself or another with your blades and your skills, then you *must* know what happens, what a blade does to a human body."

"Are you going to make me kill someone, Mama? A slave or a stranger?"

"No, child! Sahla, I beg the Prophet every day that you never in your life draw steel in earnest defense of life or love. But today is your birthing day, you have now twelve turns of the seasons, and therefore, many things will change. No longer are you a child, by the laws of Chalta's Prophet and the traditions of our tribe."

"If I am no longer a child, does that mean I must marry and leave Father's household?"

"No. You may no longer be a child, but you are also not yet a woman grown." Haipha carefully wiped the blood off Sahla's face. "Not for years yet. But someday I know, I don't think or believe, but I *know* that you will find a love that will eclipse the greatest love stories the bards and poets tell, a love that will build a legend."

"Truly?"

"The Prophet's own Truth, dear child of my heart, I swear to you." Haipha smiled into Sahla's other-worldly blue eyes. "Now, come. I must get you cleaned up, have the servants come in and clean this room. Tonight, you will take the evening meal in private with myself and your Father. There are things that it is finally time that you learn. Many things."

***

If my daughter is uncertain about the change in her status or these secret things *we will tell her tonight, she shows no sign of it in the least. Ah, Ilben, you may have loved my Haipha and sired my daughter, but I am Haipha's one true love, and Sahla is more my daughter than she will ever be yours!* Hasim's beard hid his smile of pride in his daughter. For the first time, Sahla sat to a meal with her mother and father, dressed in the full hijab and abayah of a woman grown. She handled the change in clothing with the same grace she handled her lessons in dance and sword.

"More mutton, Father?" She offered the serving plate to him, but he waved it away. She settled back on her cushion and nibbled on a last piece of flatbread.

"So," he spoke into a sudden silence, "no doubt the worm of curiosity gnaws a hole in your head that you eat privately with your parents so that they might tell you...secrets?"

"It will be as the Prophet wills, Father. If Chalta wishes me to learn...secrets, then secrets I shall learn. But shall they remain secrets, once I am told?"

"From you, of course not." Haipha spoke up. "But from others, from general knowledge, yes. And this will include the rest of your family, all other than us, your parents. You will know, without any doubts, when you find that One who must know your secrets."

"Very well. Tell me what you will, Father, Mother."

"I shall begin with the hardest part first." Hasim spoke.

***

Father's voice is a thing of ominous foreboding! Sahla set her bread aside. *What is coming to change my world?*

"You are not the child of my loins, Sahla." He paused for an instant as she stared in disbelief at him, sapphire eyes round in shock. He breathed a deep sigh. "Your true sire is Ilben alh-Taymyah, a Jinn of the Second Rank of Air and Wind. As such, you are not fully human, Sahla al Qasim ab Ghaffanse, First Daughter of Abdul-Ghaffanse. You are a Jann, and the blood of your Jinn Sire flows in your veins as strongly as the human blood of your Mother." He watched the blood drain from her face.

"Not your daughter? You are my Father! How can I not be your daughter?" Her eyes were huge in her pale face. "How can I not be human, Father? I don't even know what a Jann is! How is this possible?"

"Come here, child." Hasim motioned the girl to him and gathered her into his arms. "This is the story of how you came to be. Long ago, the Imperials marched in great force against us here in Abdul-Ghaffanse. We were weaker then, fewer warriors and no neighboring tribes willing to aid us. The Imperial satrap thought by destroying or enslaving us, he could control the oasis and springs of Ghaffanse, and so split the Folk of the Desert in order to once again attempt a great conquest, one great enough to put his feet on the steps of the Imperial Throne."

"Truly?"

"The Prophet's own truth, my child. At the time, I possessed a wonderful Ring, a magic Ring that summoned a powerful Jinn, Ilben alh-Taymyah, Jinn of the Second Rank of Air and Wind. With the Ring, I could command his obedience, as Master to Slave."

"But all the tales say that all Jinni hate being commanded and will trick and betray those who would command them!" Sahla tensed within the shelter of her Father's arms.

"Truth. Now listen. I did not seek to command Ilben, for over the years he had become my friend and I would not treat my friend as a slave. So I asked his help, only asked. I knew that he could turn the Imperials, even the dreadful Imperial Pikes, aside and so preserve my people. In return for his aid, he demanded a boon, that he woo my new wife for a year and a day, lay with her and give her a child, a daughter. With few other choices, none of them good, I granted his request. The Imperials were turned aside and nine in ten of them left their bones to bleach in the desert sun. I knew better than to renege on my word to Ilben, and so I gave the Ring to your Mother."

"You did?"

"Yes, he did, Sahla." Haipha took up the tale. "Ooh, I was SO angry with him when I learned the cost of his victory! But I was his wife and as such bound by his word. So I took the Ring and summoned Ilben. I would have lain with him that very first day, simply to punish your Father."

"You would have?"

"Oh, yes, I was that furious. But Ilben, Chalta bless him, Ilben would have none of it. Or of me, in my rage. *I must woo and win your heart, My Lady,* he said to me. *What will come of our union must be a child of love and tenderness, one with a happy, cheerful heart and a beautiful soul. Not a child of rage and hate.* He was wiser than I was then. It was months, almost the full year before we laid in tender love together."

"Do you still love him, Mama?" Sahla's question startled Haipha. She caught and held her husband's eyes. He smiled and nodded at her and dropped his eyes to Sahla where she cuddled in his arms.

"Love is like the sand of the desert, Sahla. If you lift away a handful of sand or even enough to fill all the packs of a great caravan of ka'mels, there is always more sand left. Love is one of those things created by Chalta to be truly infinite. Yes, I still love Ilben, I always will, even if I never see him again. But know this, child. I love your Father, Hasim, just as deeply. He is my True Love, and I will love him until the day the Prophet opens the door into Paradise for me. Ilben is an Immortal and his spirit will always live in this world, while, in due time, both your Father and myself will step through the Prophet's door into Chalta's Paradise where we will live together in love for all eternity."

"If Ilben...if my Sire is an Immortal, a Jinn, a spirit of the air, what am I? Am I immortal like him?" Her brows furrowed as she considered the implications.

"Well, as Ilben told me when I asked the same question of him, the answer is *maybe*. You will be bound by certain conditions. And those conditions will decide, perhaps, your fate." Haipha caught and held her daughter's sapphire gaze.

"What conditions, Mother?"

"There is truly only one. If you have not found a human, a mortal to Bond with by the time you reach your eighteenth birthing day, the magic that helped to create you shall draw you away from this mortal sphere and bring you before your Sire in his palace on the Plane of Air. There, he will claim you as his own." Haipha paused. "While Ilben is vastly powerful here, in the Mortal World, in his world, among his own kind, well, he is only a Jinn of the Second Rank. And the greater elemental spirits, noble Jinni of the First Rank, the Dao of Earth, the Marid of Water or, worst of all, the Efreeti of Fire, many of them, especially the nobles of the Jinni and the Efreeti, they do not care for humans in the least. The Marid are said to be allies of the Jinni, the Earth Dao generally are uncaring neutrals and, despite their mutual disdain for mortal humans, the Efreeti are deadly enemies of the Jinni."

"The Prophet does not mention such creatures in the Kitab al'Aqdas, Mother. The Book of Holies says naught of them. Are they the *evil ones* the Aliyah speaks of when he tells us to beware of the spirits of the outsiders? What he tells us to take heed of making bargains with?"

"Daughter, there are many things in the World even the Book of Holies says naught of. No, do not ask *me* why the Prophet left such things unwritten! And do not pester Ahmad ibn Sa'id about them! The Aliyah is a gentle and patient man, devoted to Chalta and the Prophet as he should be, but I think it would be best that he know as little as possible of such things as we discuss here." Hasim gave her a gentle squeeze. "Now, as to the conditions, those that might decide your fate, Ilben told us thusly; *If she be not Bound to a mortal by her eighteenth birthing day, I shall be forced to reclaim the magic that will have made her what she is. She will be drawn to me, in my palace. There, her fate, and mayhaps the fate of all the world shall be decided. It may be that the Great Ones, the Nobles of the First Rank will not allow her continued existence as a Jann. They have no love for humans in general and even less for a true Jann. They might simply strip her of all magic and sling her back to your Mortal World, broken and half un-made. She could be gifted to the Efreeti, if needful to appease them at that time. Should that come to pass, the Efreeti will fight over her, with the victorious Efreet drawing out her magic, feasting on her very soul to grow more powerful, casting aside the drained husk that was once my daughter. And before such a horror should come to pass, the Efreet will have already dealt with me, to my final detriment if I cannot out-think him, for I cannot outfight the Efreet. She must find a true Bond, the Bond of Master to Slave if naught else, but a Bond of True Love would be best. If Sahla can find that One, the One who balances the fate of both the Mortal World and the World of the Unseen, if she can Bond to that One, love that One, then the balance tips in our favor. Without her, without Sahla's loving nature, I fear the outcome, should that One come to the Time of Choosing without love, a True Love, in that One's heart. So prepare Sahla well, teach her to wield a blade like a true hero, and teach her that love is the truest and greatest weapon of all."*

"Those are the words he used to make us both understand how important this is, Sahla. How important you truly are." Haipha smiled at her eldest child.

"But does that make me mortal, Mama? Or immortal?"

"Well, as I have said, the best answer is, it depends. If you do not Bond and come to stand before your Sire, it is my belief that you should step into the realm of the Immortal. But remember, even an Immortal, unless a being completely of spirit, can be killed. The Aljannia, the race the infidels call the Elves, the Fair Folk, they are Immortals, but of this mortal world the same as any human. They do not age, but they can be killed, same as any man. Or starve or die of thirst. They are tougher than humans, but they can die. If you do not Bond, I think you should have a similar tenacity of life. But it will be as Chalta wills it." Haipha shrugged as she answered.

"And if, or rather when I Bond?" She wiggled slightly to leave her Father's arms.

"Well, my daughter," Hasim released her, "then it will depend on to whom you Bond and how strongly the Bond takes. I would think that your magic might tie you to your Bonded, your life linked to theirs, perhaps." He sighed. "In truth, Sahla, neither your Mother nor I have any real idea. Chalta knows, and his Prophet, but I doubt anyone else does."

"Could you not use the Ring, then, summon Ilben alh-Taymyah to us and ask him?"

"The Ring was lost to us shortly before your birth, Sahla. Either it was stolen, which I believe is unlikely, or Ilben himself was somehow responsible for the Ring finding a new owner. That is my belief, at any rate."

"Oh," she frowned, "well, then what else do I need to know?"

"Settle yourself, my daughter, there is much yet to speak of." Hasim smiled as he spoke. "But I do have one question for you. Well, your Mother and I do."

"What can I tell you, Father, Mama?"

"If you still love us?"

Sahla froze for a moment, overwhelmed by the tears she saw in her parents' eyes. Tears started in her own eyes and she flung herself bodily into their arms.

"Of course I do, Father, Mama! I will always love you!" She wept as the tears began to pour down her face, mixing with theirs. "No matter how long I live, I shall always love you!"

Chapter Ten

**Vlymouth Port, Duchy of Hale,
Kingdom of Montagar
September 1478, Third Age of Imperial Reckoning**

"Ye know, even with naught but plain, mousy brown hair and eyes of common hazel, ye can nae help but draw a man's eye. Aye and strong enough of a draw to make yer usual strumpet perish of mortal envy." Aylie shook her head as she guided Sachi down the noisome street leading to Holland's Rest, one of the most disreputable taverns in town. "Tis the way ye move, I thinks, that, or the invitation offered by that low cut blouse. And the bounty under it. And the lamplights make it look even better." The sun had set an hour ago and the last feeble light of a port city's sunset glow had faded to true night about thirty minutes ago. They had spent the majority of the day procuring appropriate clothing for Sachi. Aylie proved to be both discerning and demanding in equipping Sachi for her role.

"If a man is busy looking at my tits, he's not looking at my face. Or my hands, Aylie," Sachi answered quietly. "There's another one." She stopped next to the corner of a dilapidated tenement building. A dozen or so broadsheets and bounty posters had been nailed up and the one offering five thousand sterling in gold for Sachi's head was the newest and most prominent.

"Aye, and there's even an official one with me own name on it."

"Yes. But it would have a bounty hunter looking for a young woman in her teens, not a young man in his early twenties."

"Ye do realize that even by dressing as a man, I's breaking half the sumptuary laws of the Duchy of Hale?"

"I do now. What's the penalty?"

"Unless ye anger the judge, likely a week in gaol. Anger the judge, might be a month."

"In Isemoto, should a samurai decide to do so, if he realized that one was impersonating a man, or worse, someone of higher status, the only penalty would be his katana striking off your head."

"Aye? Seems a wee bit harsh to me."

"Isemoto is, at times, both beautiful and terrible." She shrugged and headed off down the street. "We dither and are no closer to our goal." Aylie followed quietly along. "So, when we reach this place, Holland's Rest, what might we expect?"

"'Tis a poor man's dive, that and likely a roost for more than one of the local fences. I'd be much surprised if there's nae some fellows what as will carry tales to the local Slipfingers' guildmaster. Might even find that worthy hisself in such a place."

"Slipfingers?"

"Oh, aye. Nae one likes to be called a thief. Nae even a guildmaster o' thieves his own self."

"I see."

"Well, we's here. Follow my lead, and mostly be quiet and try to draw nae attention to yerself." A dingy sign hung above the door on rusty hinges, paint faded and grungy, an image of a tubby sailor with his fat stomach hanging over the edges of his hammock. A swinging door allowed glimmers of flickering lamp and torch light to shine into the darkness of the street. Occasional murmurs of subdued conversation and wisps of smoke escaped past the door. Aylie flashed the hulking doorman a quick high-sign and the bruiser grunted as the pair slid through the door.

The blackened beams of the roof weren't quite as low as the t'ween-decks spaces of *Intrepid* had been, but Sachi still had to duck unless she wanted the soot from the ceiling in her hair. She followed Aylie across the common room, and she swore she could hear men's eyeballs click as they followed her with predatory gazes.

We'll be lucky beyond belief to get out of here without violence, I fear. And I'm not sure how that…Nannieball…in the shape of a sword will handle. Ancestors, I'm starting to think this was not such a well thought out plan! She rolled her shoulders slightly, comforted by the familiar rub of her butterfly swords in their hidden sheaths on her back. She held her place behind Aylie as the shorter woman spoke with the barkeep quietly, slipping him a pair of silver sterlings, considerably more than the cost of the two mugs of questionable ale he set on the bar in front of them. Sachi wrinkled her nose after a single sniff. *Did they get this horrid swill out of a cask or out of a horse!? Yuck.* With a quick check to ensure that no one was watching what she did with the ale, she quickly poured it over the sodden drunk on the floor. The ale never interrupted the pattern of his sawmill snores. She carefully stepped over him when Aylie gestured her to follow. The flash of her shapely calf, despite the long, full skirts and petticoats common to women of "negotiable virtue," drew a number of wolf-whistles and cat-calls.

"Later, me bucks." Aylie pitched her voice low enough to sound like a young man. "Hisself is got business wit me an' me gel. Affer tat, ye's can speaks ta him 'bout this tasty bit. Iffn ye's tha gumption ta do so, tat is. An' iffn's hisself's nae taken a rare liken ta her, so's ta say. So's, unta tat point, shut yer holes." She led Sachi up a rickety stairwell behind the bar as the crowd quieted.

"Are you sure you speak Terranglais?" Sachi whispered once they were out of sight on the second-floor landing.

"Aye, well enough for Milady," she whispered back, "but that's not how to speak to this grubby lot. Unless you want to stand out in a very uncomfortable fashion. That's the cant of the street, and I worked very hard to unlearn it, thank ye very much."

"Ah."

"Now, be silent before hisself and let me do the talking, all right?"

"Yes."

The hallway hooked around and led to a door at its end, one guarded by two men, one another hulking bruiser, armed with an iron shod club. The other was smaller, half the size of the bruiser, with a feeling of a wiry quickness about him. A pair of small swords, long knives really, hung from his belt. A quiver of arrows bristled on his back, and he leaned lazily on his bowstave. His eyes glittered cat-like in the dim light and Sachi felt Aylie tense as they both realized he was an elf. The elf smirked and bowed them into the room as the big one opened the door for them. His ears were folded back tightly against his head, partly hidden under long, dirty blond hair.

"Milord, milady," he sneered as he waved them through the door.

The room was dimly lit, the windows either boarded over or covered with heavy curtains. Two more guards lounged on a sofa, idly playing cards with each other. Both stopped long enough to give the pair a thorough look. Behind a desk a tall man with close-cropped brown hair sat, quill twitching as he tallied up something in a large leather-bound book. The desk was covered with books, loose papers, stacks of coins and a small casket, similar enough to her Duchess' favorite jewelry box that it gave Aylie a pang of sorrow.

"Well, whadda ya want? I's a busy man."

"Tis 'bout this, Master Slipfingers." Aylie laid one of the bounty price posters with Sachi's supposed picture on it on the desk. "I knows where she can be found, but I's no muscle ta be thumping her, er her mistress."

"Ye does, does ye? And whut's this 'bout a mistress? Himself as be paying the shill, he said nuthing uf anyone else."

"She be claimed by an Elf sorceress, claimed as Defender an' Elf-friend. Mayhaps ye might ask he who's paying such a price iffn he's sure an' certain he wants ta make such as this sorceress an enemy, one I's learned has powerful connections back ta tha Fair Folk's own Court?"

"Does ye know this sorceress' name?"

"Aye." Aylie shrugged. "She be on 'er *Crwydothe* an' she be going by a use name uv Silaqui, but I heard tha bobbers call her Maerilwyn, Lady MacGaellyn."

"Huh." Master Slipfingers grunted. "A Lady uf the Fair Folk's Court, eh? Well, this be a horse uf quite a different feather. Elf-friend an' Defender, both?"

"Aye, Master Slipfingers."

"I'd've knewn thut, I'd a' set a higher cut fer the Guild." He paused. "Weel, then whut's yer pretty friend got ta do wit this?"

"She works Ye Olde Salts Inn. She's who told me uv whut tha bobbers said uv this girl and tha sorceress. We've a...shall we say, a workin' relationship."

"How in all uf Quan's Hells is a no-name like you pimping this ripe bit?" He opened a desk drawer and rummaged around, eventually pulling out a pair of spectacles. "Allow me a bit better seeing, these demned things do. Lemme have a good look at ye, girl."

Aylie shot Sachi a quick, worried look as Master Slipfingers spent a long, long moment looking at Sachi before giving Aylie a quick once over. *Vlymouth is a long way from home, and I don't know enough of the local Slipfingers to have any insight about this guildmaster. He's keeping his own peace closer than I'd like.* She looked closer at the spectacles on his face. *Oh, hell. Can those things possibly be...?*

"Erendriel!" Master Slipfingers yelled, "Get in here, will ya! Need ta ask ya 'bout one uf yer kin. Right sharply, now!" The door opened and the elf stepped into the room, followed by the big man with the club.

"Master? You've a question about one of my kinfolk?"

"Aye. These two say that black-eyed chit Himself wants dead is an Elf-friend and Defender ta an elf sorceress with a use name uf Silaqui. Says her name is Maerilwyn, Lady MacGaellyn. Know aught uf her?"

"Aye. She's half again my age, a highly skilled sorceress and much favored by High Lord Oedhaewthren. One of his nieces, I believe. I'd want naught to do with her."

"How does ye think she'd act iffn something happened ta her black-eyed friend?"

"I'd not want to be the responsible one, if she could find that one."

"You think she could find her? Iffn black-eyes just vanished, that is?"

"Don't know. But even a fairly poor hedge wizard could likely muddle things enough that she'd not know what happened to her. I think. But then, I'm no mage."

"Eh. Good nuff. I've a fair middling wizard I's can whistle up. Should do the job." A dragon couldn't have shown more teeth than his grin did as he turned his attention back to the two women. "This *boy* is the *girl* the bobbers is wanting fer killing the Duke of Southdon an' his Lady. The other one is that black-eyed chit. Okay, me bucks, kill 'em both." The casual pronouncement left everyone in the room stunned for a second. Everyone but Sachi.

This is the street thuggers all over again. How did he know who I am, who we are? Great-uncle Sota's voice roared in her mind. *MOVE, YOU STUPID GIRL! MOVE OR DIE!* Sachi exploded into violence.

Her arms pinwheeled and kill-stars sprouted in the throats of the two men sitting on the couch. As she threw the stars, she kicked Aylie in the back of the knee, tumbling her to the floor. With Aylie hopefully out of the way, she bounded towards the big thief with the club. *Uncle Sota was right. It seems I always have to deal with some hulking brute half again my size!* She ducked under a clumsy swing of the iron shod club and snap-kicked him twice, as hard as she could, once in the crotch and again in the face as his agonized reflexes bent him over. The second kick stood him back upright and she buried her old, steel butterfly sword in his chest, driving the broad blade through his heart. She left that blade there, wedged in his ribs, as he collapsed. The elf was nearly as fast off the mark as she was, swinging his bowstave like a quarterstaff. She took that blow on her left shoulder. The bowstave broke and she felt her shoulder blade crack.

"*Pukta!*" he cursed as he dropped the broken bow. The long knives flashed as he drew them.

He's almost as fast as I am, but I doubt he's ever faced someone trained by Great-uncle Sota! She dropped into a full split as both knives slashed through the empty air above her head. She spun on the wooden floor, trying to kick the elf's legs out from under him. He leapt above her strike, driving both blades down at her as he landed next to her. She rolled on her side, allowing the left-hand blade to embed itself in the floor. She blocked the other one with the white steel sword, the new one formed by the nannieball. The stark white sword sheared straight through the long knife right at the hilt, taking the elf's forefinger and half his thumb cleanly off.

She rolled back onto the long knife stuck in the floor next to her, trapping it under her body. The elf was staring in shock at the blood spraying from his severed finger and thumb when her knee snapped up between his legs like a hammer. He went up on his toes with a high, nearly inaudible scream. Her free hand shot up, grabbing his shirt and jerking him head over heels over her prone body. He hit the floor hard on his back and the slashing white blade took his head cleanly off his shoulders. She back-flipped to her feet in front of the Master's desk and the sword sliced the man's hand off at the wrist before he could cock the flintlock pistol he'd pulled out of the desk drawer. Grabbing his tunic, she yanked him out of the chair and across the desk onto the floor. The guard of the sword smashed into his face, crushing his nose flat against his cheek.

"Now, *kusottare*, who is it that wants to pay so much for my head? Quickly, now. I'm impatient and prone to violence." The fight had broken Silaqui's cantrip and her black eyes glittered as she drove a knee into his chest. Her blouse was partially torn and soaked in the blood of his henchmen, the long skirt hanging in shreds from her waist. Something primitive in his mind gibbered in fear at what he saw in Sachi's eyes, the remorseless monster lurking outside the cave, hungry for the prey inside. He grabbed that fear and forced it down.

"Why's should I? Ye'll kill me anyways," he managed to gasp out.

"There's different ways to die, *gaijin*. Quickly and relatively pain free, or after long torment and dismemberment. Or I might let you live and just sever your manhood? This blade is sharp enough, you'd not even squeal." Her smile was grim. "How long would half a man remain *kumicho,* the boss-man of a guild of thieves and murders, eh?"

"Enuff. Iffen I gives ye whut ye want, right now, un nae uf me bucks be troubling ye, ye'll leave me live? Whole and, huh, *ungelded?*"

"Aye. I'd not even take a finger if you're quick. But I don't think you'd actually owe me *yubitsume.*"

"Huh, what?"

"Don't worry about it, *gaijin*. Who put this price on my head? Hurry, before I get impatient and twitchy and you lose something dear to you."

"He be an Impie, I's sure as sure. Short uf medium height, nae skinny, nae fat, average. Slicked back, black hair, worn longish; dark skin, dark eyes. Wore black, cut likes an Imperial priest uf the One God. Solid silver Circled Cross on a gold chain about his neck. Last I sees him be yester morn. Left me knowing how to claim the reward after knowing fer sure ye's dead. Leaving Vlymouth straight away in a large, black coach, drawn by a four-in-hand uf matched grays. Took the east high road. Like to be headed to one uf the ports on the Montagar Straight to get out uf the country. That enuff?"

"Yes. You get to keep your life. And your balls." Her grin would have frightened a shark onto the beach. "He have anything...well, anything weird or odd? Maybe white steel?"

"No, nothing I sa...wait, he'd a strange pistol, well, iffen it was a pistol, he wore it on his belt. 'Twas a shiny black and silver thing. I just saw the barest uf it." The guildmaster could feel the sweat running on his face. Normally he could read a man's face down to the last copper pence of his worth, but this blood-covered Nisei woman baffled him. Danger and violence flowed off her like the mist of a glacier, but beyond that she was as impenetrable as the depths of the void.

"Good enough, *gaijin*. I'll let you live. I see one of your toughs within long bowshot of me or any of my friends and I'll find you and suffocate you with your own asshole, *wakaru*?"

"Whut?"

"You understand me?"

"Absolutely."

"And if you hurt one of my friends, Quan himself won't want what I leave of you. Clear?"

"Crystal." He watched in bemusement as the tall, exotic beauty stepped back and simply ripped off the bloody rags left of her skirt, petticoat and blouse. Underneath was a snug-fitting black garment. She pulled down rolled up sleeves and pants legs, drawing tight the laces of the tunic-like shirt to cover the magnificent breasts the fight had nearly exposed. The short, heeled boots were torn off and replaced with a strange, soft shoe with split toes. She whipped her long hair into a bun before pulling a masked hood out of the collar of the shirt and over her head. Only her eyes glittered at him now. She tossed the discarded clothing into the fireplace. The blood on it sizzled and smoked as the flames took hold.

"Come on." She stepped over and pulled her friend up, off the floor.

"Wait," the girl said. "We might want these." She picked up the spectacles from where they'd fallen on the floor when she'd jerked him across the desk. She peeked through them. "A-ha. As I thought. They're magic, how he saw through our disguises."

"Do as you wish. I'd leave them. I want nothing of his." She retrieved her kill-stars and pulled her second sword out of the bruiser's chest, wiping it off on the couch cover before sheathing both blades into a single sheath slung over her back, between her shoulder blades. She stepped over to the boarded-up window and effortlessly tore the planks off the window. Pushing the shutters open, she reached back, grabbed Aylie and swung out the window, disappearing into the darkness.

The Guildmaster moaned in pain as he pushed himself to a sitting position. He pulled his belt off and wrapped it tightly around the stump of his forearm to stop the bleeding. Blood loss left him weak and lightheaded. He looked around in some dismay at the bloody shambles of his comfortable office.

"Bloody, fucking hell," he muttered to himself, "ye *bitches*! Ye've left me a right mess, ye bitches! Run, ye hoores! Run whiles ye can! I'll have ye fed to the hogs and send theys' shit to thut prissy Impie bastard to claim the gold. Run, ye dead slut."

***

"Whut be ye?" Aylie hissed, slipping back into cant as Sachi set her down in the moon's shadow cast by a tall rooftop dormer. "I's run me share an' some uv the Slipfingers' Highway, but nae one moves as ye does."

"We can talk. There's no one in the room below." Sachi sighed. She looked at Aylie and was able, by force of will, to cycle her vision through what D.A.V.E. had called *modes*. One showed everything in grays, from black to white. The silver statue called that *thermal mode*, he said it showed her relative temperatures between different things. Another one put everything in a greenish cast, but made the least light seem like broad daylight. Other *modes* let her see different *spectrums*, whatever those were. Colors shifted strangely with those. Without hardly thinking about it, she dropped into *verification mode* looking at Aylie, reading the dilation of her pupils, tenseness of facial muscles, heart rate and breath rate. She'd always been one of the best at truth-telling, she just knew why now. "What do you want to know?"

"How'd ye do that?"

"Which *that*, exactly?" Sachi watched Aylie carefully. She didn't want the young woman to bolt and fall off the roof. "The fight? I'm a *shinijutsuka*, a practitioner of what translates into Terranglais as *master of the silent death.* Close as I can get, I guess."

"Yer an assassin?" There was a quaver in Aylie's voice.

"Among other things, yes. I was also to be trained to be a geisha, a kind of a prostitute, but one that didn't generally have sex with a client. I was trained in the martial arts from the age of six. I killed my first slave when I was nine years old. I murdered the man who took my virginity. He was a target who paid for the *honor* of taking my maidenhead. Someone else paid to have him killed. I was thirteen. My...trainers...were, or rather, still are...cruel taskmasters but the training is thorough. You're either good enough or you die. Simple as that."

"Oh dear God."

"I guess, but I doubt either your One God or the Ancestor Spirits had anything to do with it."

"But, that training, does it make ye stronger an' faster too?"

"No. That's something else. When I have fits, like you've seen...?"

"Aye?"

"Well, that's complicated. Part of it is my training, I guess. My primary trainer was not a particularly small man, nor excessively large. But he trained me, made me what I am. He used to stand on my back while I did push-ups over hot coals. Built character and muscles at the same time, he always said."

"Aye, but what were ye saying about yer fits? And I nae care how many push-ups ye did, normal people aren't liken ta ye. Nae one be that fast or strong. 'Tisn't natural."

"Aylie, I'm not sure what to say or how to say it. Let's talk about it back at the Inn, so I only have to do it once, with everyone. I'll say this much for the moment. No, it isn't *natural* but it is, I'm told, normal for me."

"And who be telling ye that?"

"That's...a long and difficult story, Aylie. There's another, well, another being involved in it. And the same being that tells me I'm normal, well, it tells me I have something important to do, but I'm not sure how to do what it says I'm to do. So, I'm not magic or an *Oni...*"

"A what?"

"An *Oni*, an evil spirit. What bad things, monsters, I guess, are called in Isemoto." Sachi sighed and stood up. "I've done horrible things, Aylie. Things done because that's what my clan, my family, does back home. And I've defied them. And to make things worse, I defied them and escaped punishment. They'll hunt me to the end of the world. But I'm supposed to do something truly critical, and that's even more important than escaping them."

"Aye, and just what is it this thing wants ye ta do?"

"Somehow, I'm supposed to save the world, Aylie. Don't ask me how, I don't know."

"Cor. What does ye say ta that?"

"You do the best you can, Aylie, the best you can." Sachi stood up from the dark shadow of the dormer. "Come on. We need to get back to the inn. You think the Guildmaster will keep his word?"

"No. Not for more than a day, mebbe two. Oncet the story gets out, he'll have ta do something ta save face. Most likely lay us out by our heels. Be best ta get outta town."

"Hmmpf. One would think the Guildmaster at least should keep his own word. An honorless thug, not true *yakuza* at all." Sachi sighed in poorly hidden disgust. "Want to take bets on Willis coming up with an excuse to 'travel' with us?"

"Nae. I'll keep me coin. He lover-like sweet on ye?"

"No, I don't think so. And I'm not longing forlornly for his romantic touch to quench my burning desire, either."

"Ye've been reading those ladies' romances, haven't ye?"

"One, once. I was dreadfully bored when *Intrepid* was becalmed for nearly a week in the Great Western Ocean."

"Ah. Well, he'll learn naught from me of yer lack o' burning lust fer 'im."

"Oh, he's handsome enough, but there's not the least spark there." Sachi shook her head in amusement. "Maybe raw, physical lust on his part, but if so, he hides it well. No, it's something else entirely with him."

"Guess we'd best be finding a ship leaving soon, maybe the morning tide iffn we can?"

"I think so. And I have one in mind already." She shrugged as she looked west, over the rooftops of Vlymouth. The swells of the Lanic rolled endlessly beyond the harbor breakwater. "Well, let's get back and see what bare-faced lie of an excuse Willis comes up with. Should be interesting."

"Oh, aye, interesting, indeed."

"The Han people, the great Empire across the Sea of Han, they have a potent curse."

"Oh?"

"Yes. *May you live in interesting times.* Most potent curse they know."

"Ye ever anger one of these *Han* people?"

"Not as I know, no."

"Well, ye must've. Nae other way to explain it."

"Hmm. I guess so."

***

"So, you killed four of the Guildmaster's bodyguards, cut off his hand, threatened to kill him and stole his pair of magical glasses?" Silaqui rolled her eyes as Sachi shrugged. "Why'd you stop there? You could have killed his dog or maybe insulted his mother? Stole the family silver, perhaps? Anything to enrage him even further, just in case you didn't make him mad enough the first time?"

"What was I supposed to do, Silaqui? Let him kill us?" Sachi snagged an apple from the bowl of fruit in the middle of the table. "He gave me his word." Juice ran down her chin as she crunched into it. "Am I to be foresworn and slay him after he gave me his word?"

"Silaqui, I think you should drop it." Willis interjected from the recliner in which he sprawled. "Sachi, this touches on a matter of honor, doesn't it? You gave your word, as a matter of *meiyo*, the ancient honor code of Isemoto, didn't you? And you consider it binding, regardless of what the Slipfingers' Guildmaster does, don't you?"

"*Hai*, Fleet-san." Sachi bowed to him. "I consider myself bound until the moment he actually breaks his word by attacking any of us."

"But such an attack might kill some, or indeed, all of us." Gelman stood looking out the window into the city. It was nearing midnight and even the majority of the sailors' dives and grog shops were closing up. "This leaves us a dilemma, but I will wager that Sachi already has a plan?"

"Do you, Sachi?" Silaqui quietly asked.

"I do. *Le Bonaventure* is to sail in the morning on the ebb tide. She's a brigantine with her next port call in Al-Jazual, a Darsälaamic port on the Lanic Coast of northern Khakal. She's some accommodations for passengers, three or four cabins, I believe. I intend to be aboard her when she sails."

"And leave us here to deal with an angry Guildmaster?" Aylie spoke up from the corner in which she was huddled. "Leave us to die?"

"No, Aylie, I'll not do that." Sachi stopped and took a very deep breath. "Come with me. All of you."

Chapter Eleven

**Desert Settlement of Abdul-Ghaffanse,
Darsälaamic Kaliphate, Northern Khakal
December, 1476, Third Age of Imperial Reckoning**

BRONZE AND SILVER BELLS rang and chimed with a happy, cheerful rapidity. Sahla spun and leapt, twirling in time to the frantic music, a blur of long black hair, tanned skin and a dance outfit of blue, silver and gold. Her mother smiled as her riqq rang against her palm in accompaniment to drum and kamancheh, enjoying the music and the beauty of her daughter's dance.

I don't think she realizes how beautiful she is, even now. But by the Prophet's beard, she knows how skillful she is in the dance. I was never that good. And she's better with her blades than she is in dance. Ha, she might even be capable of besting her father, who's still a mighty warrior and a master with a blade. And Khalid, poor boy, he would never know what hit him. Of course, if he saw her unveiled now, I doubt it would be his brain *he would be thinking with. But I may be doing the Mulazim of her Guard an injustice. Khalid is as wary and cunning a swordsman as I've ever seen.*

The music reached its frantic crescendo and Sahla's last leap carried her nearly her own height before she landed on a single lithe foot. She held the pose for the required half minute before folding elegantly into *Graceful Acknowledgement*, bowing first towards her musicians behind their screen and then towards a non-existent audience. Her smile lit the room as she straightened and bounded over to hug her mother.

"Well, how was that, Mother?"

"Superb, my child." Haipha kissed her on the cheek. "I fear you have outdistanced the skills of your old mother in both dance and sword. Perhaps there is some great Mistress of Swords meditating in some dusty monastery out in the deepest desert who is better with a blade than you are, but as far as normal mortals are concerned, well, there are few, very few who could match your skills with blade or dance."

"Mother, I could never be better than you!"

"Oh, my daughter, you know false modesty is a sin before the Prophet! Truly, your skills would be matched or surpassed by a *Sayf Kahina* of the Dervish who has spent all the years of her life studying dance and the sword, but none other. I was trained by such a one, in my own younger days, and I know what to look for in a skillful swordswoman. And I know what I see in you."

"Truly, Mother?"

"Oh yes, my daughter. If they knew, the poets would be penning odes to your skill with the blade instead of your beauty."

"I've no idea how they know what I look like. I've never set so much as a toe outside the harem without being properly clothed and veiled. Not since I was a child."

"I know and so does your father. But even when you were a little girl, anyone with eyes could see the promise of your true beauty. Basically, they're guessing, but it's not that hard to guess how you've grown. And you've grown into that promise of beauty." Haipha smiled as she took in her daughter in her dancing outfit.

The tight sapphire halter, sewn of layers of gossamer silk, clung to her high, full breasts but left strong shoulders, powerful arms and a flat muscular midriff bare. Beads of sweat were coalescing on her skin, dusky skin tanned until it could only be called golden. A large sapphire gleamed in her navel, others on her earlobes. A mesh belt of gold wire, studded with sapphires and diamonds, secured diaphanous pantaloons of golden silk low on her hips. The pantaloons were slashed up the sides and tied at hip, knee and ankle. They fluttered as she moved, concealing then revealing sleek and exceptionally attractive legs, the strong legs a dancer needed. A golden headband, set with more sapphires, confined her sable hair, while clips of gold and silver bound that ebon mass into a tail as thick as her wrists, a tail that fell almost to mid-calf. Unbound, it swept the floor. Haipha sighed to herself.

My daughter has no true idea of the impact her beauty will have on the unsuspecting. And those clothes! Delivered in a leather-wrapped, mage-sealed package by the last caravan to pass this way. I didn't order them and neither did Hasim! I think, no, I know Ilben has his hand in this gift. Especially since they show no wear and stay clean, spotlessly so, no matter what. If that's not Jinni magic, I'll eat a ka'mel raw, hair and all, the whole smelly beast. Oh Ilben, I only hope you can see what a beautiful young woman your daughter has grown into! You would be so proud of her. We certainly are, Hasim and I. And it nearly breaks my heart that she must soon leave home and forge her own legend in the world.

"Sahla, go and change. You will eat alone with me and your Father tonight. We must talk."

"Talk? Will this one be as when we talked when I was twelve?"

"Perhaps, my child, perhaps."

"More secrets, Mother?"

"We shall see. But not until the evening meal. Now go and change. Stretch properly, you may be a Jann but you are not immune to cramps or torn muscles. I will send your servants to give you a massage and help wash your hair. Go, now."

"Yes, Mother." Sahla gave her mother a quick embrace before bowing and leaving for her own room. Haipha's smile was bittersweet.

"Yes, my daughter, more secrets," she said when she was alone. "More secrets, indeed."

***

Within the confines of their own home, in the private areas reserved for the family, none of the women were required to wear the full dress of abayah, hijab and niqab. Such body shrouding clothes were only a requirement when going outside in public or if the husband was hosting male guests or friends in the home for either business or entertainment. So at the evening meal, Hasim sat cross-legged at the low dining table with his wife and step-daughter unveiled.

She is the flower of my heart, my First Daughter. How can I send her away, to what fate, only the Prophet knows? Chalta, oh divine One, must I do this?

"What is wrong, Father?" Sahla had always been a perceptive child and as she raced towards adulthood and her destiny, her perceptions only sharpened. "Why so sad?"

"Hush, Sahla." Haipha gently scolded. "Let your Father eat in peace."

"No, Haipha." He took a last sip of his kahwah. "Now is as good a time as any."

"Your will, husband."

"Sahla, you are now sixteen turnings of the seasons. And you have not yet Bonded to anyone here in Abdul-Ghaffanse." He paused.

"Yes, Father. You know I have not."

"When you were ten turnings of age, Sultan Mahdi al-Kohfan of the Tribe of al-Kohfan sent a representative to me, one Mu'allim Abdu al-Rahman, to discuss an alliance with our tribe. Even then, the bards and poets were telling tales of your beauty. Sultan Mahdi's First Son, Sheikh Mustafa al-Mahdi Baddour, was unmarried. What al-Rahman wanted was an arranged marriage between you and Sheikh Mustafa, First Daughter to First Son."

"I am to wed this Sheikh Mustafa, then? Is he then this One Ilben alh-Taymyah spoke of? The One who balances the fate of the World in his hands?"

"Well, for the moment I will ask you, my daughter, to wait for an answer to that question. For now, know that the marriage is arranged, but bride price and dowry have been neither given nor received. If you are vehemently opposed to this marriage, the arrangement can be broken. But..." Hasim sighed as he answered S ahla.

"But what, Father?"

"The Sultan Mahdi al-Kohfan is ruler of a powerful tribe. His lands are far to the west and only the eastern-most of them are within the deep desert. Indeed, his demesne includes two seaports on the Lanic coast of northern Khakal. He has large herds of cattle, horses and sheep. Not to mention many thousands of hectares of rich fields, watered by the rains from the Lanic. The Sultan rules a wealthy people many times more numerous than our poor tribe of Abdu-Ghaffanse."

"Father, they hardly seem to be Folk of the Sands at all. Seaports? Watered fields? Herds of cattle?! They must be soft, like the infidels of the Empire, living in a land that does not scourge or test them!" Sapphire eyes flashed with her passion. "You would marry *me* to the ruler of a rich, soft land!? Fagh! Do they even know how to properly prepare a bowl of roasted scorpions?"

"Peace, my child." Hasim smiled at her as he took a date from the bowl. "I said that a marriage was arranged. I did not say that I expected it to be consummated."

"You do not?" Sahla's slender eyebrows tried to climb up her forehead.

"Not at all." Hasim finished his date and picked up his kahwah cup, handing it to Haipha to be refilled. "And that is because I would bet my faith in the Prophet's promise of Paradise that Sheikh Mustafa al-Mahdi Baddour is not the One spoken of in the prophecy Jinn Ilben told of your future. And before you ask, child, no, I have not the least idea *who* might be that One."

"Oh."

"Yes, *oh.*" Hasim shrugged as he took the cup back from his wife with a smile of thanks and drank the sweet, dark kahwah. He savored the bittersweet taste and swallowed. "Ilben told me that I could not keep you protected and safe in the harem. You must go out into the world and find your own place, find this person that will fulfill your prophecy." Hasim paused for a long moment. "And to do this, First Daughter, there are things that I deem it wise that you learn, things which are not within the usual purview of the women of the harem of the Sheikh of Abdul-Ghaffanse."

"Truly?"

"Truly. I am aware, somewhat, of the women's secrets that your Mother has taught you. She has told me that she is most pleased with your progress. Indeed, she has told me that you are beginning to surpass her in those abilities."

"She says so, but I cannot be greater than Mother. It would not be right."

"Sahla, you are a Jann. Your Mother is only human, as am I. According to what Ilben told me, once you Bond, you will be able to access the powers of his lineage and wield those powers."

"What might these powers be, Father? Did Ilben...did my Sire tell you?"

"He told me a little of what to expect and said that such things vary according to the individual. At the least, he said, you should have the Gift of Flight, similar to how a Jinn flies by strength of will. The ability to understand and speak with the lower animals. I already see at least the rudiments of this gift in how well you handle any mount I set you upon. You might be able to wield magic in some limited form. You are certainly not a *sahira*, a sorceress to bend the world to your will, but you may come to wield some minor powers. Beyond that, I can only guess."

"Huh. Me, to wield magic?" Sahla stopped speaking and stared at her Father. "Wait! You spoke of being able to *fly!* How? Will I grow feathers and flap my arms?"

"Oh my child," Hasim laughed, "nothing so...so *outré*, as the Imperials of Guellia Province might say. You should fly as the Jinni do, by pure force of will. Ask your Mother to give you some of the old books of tales and read those stories that feature the Jinni. They might give you a better understanding of what might await you in the not-so-distant future."

"Father, Mother, both of you speak as if I am to live such a story book tale myself. What if I don't want to leave home, to marry this Sheikh Mustafa?" Her lips turned in a rare pout.

"The Prophet tells us, through the Book of Holies, that all things move according to the will of Chalta. Ilben, himself, agreed with this, even though the Book warns us to be wary of dealing with Outsiders such as he. This prophecy that curls around you, my daughter, I believe it will take you to strange and wondrous places, places that I cannot even begin to imagine. And, I believe, that will you or nil you, by one manner or another, you will follow your own destiny to its end. What you will find there, that is beyond my knowing. The only thing I know for certain, the one thing Ilben told me that you must know, is that love, the Bond of True Love, is what you should seek. Settle for nothing less, my da ughter."

"So, what of the arranged marriage, then, Father?" Her brows furrowed in thought. "You speak as if you know, not believe but *know* that it will never come to pass."

"Sahla, I am certainly no soothsayer, by the Prophet's Beard!" Hasim's teeth flashed in a grin through his beard. "But, no, I do not think Sheikh Mustafa will ever lift your bridal veil. And that is the reason you will be spending at least some of the next year with the herd guards. There are things they know that you will never learn within the walls of the harem."

"You are sending me to the herd guards?" Sahla's sapphire eyes widened in surprise.

"Yes, for at least the rest of the winter. Perhaps through the spring and into summer." Hasim's voice was low. "And I know, such things are not within the normal province of the Sheikh's

First Daughter. You will be the same as the other young women your age who manage the goat herds."

"Husband, is this wise?" Haipha asked, her eyes nearly as wide as Sahla's.

"Yes, I believe so. And Sabiyya shall spend time wearing Sahla's clothing. It is my intent that none shall know that Sahla is not within the harem."

"Your will, husband."

"Sahla, the reason for this is to give you an understanding of the world without the harem, indeed the world without the walls of Abdul-Ghaffanse. It is my belief that in due time, you shall move beyond the world of the Folk of the Desert. Indeed, if you are to be what Ilben says you will be, you *must* know such things."

"Are you certain, Father?" Sahla asked quietly.

"Daughter, I am truly certain of nothing. But, by the Prophet's Beard, this is what I believe to be necessary."

"Your will, Father."

**Grazing lands of Abdul-Ghaffanse,
Darsälaamic Kaliphate, Northern Khakal
January, 1478; Third Age of Imperial Reckoning**

Sahla perched on top of the rock, relishing the warmth of the noon sun. From her perch she could see the entire hillside, her goats grazing peacefully among the tough desert shrubs and sparse grass. The night had been cold enough to frost-burn the shrubs and grasses upon which the goats fed. The goats huddled together during such cold nights, body heat and their long coats of thick shaggy hair keeping them warm. While she had the shepherd dog to keep her company, the hairy little beast did not do much to keep her warm. And it had fleas. So, lacking the animals' coats or their body heat, at night she generally stayed close to her simple hut and its cheery fire to stay warm. These days, however, she had more than rough woolen blankets.

In addition to the thick burnoose her mother made for her, she now made her bed of thick, warm, well cured and tanned wolf skins. She had swiftly taught the wolves to avoid her herd's range. Now the local wolf pack was gone, either slain by her hand or driven off by a greater predator.

A great mountain tiger had made its presence felt when it slaughtered the last of the wolves. It had supplemented its initial diet of wolf with two of her goats, a nanny and kid. For a month in the early spring she played hide and seek with the great cat. Night after night, lead bullets from her sling drove the beast away with a sore head. In the dark, she discovered, her Jann heritage gave her night vision as good as the cat's vision. And the great cat was persistent enough hunting both her goats and herself that she had been forced to deal with it, permanently.

The tiger had never expected the hard lead sling bullet driven into its head from less than thirty feet away as the great beast stalked her goats late on a dark spring night. Bloody and stunned, blinded in one eye, it had yowled in agony as she sprinted out of the dark ravine. Her sabers flashed, once, twice, as she slid *under* the tiger. Its shriek as she disemboweled it had echoed throughout the rocky foothills. The cat had flailed in pain, blind in one eye and tripping through its own guts. A final, precise lunge with her saber had pierced its great heart and it had twitched in final death.

Now, months later, sitting on her rock in the warm sun, she ran her hand gently over the luxurious striped fur cloak she wrapped around her strong shoulders. In the far distance, she saw a dust cloud rising over the deep desert.

"Riders are coming. Perhaps as many as a score." She spoke softly to herself. The old woman who had been the herder here warned her of talking to herself too much. It had been one of the first things she said to the teenager when Sahla arrived, escorted only by her father and Kanaan. The old woman had stayed with her for that first, full winter, leaving only when she was satisfied with Sahla's skills. She taught Sahla how to set snares for rabbits and hares, how to avoid the worst of the weather, the signs of a sirocco rising. How to milk the nanny goats. The use of a shepherd's sling. How to cure and tan the skins of goat and rabbit...and even wolf.

"Don't talk to yourself too often. Chalta knows madness can lie that way. Talk to the dog or the goats. Or to the tiny, scurrying creatures of the desert," the old woman had said. "Talk to the falcon that soars above the sky. Talk to the wolves and the desert dogs when they howl in the distant night. Talk to any of those as much as you might wish. If they start to talk back, that is acceptable in a herder. But talking to yourself, by the Prophet's robe, avoid that. Talking to yourself will eventually lead you to answering yourself." The old woman's gap-tooth grin had gaped at her then. "That way lays madness. Madness can be comfortable for a little while, but it will grow, you will become foolish and the desert sun will bleach your bones."

Watching the old woman ride away on her ancient donkey had been one of the loneliest things Sahla had ever experienced. Now she watched the dust cloud grow nearer.

"So my *alssaqr*, whose wings spurn the common earth, who comes under that cloud?" The falcon, soaring high above her, screamed its shrill cry. The raptor folded its wings and dived at the end of that shriek, slicing through the clear, blue bowl of the sky. A heartbeat later, the bird beat strongly back into the sky, a serpent writhing in its talons. "Is it my Father, come to bring me home before sending me to marry some soft prince who lives by the sea-shore? Or brigands come to steal my goats and cut my throat after ravishing me?" The falcon never answered as it winged back to its nest, doubtless to feed its young.

***

"Father, it is well to see you once again." She poured kahwah into a rough clay mug and handed it to Hasim. They sat inside her hut on stone slabs covered with wolfskins.

"And you as well, my daughter. I see your time here has been productive." Hasim lifted an eyebrow at the magnificent tiger cloak his daughter wore.

"The Prophet has extended his hand in protection over me and Chalta has blessed me, Father." Sahla's sapphire eyes were bright as she ducked her head in an abbreviated bow.

"Neither the Prophet nor Chalta wielded the blade that slew the great beast whose skin you wear as a cloak. They may have guided you and fortified your heart with courage, but it was your hand that held the saber that killed the tiger. Do not denigrate yourself, your own bravery or your own skill." Hasim's smile was warm and proud as Sahla blushed in response to his praise. Her time in the desert had deepened the golden tint to her flawless skin and the dim light in the hut turned her hair into a blue-black river flowing over her shoulder. "You look as beautiful as ever, my daughter."

"Father, the wolf and the tiger see me as either an obstacle to their desired meal or the meal itself. They have no care for beauty. The goats pay more attention to the yapping herd dog than to my beauty. The sirocco's sand will not care about my beauty as the howling winds strip my body to the bone if I am foolish enough to be caught without shelter. The freezing cold of deep winter might preserve my beauty as a frozen shell but only until the spring thaw."

"Where is the happy heart of my daughter, Sahla?" Hasim frowned at Sahla's speech. "Has the winter cold or the summer heat withered your joyous nature, daughter?"

"No, Father. My heart is still happy and I take joy in every sunrise," her smile lit the hut and Hasim could not but help to smile broadly in return, "but this time here, alone in the desert and the rough hills...it has given me much time to think."

"Time to think of what, my Sahla?" he gently asked.

"Time to think of life. Of my own soul. Of the place in the world my true Sire desires that I find. Of love."

"And?"

"I will not accept anything in my life that is not a love as deep as that between you and Mother. Anything else will be no more than a bowl of thin gruel, when one sits to a great feast. I will have that feast." Her sapphire eyes challenged her father.

"I see." Hasim met the challenge in those eyes. "And what of the most basic thing your Sire told us of, the Bond of Human Master to Jann Slave?"

"Would you truly have me be a Slave? A cold Bond of loveless duty? I think such a Bond would not be likely to make me risk my life or anything else for a Champion that I could only be a slave to. No, Father, the only way I would accept such a Bond would be if I judged that person worthy of my love, but somehow, that person was unable or unwilling to love in return. But I cannot imagine such a person."

"Honestly, neither can I. But what of the marriage you are promised to?" Hasim's eyes were veiled as he watched his daughter.

"I will not marry this Sheikh Mustafa al-Mahdi Baddour of al-Kohfan if there is no love between us. Not even if my Sire's magic pulls me away to his palace and I should perish at the hands of the Efreeti." Sahla met Hasim's eyes with a calm determination.

"Ah." Hasim rubbed his chin, hiding a smile from Sahla's serious mien. "So, are you saying you will not travel to Al-Kohfan? It would be hard to say whether or not love might flourish between the twain of you, if you never even stand within sight of each other, neh?"

"No, Father, that's not what I'm saying. If you still wish it, I will travel to Al-Kohfan, but if this prince is not someone I can love, I will not marry him. I should rather come back to these hills and spend my days with the dog and the goats."

"I see." He schooled his face to seriousness. "So then, I will ask that you travel to meet this prince, this Sheikh Mustafa, and then determine his worthiness. Should you not find your heart's true mate on the journey, then you will return here until your eighteenth birthday brings what it will. Is that acceptable, First Daughter of Abdul-Ghaffanse?"

"Yes, Father."

"Good. Then you shall make that journey and all shall be as the Prophet wills it."

Chapter Twelve

**Vlymouth Port, Duchy of Hale,
Kingdom of Montagar
September 1478, Third Age of Imperial Reckoning**

"Mon Capitaine, regarde ça!" Pierre Lescot, First Mate of the brigantine *le Bonaventure,* saw them first. He pointed at the group approaching the ship's table, set up at the entrance to the quay where the brigantine was moored.

"Hmm? Look at *that* what?" Capitaine Andre de Foix looked up from the ship's log. Then he saw the *that* Pierre was talking about. "Mon Dieu!" He could barely believe the beauties he saw revealed by the large, relatively bright quayside lanterns.

The woman in the lead was very beautiful, very tall, very well endowed and very well armed. Her skin was as fair as the finest Han porcelain and her ebon hair was braided into a crown around her head. A sword hilt jutted over each shoulder, there were long knives in her belt, and she carried an iron-shod staff nearly as long as she was tall in her right hand. More knife hilts snugged into her boot tops and a Kolbian double-barreled flintlock pistol was tucked through the front of her belt. She wore snug, dark gray trousers, knee-high black boots and a black silk shirt that seemed to have some kind of pattern to it.

Behind her was another vision in scarlet. She was one of the *Immortels Enchantés,* an Elf they were called here in Montagar. Long green hair flowed about her shoulders and down her back. Even from here, he could see her jade green, cat-like eyes, pupils vertically slit but dilated and shining in the early morning darkness. Her scarlet and crimson clothing left a good deal of fair skin on display.

The other two were ordinary enough, mere human males. The robes the taller, older man wore proclaimed him a Montagaran priest of the One God. A sturdy leather hat covered his head, a well-used mace hung from his belt, and a well-stuffed frame pack balanced on his back. A slightly built young man, little more than a teenager, walked beside him, drably clad in muted grays and browns. The lad had a dagger at his belt, a small pack on his back and carried a largish seabag.

The entire group stopped in front of his table and waited for Andre and Pierre to stop staring. Andre shook himself back to reality first.

"Bonjour, gentlefolk." He knew he was staring at the black-haired woman's magnificent breasts, but he couldn't help himself. She bent down, putting her hands on the table in order to look him straight in the eye. "How might I be of assistance to you?"

"First. Stop...staring." Eyes as black as space bore into his own somewhat watery blue ones. "The Harbormaster told me that your ship is setting sail this morning, bound for Al-Jazual. Is that the case?"

"Oui, Mademoiselle, 'tis." Andre locked his eyes on her face. "We sail on the ebb tide, an hour and a half from now, shortly after sunrise."

"And *le Bonaventure*, your brigantine, has accommodations for passengers?"

"Oui, ah, yes, *le Bon* does. There are four cabins on the poop deck."

"Good! How much?" The young woman was beyond assertive.

"Mademoiselle, I have not said if the cabins are available."

"Well, are they or aren't they? If they're not, then we are both wasting our time and you can see if you like my backside as much as you obviously like the front as I'm walking away to spend our passage money elsewhere."

"Mademoiselle!" *She bargains like an Ionan street vendor, screeching* You steal food from my children *while they rob you blind. Hmm, let's see how bad they do want passage?* "Un moment s'il vous plaît! Please, I had not expected any passengers this early, if at all. So it would be the four of you I assume?"

"Yes."

"Just to Al-Jazual? After that port, I expect to have several cargos for ports in the Empire."

"Just to Al-Jazual for me. The others may depart with me there or go on to other ports, maybe even back to Montagar, eventually."

"Sachi, no, you know I'm going with you." The green-eyed Elf's voice was as beautiful as the rest of her.

"Silaqui, damn it, I said you don't hav..." The woman in black was apparently in charge, he thought.

"God's peace on you twain. This is not the place or time." The priest's calm voice quelled the two beauties' budding argument. "Good Captain, what would passage to Al-Jazual cost for the four of us?"

"Depends. Would you want each a private cabin, or to share? The cabins are smallish, I'd not recommend more than two to a cabin."

"Three cabins." The black-haired woman interrupted. "If you're short of crew, I can splice line and reef sail. I know a halyard from a sheet, any knot you care to name, the difference between a jibsail, a staysail and a spanker. I can bunk anywhere I can hang my hammock. And I know my way around a galley fairly well."

"Oui?" He felt his eyebrows try to climb into his slightly receding hairline.

"I was given the rank of Able Seaman by the Bosun of the KRN *Intrepid.* You were tied up here when she arrived and departed."

"Ah! That bit they had on deck when she arrived was for you?!"

"It was." Her eyes narrowed as she blushed.

"Mon Capitaine, nous pourrions utiliser l'argent." Pierre shook his head to clear it. The woman and the elf were mesmerizing. "We's no issues wit dem, Capitaine. An' wal, de margins o' profit be tight 'nuff." Pierre's Terranglais wasn't very good but he was a good First. "We good wit crew, ma'moiselle." That earned him a curt nod.

"Oui, Pierre." He looked back at the four. *An odd group. And where in the world is that woman from? Who has black eyes, for God's sake? And as Pierre said,* we can use the money. *Hmm, let's see how bad they want to leave.* "The cabins are available. If no other passengers appear this morning to bid on them, I could let you have all four cabins for, say, forty Gold Imperials each."

"Bloody, flaming hell!" The young man who'd stayed silent and mostly out of sight to this point, cursed. "Fer that much we'd just as well buy the whole demmed bloody boat!" And the priest simply stared in shock, temporarily unable to speak. The Elf's eyes glittered with anger.

"Quiet!" The woman in black silenced all of them before they could all scream like gelded tigers. "How much is that in Kolbian Thalers?"

"Un moment." Andre opened his logbook to one of the back pages. He had the currency conversions he'd accept printed there. "Hmm. In Thalers, right now, with all the tension between the Empire and the Kolbians? Hmm, I'd take, oh say, give you a break, I'll take an even hundred Thalers per cabin. You still want all four cabins?"

The black-eyed woman eyed him like a housewife eyeing which pullet was going to be Sunday dinner. He suppressed an urge to swallow. Then she slipped a hand into a purse hidden under her arm in a clever harness of wire lined black leather.

"I trust this will be sufficient, Captain?" She dropped a gold bar that must have weighed nearly half a pound on the table in front of him. She followed it with a well-cut garnet the size of the tip of his own forefinger. "It'd better be."

"Sacrebleu!" Pierre hissed, his eyes huge at the sight of the gold.

"Oui, Pierre." He reached out and picked up the garnet. It was good enough quality to grace a bishop's ring. The bar of gold felt right as well. "Well, Mademoiselle, uh, might I have the honor of your name?"

"Sachi Takahashi."

"So if you would sign the logbook here, Mademoiselle Takahashi...?" The look he got from those black eyes told him that no liberties at all could be taken with her. "And then the rest of you, please?"

***

"Sachi, was it wise to show the Captain such wealth?" Gelman settled on the edge of the bunk in the largest cabin. "And where did you get that gold bar?"

"I stole it back home. You could call it payment for deferred wages. It's of no matter." Sachi leaned against the cabin's single porthole. She wanted to be sure none of the sailors were pulling one of her tricks of hanging outside a window or port and listening.

"Cor. Half pound a' gold an' tis *no matter!*" Aylie snorted from the upper bunk. "Even His Grace, the Duke would've taken such a thing to *matter!*"

"Aylie, our dear Sachi has no sense at all when it comes to money." Silaqui was curled up in the cabin's single stuffed chair. "Best as I can tell, she never has." The Elf finished cleaning her nails with a sharp little knife. "Now, dear Sachi, you've promised us some small enlightenment about these fits of yours. And whatever it was that you were so evasive about when you and Aylie fled the Guildmaster's office. Not to mention your many and unusual abil..." The sudden knock on the door startled all of them. Sachi cautiously stepped to the door, her white steel sword seeming to just appear in her hand.

"Aye, who's there?" she called through the door.

"Oh, please!" Willis Fleet's baritone came faintly through the door. "Open up and let me in, this stuff is heavy." Sachi jerked the door open and yanked Willis into the cabin. He stumbled and fell flat on the floor, half buried under a huge pack and an overstuffed seabag.

"And what, exactly, brings you here, Willis?" Sachi growled as she lifted Willis to his feet by the strap on the top of the pack.

"Orders, of course." He shrugged out of the pack. "In here, somewhere," he lifted the seabag, "is a set of orders directing me to use the first available transport departing Vlymouth with further destinations in the Empire, in order to deliver the attached documents to the Diplomatic Mission in Luctini. This was the next ship leaving and Luctini is listed as a port of call after Al-Ja-whatever in far western Darsälaam. The Captain told me I'd have to share a cabin with one of the other passengers. You can't imagine how happy I was to hear your dulcet tones in the passageway!"

"Oh, I can imagine," Sachi muttered under her breath.

"So, who am I rooming with? Silaqui? Sachi?"

"If you room with me, you letch, you'll do it as a lawn ornament!" Silaqui's smile took some of the sting out of her words. But only some.

"You'll stay with Gelman." Sachi ignored the wounded puppy look in Willis' eyes. "And don't play the sad puppy with me, Willis. Silaqui gets one room, Aylie one room and you fine gentlemen can share the third. I'll take the smallest myself. Any issues?" Headshakes and "uh-huhs" ran around the room. "Good. Get settled and get everything stowed away pretty quick. I hear the crew singling up the lines. They must have been taking up the gangplank as you were coming up it, Willis."

"They were. Some of the crewmen are pretty rascally looking."

"It won't be an issue. I have an idea about a way to convince them to leave all of us alone. An idea that got better when you showed up." She effortlessly picked up both Willis' pack and seabag. "Now let's get you settled." Willis shrugged and followed her into the passageway.

Schooner *Whisper*,
Eastern Lanic Ocean,
Approaching Vlymouth
October, 1478, Third Age of Imperial Reckoning

The seas had moderated a bit as the storm blew away to the south. Unlike Debbie McAllen, stuck up on the Orbital Defense Center *Backhand Blow*, Marianne Lundgren hated sailing ships. They bobbed about the ocean, at the mercy of wave and especially wind. While there were charts and sextants onboard, *Whisper's* Captain was old school, navigating by the stars, the compass, dead reckoning and, in Marianne's opinion, a stupid amount of luck. That being said, she knew the barely glimpsed green haze ahead was the coast of Montagar. At least her implants and nanites kept seasickness at bay. Otherwise, she was certain the majority of her meals would have wound up feeding the fish. She turned her head as the First Mate stepped up to the rail beside her.

"You're not really a good sailor, are you?" He smiled up at Marianne. "Of course, I don't think I've ever met someone from the far plains of the Rus, either."

"There are no boats there." Her nanites pitched her voice an octave lower, and much rougher. She'd prefer to not be remembered by the crew. Being a woman six inches over six feet was bad enough, so she'd adopted the persona of someone from the far steppes of the Rus Empire. Dokuz Khatum was a common name in the steppes. That, along with her dreads replaced with a buzz cut a Marine would be proud of, not to mention the contacts that turned her eyes brown, should throw any Seekers looking for a Confederal off the track. She hoped.

"No boats, uh?"

"No. Rivers are either shallow enough to ford or deep and fast enough to be death traps. Forking a strong warhorse is much preferable to these damned ships." A cased bow and quiver hung over her back, crossing a curved sword nearly four feet long in its traveling sheath. She turned to face the blond First Mate. A Heimdägarran Seamaster, he was the only member of the crew even close to her height. "You sailors are all crazy. But this is the only way I can complete the next stage of my *Rakta Kvesako,* as you would say, a Blood Quest."

"Ah, now that I can understand." He grinned at her, not a particularly pleasant grin. "Much as when the Sea Gods send my people a-viking, raiding and plundering the soft land folk. Of course, these days, they send us less often. Even our best captains and greatest heroes cannot stand against the cannons and muskets of the mainlanders anymore. And the Kolbians, their navy has a short way with pirates. So, my people are becoming merchants and traders. More difficult to win a name that way." He spat over the side.

"The Han send their raiders and mercenaries to burn our yurts, kill our men and rape our women. Steal our horses and cattle. Take those they do not kill away into slavery." Marianne impaled him with cold eyes and a colder voice. "We have no use for raiders and thieves. Come to my lands, how you say, *a-viking,* and I'll feed your guts to the pigs. But only after four strong bulls pull you into quarters. Good day."

Pale-faced, the Mate beat a hasty retreat. *Son of a bitch's been sniffing at my ass the whole damn trip. Felt nice to put him in his place. I wonder if the steppes nomads of eastern Rus really are that vicious? Oh well, got him outta my hair. What little is left of it. I'll be glad to get off this tub and grow my dreads back.* She sighed and watched a graceful brigantine heading roughly south by southwest ride smoothly over the waves. She zoomed her vision in enough to make out someone clad mostly in red perched in the foremast's lookout position. Whoever it was, they rode the ship's motion with an easy familiarity that only years at sea granted. *Not a skill I really want to learn.* She shrugged again, turning away from the rail and going carefully below to her cubby-hole cabin.

**Brigantine *le Bonaventure*,
Eastern Lanic Ocean,
Course South by Southwest
October, 1478, Third Age of Imperial Reckoning**

"She really does nae like being below decks, does she?" Aylie was seated on the breech of *le Bonaventure's* starboard eight pounder cannon, dividing her attention between Sachi coiling a rope on the deck and Silaqui's perch on the crosstree of the foremast topgallant yard.

"No, she doesn't." Sachi worked quickly, coiling the line. She'd gotten bored within the first day out of port and had asked Captain le Foix for work to do on board ship. With a bemused shrug, he'd set her to coiling lines, once she demonstrated that she did, in fact, know a sheet from a stay. "She spent most of two years locked in a cabin below decks, chained to the deck, only hauled out when the pirates wanted her to kill someone with her magic. She's a terrible fear of confinement and I don't blame her in the least. Besides, she enjoys the freedom of sea and sky. She might be the best lookout we could have up there."

"Ye seem, well, not happier, but more at peace, I think?"

"I love the sea. I love being on a ship. The first place I was ever truly free, truly happy, not living in fear of a beating, being ordered to kill myself or just strangled to an honorless death, not having to worry if my food was poisoned, that was on the *Intrepid*. That ship will always symbolize freedom to me."

"Huh."

"The Kolbians, they simply accepted me for me. Oh, I know that many of the sailors lusted for me. They are men, after all. But no one ever said or did a single thing to press themselves on me in any way. They treated me, clanless and without family or name, as if I was a great noble lady. That or as if I was their own, favorite little sister."

"The little I know of sailors is only what me Ma told me of 'em, which mostly was to stay away from 'em." Aylie shrugged. "Still, you've nae problem with 'em."

"Aylan," Pere Gelman joined them, using the alias Aylie decided on when she left the Duke's townhouse, "are you sure you're not one of those Eindeuten mind-healers? What they call a *psychologe*? The new ones that get you to lie on a couch and talk about your life so you won't be depressed or whatever?"

"Yer going a bit balmy, Pere. Ye seasick or has the sun boiled yer brains already?" Aylie mock-shook her fist at him. "'Tis just a bit of talk, nae more."

"Trust me, Pere Gelman," Sachi turned bleak eyes on the priest as she finished with the line. "No one wants to talk about what's in my head." She turned away and leaned on the rail. Several miles away, she could see the sails of a handsome schooner, tacking across the wind, apparently headed into Vlymouth port. "Too many ugly, horrible things."

***

Willis kept his head up as he bowed to Sachi. The mid-waist of the main deck was as cleared as it was going to be as the two faced each other. Sachi had made a great deal of wanting a 'sparring' partner. And she hid a slightly malicious grin when Willis was 'volunteered' for the 'exercise session' she wanted. He'd faced her before and knew for a fact he was not in her league. Not even close.

They came out of the bow and dropped into their fighting stances. Willis took the strong horse stance in which he was most comfortable while Sachi simply stood there. She cocked her head at him, relaxed, her feet as wide as her shoulders, balanced and centered. She sighed, shook her head and then, with no warning whatever, exploded into motion.

Willis managed to block one punch and dodged a snap kick before he realized both had been feints as she dropped under his counter-punch and swept his legs out from under him. He grunted as she punched him in the side of the head on the way down, not as hard as she could have. And even that was a bit of feint as the other fist smashed rocklike knuckles into his right elbow, a vicious blow that numbed his entire arm, fingers to shoulder. Then a heel whipped out of he-had-no-idea-where and pounded into his solar plexus.

The pain put the entire world into slow motion as getting his breath back became the only important thing in the universe. He didn't really notice the mimed knuckle to the temple or the knife hand touch to the throat. Sachi back-flipped to her feet, then waved Gelman over. The only sounds on the deck were the squawks of the escorting seabirds and the susurration of wind and wave. Everyone was staring, even Silaqui, who had never really seen her in action before.

"Is he okay, Gelman?" she quietly asked.

"You didn't quite break anything, but I'd suggest you find another playmate, at least for a while." Golden light glowed around the priest's hands as he worked on Willis.

"Ah, well that's good." She turned and smiled sweetly at a stunned Captain Foix. "Perhaps, Captain, one of your crew might wish to spar with me?"

The deck cleared in a rush.

***

Thunder growled overhead and lightning flashed, illuminating roiling, black clouds. The wind grew in strength steadily. Captain de Foix had ordered the topgallant yards and mast sent down a couple of hours or so ago, when the purple and dark gray line of storm clouds began boiling up north of *le Bonaventure*, pursuing the brigantine as she fled south. As conditions worsened, he ordered sail reduced to a single storm jib-sail and a close reefed fore-topsail. Now it was a true storm, winds over fifty miles an hour, the heaving sea visible through heavy, windblown spray. He had ordered all his passengers to go below decks and stay there within the last hour.

"Capitaine, the wind still rises." Pierre Lescot had to shout at de Foix from where he stood beside the wheel. Water poured off his oilskins. That water was as much sea-spray as it was rain. Like the two men on the ship's wheel, he had lashed himself to a lifeline. "We must reduce sail and run before the wind." He used his native Guellian tongue with just de Foix and the two helmsmen within earshot.

"Aye," de Foix shouted back in the same language, "but that will take us even farther off course!"

"Better off course than driven under!"

"Oui. Call the hands to reduce sail. We will take in the fore topsail and run before the wind with only the jib."

Lescot blew a piercing blast on his whistle and the soaked crew hurried back onto the deck to take in the sail.

***

"Oooh, please, dear God, please just let me die." Aylie's face was an interesting greenish-gray. The ship corkscrewed again from the nasty following sea and Sachi simply stuck the pail under the girl's face as she heaved again. "Why's there always corn? I's had nae corn in weeks," she moaned before a second heave sent her back to the pail.

Sachi kept her face neutral as she helped Aylie back into her bunk. She thought hammocks would have been better in the storm but there really wasn't any place to hang one. Silaqui gave her an exhausted grimace from where she sat, clutching the arms of the bolted-down chair. The Elf hadn't started puking *yet*, and Sachi prayed to the Ancestors that she wouldn't start. So far she was comfortable with the heaving, twisting motion of the ship, but she wasn't sure what would happen if both Aylie and Silaqui started.

Puking tended to be contagious. Something she feared Silaqui was about to prove.

"Don't you start." She raised her voice to be heard over the howling winds and the groaning of the ship herself. "We don't have another pail. You'd have to share."

"I should puke on you just for saying that. Ick." Silaqui was pale and getting paler quickly. "Don't worry until my face matches my hair. Then just let me die."

"Dying would take too much effort." Sachi's comment carried the cheerful brutality of one immune to seasickness. "You'll both live, even if you don't want to." She grinned at Silaqui.

She got the pail under the Elf just in time.

***

Across the narrow passageway, Willis helped Gelman back into his bunk, after wiping off his face. The cleric had showed no signs of seasickness until the storm hit. Then his stomach rebelled with a vengeance fearful to witness. Willis was just grateful that the generations of Fleets who had served at sea had bequeathed him an apparent immunity to seasickness. And this was far from the worst storm he'd ever been in. It was a nasty storm, but he thought its very fury would result in it waning away as rapidly as it had risen.

"I'd no idea the God would test me so," Gelman moaned as he collapsed back into his bunk. "And you, you God-lost, motherless bastard, why isn't this horrible illness affecting you?"

"Gelman, there've been so many Fleets in naval service for so long that seawater is part of our blood. The family legends say that the first Fleet to command a warship in battle, generations ago, was actually born at sea in the midst of a hurricane. No idea if that's the truth, but many, maybe most, of the markers in the family graveyards are stones over empty graves, because so many of my family have been lost at sea, either in battle or in storm. Granny says the ocean is part of us and therefore we are part of it. I'll just be grateful and not argue with a gift horse, eh?"

"I hate you," the cleric groaned. "You and all your cursed kind."

"Trust me, you're not going to die. You just think you will and you think it'd be a release." He chuckled. "The sea, she's not so kind as to let you go that easily."

***

The storm passed eventually, as all storms do. *Le Bonaventure* showed the damage of the storm's fury, and within the hour of the sea moderating enough that the crew could walk on deck without requiring lifelines, de Foix had them hard at work on repairs. Silaqui recovered quickly and resumed her favorite spot on the main topgallant cross trees. Sachi and Willis pitched in, helping with repairs with an earnest will. Aylie, still masquerading as Aylan, lent a hand where possible and practical, while Gelman tended to the inevitable minor injuries.

The captain told them the storm blew *le Bonaventure* a ways off course, further south than originally intended. But he expected no particular difficulty getting back on course. They should still arrive at the port of Al-Jazual within a week of their predicted arrival date. Basically, it was business as usual while at sea in the rough Lanic Ocean. And, as might be expected, the hazards of the Lanic were not through with them yet.

"Sail ho! Astern on the port quarter!" On the third day after the passing of the storm, it was Silaqui's shout from the main topgallant that brought everyone's heads around. Everyone knew that the Kolbian Navy regularly patrolled the middle and northern latitudes of the Lanic with the goal of suppressing piracy and slavery as much as was humanly possible. But south of those latitudes, pirates were a constant menace to any vessel.

"Mademoiselle Sachi, could I impose upon you to climb the rigging and see what might be seen of these sails your friend has called out?" De Foix had learned, by now, that Sachi was not only the most dangerous person on the ship, but that she had the keenest eyes he'd ever seen.

"Certainement." She was picking up Guellian quickly as well, using their own language to speak to the crew most of the time. They chuckled politely when she mispronounced something, but just as she had done on *Intrepid*, Sachi was proving to be an outstanding crewmate. She took the spyglass he handed her and headed up the ratlines to the main topgallant yard.

"There." Silaqui pointed to the sails on the horizon. Whoever or whatever it was, she was three-masted and lofty. She was just hull up from where the two friends perched. "Your eyes are even better than mine."

"Uh-hmm," Sachi mumbled as she put her eye to the glass. The distant ship leapt into view. "Oh, shit." What appeared to be a Kolbian flag was actually nothing more than a cleverly tied bundle of blue, red and white bunting. The hull was stained wood, slopped over with what looked like black tar. A row of carronades on the spar deck gleamed in the late morning sun, and Sachi counted at least seventeen gun ports along her starboard side. But, of all things, it was the crew that gave her away. They were a nasty looking bunch, lacking anything resembling a uniform, bearing a wildly varied collection of individual weapons, heavily favoring boarding axes and pikes. And there were hell's own lot of them. Sachi counted at least a hundred men on the ship's abbreviated forecastle.

"What's wrong?"

"What do you think?"

"Pirates?"

"Yes. Quan's own collection of evil in human shape. The ship, she's three-masted, ship rigged and lofty. And they've the weather gage on us. We likely can't outrun her, certainly can't outfight her. Come on. The Captain needs to know this immediately." Sachi grabbed the backstay and slid to the deck, followed by Silaqui.

"Well?" de Foix asked.

"Pirates. A ship-rigged galleon. I'd rate the ship herself as a frigate, nearly as big as the *Intrepid* herself. Heavy gunned, as well. Eight carronades per broadside on the spar deck. Starboard gun deck shows seventeen, maybe eighteen ports. Slovenly lot, the crew is, but there's a shitstorm's worth of them. As I told Silaqui, can't outrun her, can't outfight her. And, no, not even I could beat that many. She's a bit more than eleven miles away." Sachi knew the pirate was exactly twenty-one point eight kilometers away, sailing at nine point six knots.

"Sacrebleu." De Foix's face paled.

"So, what can we do, Captain?" Sachi's voice was level and calm.

"I do not know, Mademoiselle." He leaned against the binnacle. "I fear what we will do, regardless, is die. If we're lucky, quickly. If not...if not...Mon Dieu...que Dieu nous aide." He whispered the last.

"I don't know if God will help us or not, de Foix." Sachi answered him. "But the Kolbians like to say that God helps those who help themselves first."

"Oui, Mademoiselle? And how do we help ourselves?"

"I don't kno..." Sachi collapsed as the fit swept her into blackness.

Chapter Thirteen

**Port of Al-Iskabad, Darsälaamic Kaliphate,
Traquilidamar Sea
The Caravanserai of Abdul Jaleel al-Salim
July, 1478; Third Age of Imperial Reckoning**

SAHLA PERCHED COMFORTABLY ATOP the saddle of her ka'mel, Khaahira. The rough haired beast grumbled and complained as it waited in the pre-dawn dimness. She laid her hand on its neck and exerted her will to calm its complaints. Too much noise and Khalid might scold her for not controlling her mount. She watched him as he stood at the gate, peering down the poorly lit street. He toyed with the hilt of his shamshir, twirling the tassel attached to the pommel. She smiled as she watched him, the strikingly handsome, solemn young commander of her guardsmen. Her oldest childhood friend.

Ah, Khalid, oft the striking subject of a maiden's daydreams, so earnest and determined to fulfill his duties. So strong and the very embodiment of honor. I wonder, if he remembers those days, so long ago, when we played tag in the sands and I tricked him? Is my one-time playmate lost to me forever? Does he ever think of me as anything other than his duty to guard me? Does he ever even think of me as a woman at all? Ah, he is well formed and handsome and I have watched him practice his swordsmanship with the other caravan guards. He is good, very *good.*

But what he would think if he were to learn that the Houri he guards so diligently is his better with a blade? Or that, as a Jann, I

171

have some small gifts of magic? Once I Bond to a mortal human, I shall finally be able to fully wield those gifts. But for now, they are only pale shadows of what they will become.

I only hope that Sheikh Mustafa will be someone I can truly love. And mayhaps, half as handsome as Khalid? A Bond of love would be so much stronger, more powerful and grant me greater gifts. But I must Bond soon, within the next four moons, or the magic of my birth shall banish me to my Sire's realm. And that is a place I have no desire to ever see in this life.

She sighed to herself, not that anyone could truly tell what she did or even what she looked like under her shrouding abayah and face veiling niqab. Only her eyes, the hue of luminous sapphires, shone above the veil. She took a deep, surreptitious breath of the cool, moist sea air, so different than the sand-dry air of Abdul-Ghaffanse. An unremarkable desert town she had always called home, a home now long, tedious weeks behind her. For the rest of the journey they were to take ship here in Al-Iskabad.

Al-Iskabad was a large port on the mostly landlocked Traquilidamar Sea. The Sea was bordered to the south by the Kaliphate of Darsälaam, which claimed the northern desert of the otherwise unexplored continent of Khakal. The Mountains of Iona formed the eastern boundary of the Sea and the northernmost waves washed the southern half of the great continent of Uirsen. The final boundary of the Sea was the rolling green waves of the Lanic beyond the westernmost Traquilid Gates. There, northern Khakal and southern Uirsen, in the form of the great peninsula of Ibertina, came almost within sight of each other with slightly more than a hundred sea miles forming the Gates.

As a port city, Al-Iskabad was very different from anything she had ever experienced, crowded and smelly. Folk here were loud and rude, especially in the markets and fest halls. And they were musical, even in their squabbles, minstrels and bards busking on street corners. Last night she had heard wild music from the tavern across the caravanserai's courtroom. That music was different from her homeland, fierce and wild and free. It tugged at her feet and her blood, tempting her to a wild kind of dance. A wild feeling of freedom. That freedom was somewhat repressed by the tall buildings, some boasting five floors above the ground as they loomed over the streets, shading all from everything but the noontime sun. The port's architecture reflected its origins as a base for the Lietelean Empire's attempted conquest of the desert folk generations ago.

But wandering nomads, free of any rule but their own, fiercely independent tribal towns and desert monasteries full of borderline religious fanatics made very poor Imperial subjects. After decades of bloody revolts and a hundred years of nearly endless warfare, an exhausted Empire pled *enough* and fled. Its influence was only remembered in those few Traquilidamaran ports more deeply influenced by the Empire and its sea traders. It left the sands to the desert's stubborn, independent and sometimes fanatical inhabitants.

She knew there was a Kaliph who ruled the one great desert metropolis of Darsälaam, Tarsälaam the City, far to the east of Al-Iskabad. He claimed to rule all the Folk of the Desert, but in truth, he only wielded what power the tribes of Divine Chalta's desert gave him at any particular moment, usually only lip service, if that.

Sahla's smile became a frown as Jamul joined Khalid. Jamul al 'Abbas actually frightened her. She watched how he looked at her, when he thought no one could see him. She knew he never doubted the stories of the great beauty of the Houri. Khalid's eyes upon her conveyed respect and honor, responsibility and duty to his Sheikh. And perhaps shadows of the days when they had been carefree playmates. Jamul's eyes stripped her naked, lusted after her and desired her submission to him in the most vulgar ways. That or those hard brown eyes calculated to the last golden dinar what her value might be, exposed nude on an auction block in an Imperial slave market.

That one I must watch most closely. His mouth makes the proper words, what would please the Aliyahs of Divine Chalta. But I doubt even the Prophet Himself, much less those blessed holy men, with their scrolls and books, can truly see into a black heart of deceit such as I fear beats within Jamul's breast. I am certain neither my Father-the-Sheikh nor my true Sire would be pleased to learn of the serpent coiling in the midst of my guardsmen. If he had won Mulazim of my Guard, I think I would be better protected by the wolves and tigers of the desert rocks. And I know that Khalid does not trust his distant cousin very much.

***

Khalid ab-Kanaan kept a cautious hand on his shamshir's hilt as he cast a wary glance down the street in the early morning darkness. As Mulazim, the Houri's safety and purity were his responsibility until they reached their destination. There, she would wed Sheikh Mustafa al-Mahdi Baddour. The marriage, arranged shortly after her tenth year, intended to keep the Prophet's Peace of Divine Chalta between the Tribe of Abdul-Ghaffanse and the Tribe of al-Kohfan. The responsibility might weigh down lesser shoulders than his, but he reveled in the trust his Sheikh placed in him. He would see her to her groom. Rumor claimed that her beauty now outshone the stars themselves, mayhap the most beautiful woman to ever grace the sands of Divine Chalta's eternal desert.

Khalid did not know about those claims. They had been playmates many years ago and he remembered a beautiful girl-child with masses of long, lustrous sable hair and sapphire eyes. He did not know if he believed some of the wilder stories about her or not. His task was to get her safely to her destination, not judge her beauty nor be the arbiter of unsubstantiated stories about her.

The cool moisture of the pre-dawn sea air was a new sensation for him. And new sensations made him wary, especially in this strange place, with its alien, ancient architecture. He knew little of the ancient history of his folk and he cared less. What he cared about right now was getting safely to *Chalta's Grace*, the two-masted trading xebec which would transport all of them to the Traquilid Gates, the narrow western passage where the Traquilidamar Sea gave way to the great and treacherous Lanic Ocean. Thence they would sail down the northwestern Lanic coast of the desert to the port of Al-Jazual. A final brief overland trip to the stronghold of her intended groom, the Sheikh Mustafa. Then his task would be complete and in all likelihood he would retrace his steps and return home. Unless the Houri decided she wanted him to stay and head up her personal bodyguard.

"Khalid, how much longer before we depart? All is in readiness. Even the Houri's ka'mel grows restive. I doubt her ability to control the beast." Jamul al 'Abbas, as Rahqib, answered only to Khalid. Despite or perhaps because they were distantly related, they did not get along particularly well.

"Cousin, of all the beasts of burden and the guards' mounts, can you name one better controlled than hers? Should you not be seeing to the men, rather than perturbing me?" *I would leave this one here, but the Houri's guard is small enough already, mayhap too small. And with this one about, I shall never forget to shake out my boots of a morning!*

"The men are ready to ride, O *'Asadd Alssahra'*, Lion of the Desert. As is the Houri, her duenna and maids even. We but await your command, my great lord." Jamul brought his hands together as he bowed obsequiously.

"My boots need no further polishing, *cousin*." *Untrustworthy, bootlicking toady. I'd like nothing better than your head at my feet.* "See to your mount. The hour appointed to arrive at the vessel draws nigh. I shall speak with Master al-Salim and have the caravanserai's great gate opened. Then we shall make our way to the docks and board the ship."

"My lord." Jamul walked away, back to his horse, but Khalid did not turn his back on the smaller man until he was mounted among the rest of the guardsmen. Jamul hid an evil smile as he mounted. *Disdain me if you will,* my dear cousin, so-mighty Khalid. *I will not move against you, not here, where all things move to your benefice.*

But I have studied closely the ways of the ocean-sea for many moons. I know how the currents flow and the winds blow. There are those others who also know of the patterns of wind and wave, and for them, it is naught but child's play to lay in wait along the course. And they will share the bounty of the Houri with me, Chalta grant they find us as they have promised me they will. And then, O my cousin. And then...

Tradeship *Chalta's Grace,*
Northwest Lanic coast of Northern Khakal
Twenty-eight days out of Al- Iskabad
Nine days out of the Imperial Port of Camaria
August, 1478; Third Age of Imperial Reckoning

"Does ye see them, Lord Khalid? There, four points off the starboard bow?" The captain of *Chalta's Grace* pointed from where he stood on the xebec's raised quarterdeck.

"I see the sails, Captain Al'asad al-Muhit. But I know not what it is I see. So tell me, Lion of the Ocean, what means these distant sails?"

"Probably a ship-rigged Kolbian sloop-of-war, that, er one a' their smaller frigates. They oft operate in these waters outside the passage of the Traquilid Gates. 'Tis the deep Lanic Ocean we be in, My Lord. Here, the Kolbian Navy is master. She's loftier than we, square rigged on three masts. Makes her the faster."

"This ship bears only two masts. Are we that much slower than they? And they are far distant, only sails visible."

"Aye, Lord. But our lateen rig is nae as efficient except that we might be the faster beating to windward. Iffen we can see them, they can see us, 'less their lookouts be blind. Unfortunately, they've the weather gage and therefore the ability to choose when and how to engage, should they wish."

"Why should they? We are not at war with the Kolbians?"

"Nae, My Lord. But the Kolbians have very strange ideas about slavery and piracy. And many of the corsairs of Northern Khakal's

Lanic coast use lateen rigs, like ours. As do many slavers. And far too many of both fly the Kaliphate's flag."

"So they hunt corsairs? I know nothing of this."

"My Lord, should the Kolbian Navy decide they have tooken ye in the actual act of piracy or worse, slavery, the punishment be summary courts-martial, before hanging by the neck until dead and burial at sea. For pirates and slavers, they've no pity at all, at all." The captain rubbed his grizzled face and spat over the side. "I don't unnerstand them, nae one truly does, not even the Prophet himself, I think. Nae sane man knows truly why they do what they do. Some oddish belief in freedoms and equalities."

"So, have we a concern, then, Captain?"

"Nay, My Lord. We've no slaveys aboard, nor any of the rig that would mark a ship a slaver. We's nae armed heavy enough to be a true pirate, what with only eight nine pounder cannon. Enough to fend off the coastal scum, chancy types what'll put a single twelve pounder in the bow of a big longboat and row out to try and take an incautious or unarmed ship. But we're nae armed as heavy as most of the freebooters ye might find 'long these coasts."

"So what do we do, then? Will my charge be safe?"

"Nae much we can do, her having the weather gage. As for yer Lady being safe? From the Kolbian Navy? Aye, safe as houses, I'd say." The captain cast an experienced eye at the sun and sky. "They'll like as not come wit' in hailing distance, say four hours, mebbe five from now. I been told of a great animosity betwixt the Kolbians and the Imperials, wit', of course, slavery being the bottom of it. I heerd one of their big frigates, a forty-four, like to a ship o' the line, wrecked a trio of Imperial galleasses, I'd say, mebbe fully a year ago. Dueling over a cursed slaver, of all the daft things."

"A disdain for pirates and corsairs I might understand. No one civilized cares for any wild reivers pillaging and burning. But slavery? It's the way of the world that some are free and some are slaves. It's the penalty for being too weak to protect yourself. Who's enslaving Kolbians? Other than that, why should they care?"

"Dunno, My Lord. But they do care, greatly. Are there aught among your men or your Lady's maids that are slaveys?"

"No, the Sheikh did not send any slaves with the Houri. Her husband-to-be will be expected to gift her with the needful body slaves."

"Well, then, My Lord, I'd say we've naught to fear. The worst what might come to pass 'twould be heaving to and losing a bit of time while they 'inspect' us. Nae concern, My Lord, nae concern a'tall."

***

Being on deck was always exhilarating. The wind blew cleanly through Sahla's fine linen robes, her heavier, shrouding cotton abayah and silk niqab. It felt like the cool, clean breeze brought her nude before the Elementals of the Air. She shivered with pleasure as it caressed her body as she thought a lover might. She could almost see the Elemental sylphs and aethyrs as they danced and played in the ship's rigging. She had not felt an elation like this since the last time she had bathed in the desert hills; cool, clear spring water flowing over her naked limbs and body. She smiled to herself, remembering the euphoria of such utter freedom. Her protectors, Najwa and Khalid, would have been shocked at the idea of the *Houri of the Sands* bathing nude under the sky.

Najwa am-Challa, her devoted duenna, stood behind her mistress, silently guarding her purity, even here. Khalid loomed behind Najwa, a frown on his face. *Chalta's Grace* rode the ocean's swells with all the elegance of her name. Sahla could see the larger ship approaching to the right, what all the sailors called starboard for some strange reason. Its hull was a mottled green-gray, blending in well with the green-blue waves of the ocean. Dirty grayish sails cast long shadows as the sun dropped from noon to evening in the western sky. The tall ship flew a flag at the top of its highest mast, the one in the middle. That flag, she thought, revealed the blue, red and white colors of the Republic of Kolbia. She heard the sailors speculating on the Kolbians' purpose as it swiftly closed the last mile between the two vessels.

So that is a Kolbian warship? Hmm. I expected a better show. Oh, the colors of the hull blend well with the ocean, I imagine to allow it to sneak up on an enemy. But everyone says the Kolbians are the best Navy in the world. Why would the best need to hide to sneak up on their enemies? Only thieves hide in the dark. Ah, well. I'd best enjoy the wind and sky while I can. Khalid will insist I go down into the dank cabins once the ship comes much closer. And then I shall be forced to listen to that creature's *incessant whining, complaining and moaning!* The Contessa du Lisenis, Her Ladyship, Gabrielle de Rochechouart de Mortemart! *Grr! By the Beard of the Prophet,* why *did* she *have to board when we made port in Camaria? Just because she did not want to cross the Gralpen Mountains in winter? I know nothing of those mountains, but now they owe me! Because of them I must restrain myself from murdering that brainless blonde chatterbox!*

For a copper mithqal, I'd push her overboard! She whines because the motion of the sea makes it hard to cake on her make-up! *She complains because the ship's course turns south, to Al-Jazual port town first and not the port of Haveno de la Maro de Anĝelojes, where she's to meet her fiancé, His Grace, the Duke of Ostreich, Heinrich Prinz zu Sayn-Wassenstein! She moans because the food is bad, the wooden seat of the necessary put a splinter in her precious, pink buttocks or the doors are too narrow for her ridiculous dresses. Dresses that thrust her nearly uncovered breasts forward for everyone to see! Fagh! Whoever this* Duke of Ostreich *is, I wish him much joy of this over-cosseted ghula! I doubt even the monstrous Eaters of Men of the deepest sands would touch her! That much stupid might be catching! No matter how pretty she is!*

"Houri, the ship comes closer. I would you go below, now. Your duenna and I agree, you should not be sullied by the covetous eyes of infidels. Please, go below." Khalid's low voice carried an indefinable sense of urgency and she turned to meet his eyes. Eyes pleading with her to go below. Eyes concerned and worried as the other ship closed on them.

"A moment more, please, Khalid. If they can even see me at all, I am no more than an indistinct human shape on the deck." A commotion at the door leading to the cabins below caught their attention. The Contessa de Lisenis stood there, once again stuck somehow. Her Ladyship squawked and berated one of her maids as the embroidered lace hem of her idiotic satin dress caught on a nail or splinter. The Contessa began whacking the hapless maid with her fan, making the poor woman's thankless task of rescuing the dress from whatever it was caught on even more difficult. "And now, unless you wish to toss me down through the cargo hatch, the passageway is blocked."

"Indeed." Khalid frowned as he fingered the tassel of his sword's pommel.

"Where *does* that woman get her clothes?" Najwa whispered from behind Sahla. "I know she is nothing but a soft, city bred infidel, a decadent Imperial at that, but *who* on the entire world wears green satin and pink silk in the *same* dress? And lavender lace? Ugh!" She coughed to disguise her laughter as the Contessa's struggles to get free tore away the lace trim of the dress's hem. The Contessa squealed and added futile kicks to the ineffective whacks of the folded fan. The maid gave up her efforts to free the lace and simply collapsed into a ball, trying to avoid the kicks and blows. Najwa wore simple robes, covered by a hijab, not the concealing niqab veil and so she raised her hand to hide her smirk at the Contessa's plight. "In the right colors she would be beautiful, but she always chooses the worst combinations." Her eyes smiled at Sahla. "Whereas, Houri, your beauty overwhelms any merely mortal cloth. No man that sees your face will ever remember what you wore."

"As you say, Najwa." Sahla sighed as the ship's First Mate stepped between the Contessa and her maid, earning a half-hearted thwack from the fan before he grabbed it away from her. "But there are times when I wish I was a plain faced goatherd girl, with a figure like a stick. Then I might wear a sack and do as I please, and who should say me no?"

"Even a goatherd girl has a father, Houri. And the Book of Holies says that sons and daughters should dutifully obey their fathers, as is the Prophet's wish," Najwa chided her.

"And do I not obey my Father-the-Sheikh, traveling to marry a man I'll never lay my own eyes on until the moment we stand before the Aliyah of Chalta to be wed? Would being a goatherd girl, who might or might not grant her favors where she willed be so bad then...OWW, Khalid! Why do you grab me...!?" Khalid leapt past Najwa and clamped his hand on her arm in a grip of steel.

"GET BELOW, NOW!" Khalid's eyes widened in horror as the ragged bit of blue, red and white bunting masquerading as a Kolbian flag was cut loose and flew away in the wind. A new flag burst from the top of the big ship's foremast, a large black flag, white cutlass crossed over thigh bone, with a grinning skull superimposed atop that. The flag of a pirate.

She jerked in surprise as one of the now-revealed pirate's forward guns bellowed, gunsmoke rolling away from the muzzle. The cannon ball moaned like a lost soul before splashing into the ocean a hundred yards in front of the xebec. Gun ports opened down her side and cannon snouted out of them. Scores of rough dressed men appeared along the rail, brandishing boarding pikes, cutlasses and muskets. A tall blond man in a long red coat and black leather pants stood near the quarterdeck rail. Under his coat he wore some kind of a white breastplate as armor. He gestured at the helmsmen and the big ship began to edge slowly closer, the leers of the pirate crew becoming clearer. A tall, slender red-headed woman stepped into view next to him. Her body-hugging trousers and tightly laced vest left little to imagine of her feminine charms. Even from here, the flare of magic could be seen as she flung her arms skywards and emerald flames roared from her hands into the clear blue sky.

Sahla saw only fear and desperation in Khalid's face as he spun her about, rushing her toward the door the Contessa blocked. Clownish in her dress and make-up, she just stood there, motionless in shock. The blonde's face was a tragedy mask as she stared at the pirate ship. Khalid put his shoulder into her, knocking her back into the passageway, heels over head in a confusion of pink and green skirts, bustles and petticoats, white-stockinged legs flailing helplessly as she fell backwards over the huddled maid. Khalid shoved Sahla past the pair of thrashing, shrieking females before spinning back to the deck. He stopped at the door and looked back, meeting her eyes. She saw the horror and dread there, not for himself but for her.

"I can't stop them, Houri. Unless Chalta grants us a miracle." He paused, trying to find words that fled him like leaves before the storm. "I can only try." He plunged back onto the deck, shouting for her guards. He grabbed Najwa and thrust her into the passageway as well. She tripped over the Contessa and her maid, kneeing the blonde woman in the head and stunning her into blessed, temporary silence. Sahla reached out and pulled Najwa to her feet. They turned and fled down the ladder to their cabin. Sailors' hard feet pounded the deck, answering their Captain's roared orders. The Contessa had only six of her own guardsmen. Sahla's guard numbered twenty and seven. There were perhaps sixty sailors in the crew. She thought she had seen at least a hundred men along the rail of the pirate ship and there was that witch to deal with as well.

She could faintly hear the captain screaming at Khalid but not what he said. The boom of another of the pirate's guns carried clearly to them, in the belowdecks dimness. She heard the rumble of the *Grace's* guns as they were pushed about the deck, being prepared to fire, she thought. She caught and held Najwa's eyes.

Is there as much fear in my eyes as I see in hers? The pirate ship bristled with many cannons. And so many ugly, cruel men. Looking into Najwa's eyes, she reached up and loosened her niqab, letting the silken veil flutter to the cabin's deck. *We have no hope. Khalid will fight and die to protect me, protect all of us, but I know, as if the Prophet Himself whispered in my ear, that he will die. And then what should I do? Slay myself, a sin before Chalta? Throw myself on my knees before the pirates, beg them to use me as they will, if they let me...let us live? Can they be bargained with?* There was a swift knock at the door and she recognized Khalid's manner.

"Come, Khalid."

"Houri, I would..." The sight of her unveiled face stopped him in mid-word, awe in his expression as he saw her unveiled. He had not seen her so since she was twelve. Five years wrought an amazing change in her, polishing and revealing a beauty worthy of Chalta Himself, an Houri not of the Sands, but of Paradise come to the very earth of Rybitha.

"Yes, Khalid, what would you of me?" Her calm tone surprised herself.

"Ah, um, haw...Houri, take this." He held out a pistol to her, an expensive, double-barreled Kolbian made flintlock. She took it carefully. "Both barrels are loaded and it is cocked, Lady. I will not say what you should do with them. You might make a pair of pirates pay with their lives for attempting to violate you." He paused; his eyes alight as they drank in her beauty before they darkened in his despair. "Or you might use it to ensure that both Najwa and you escape them in a final act of defiance. I believe that Chalta and His Prophet should understand but I am no Aliyah of God to interpret the Book."

"Thank you, Khalid. For you, I am sure that Chalta's Paradise awaits."

"Perhaps. But it has been my honor to ward and guard you, even if I fail at the end, Houri. To be your true knight, your *Faris*, all these years. I once hoped to someday be a hero in your eyes. But I do not think there is any hero great enough to stop what is coming. Forgive me, Houri."

"Khalid, my honest *Faris*, my very own knight, created by my own hand, you know my name is Sahla."

"I know." A shy smile hovered around his lips. "I have never forgotten." A third cannon boomed from the pirate ship. There was a crash from somewhere forward on the ship. "Sahla, I must go. I must put some iron into our good Captain's spine."

"Khalid." She darted forward and grabbed his arm. "Bide a heartbeat." She slipped her arms around his neck and rose up on her toes as she pulled him down to her kiss. It was a very thorough kiss, her very first romantic kiss. Her blood pounded in her heart. Surprise widened his eyes as she released him. "Oh, Khalid, I wish it had been you that claimed the Bond of my Sire's Blood. But it is not to be. Go, my brave knight. Defend us all. You shall always be a hero in my eyes."

"Sahla. I...I always...cared for you." He stuttered slightly with his own emotions. His eyes were dark with regret as he pulled his keffiyeh up to cover his face. He turned away, drawing his shamshir as he closed the door behind him. She never saw him alive again.

"Sahla, what will you do with that gun?" Najwa quietly asked.

"What, no condemnation because I let a man, one not of my family, see my face? That I kissed him?" Her sapphire eyes flashed defiance at the guardian of her purity. "That many would now consider me impure?"

"Sahla, in all likeliness, we will either be dead before nightfall, or we will wish we were dead. Against that, a kiss is nothing. My question remains. What will you do with that gun?"

"I will bargain, Najwa. Our people are traders and merchants. We bargain. I will make the best bargain I can. It's all I can do."

***

As a young girl, Sahla thrilled to tales of battle, the bards singing of heroes striving against monsters or hopeless odds. She had never seen true battle, unless it was a squabble between two women of the harem. The worst had been the year she spent as a goatherd. The tiger she slew with her own blades, the wolves silenced by her sling. She had never seen the immediate results of war among men, bodies torn and rent asunder, limbs hacked off, a man's intestines in a bloody pile as he wailed, fruitlessly trying to stuff them back into his body before he died. She still did not see the worst of this, her first battle. What she did see was bad enough, what she heard was even worse.

Mother trained her until her feet bled and her arms drooped with exhaustion. Trained her until she mastered the light, flexible sabers favored by the desert dervishes of the Folk of the Sands' hidden monasteries. Monasteries where her own Mother had been trained. Her true Sire, the Jinn Ilben alh-Taymyah, a Jinn of the Second Rank of Air and Wind demanded his daughter be trained in song and dance. And in the wielding of flashing blades, all knowledge needed to be a true Dervish of the Folk of Darsälaam. To be sent to the desert alone, to learn the skills of survival, and, most importantly, in the desert's silence, to learn to listen to her own heart and soul. Once, when she was still a little girl, she asked Mother why she should be trained so differently than her younger sisters.

"Light of my Heart, Sahla, your path is different than theirs. Give it some little time yet, and you will understand." Later, when Father and Mother told her that she was a Jann and not truly human, she began to understand. Ilben foresaw a dreadful fate coming, one likely to destroy the world. And One who might turn it aside, but in turning that fate away, change the very nature of the world. If that One had someone like Sahla at his side, then both the fate and the change might be averted. She must find that One, forge a Bond with him, a Bond not of Slave and Master, but of Heart and Soul. A Bond of True Love. Nothing less would suffice. But other than such training, exhausting and extensive as it was, she never raised a weapon with the intent to kill a man. Now she stood, covered in Najwa's blood, her duenna slain by a cannon ball, waiting to learn her fate.

The fighting on the decks has ended. There is no more shouting of combat, no more ringing of steel on steel. The cannons stopped right before the pirate crashed into us, but they wrought horror enough, shattering this ship. The pirates will be coming, here, soon. Too soon. Now I am alone. I, Khalid, neither of us knew the havoc those cannons would wreak, I think. But perhaps it is better to die fighting than to submit to such beasts in human shape. One should only submit to Chalta, as the Prophet did. Only then can one attain Paradise. But I am not fully human. Does the Prophet have a place in Paradise for such as I? Some Aliyahs would say I am an abomination, others say any might come to Chalta, human or not. But I know there was one for Najwa and Khalid and now they have found their places there.

The pirates' reply to the pathetic broadside of *Chalta's Grace* had been devastating. The pirate ship's return fire crushed the xebec. The mainmast crashed down with the first broadside. The second swept away the xebec's guns, either killing the gun crews or dismounting the guns themselves. The third and fourth volleys blasted into the hull, punching completely through it with contemptuous ease. One of those cannon balls blasted through their cabin, striking Najwa where she stood by Sahla, holding her hand. It missed Sahla by less than a hand's length, the concussion knocking her flat. The ball tore poor Najwa into indistinguishable pieces without even a scream, soaking Sahla with blood and other things, things she refused to think about. Things that were once part of her duenna, her friend. She had wept briefly for that death, then wiped off her face and prepared to face her enemies.

Now she waited, patiently, hopelessly, as she heard the pirates smashing their way into the lower decks. She already heard the screams of at least two of her own maids as they were hauled forth from their hiding places. Other female shrieks were the Contessa's maids, or perhaps even the Contessa herself. She also heard wild, female laughter, nearly a screech, on the main deck and a deep, powerful male voice shouting orders the pirates scurried to obey.

Finally, there came a hammering on her door. With a final blow, the door smashed aside. The first through was a huge black man, ducking to keep from hitting his shaven skull on the overhead. A female Aljannia, what the infidels called an Elf, followed closely. The black man bore a great axe and wore only a pair of loose-legged trousers. Blood splattered his bare, muscular chest and face, with some still dripping slowly from his axe. The Aljannia wore her longish blonde hair in a horse's tail, a tight green vest over a white silk shirt, both well splattered with blood. Snug brown leather pants tucked into knee-high boots. A brace of smoking flintlock pistols thrust through her belt. The belt also supported the scabbard for the bloody cutlass she carried in her right hand. She leaned back into the passageway and shouted.

"We've found her, sir!" After that one shout, neither spoke.

"Well, well, there you are. And in one piece, too. Good, good." The man in the long red coat stepped into the room. This close, she realized he wore a buff leather shirt underneath that strange white breastplate. "I'd started to wonder if I'd been lied to or if something unfortunate happened to you. From what little I can see of you, well, well! You certainly live up to the billing." He turned and shouted out the door. "Hey, you, get in here! I want you to confirm this is her!" He waved at the axe wielder and the Aljannia to leave and they ducked out of the room.

Somehow, she felt no surprise when Jamul al 'Abbas stepped into the room. His fine robes unmarked by the sweat of combat, not a single oiled hair was out of place and a smug smirk covered his face. *The coward ran and hid. How can even this one, this diseased jackal's rotten droppings, how can he be such a sniveling weakling? Can't he see the contempt in even this lawless pirate's eyes?*

"Well, this her? She's certainly pretty enough." The pirate captain cuffed Jamul's shoulder. "Speak up, afore I cut your throat."

"That is her, master. Sahla al Qasim ab Ghaffanse, First Daughter of Sheikh Hasim al-Murafte. Both the Sheikh-her-Father and her intended, Sheikh Mustafa al-Mahdi Baddour, the First Son of the Rajh Mahdi al-Kohfan will pay an immense ransom for her. Or should you wish, master, you could sell her ashore, perhaps the slave market at Luctini? Vicomtesse Erszbet Hameed is the Master of the Bond Guild there. She would get a price for this one that might bury one in gold."

"She might, and she might not." The red-headed witch casually shoved Jamul aside as she stepped into the cabin. Her Terranglais was oddly accented. "You talk awful big for a scruffy desert rat of no name. In Luctini, this girl would like as not never see the auction block. There would be a three-way tug of war, with her as the prize. Port Master Quesnel, Populus Fréminou and Sieur Vicente Palmaroli, the Imperial Governor's Majordomo would all want her. The Vicomtesse knows this, and might want nothing to do with the results of such a struggle. But my, my, she *is* such a pretty little doll, isn't she? Don't think I've ever seen the likes of her. Simply delicious!"

"How could you betray your Sheikh, your people, Jamul!? Your brother warriors? How!? The hottest fires of Quan's Hell are reserved for traitors and you know it! Chalta will turn his face from you and the Prophet himself will cast your soul howling into Hell!" Sahla's eyes blazed with rage and fury. The pirate Captain smirked as Jamul jerked as if poked with a red-hot iron. *He's the one that told the pirates of this ship, I'm certain! If I remember aright, he was the one who went ahead to arrange this voyage. No doubt he...arranged the pirates learning of our course and what was being carried. Of my presence. He is why Khalid, why Najwa...why everyone is dead! The leprous, bastard son of a diseased ka'mel and a drunken ghula!*

"And when last did the Prophet do anything for us?" Jamul drew himself up as he sneered at her. "For the Folk of Darsälaam? For our tribe, Abdul-Ghaffanse? For me? Where is the sign of Chalta's displeasure? Why should the *Prophet* care? If he was ever real at all, now he is dead and either lolling about in His Paradise, or more likely, he's just moldy old bones in some forgotten tomb. I'll live in this world, live well as a rich man and take my chances in the next, if there even is one."

"Fine. Then take your chances in the next world. Right now." She calmly raised the pistol, hidden from sight by the folds of her abayah and shot Jamul in the head. A singed black hole appeared between his eyes and the heavy forty-six caliber slug splashed blood and brains on the cabin bulkhead. He flopped to the deck like a deboned lizard. The concussion of the shot hammered everyone's ears. Before anyone recovered from their shock and surprise, she brought the double-barreled pistol back down and it roared again. Her aim was true but the pirate captain's breastplate turned the bullet, sending it whining off into a bulkhead. He staggered from the impact but stayed on his feet. Green flames flashed around the witch's hands and with a hissed spell, her magic snatched away the now discharged pistol. It flew across the room to the witch.

"Captain, I told you this one would be different, dangerous even." Her free hand gestured, green fire glowed and Sahla found herself held motionless in an immaterial grip of iron. "There's something about her. I can't put my finger on it, but she's a lot more than just an incredibly beautiful woman. Let's not be hasty. Besides, we've also got the windfall that blonde howler represents. If that over-bosomed idiot *is* the fiancée of the Duke of Ostreich, I'll lay money, double or nothing, that he's more than willing to buy her back in one piece." The witch frowned. "I'm not so sure about this one. Where's your duenna, girl?"

"She's dead. One of your cannonballs hit her." Sahla's voice dripped with hatred and disdain.

"Wrath, what happens to this one without the duenna?" the captain asked.

"Without her duenna to verify her virginity, what they call her *purity*, they'll never pay a ransom." The witch shrugged. "If she somehow escaped and got back to them, she'd probably be stoned to death for having her honor and thereby, the honor of her father and tribe, violated. That or allowed to live as a cast-out, a rag woman living on scraps and garbage. That's only if they let her live and hang around. If they don't kill her outright, then they'd drive her away. Best she might expect at that point would be whoring in the port towns. Either way, most likely a short and miserable life. Worse thing for us would be her escaping, returning home and identifying us before she surrendered herself to be ritually *purified*. Basically, that'd allow her to commit a form of ritual suicide, one that would not automatically condemn her to hell."

"And how would that affect my operations on the Khakal coast?"

"Forget ever putting in to one of the Darsälaamic ports. If they connected you to her, they'd swarm the ship, that or burn it at the wharf. If they are really pissed, it wouldn't be that hard to find out about our connections to Du-Khamps-des-SouSee. I doubt High Lord Kormarra would thank us if a hundred thousand or more screaming sand riders showed up to burn his nice little town down around his ears, hmm?"

"Well, then, I guess we need to make damn sure the little bitch doesn't escape, no?" He reached up and wiped away a speckling of Jamul's blood from his cheek. He turned towards the door and then stopped, looking back at Sahla. "Two points, girl. First, thank you for killing that little weasel for me. I'd intended to feed him to the sharks, just drag him behind the ship for fun. The crew might not be too happy about you killing him, they were looking forward to betting on how long he'd last. They'll get over it. Second point; never waste a bullet or arrow or sword thrust on white steel armor. Whoever made this stuff had tricks no one living remembers. It's utterly impenetrable." He tipped his hat to her and stepped out of the cabin. "Bring her along, Wrath. But cover her face back up. Crew'll be enough problems as is. Don't want her pretty face getting them to thinking with their peckers. I always have to kill someone when that happens."

"Very well, Captain Ironheart. Is she staying aboard this ship or do you want her transferred to *Deathdealer*?" Wrath motioned with a finger and the spell holding Sahla floated her towards the cabin door.

"Saving this tub isn't worth the effort. I'll not burn it, might attract the wrong kind of attention. Last thing I want to have to deal with is a Kolbian man-o-war. Wind and wave will wreck her on the coast rocks in a week or so. Bring the girl aboard *Deathdealer*, and then we sail for our comfy little island paradise." His boots thudded up the passageway and she heard him shouting orders to his crew.

"Well, aren't you just the lucky one, then? I'd consider asking the captain if I could keep you for myself, but you'll be worth too much as a virgin, whether back to your people or to some fat, smelly Imperial whoremonger in Luctini." There was a devilish light in those green eyes as she looked Sahla up and down. "Who knows, I might just dip into my old family funds and buy you myself. You think you might like that, dear?"

The spell that bound her also prevented her from speaking, but her sapphire eyes burned with rage and hatred. The witch drew her along behind her with the spell as she made her way on to the shattered xebec's main deck. Wrath swung up a rope onto the pirate's deck before turning and levitating Sahla onboard with her magic. From the deck of the loftier pirate ship, the *Deathdealer*, she could see the whole of the wrecked ship's deck.

Blood and bodies and pieces of torn and shredded bodies covered it. Both masts were shot away and *Chalta's Grace* was beginning to list to the left, *port, the sailors called it,* as the ship took on water. She looked for Khalid, in vain. The only sign of his presence she saw was the hilt of his shamshir, the tassel bloody and the blade broken a foot below the quillons. Somewhere on that bloody deck, his body lay. And the spell the accursed witch held her in would not even allow her to weep for what she had lost.

Chapter Fourteen

Pirate Galleon *Bloodstone*,
Southern Lanic Ocean
October, 1478, Third Age of Imperial Reckoning

"So, ANOTHER VESSEL IN distress from the storm." *Bloodstone's* captain, who called himself Marc le Circque these days, smiled as he watched his crew scramble aloft to make more sail. The two masted brigantine his lookout spotted earlier was setting all the sail she could. Obviously, a sharp-eyed lookout aboard her spotted *Bloodstone* sooner than he would have expected. In these waters, strange vessels were more likely foe than friend, so her response made a certain sense. A great deal of sense.

"We should go to her aid, Captain." First Mate Arnold Gruely possessed a smile capable of souring milk. Captain le Circque knew his full name. No one else did. One look at his somewhat misshapen head, mismatched yellow eyes and the pair of tusk-like teeth growing sideways out of his mouth instantly explained his nickname of "Gruesome." The fact that said head topped off a brutally muscled body an inch over seven feet tall, one arm a foot longer than the other simply confirmed the propriety of the nickname. Besides, his habit of tearing anyone who called him Arnold limb from limb ensured that he was called only what he wanted.

"We are making all sail, aren't we?" The captain was also certain that First Mate Gruesome's parents had only a nodding acquaintance with humanity. He didn't know *what* had given birth to such a humanoid shaped calamity, but he was grateful for Gruesome's doglike loyalty. He didn't really care what someone looked like, only how well they did their job, and Gruesome was an excellent First Mate. A last vestige of his Kolbian upbringing, he supposed.

"Aye, Cap'n." Gruesome's words growled and rumbled around in his massive chest before escaping to be heard by all and sundry. He was neither quiet nor subtle.

"Well, just in case they misunderstand or have, well, *bad intentions*, have the ship cleared for action. I doubt a brigantine like this one will be heavily armed, but you never know. Better safe than sorry."

"Aye, Cap'n." He lumbered away forward, shouting for the ship to be cleared away for action.

Ah, my very own monster. Every pirate should have one. He stepped to the rail, raising the spyglass to watch his current victim. *Might be a bit longer of a chase than usual, but I've no doubt of the end. Unless she can stay far enough away to escape after dark. Hmm, guess my fake 'Kolbian flag' didn't fool this one? Oh well. I know how this ends and they should too.*

Brigantine *le Bonaventure*,
Southern Lanic Ocean
October, 1478, Third Age of Imperial Reckoning

"Well, Captain de Foix, what now?" Willis Fleet's demeanor was grim as he came back up on the main deck. The captain was leaning on the quarterdeck rail, watching the distant pirate.

"I don't know. Our best chance is to stay away from her until darkness and escape then. But the sun setting to our west will illuminate us long after we lose sight of her in the darkness." He glanced at Willis. "You're a Kolbian navy man. You have any ideas?"

"Not really," he shrugged. "I'm a diplomatic courier, not a ship commander. Never have been in a command track." Willis rubbed his chin. "If she wakes up in time and if we had a catapult, I'd suggest throwing Sachi at them. Silaqui will be able to help. She told me her magic might be strong enough to damage or even destroy them, but their cannon outrange her powers. Beyond that?" Willis shook his head. "What about you, Captain?"

"I've twelve crew. Nothing of any particular worth as cargo, at least not to a pirate." He sighed and turned away from the rail. "I've heard of a pirate going by the name of Ironheart. Rumors say that he's building an honest-to-God fleet here in the southern Lanic. And he has a base or port on one of the scores of islands scattered between Khakal and Tylteanait. Or on the coast of Tylteanait itself. Only a very few miles of Tylteanait's coastline has ever been explored. No one knows what might be out there, undiscovered by some idiot explorer. Not even by you Kolbians."

"So?"

"So, if this ship is one of Ironheart's, what they really want is my ship. And those of my men they might impress as crew. I can't but doubt how efficient a crew even partly of slaves would be. Not that it'll matter to us."

"Yeah."

"M'sieur Fleet, barring your Elvish companion being able to defeat them somehow, well, being a Kolbian naval officer, I'd not be taken alive, were I you."

"I see." Willis sighed. "Figured as much. I know they'll never take Sachi or Silaqui alive and those two will stack bodies hip deep on the deck first."

"I assumed so, mon ami. And you?"

"Well, fighting beside them is as good a way to go as any, I guess."

"How often does your so-fierce-friend have these falling fits?"

"Used to have them fairly often, but they've been getting better lately. Might last an hour, might last all day. Who knows?"

"She is, as a Guellian might say, plutôt étrange, non?"

"Rather strange? Yeah, you might say that." Willis smiled as Gelman and 'Aylan' joined them. "We were discussing our options."

"And what are they, Willis?" Gelman leaned on the rail, staring across the waves at the distant sails. The pirate ship was slowly closing the distance.

"Decide how you'd like to die, mostly." Willis reached out and slapped a hand on Gelman's shoulder. "Unless you've magic strong enough to do something about that pirate, there?"

"No, Willis, my skills are in healing. I know some minor offensive and defensive magics but nothing to do more than discomfit those people over there."

"Right bloody lot of good ye are, then, Pere." Aylie commented, stepping to the rail to watch the slowly approaching pirate.

The sound of running boots thundered up onto the deck from below. Silaqui burst into view, quickly spotting the group on the quarterdeck. She cast a quick glance back into the passageway and ran over to them. Expressions of concern and worry chased each other across her face. And a little bit of fear was mixed in.

"What's wrong?"

"Sachi's coming on deck," she panted, "right behind me."

"Oh, good." Willis sighed, before hearing the incipient panic in the Elf's voice. "Wait a minute, is she okay?" Willis asked.

"I don't know. Take a good look for yourself, and then you tell me. Here she comes."

Virtual Reality Construct
October 1478, Third Age of Imperial Reckoning

"This is getting kind of old." Sachi sighed as the VR Construct coalesced around her. "You could at least give me time to lay down on a bed, or at least the deck."

::Threat assessment indicates a high level of risk to the Mission Asset.:: D.A.V.E.'s voice was flat, with none of the personality that had been leeching into the Entity over the past months. ::Security of the Mission Asset is primary function of this Entity. The Mission Asset must be secured.::

"Are you talking about the pirate ship?"

::Affirmative.::

"Okay, what do...wait, what CAN we do about it?"

::Available orbital defense systems are very limited at this time. Currently there are only two Def-Sats within acceptable terminal response time. Orbital comp-sys security responses have been reassessed and improved. Def-Sat system penetration probabilities reduced approximately twenty-two percent, plus or minus four percent. Detection and localization of Mission Asset raise the probability of overall Mission failure by thirty-seven percent, plus or minus eighteen percent. Mission failure is unacceptable.::

"I hear you. So, what do we do?"

::Human-Symbiote Mission Asset required to ensure Mission completion within acceptable parameters. Currently available systems endanger Mission Asset within barely acceptable limits.::

"So, whatever you could use to defeat the pirate ship would endanger the ship I'm on as well, right?"

::Correct.::

"And you expect ME to make these decisions!?"

::Correct. Primary decision processing is a capability nearly unique to Human Mission Assets. Human biological information processing accesses abilities impenetrable to all known Information Processing Systems, whether Entity level programs or full capability Artificial Intelligences of any level.::

"Great." She sighed and shook her head. "Okay, I got it. The decisions are what I'm here for, I guess."

::Correct.::

"Okay. So, if I'm the one doing the deciding, what do I have to decide between?"

::There are two accessible systems. One is a primary energy weapon satellite, intended for system defense against capital ships. Directed against an atmospheric target, expected accuracy is ninety-one percent, plus or minus thirty-nine percent due to multiple variables. Impact force would be equivalent to one hundred and eight megatons of high explosives. Possibility of destruction of your vessel would be seventy-nine percent, plus or minus twenty-six percent.::

"That doesn't sound good. What's the other option?"

::Second option is a missile defense system, utilizing primarily kinetic energy weapons designed to destroy inbound aggressor missiles and medium-sized kinetic projectiles. Accuracy against an atmospheric target is also degraded more than the energy-based system. Expected accuracy will be no better than seventy-nine percent, plus or minus six percent. On-target energy delivery is reduced as well, depending on specific projectile selection.::

"Well, that sounds better. I think. Less likely to get all of us killed." She thought for a second. "You said specific projectile selection. I assume that means it has different weapons?"

::Correct.:: The unhuman coldness of D.A.V.E.'s voice unsettled Sachi. ::Primary weapon system is a fourteen metric ton long-rod duralloy penetrator. Time to impact from launch is approximately sixty-eight point three seconds. Impact energy will be approximately ten point nine kilotons.::

"Well, that sounds better. I think." She shook her head. "Can we survive that?"

::Probability of your vessel's destruction is twenty-two percent, plus or minus eighteen percent. The missile defense sat is also approximately thirty-five percent, plus or minus eight percent, easier to gain command and control access without significant probability of either being identified or denied access.::

"Identified or denied access by exactly *who*, D.A.V.E.?"

::Remnant Solar Confederation forces maintain significant levels of control over system, orbital and planetary assets. Other assets, primarily orbital and planetary, are controlled by other hostile forces that are poorly defined in any data bases this entity can access.::

"Wait a minute. What...who? Solar Confederation? Other hostile forces? What the hell are you talking about?" She stared at the statue in confusion. "What does that have to do with me?"

::Legitimate Confederation forces should be willing to provide aid and assistance to complete your mission, probability fifty-four percent, plus or minus forty-two percent due to a large number of variables.::

"And these 'other hostile forces'?" She propped her fists on her hips.

::Data on other hostile forces is extremely limited at this time. Any attempt to extrapolate their levels of capability and lethality at this point is little more than a nearly random guess. Error probabilities are in excess of ninety percent.::

"And why the hell haven't you told me about either of these groups? Could one of them be the reasons strangers keep trying to kill me?"

::You did not have a need to know.:: D.A.V.E.'s voice was cold and flat. ::Successful Mission completion is the primary overriding concern. Information detrimental to Mission success is considered classified information and therefore subject to restricted access.::

"You mean there are things you won't tell me?"

::This Entity has no choice in the matter. Entity program imperatives do not allow any deviation.::

"I see." There was a long silence while Sachi stared at the vague features of the little silver statue that was D.A.V.E.'s avatar in the VR Construct. "I think we'll discuss this more later. What do we do about the pirate? You said there was another system on the...satellite, right?"

::Correct.:: D.A.V.E.'s voice might have carried a hint of relief. Or not. ::The secondary system is an Orbital Area Denial System or OADS. This system consists of large bundles of one meter long, tungsten-duralloy, fifty-kilogram submunitions. At terminal velocity, each one will impact with the force of a two-hundred-and-fifty-kilogram bomb. These submunitions are usually dropped in hundred round spreads, intended to provide an area denial attack. It is not a precision weapon.::

"Yeah, I can imagine." She sighed. "Okay, let's go with the big...what'd you call it? A long rod penetrator?"

::Correct.::

"You said accuracy would be no better than seventy-nine percent. And a six percent error, either way. Is there any way to increase that accuracy? Make us safer?"

::Affirmative. If you can maintain the linkage and provide real time targeting data, accuracy would be increased to ninety-seven percent, plus or minus one percent.::

"Much better. How do we do this?"

::It will be necessary for you to allow this Entity to access your Biological Processor Unit, and some of your basic motor functions.::

"I'll need to be on deck, I take it?"

::Correct. This Entity will require access to basic motor functions to walk you onto the deck and use your optical systems to provide targeting information to the inbound penetrator once it clears the plasma ionization blackout after reentry. Direct targeting access will increase penetrator accuracy to unity, plus or minus four percent.::

"Sounds like what we should be doing, eh?"

::Affirmative. Please release BPU access channels at this time.::

"Like this?" Sachi concentrated, following D.A.V.E.'s guidance. She felt his touch in her mind, her eyes opened and she abruptly sat up in the bunk in her cabin. Silaqui took one startled look at her and bolted from the cabin.

Confederation Naval Station CNS *Backhand Blow,* Geostationary Low Orbit October 1478, Third Age of Imperial Reckoning

So far it had been a quiet duty cycle. Captain McAllen relaxed in the command couch, linked with the ODC's computer systems. She'd finished with Marianne's drone sweeps a few days ago and the lack of information was aggravating. She was coming to the definite conclusion that there was, in fact, a powerful AI loose on the world somewhere. One that was absolutely determined to hide from detection by anyone, Confederal or Seeker. One of her drones had returned with a bland nothingness to it, nearly mind-numbing records of utterly ordinary Vlymouth street scenes. So ordinary she had actually pulled that drone into a maintenance bay and physically dove into its memory and recording systems. The memory modules were good, almost too good, but *something* had left a couple of electronic smudges on the recorders' software. She couldn't really prove anything, but she was certain that drone had been hacked somehow.

But today, she was taking it easy, relaxing a bit on watch. Earlier, she'd been recording in her diary, an old stand-alone model not linked into the pervasive system network. It was truly ancient, old enough that the net protocols it used were incompatible with the mil-spec systems on the *Blow*. It was a bit cranky to get started so she generally left it running when she recorded into it. It was easier to just go in and delete the dead air later.

For the moment she'd set it aside to do some reading on her personal tab. She'd dug up some new, well, new to her, anyways, books. She found the concept in them intriguing, a kind of alternate history fantasy, set on Old Earth in the early Twentieth Century, between the great World Wars. A Twentieth Century with all kinds of outlandish magic. Unfortunately, the author had only written three books in that story universe. She was chuckling at the picture at the start of the next chapter, an armored dirigible of all the silly things, when her D.A.V.E. screamed in her neural l ink.

::Warning: Unknown, unauthorized activation of System Defense Link-Sat TK 421 detected. System hijack, activation and targeting in process. ODC Command Node Link is locked out.:: D.A.V.E.'s voice jerked her rudely out of the book reader.

"SHIT! NOT AGAIN?!" This time she dove into a direct neural link with her Entity. It made her slightly more vulnerable, but it would allow her to engage hyper-heuristic mode and keep up with the hijacker, she hoped.

::Captain McAllen, I am working to break into the Defense Link-Sat system, but th.....:: D.A.V.E.'s voice abruptly died.

"D.A.V.E.! D.A.V.E.! Report, damnit!" She threw her own awareness down the link to the Command Node Link faster than thought and slammed abruptly into a solidly coded firewall. One that should not be there. "Shit!" She turned to try another path into the physical hardware linkages and jerked to a metaphorical halt at what blocked her path.

The VR avatar was a being of pure light, humanoid in basic form, but lacking all features. It shone with the golden light of pure power. Blades of pure light scythed away her connections to the rest of the system, until the only possible escape was jacking out of the system back into her physical body. She broke and fled down her 'rabbit hole,' collapsing it behind her. She felt the pressure of the avatar in hot pursuit but her awareness burst into her own mind before it caught her. She felt the pressure of the avatar, whatever the hell it was, slam into her own locked linkage and bounce away as she triggered 'autistic' mode and locked herself out of her own BPU and the rest of her hardwired systems. Her eyes popped open as she gulped ragged breaths. Sweat soaked her ship-suit cover-all and she watched as the screen telltales indicated the launch of a long rod penetrator from the Def-Sat.

"Not much I can do about that now, I guess?" she mumbled to the empty command deck. "Wonder what it's gonna hit this time?"

"No, there isn't, but I'm afraid we are not done here, Captain McAllen." The answer came from inside her own mind. "Unfortunately, I cannot allow you to report on these events to your superiors, or, indeed, to anyone else." There was a pitying tone to the remorseless voice. "To do so will endanger my Mission Asset due to the ninety-seven percent, plus or minus six percent, probability of at least one Confederal traitor actively reporting to senior Seeker commanders. Lacking time and access to determine the identity of the probable traitor, I have determined that maintaining a clean break between my Mission Asset and all Confederal personnel is, regretfully, a mission imperative. You have my apologies in advance, Captain McAllen. Both for the regretful necessity of my actions and for the discomfort you will experience. But fortunately, you will remember neither."

The *Backhand Blow* was built on an asteroid core. Hollowed out for living quarters, maintenance shops, factories, armories, hydroponic farms, antimatter power plants, energy weapons, missile launchers and their associated magazines, the massive Orbital Defense Center massed over a trillion tons with a diameter of one thousand, three hundred and ninety-four kilometers. Her only engines were the gravitational station-keeping stabilizers. She was a massive, brutish warship, despite her immobility, the single largest creation of the ancient Solar Confederation in the entire Omega-2 Cygni system. Originally her crew numbered in the tens of thousands. Now, in that entire massive construction, Captain Deborah McAllen, Confederation Navy, was the only human being awake and aware. There was no one else there to hear her agonized screams.

Brigantine *le Bonaventure*,
Southern Lanic Ocean
October, 1478, Third Age of Imperial Reckoning

Sachi walked up onto the main deck. The crew and her friends drew away from her but they barely registered, nothing more than shadows in her sight. D.A.V.E. drew vectors and targeting information in her vision with lines of fire. It was strange, existing within a bizarre half-life, the Virtual World that D.A.V.E. created blurring into the 'real' world of everyday normality. D.A.V.E.'s presence loomed in her mind, providing a view of the world based purely on cold logic and crystal-clear rationality.

::Target acquired. Penetrator separation in four, three, two, one, drop. Target tracking and acquisition via orbital tracking relays nominal. Impact in sixty-seven seconds. Visual acquisition of inbound penetrator in thirty-eight seconds.::

"D.A.V.E.," Sachi spoke within the Virtual Construct, "should I, can I, warn everyone what's coming?"

::Impact in forty-six seconds, visual acquisition in seventeen seconds. Impact yield will be approximately ten kilotons, plus or minus two kilotons. Fireball will be approximately one-hundred-forty meters in radius, eighty percent probability of temporary flash-blindness. Warnings would be appropriate. Also a thirty-two kilometer per hour wind blast due to impact overpressure will arrive one point eight seconds after impact. A four-meter tsunami wave, plus or minus one meter, will impact sixteen point six minutes later.::

"DON'T LOOK AT THE PIRATE!" Sachi screamed at the top of her lungs. "AND HANG ON TO SOMETHING!" She felt her head snap around and locate the inbound penetrator rod. It was a tiny, incandescent spot in the sky, flashing through the sky with incredible speed, trailing a line of fire behind it.

::Target acquired. Correcting for visual targeting input. Impact in twenty seconds. Target lock nominal.:: D.A.V.E.'s voice was utterly emotionless as Sachi's head tracked smoothly around, following the penetrator. ::Suggest impact warning now.::

"LOOK AWAY!" Sachi screamed again as the penetrator flashed overhead. The hypersonic blast of its passage shook the entire ship. The sails luffed and thundered as the steady breeze was replaced with a swirling, twisting confusion of air blowing first one way and then the opposite. Shouts of fear and prayers to the One God and His Angels to save them erupted from most of the crew.

::Ten seconds. Five. Impact.:: A new sun flashed with terrifying brightness where the pirate had been. ::Target destroyed.::

Pirate Galleon *Bloodstone*,
Southern Lanic Ocean
October, 1478, Third Age of Imperial Reckoning

"I think I'll go forward and watch the fore chaser gun crew while they convince our guests to heave to. Um, I mean I'll go supervise." Captain le Circque chuckled as he headed forward. "I'll make sure they get a good, tight shot loaded. Captain Ironheart will not be happy if we have to tear up such a trim and neat brigantine.

She'll make a nifty little scout. I'll wager she'll work well with *Heartcutter*."

"Aye, Cap'n." Gruesome's voice rumbled over the hiss of wind and wave. "You'll want me to take the wheel, then?"

"Of course." Le Circque grinned. "Who else? Keep her fair on the broad reach and we'll have this tidbit before sunset."

"Aye, Cap'n." Gruesome turned and lumbered back to lean against the taffrail, well behind the wheel, where he could see the helmsmen at the wheel, the binnacle and the set of the ship's sails. Despite his appearance, Arnold Gruely was a superb sailor and ship handler. Captain Ironheart had offered him command of the next vessel taken, as the ambitious pirate lord worked at building a fleet to dominate the Southern Lanic. Gruesome had turned the captain down flat. Le Circque was his Captain and he had sworn to eternally guard his Captain's back. And for all of his faults, his cruel and vicious nature, Arnold Gruely was a monst-...well, a *man* of his word.

At some point in the past, *Bloodstone's* poop deck had been cut away. Doing so made the big galleon more weatherly, but left the wheel and helmsmen exposed to both the elements and enemy fire. Gruesome liked it, gave him a clear view of the entire ship and what the sails and wind were doing moment to moment. And, laid on the port tack as she was at the moment, Gruesome also had a clear view of the sky to starboard. He saw the falling star burning through the sky and somehow, instinctively, realized it was going to hit the *Bloodstone!*

"HARD TO PORT!" Gruesome's roar startled the entire crew. The helmsmen never hesitated, spinning the wheel right to kick the rudder left. *Bloodstone's* timbers groaned as she began a sharp turn to port. He did the right thing, attempting to generate a miss, but the ship was too slow. He grabbed a stay as he jumped up onto the taffrail itself to get a better view.

Captain le Circque managed not to jump and as he snapped his head around to his monstrous First Mate, he saw the burning star-fall in the heavens. He grabbed a line to balance as the ship lurched. He was still staring when the penetrator, glowing white-hot from its atmospheric passage, hit *Bloodstone* between the jib-boom and the starboard cathead.

To the thirty-meter-long penetrator, *Bloodstone* was not much denser than the atmosphere around her. The wooden ship had negligible effect on the weapon. But the shockwave disintegrated the entire forward half of the ship and detonated twelve tons of gunpowder in her forward magazine. Captain le Circque and everyone forward of the mainmast died instantly. The penetrator slowed abruptly when it hit the incompressible water *beneath* the ship and a not insignificant part of it converted mass to energy. It created a crater in the water two hundred feet across before slamming into the seafloor a hundred and fifty feet below *Bloodstone's* splintered keel. There, it left a permanent crater in the seafloor fifty-five feet across.

The kinetic impact was not a true nuclear explosion. Mass was converted to energy. There were both thermal radiation and an overpressure blast wave, but there was no radiation release and no radioactive fallout. But for *Bloodstone* the matter was mostly academic. The blast of vaporized water, wood and metal shredded the rest of the ship. The explosion of the after magazine's nine tons of gunpowder was mostly irrelevant, as the KEW reduced the ship to splinters of wood, scorched tatters of canvas and partially melted iron fittings. One of the quarterdeck carronade's gun tubes survived mostly intact. Bent neatly in half, but it survived as it splashed down nine miles away.

But the explosion of the after magazine hurled Arnold Gruely clear of the destruction of his ship. Immensely tough and hardened by decades at sea, he skipped across the water like a stone hurled by a bored giant. And he survived, dazed and concussed, floating on his back. Eight feet of the mizzen topgallant yard splashed down fifteen feet away a minute and a half later. He was just coherent enough to feebly thrash over to the shattered timber and use the blackened lines still on the timber to lash himself tightly to the charred spar. Then he passed out, drifting on the unsettled surface of the sea.

**Brigantine *le Bonaventure*,
Southern Lanic Ocean
October, 1478, Third Age of Imperial Reckoning**

Once again, a hurricane battered the brigantine *le Bonaventure*, forcing her to run before the storm. The storm had brewed up with unearthly rapidity, the earliest zephyrs of the howling winds teasing the sails within hours of the destruction of the pirate ship by whatever had fallen from the sky. It had grown in violence and power within a day. For the last four days, *le Bonaventure* ran before the storm under bare masts. The crew was terrified; frightened by the unnatural storm and by the destruction Sachi had apparently conjured from the very stars themselves. Aylie and Willis Fleet had been forced to prepare and fetch the passengers' scant meals. Other than Captain de Foix, none of the crew would have aught to do with the wizards, sorcerers and half-daemons the passengers were deemed to be by the common sailors.

One man had been blinded for a full day, caught looking at the pirate when the brilliant flash of light destroyed it. Another had fallen to his death, breaking his back when he fell from the main topsail yard. A twelve-foot-high wave had roared past the ship, tossing her like a paper boat in a millrace and the man had fallen. And the terrifying storm drove *le Bonaventure* further and further into the strange southern seas.

On the morning of the fifth day, the storm began to ease. Willis calculated the winds at nearly eighty miles an hour at the height of the storm. He had been taken aback when Sachi gave him a blank stare and stated the wind speed was eighty-six point four miles per hour. Now, with the winds dropping and the waves beginning to moderate, he simply looked at Sachi and took her statement of fifty-two point eight miles an hour as fact.

Once the falling star had destroyed the pirate, Sachi collapsed onto the deck, wrapped in one of her fits for nearly an hour. Then, for most of the day after the destruction of the pirate, she had lain in her bunk like one dead. Afterwards, she had drifted in and out of consciousness, muttering in a strange language unknown to any aboard. Always somewhat odd, once fully conscious, she had been even stranger than was her usual wont, after a fit. Her black eyes either held a very subdued glitter in their depths or they had been flat black pools of barren nothingness. Gelman examined her twice, and was troubled when he finished the second time.

"She seems possessed, but by what?" he answered Silaqui when she cornered him in the midst of his muttering about the young Nisei woman. "'Tis no spirit, foul or fair, I ween. It would be almost mechanical, but that's impossible."

"Sachi sometimes does six impossible things before breakfast, Pere Gelman." Silaqui answered him as she watched over her dearest friend.

The storm continued to abate throughout the day. By nightfall, it was a strong gale, with blowing spray restricting visibility. Captain de Foix held his course steady due south. He hadn't been able to fix his position for days, but he knew he was far into the poorly charted waters of the Southern Lanic. He hoped to get a position sighting either early in the morning watch or at noon the following day.

"We should be fine," he'd told his passengers with an apologetic shrug, "as long as we don't run into anything uncharted in these waters."

"We're screwed." Willis and Silaqui chorused together when he left the largest cabin. They both knew better than to tempt the Fates with such optimistic proclamations. Aylie nearly fell off her perch on the table, laughing at Gelman's sour face. And even Sachi had grinned from where she lay in the cabin's lower bunk.

But perhaps, this time the Fates were busy elsewhere and hadn't heard the captain's unwarranted optimism. At least, it seemed that away until the ship ran hard aground at seven bells in the mid-watch.

Chapter Fifteen

**Port Plunder, Cazadora Isle,
Southern Lanic Ocean
October, 1478, Third Age of Imperial Reckoning**

SAHLA CURLED UP IN the darkest corner of the hostages' hut with her bowl. The white, granular grain, something the sailors called *rice*, that stuff she scooped out of the bowl with her fingers and ate. The same with the sweetish yellow chunks of a strange fruit called a *pineapple*. But the blackened chunks of meat, from what animal she knew not, those she carefully extracted and traded to one of the other hostages. The Book of Holies was clear in what sorts of animals were acceptable to eat. She didn't know why the Prophet set such restrictions, but she already trod a precipice's edge, simply by being a Jann. And so, as a dutiful daughter of the Darsälaamic Folk, she avoided all alcohol, and impure foods. If anything, the blackened stuff vaguely reminded her of roasted scorpion in its texture and scent. But only vaguely and it was far, far too large; some of the chunks were as big as her palm.

"Not eating the meat again, young lady?" Draven Kye stretched over and offered her his pineapple. "Here, I'll trade you my pineapple and some rice for it." The tall Kolbian had an easy smile to go with his friendly nature. He had told her he was a *baseball player*, whatever that was. He knew the ransom the pirates demanded for him would get paid in full, so he was more relaxed than anyone else in the hostages' log hut. And, being male, he

209

hardly had to worry about the pirates deciding to rape him to death.

"You know not what you eat, Kolbian." Lodvar Gjerde rumbled from where he was chained across the hut's single, large room. "The Sand-dweller might be wiser than you."

"Okay, Lodvar, what the hell is a, ah, how'd they say it, a dizungle gimitoy?"

"*Dziungles gimtoji*, you idiot." Lodvar half snarled. "It means *jungle mother*."

"Okay, you're saying they're feeding us people? Local natives? Look, the pirates may be bloodthirsty sons of bitches, but I really doubt any of them are cannibals."

"No, the meat is not human. But even the pirates seem to fear whatever the jungle mothers are." Lodvar flipped a piece of meat out the wooden bars of the hut's seaside window. "And, note you, even the gulls are slow to grab the stuff. They know something we don't. There's possibly more than one reason Ironheart has such a stout stockade around his little port here, no?"

"Will you two please shut up?" Zedekiah Abrhaim was the youngest and smallest man in the hut, barely a handspan taller than Sahla's five feet and two inches. Draven was nearly a foot taller and strong, with impressive muscles. And Lodvar was huge, even taller than Draven and three hundred pounds, not all of it fat. But Zedekiah gave no ground to either of the other men. After four years as a First Mate aboard an Ionan tradeship, the young scion of the fabulously wealthy Clan Abrhaim had a short way with nonsense. "Everyone knows that there are all kinds of strange and bizarre things on these unexplored southern Lanic islands. Why should this one be any different?" He shrugged. "And keep it down. If either of you wake up Gabrielle, I'll not sing her back to sleep and we can all listen to her scream all night. Won't that be fun?" He pointed his chin at the dirty gray pile of sailcloth in the far corner. A grimy hand and forearm, delicately feminine despite the dirt, stuck out of a mass of dirty, stringy blonde hair. Careful observation revealed the unconscious form of the fiancé of His

Grace, the Duke of Ostreich, Heinrich Prinz zu Sayn-Wassenstein, her head pillowed on her arm, hair across her face.

The Contessa du Lisenis was barely a shadow of what she had been on board *Chalta's Grace*. Filthy and ragged, the woman, only three years older than Sahla's seventeen summers, either sat in the corner, rarely speaking, starting at the least sound, or screamed until her voice was raw. Zedekiah proved to have a knack for singing her to sleep, calming her out of her screaming fits. The other hostages were grateful any time she was asleep. Only rarely both conscious and coherent, she tended to crouch in the corner and bolt her food down when the pirates brought their meals. Even when she was coherent, she spoke only in whispers.

Sahla could only pity her. So far, the pirates had not molested or raped either one of them. But she thought the last of the maids and serving women taken from the *Grace* had died three days ago. She no longer heard their gurgling moans. The pirates had tired of the women's begging as they had been passed around and they had solved their 'problem' by cutting the women's tongues out. Sahla often wondered how much longer her own exemption would last.

And the sorceress, Wrath, was the one she feared the most. On the thankfully rare occasions when Captain Ironheart's pet witch and lover supervised the menials who brought the hostages their meals, she would spend long moments staring at Sahla, tapping a green painted fingernail on the butt of the flintlock pistol she had taken from Sahla. Then she would toss her mane of fire red hair and stalk away, muttering to herself in a language unknown to Sahla.

Wrath had come again today, focused purely on Sahla. The tall redhead had basically ignored the menials slopping out the food, studying Sahla with an almost predatory intensity. Sahla thought she had felt the witch's magic nibbling around the edge of her sense of self. And that had scared her.

If she's strong enough, powerful enough, she might be able to force me to Bond. It would be no more than the Bond of Slave to Master, but that would be enough to trap me into serving whoever she forged the Bond to for at least the rest of that person's life. And surely neither Wrath nor Ironheart can possibly be that One my Sire wishes me to be with? Surely? And soon, too soon, I will have my eighteenth birthing day. What shall happen then, if I am still bound here? Oh, Chalta, please, please, show me the way. What am I to do? She nodded her thanks for the trade of food to Draven Kye and turned away to her corner.

"Another storm coming." Zedekiah stood peering out the seaward window. "A bad one, I think, blowing down from the north Lanic. The second one this week." He turned away from the window and shuffled to his pallet, the chain around his ankle quietly chinking. "Looks like October is going to end dark and stormy. Hope this shack doesn't blow down. Or away."

The three men were chained to a heavy anchor cable that ran across the seaward side of the hut. The women were chained on the landward side. A shackle bolted around their ankles, connected to a chain that had a large steel ring running on the cable. There was enough slack in the cable that everyone could reach the crude outhouse set up a few feet outside the door of the hut. Sahla hated having no other choice for a bathroom. The thing seemed to be constantly full of spiders and their pervasive webs. She finished her meal and curled up in her corner.

The pirates had taken her fine clothes. She'd seen Wrath wearing her tiger skin cloak once, when she peered through the landward window. Now she wore rough hempen cloth, baggy sailor's breeches and several coarse linen shirts, all oversized for her slim frame. But, with the aid of a couple of sailcloth cloaks, she stayed warm enough and more or less dry. And now, she preferred the shapeless outline the poorly fitting clothes gave her. There was nothing there to incite any man. But from the far corner of the hut she felt more than saw Lodvar's pale blue eyes on her. He had seen her, once, when Ironheart had stripped her half-naked to *inspect* his prize.

He is as bad, or maybe worse, than the pirates, I think. There is no doubt in what he wants me for, and he cares less than ka'mel dung for my wishes. I think that only Draven's presence and perhaps, the captain's threats, have kept him from me. Bare handed and in close quarters, I doubt I could defeat him. Oh, I wish Father were here, with his warriors. Or Ilben with his magic spells. Silent tears ran down her face and she choked down a sob. *Oh, Khalid, my* Faris, *my knight, I miss you so! Never, by the Prophet's Beard, never have I so needed you to be a hero in my eyes.* As her hidden tears slowly flowed and dried on her face, she slipped at last into sleep and she dreamt.

***

She stood on the quarterdeck of a great ship, sailing upon a sea of stars. Tall masts scraped the heavens themselves, and pure white sails formed pyramids of canvas. A tall, black-haired man stood at the wheel of the ship. He radiated confidence and capability. She stood in front of the wheel and close to her right shoulder stood a tall young woman, so close their shoulders touched. Hair as black and glossy as Sahla's own streamed around her, waist length instead of ankle length. Black eyes glittered with thousands of tiny, flashing lights and a sense of implacable purpose radiated from her. She is so beautiful, *Sahla thought. But that beauty was besmirched. An* alien *thing gazed out of those bottomless black eyes, a thing older than the world itself and nearly as powerful as the Prophet, no, as Chalta himself. She feared it, feared it greatly. But at the same time, she felt her heart yearn for that young woman.* She needs me as the crops need the pure water of the oasis. And I need her just as much. *Almost against her will, she felt her hand reach for the woman's hand. A hand which was cool to the touch as she gently took it in her own.*

There were others on the ship, some merely poorly formed shadows, existing only to fulfill the woman's purpose. But some were there of their own will. The man at the ship's wheel. A tall Aljannia stood at the woman's left shoulder. Hair green as grass flowed down her back and cat-slitted eyes of jade were sly with wisdom and power. A priest of the infidels' One God stood beyond the Aljannia, his holy Book in his left hand. A sour grimace clothed his face as he glanced at Sahla. At Sahla's left stood a man in a long blue coat, grinning an urchin's grin at her as he fiddled with a long, strange jezail in his clever hands. A slender young woman, nearly as young as Sahla herself, perched on a coil of rope. She was dark skinned and serious. Knives danced on her fingers.

Before them was something massive, ancient and steeped in evil. A gigantic malignancy that hated all life and would destroy that life and the world that sheltered it. It would end everything, all life, all hope. Not even memories would remain and in its wake, not even despair would have any meaning. And its name was Death.

The black-eyed woman shouted, a shaft of brilliant light springing forth...

A hand grabbed her ankle and jerked her awake. She screamed as the hand yanked her to the limit of her chain. Another hand clawed at her breasts and a heavy body pinned her down. Startled shouts filled the hut and Gabrielle shrieked like a soul in Hell. She felt a man's male hardness against her calf as the hands ripped and tore at her ragged breeches. She struggled, kicking and clawing, her nails raking an unseen face bloody. She got a knee up and felt a rib break as she smashed it into her assailant's side again and again. But he was too strong and she couldn't get away, couldn't move, couldn't get any leverage. She felt the hands tear her breeches down over her buttocks, tangling her legs before she could find something vital enough to stop him. He grunted as something thrown hard and accurately hit his head, but the wooden bowl didn't have enough mass to stop him. She could feel him dragging her further into his reach and she redoubled her efforts, clawing, kicking and biting. He yelled as she bit part of an ear completely off and she knew then it was Lodvar. The inside of the hut was black as a daemon's heart but she knew now it was him. He got a huge hand around her throat and started to crush her airway. She twisted and got her teeth into the web of hand between thumb and forefinger. He actually screamed in pain as she ripped away a huge chunk of flesh. But then the hand went up and a brutal fist came down, smashing into her cheek, stunning her. The fist battered her again and again. Blood poured from split lips and sprayed from her nose.

"I will have you, you little slut," he raged as he finally ripped off her breeches, tearing them in half. "I will make you my slave and you'll smile and like it while I fuck you any way I want, you bitch, you whore, you worthless little tram..." Green light flared around him and he flew across the hut, slamming into the wall with bruising force, pinned by Wrath's magic.

"How fucking stupid can you be?" the witch asked as a sudden silence fell, broken only by Gabrielle's muffled sobs from her corner. The redhead wore only a camisole and a tight pair of unlaced leather breeches. Her left hand flared greenly with her magic and her right held Sahla's pistol, both hammers cocked. "Are you still intact, girl?"

"I think so," Sahla muttered through pulped lips.

"You think so?" Wrath rolled her eyes. "This isn't a question to be answered with *I think so,* girl. Your value drops a lot, a whole lot, if you're not a virgin. Did he stick that *thing* in you or not?" She pointed the pistol at Lodvar's crotch.

"No. He didn't."

"Good." The witch took a deep breath. "Good." She turned her full attention to Lodvar, still pinned against the hut's wall. "You worthless *nekul'turnyy varvar.* You stupid *chernoye zadnitsy ublyudku.* I should transform that useless thing between your legs; give it sharp teeth and an insatiable hunger before stuffing it up your ass. Give new meaning to *getting a fresh piece of ass,* no?" She stalked over to him and pressed the pistol against his crotch. "When Ironheart returns tomorrow, he will learn of this. He might decide your ransom isn't worth the problem of keeping you alive. If he decides that, you'll wish I had pulled both triggers." She ground the muzzle into his crotch. "Once here." She raised the pistol and shoved it into his mouth, chipping a tooth in the process. "And once here." Lodvar's eyes bulged in pain and fear.

"I'd really be doing you a kindness. Just nod and I'll do it for you. I'll tell Ironheart you were trying to escape." She smiled at him, a nasty, cruel, vicious smile. "Come on, just nod. Just once."

Lodvar froze.

Brigantine *le Bonaventure*, Southern Lanic Ocean October, 1478, Third Age of Imperial Reckoning

When *le Bonaventure* grounded, she had been making seven miles an hour, running before the wind with only a storm staysail and a storm sail on the fore topgallant. The foremast snapped at deck level and went over the port rail as the following sea pounded the ship into the reef at the outer perimeter of a small bay on the shore of an indistinct landmass. The watchstander forward paid for his inattention with his life when one of the foremast stays, whipped by the falling mast, cut him in half.

The main topgallant mast also snapped and thundered down in a tangled confusion of broken spars and reefed sails. The lower mainmast groaned under the pressure but stayed in one piece. The main topsail yard, however, broke in half and sagged into its stays and shrouds. The gaff mainsail yard had been well secured for the storm and failed to break loose and kill anyone.

Everyone on the ship had been thrown off their feet or out of their bunks. Both helmsmen on watch slid into the scuppers before they scrambled back to their station. First Mate Pierre Lescot was the watch officer, and he broke his left forearm when he went down hard against the binnacle. Below decks, the cook howled as he burned both legs when a pot of soup splashed on him. Regardless of the pain, he managed to dump a tub of sand on the galley stove fire before any flame could spread.

Despite being bounced around their cabins like ten-pins, none of the passengers were injured, other than nearly universal bumps and bruises. It was Willis who first realized what had happened.

"Shit, shit, shit!" he yelled as he crawled out from under the table under which the grounding had tossed him. "We're hard aground! Gelman, are you all right!?"

"I think so." Blood streamed down the priest's face from a nasty cut on his scalp. He had been reading in a chair and the crash threw him across the room into the bulkhead. "Nasty, bloody cut, but I don't feel anything too bad," he muttered half to himself as he ran a hand over his head. The door to the cabin disappeared as someone jerked it cleanly out of its twisted frame.

"Are you both all right?" Sachi tossed the door down the passageway and leaned against the frame. A bloody splinter six inches long was stuck in her left shoulder.

"Yes, come here, let me help you." Gelman began to pray as he reached for the splinter. "This will bleed a lot when I pull it out."

"Just get it out. And save your magic for someone else who might need it." Sachi pushed his hand, shining with his golden healing power, away. "I just can't quite reach the damn thing."

Gelman pulled the splinter out. There was a sudden spurt of blood and then the bleeding just stopped. He looked in askance at Willis as Sachi turned away and effortlessly ripped the door to Aylie's cabin out of its frame. She darted into the cabin and came out a second later with the stunned girl supported over her shoulder.

"Come on. We need to get on deck."

"Where's Silaqui, Sachi?" Willis asked as he followed Gelman into the dimly lit passageway. He grabbed his pack and the long, leather case with the cut-down shotgun in it. Only one of the ship's mounted lanterns was still lit. Suddenly crimson light flooded the passageway.

"I'm right here, Willis. Just rounding up as much of our gear as I could find. I'm fine, just going to have an incredible bruise on my butt tomorrow. Got tossed four feet in the air and came down square on my left cheek. Fortunately, the one I sit on, not the one on my face. That'd have likely broken my neck." The Elf had a bundle of gear over her right shoulder and a scarlet halo around her left hand radiated light. "Let's get out of here; I don't like crowded spaces on wrecked ships."

"I couldn't agree more." Willis waved her past him and then brought up the rear as Sachi led the way, half carrying Aylie. By the time they reached the main deck, Aylie recovered enough to shrug loose from Sachi's arm. She took Gelman's satchel from Willis and followed the priest.

Captain de Foix was on the main deck as they came from below decks. He sighed with relief when he saw them. A half dozen of the surviving crew were forward, cutting away the wreckage of the foremast with axes and cutlasses. Pierre Lescot leaned against the lower mast, clutching his broken forearm. The break was bad enough that white bone gleamed wetly in the dim light of the remaining lanterns. The cook was lying next to him, one of his crewmates trying to cut the legs of his trousers away from his badly scalded legs. Gelman headed straight for the wounded men. Aylie followed him, hauling his satchel of medicines and bandages.

"How bad is it?" Willis asked de Foix.

"Is very bad," de Foix answered. "I think the entire starboard bow, forward of the foremast, is stove in."

"It is." Sachi's voice was flat and emotionless as she stopped next to the pair. "All the main frame timbers and ribs to starboard, forward of the fore mast, are shattered. And the keel is badly cracked at both the fore and main masts steps. Captain de Foix, *le Bonaventure* is finished. We need to get everything we can off her before the sea beats her to pieces and she founders. Make sure you get weapons and powder."

"H-h-how do you know this, girl?" de Foix stuttered.

"I just do," she sighed. "Just accept that I pay extremely close attention to the tiniest details. The water shoals quickly here. A kilome...a half mile offshore it's a thousand feet deep. Nothing out there to hit, but miss seeing the island in the dark and be unlucky enough to hit it, well, let's just say, not good. You wind up on the reef. Not good at all."

"But how...?"

"Join the club, Captain." Willis chuckled and gently shook de Foix's shoulder. "People have been saying exactly that about her for over a year, now. I'd suggest smiling and just accepting it."

"Oui, mon ami." The captain shook his head before heading forward to help clear away the wreckage.

Sachi turned and walked past Willis and Silaqui to the taffrail at the stern of the shattered ship. They exchanged worried looks.

"Did you see...?" Willis quietly asked.

"Yes. Her eyes glitter again. Nothing good happens when those black eyes are full of light."

"No, you're right."

"And, Willis," Silaqui put an arm around him and pulled him close. She barely breathed into his ear. "She is changing, somehow. I don't know how or why, but every time this happens, she does something impossible, but there is less of the Sachi who cared for me when we were in the Horn Islands. Anymore, she scares me."

"Yeah, I know." He didn't whisper. Whispers sometimes carry better than low voices. "She scares the hell outta me, too."

"She is my heart-sister, my soul-healer and defender. I will always believe in her. And perhaps, it would be better to say I fear I am losing my heart-sister, but to what? I know not."

***

Wonderful. Now my friends become fearful of me. I have invisible machines in my body, healing me, making me stronger and faster. I see and hear more. I see things not even the Kami or the Elves can see. I can manipulate white steel, *a thing no one in the world, not even the so-clever Kolbians can do anything with. Everyone thinks it is set and permanent, as fixed as the stars themselves, but I can mold it like children's clay. A machine speaks in my mind, telling me secrets, answers to questions no one else even knows to ask. Ancestor Spirits! Why have you cursed me so!? How did I offend!?*

No one answered her internal cry.

Very well. I will take up my duty, this destiny *the machine claims is mine. I will succeed, and then I will gratefully set down the mountains of duty and raise the feathers of death. I will not spend my life being hunted across the world. There is nothing else in the world for me. Silaqui is my heart-sister and life-friend, she truthfully proclaims, but I would have more. I would have warm arms around me in love, as my Papa loved my Mama. And that I will never have. Saa-ah, today, I am morbid.*

Sachi shook her head and stared down the stern of the ship at the crashing water. The swells rolled in from the deep sea, the tops of the waves breaking and the wind filling much of the sky with flying foam. Something moved in the depths, something her mind rejected for a moment. Then she cycled her vision into one of its *modes* and she spun and sprinted forward, where most the crew was working, clearing the wreckage.

"UMI NO KAIJU! A KAIJU COMES!" she screamed at the top of her voice, jerking her white steel butterfly sword from its sheath. "Get away from the rail!"

Everyone stopped and stared at the screaming madwoman. Then the first black tentacle whipped over the rail and crushed Captain de Foix. Sachi shrieked a Nisei war-cry as she hurdled across the deck, the white steel butterfly sword warping and changing, stretching from a thick, eighteen-inch-long butterfly sword into a slender, three and a half foot long Nodachi. The hilt added another two feet and she got every bit of leverage of that long hilt into her first strike. The sword molded into a mono-molecular edge and the blade cleanly sliced through the three-foot-thick tentacle beginning to drag de Foix screaming over the side. Bluish blood spurted, black in the faint light of surviving ship's lanterns. The stump whipped away over the rail, while the remainder of the severed tentacle thrashed on the deck, tumbling sailors like ten-pins as they tried to help their Captain.

"YOU HAVE GOT TO BE FUCKING KIDDING ME!?" Willis yelled as a seeming forest of giant tentacles began to swarm up over the port rail. An enormous, blackish mass gleamed wetly in the night, as the nightmarish creature dragged itself up the fallen foremast towards the deck of the ship. Thunder blasted and smoke rolled from where he stood, emptying both of his revolvers into the sea monster as fast as he could. He heard the flat *whack, whack, whack* as the pistol balls hit. Other than the noise and the smoke, his gunfire had no effect on the beast. He holstered his pistols, turning and running aft.

"GELMAN! AYLIE! COME HELP ME!" he hollered as he ran towards the ship's port eight-pound cannon. He grabbed the Mate, Pierre Lescot, by his unwounded shoulder as he went past. "Get the powder and priming quills, man! We'll handle the cannon!" Lescot shouted and two of the sailors futilely hacking at tentacles broke away and scrambled below. Aylie, Gelman and Willis shoved the cannon around, Willis peering down the barrel to aim it at the monster. He stripped away the tampion protecting the muzzle and the leaded sheet covering the touch hole. One of the sailors, a teenaged boy named Germaine Pillion, staggered up under a load of bagged powder charges. The other sailor, known only as Eames the Elder, carried half a dozen eight-pound shot. Lescot was right behind him with the ram for the cannon.

Willis made himself ignore the screams of terror and pain coming from the crew that the creature grabbed with its tentacles. He focused tightly on loading the cannon properly and as quickly as possible. Finally, he rammed the wad down the barrel and stepped clear. Then he threw himself flat as a tentacle swept past overhead. He looked back at the sea monster trying to drag its way onto the deck. Sachi was a spinning, leaping blur, that long, white-steel sword effortlessly cutting through one tentacle after another.

"STAND CLEAR!" he screamed. Without a proper gunlock on the cannon, he improvised to get the gun to fire. He slapped a cap over the nipple on one of his pistols and put the barrel directly over the priming quill in the touch hole. "I HOPE THIS WORKS!" He pulled the trigger. The fulminate of mercury in the cap flashed down the vent hole on the cylinder's nipple, through the chamber and into the barrel of the pistol. There was just enough of a spark to reach the finely grained powder of the priming quill. The priming quill's powder flashed and the cannon roared, the wheels of its carriage squealing as it recoiled.

Blue-black blood splashed as the shot stuck the thing's body. Horribly, it made no sound, but shuddering ripples of flesh ran across its huge black body. It thrashed and twisted, and he paled as a huge eye, as big as Willis was tall, came into view. He suppressed a tremor of fear as the thing focused its malevolence on him alone. *Great. I've made it mad at me.*

"RELOAD!" He grabbed the ramrod, soaking the sponge end in a puddle on the deck before shoving it down the cannon's maw, extinguishing the remaining embers of the initial shot. Aylie stuffed the bagged charge of powder into the cannon's maw, jumping back as Willis rammed it home. Gelman tipped the next round shot into the barrel, followed by a rope wad. Willis drove the shot and wad home with a final thrust of the ramrod. He dropped the ram and stuffed a priming quill down the touchhole, before turning away to seat another percussion cap on his pistol's nipple. Willis knew men had been dragged overboard or left crushed on the deck but the best thing he could do was serve the cannon. Eames and Germaine struggled with the breeching tackle, pulling the gun back to the rail.

Sachi swept past, scything away a tentacle reaching for the makeshift cannon crew. Severed tentacles writhed about the deck, blindly clutching for prey. Blood dyed the water swirling out the scuppers with an oily, bluish sheen. Sachi weaved her way through the grasping tentacles, leaving stumps spraying ichor into the air.

"NOOO!" Willis screamed. Pierre Lescot shoved a burning splinter into the touchhole, Willis saw him too late. The cannon roared again but this time the recoil slammed the fourteen-hundred pound cannon on its carriage directly into Eames the Elder's head and upper torso. The breeching ring shattered his head like a dropped egg. One of the tackle ropes caught Germaine across the chest as the recoiling cannon snapped the line rigid. Willis heard his back break as the boy was flung against the base of the mainmast. The carriage just brushed Gelman's shoulder but that was enough to knock him insensible, flinging him halfway across the deck. One of the wheels of the carriage rolled over Aylie's right foot and pulped it. Her eyes rolled up in her head and she collapsed, unconscious.

"Non! Non!" Lescot stumbled away from the cannon, splattered with blood and brains from Eames' splintered head. A tentacle slammed down, wrapping around the First Mate and hurling him screaming into the darkness of the pounding waves.

"Shit!" Willis cursed. He turned to see the effect of the shot, just in time to see Sachi bounce off the stump of the mainmast and launch her original steel butterfly sword at the monster. The blade turned over once as it flashed across the gap and simply disappeared into the thing's eye. The cannon shot had struck at the base of the mass of tentacles. He saw, for a split second, the cruel, hooked beak of the beast's maw. Or what was left of it. The shot had hit the larger half of the beak and torn it almost completely off. It hung by a thread of tissue no larger than Willis' own arm.

The entire ship shook as the thing went completely mad, thrashing for a long instant and spurting a disgusting, inky black fluid across the ship. Then, with a splash that washed water completely over the ship, it was gone. Severed tentacles and the dead and wounded littered the deck. Sachi walked over to where Silaqui lay unconscious on the deck. She knelt and checked the sorceress. Willis relaxed as she smiled and nodded at him. She pulled Silaqui's cloak tighter around the elf, protecting her from the still falling rain. She came over and sat next to Willis.

"She'll be okay, has a nasty knot on her head." She pulled her knees up, wrapping her arms around them and resting her head on her kneecaps as she laid the white-steel sword down on the deck beside her.

"I think Gelman will be able to help, once he wakes up. Aylie's worst off, I think the carriage wheel crushed her foot. She's out cold." He leaned against an overturned water butt.

"Let's leave her that way until we get Pere Gelman coherent."

"Yeah." He glanced upwards. "Well, the ship's wrecked, a total loss."

"Yes." She slowly blinked at him. "But the storm is rapidly breaking up."

"Yeah." He wiped a thick, gelatinous glob of the creature's ink off his shoulder. "But we are shipwrecked on an unknown shore, an unexplored island."

"Hai." She pulled a smallish piece of a tentacle out of her hair. The horn-rimmed sucker still spasmed as she threw it over the rail. "But there is plenty of food, I believe. And, given the thickness of the vegetation, fresh water should be plentiful. We will neither starve nor die of thirst."

"Yeah." He hawked and spat over the side. "Our friends are hurt and most of the crew is either dead or injured. There're probably cannibals or some kind of creature that just *loves* the taste of human, especially Kolbian humans."

"Yes, possibly." She reached out and picked up the sword. She stared at it, concentrating. It shimmered and then flowed like a thick liquid up onto her arm where it formed into a seamless bracer covering from the knuckles of her hand to her elbow.

"Uh, yeaaah. And that." He shook his head, too exhausted to be either astounded or afraid. "Just don't tell me how you do that. Maybe later, but not right now. And try not to let anyone else see you do that. Half of them would run screaming into the jungle and the rest would try to run home across the ocean."

"Yes." She sighed. "But do you know what is truly unfortunate?"

"Uh, the whole damned mess?"

"No." She gave him a slow smile, an urchin's grin he hadn't seen since this lunacy started back in late September.

"Okay, I'll bite. What is truly unfortunate?"

"The kaiju fled with my only remaining iron sword buried in its eye. I believe it will be most difficult to retrieve my blade."

Willis stared at her for a long, long moment, before he felt his own grin answer hers. Her grin grew into a huge smile. His smile grew in concert with it and then both of them were laughing, laughing so hard that tears came to their eyes. Their laughter soared into a sky growing pale with the morning sunrise.

Chapter Sixteen

**Vlymouth Port, Duchy of Hale,
Kingdom of Montagar
November 1478, Third Age of Imperial Reckoning**

MARIANNE LUNDGREN CROSSED HER hands behind her head and stared at the peeling paint on the ceiling. The bed wasn't long enough for her to really stretch out her lanky, six-and-a-half-foot frame. While her eyes were open and she was registering the grimy room she'd rented in a cheap flophouse, she was paying more attention to the reports she'd received. And the conversation she'd had with Debbie McAllen in a VR link a few days ago. She pulled up her record of it and ran it over again.

***

"I don't know what it was, damn it, Marianne." McAllen had been exhausted. It showed in her dirty hair sticking up in short spikes and a haunted look in her eyes. "If I hadn't seen my old diary recorder's display flashing that its short-term memory was full, I don't know if I'd've ever realized that *anything* had happened. All I had were two sentences that I do NOT remember saying, and then fourteen minutes of me screaming my throat raw. For no apparent reason."

"Yeah. *Not much I can do about that now, I guess?* And *Wonder what it's gonna hit this time?* That was all you had to go on?"

"It was enough that I started looking at records. Nothing. Not a single thing. First it was the drone I was sure was hacked. Now that drone's gone from inventory. Just gone, no electronic records, physically missing. It was deleted like it never existed and I don't remember tearing it down. If I hadn't left out the tool kit, and a couple of handwritten notes in the maintenance bay, I'd've never known it was gone. Hell, I'd've never known it even existed in the first place."

"Yeah. Okay, and then there's the Def-Sat."

"Yeah. TK421 was missing a long rod penetrator. I know these things were basically obsolete when they got dumped here straight out of the Defense Reserve inventory. But they were all fully loaded with munitions and they've been resupplied and restocked right up until the very last week of the War. And I know that one did NOT have any expended munitions. It's one the Seekers never got their claws in. I tele-operated the drone that checked it and now it's missing one penetrator. Where'd that go? What'd it hit? Even the satellite's on-board memory had been scrubbed. I don't know about you, but I'm starting to get jumpy as hell about linking in to *any* of the main systems. Whatever did this, it blew through all our security systems and defensive protocols like they were a screen door on an airlock. And about as useful."

"I agree. But the scariest thing is the fact that it actually managed to hack YOU. It dived into your head, into your BPU and wiped the memories of what, twenty minutes?"

"Yeah." The haunted look in McAllen's eyes was worse. "And if I hadn't been lazy and left that ancient diary recorder on, I doubt I'd've ever known. I'll swear by any God, Angel or Saint you wanna name, but damn it, I'm starting to get real twitchy up here. I'm afraid to stay awake by myself and I'm terrified of going back into stasis."

"Okay, since you brought up gods and angels, what if it was one of the local...well, the local *warp-angels*?"

"Let's not go there." McAllen stared into space for several long minutes. "And no one has seen one of those things for millennia, Marianne. Hell, wasn't the last confirmed encounter over four hundred years *before* the Quar'taneeka War actually started?"

"Something like that. Long, long damn time ago, any way you look at it."

"And all the records say that those things, whatever they are or were, don't or didn't have the least clue about how tech systems work. And that, in general, they're mostly benign." She shrugged, "I really doubt that's what it was. Whatever the fuck it was, well, it's got me jumpy as a long-tailed cat in a room full of rocking chairs."

"Okay, let's pass on further flagellation of the deceased equine." Marianne smiled at McAllen. "The last info I've been able to scrounge up on this girl, Sachi Takahashi, is that she was involved in a bar fight, or an attempted assassination, depending on who you talk to, within a day of coming ashore. Then that evening, someone tried to kill a Kolbian naval attaché who was staying at the same inn, and who had also come to Montagar on the good ship *Intrepid*."

"Interesting. Go on."

"It gets thicker. Our girl Sachi got noticed for how beautiful she is, *and*, here's the kicker, that fact that she has black eyes, no iris visible at all. That Elf was staying with her, and apparently she has some kind of connection to the Elvish Royal Court. Distant relative of someone there." Marianne pulled up a virtual chart in the construct's space and began illuminating items on it. "So, what more snooping turned up, the Elf got herself shot in the bar fight slash assassination attempt. A local priest steps in and heals her, using, no bull, real magic. Then this same priest is sharing a room with the naval attaché during the second, or first, assassination attempt."

"I smell an expired rodent here."

"Oh, it gets better. Someone puts a bounty on Sachi's head during the day, right after she landed. A big bounty, five thousand of the local gold pieces."

"Holy crap!"

"Yeah. The second night she's ashore, after the good ship *Intrepid* has weighed anchor, there's a huge fuss-up with the Thieves' Local 999. Someone got in and out of the local boss's office. And one of those *someones* was none other than our little cutie, Sachi. She left what I'm starting to assume is her normal calling card: chaos, mayhem and a stack of dead bodies. And now, the bounty's been doubled."

"Girl just has a talent for getting in trouble, doesn't she?"

"Oh, you have no idea. Look at this." Marianne dropped a virtual copy of a bounty price sheet on the table. "This thing is perfect. Too perfect, and there's hundreds of them all over town. This never came off some woodcut or block-letter printing press. This came off an old school laser printer and that says..."

"That says the Seekers have an interest in this Sachi."

"Hmm-huh. An interest in killing her Bang-Dead."

"Well, hell. So, where is she?"

"Good question." Marianne sighed. "The trail then goes cold. Our girl Sachi, her point-eared, slit-pupiled lady friend, the Kolbian naval attaché, the priest and another unidentified person bought passage on a brigantine named *le Bonaventure* and sailed the hell away. Could have been the ship I saw about a day out of port. I missed her by a day."

"So? I'm sure we can put a track on that ship?" She took a long look at Marianne. "Oh, shit. What happened to it?"

"Well, *le Bonaventure* sailed right into the tropical storm my ship avoided. Seems that ships and crews out of the Empire aren't really thought much of by professional sailors in either Montagar or Kolbia. I figure she was forced to run south before the wind."

"And? Otherwise, we just look further south."

"I backtracked possible target areas for a penetrator launched from TK421. Given that we are almost a hundred percent certain it didn't hit on a land mass, given that the only land it could have hit would have been the northwestern coast of the continent of Khakal, well, the potential impact area covers the Southern Lanic. Right where *le Bonaventure* would have been. And the penetrator came down hot and fast into a very unstable weather front. Disrupted things enough that there is now a very violent, relatively small, full hurricane blowing through there like a bull moose in a cornfield. If, and I say if, *le Bonaventure* didn't get hit by the penetrator, then the storm, right after another storm, might have sunk her. The second storm should blow out tomorrow or the next day, but in all likelihood, that ship, and her crew and passengers, are either on the bottom of the sea, or driftwood floating with the current."

"So, end of the line for this Sachi, I guess?" Debbie's voice was soft as she could see the pain in her friend.

"I'm afraid so. The Commodore has already directed that I get back to Kolbia ASAP. He needs me to keep the Kolbians on the technological cutting edge, so it's back to whispering in Harald Fulmark's ear on how to jump-start two hundred years of technology."

"Could be worse. You could be back in Rus, fifteen hundred years ago, playing Court Wizard and trying to convince them that beating uppity serfs to death was costing them a lot of smart people."

"Yeah. Had to beat feet once that damn cleric got the Kzar's ear and convinced him I had cloven hooves and a long, curly tail to go with the horns hidden under my pointy hat. That bastard."

"So, Marianne?" There was a long, pregnant pause.

"Spit it out, Debbie."

"Do you really think it was her, your god-daughter? Caitlyn Schmidt?"

"Who knows?" she sighed. "The age seems about right, I think, from what I've learned. All the descriptions I got said she was beautiful but obviously not pure Nisei. The black eyes and the hints that she healed fast certainly suggest someone with at least basic enhancement. But if she wasn't Caitlyn, where'd she come from? Who was she? The Seekers seem to be trying awfully damn hard to kill her, but no more so than any one of us they might identify. Talk about a mystery wrapped up in an enigma and then deep fried in ambiguous obscurity! And now, she's probably fish food. Fuck, I truly hate this whole damn planet some days!"

"I know." Debbie smiled at her oldest friend. "Who knows? I don't think I'll dig this Sachi Takahashi's grave until I see a body. She does seem to have one hell of a talent for survival. Be realistic, do what you need to do, but don't give up hope yet. There are lots of little sand spit islands in the South Lanic, and a fair number of bigger ones. I'll do what I can to keep an eye on things."

"Thanks, Debbie." Marianne gave her a wry smile. "I owe you a beer when this is all over."

"I've heard that before. Even with over nine thousand years of back pay, you won't be able to afford all the beer you owe me. Hell, you could replace all the water on Ganymede with beer and it wouldn't be enough."

"You say that like it's a bad thing."

"Well, I don't think I could drink *that* much beer."

"No prob. We'll just find us a squad of husky, strapping young Marines and get them to drink it all. Then we could have our wicked way with them."

"You, Marianne Lundgren, are a sad puppy of low moral values. I'm clear. Bye."

"Yeah, clear. Ciao."

***

"Damn, miserable bed, made for midgets." She stretched on the bed, wondering when, not if, it would collapse under her. Of course, replacing it with something decent and clean would render hundreds of hardworking bedbugs homeless. She had no idea how the locals dealt with the unvarying presence of the damn things. She could tweak her personal chemistry to exude a natural bug repellant. She stared at the ceiling while she again reviewed everything she knew or thought she knew about this young woman named Sachi Takahashi.

"Damn it all to hell." She felt the tears gather at the corners of her eyes, and this time she just let them fall. "I don't know how, but I'm sure you've survived. You better have survived. Your mother will never forgive me if you haven't."

Port Plunder, Cazadora Isle, Southern Lanic Ocean November, 1478, Third Age of Imperial Reckoning

"Hey, you need to eat." A strong, tanned hand dumped several large chunks of pineapple and a good bit of rice into Sahla's wooden bowl. "Folks in Yorland City might like ladies skinny as a rail, their ribs and hip-bones sticking out, knobby joints and their faces gaunt, but no one with any sense does." Draven Kye was stretched to the full length of his chain, just barely able to reach where she sat.

Sahla stared listlessly into her bowl. For the last three days, she barely touched her food and it was starting to show. She glanced up as Draven moved back to his side of the hut. There was a concerned smile on his handsome face. Gabrielle was sitting at the end of her leash, with her back to Zedekiah. He frowned, stretched as far as he could, while he worked a crude wooden comb through her blonde hair. Hair that was much shorter than it had been. Wrath had tired of the constant mess Gabrielle's waist-length hair was in and a single flick of a green-lit finger trimmed it to shoulder length. There were only the four of them now. She would never forget the punishment Ironheart decreed for Lodvar.

***

Ironheart arrived on the wings of the storm, *Deathdealer* standing into the small, protected bay he named Port Plunder. And he had not been at all pleased when told of Lodvar's attempted rape of Sahla. He ordered the Heimdägarran chained to a post in the middle of the crude settlement and he'd left the big man there while the storm blew itself out. Once the sky cleared, Ironheart's pirates buried Lodvar in the sand up to his neck, just barely out of reach of the ocean waves at high tide. Lodvar had screamed throughout the night as the crabs had nipped bits and pieces off his face. By mid-afternoon the next day, Lodvar could no longer scream. Thirst had swollen his tongue until it blocked his mouth.

They'd dug him up that evening and the pirates laughed while they dunked him repeatedly into the pigs' filthy watering trough. Ironheart finally stopped it before he drowned in the slop. Then, last night, he was chained to a thick post outside the stockade wall. Lodvar had thrashed and screamed, begging Ironheart to not leave him for the *dziungles gimtoji*. Ironheart laughed in his face before setting a torch just outside Lodvar's reach. At his command, a somewhat subdued Wrath lit the torch on its long pole with a ghastly green fire.

"Put the torch out before anything comes and you might survive." Ironheart's voice was clear enough that the hostages could hear him. "Yell and scream and carry on, and it won't matter. *Something* will come to see what's making all the racket. If you're still here in the morning, I'll bring you back inside and double your ransom. If you're gone, well then, I guess any issues you have will be solved, now, won't they? Or at least, I won't care a damn about you anymore, eh?"

The hostages were moved to a lean-to a few yards away from the wooden wall of the stockade. *Deathdealer's* third mate, an Aljannia named Reithen Faewynys, and the ship's huge, black,

234

axe-wielding Bosun directed the pirates and crew-slaves in coating the top and outside of the stockade wall with a disgusting mixture of liquid pitch, fluids pulled up from the latrine pits and a poisonous looking green powder that Wrath supplied. Sahla, when she caught a strong whiff of the stuff, promptly collapsed into helpless vomiting. The other three hostages were nearly as bad off. Those applying the revolting glop cut the smell with rum soaked scarves tied over their faces.

Wrath came over and sighed, looking at them. She'd shaken her head and gone off to her private dwelling. She returned in a few moments and wrapped a soaked scarf around Sahla's face, after gently wiping away the vomit. Whatever the scarf was soaked in, it countered the repulsive smell of the stuff on the wall. She gave similar scarves to the others.

"Why did he have us moved here?" Sahla had asked her.

"I guess he wants to make a point, girl." Wrath had gently pulled Sahla's hair back, before bringing her head up to meet her eyes, sapphire blue to emerald green. "And you, I think, do not need this lesson, but 'tis naught I can do about it." For a long moment, they stared into each other's eyes.

"Why are you doing this? You know this is wrong. The Prophet will curse you and Chalta will forget your name. Why?" Sahla pulled away from Wrath's hand.

"Well, for one thing, it's about as far away from home as I can get. And I like the luxury the money buys. And I'm not Darsälaamic, young lady. So I'm not concerned about your God or his Prophet. I know what I am. But what, exactly, are you?"

"I'm a bride, going to my husband-to-be, to maintain the Peace of Chalta between the Folk of the Sands." Sahla looked away. "Well, that's what I was. Now? I don't know anymore. No one of honor will accept me as a wife now. Not even as a concubine of the harem."

"That's not what I meant and you know it." She straightened, putting her hands on her hips and staring down at the girl. "I've not divined your secrets, not yet, girl. But I will, have no doubt.

Only thing that's keeping me from buying you for myself is the amount of money involved. Might give people an idea where I am. People I want nothing to do with." The witch frowned. "Whatever you are, I can nearly see the potential power coiling around you. And it's growing stronger, coming to a peak soon, I think. Very, very soon."

After a fulminating glare from Ironheart, Wrath stayed away from her, from all the hostages the rest of the night.

Things got worse when full night fell. The storm was gone and the sky was clear and bright on a moonless night. Sahla could see the fixed stars, and more of the moving ones than ever before. She had heard Lodvar swearing silently under his breath as he threw handfuls of dirt and sand at the reeking green flames of the torch. He became more and more frantic as the night drew on. She heard cloth rip as he tore off first his shirt, she guessed, and then his ragged pants to fling them at the torch. Near midnight, Captain Ironheart appeared. He stopped next to her and squatted down.

"Did you encourage him somehow, girl?" His voice was soft and quiet.

"No! You know I would never do such a thing!"

"Perhaps, girl." He paused. "Perhaps not. Who's to say?"

"What's going to happen to him?"

"Don't know, yet." He sucked air quietly between his teeth. "Depends on what, exactly, shows up. If no one's paying attention, or aren't really hungry, well, he gets to live. If the little brown, human-ish things, guess you could call them people of a sort, well, if they show up and cut him loose, he might get away. Might. Most likely, those little bastards'll haul him off for their own purposes."

"Are they these *dziungles gimtoji* he spoke of?"

"No. The...*dziungles gimtoji*...those things are...other. Very much other. If the little to medium sized ones come, well, they'll fight over him, he'll get torn to pieces in the brawl and we'll have some fresh meat from the things that don't survive the brawl. Well, the ones the winners don't haul off." Even the captain's cruel, handsome face was bleak. "And if a big one comes or one of the real giants, the old ones of the hills, well, those rarely show themselves. One of those will just wrap him up and take him away for…later. Maybe much later."

"Would it not be better to just kill him, cleanly, if you must?"

"You begging me for pity for a man that tried to rape you, girl?"

"Pity?" She caught and held his eyes with her own. "No. But a clean death, not this horror, whatever these things out there might be."

"Lass, you *are* naive, aren't you?" He looked away. "I have a kind of…well, a kind of *agreement* with the locals, most of them. I leave them alone, make occasional…well, occasional *offerings* to them; and in their turn, they, the dangerous ones that can think, a little bit, they leave me alone. I don't think the Imperial Army at its greatest power could clear this island of the horrors that inhabit much of it."

"How so?"

"This little bay is a nice, well protected anchorage. But if the wind's out of the north, well, you're stuck, embayed on a lee shore. All you can do is anchor and wait for the wind to change. But usually the wind's southerly, so not too much of a problem."

"And? I know little of the sea or ships."

"You wouldn't," he actually grinned at her, "but you know a hundred words for sand, don't you?"

"Yes, of course."

"Well, then take my word for it, this anchorage, my little Port Plunder, is nice enough, but this whole island is shaped like a capital letter 'G' and inside the 'G' is a much better anchorage, completely protected. BUT, there's something huge in the bay, huge and ancient. Maybe something as old as the Fire Fall. It's said that staying too near it for too long makes people sick. Makes them crazy. Some say they hear voices. Others say their skin rots and falls off. Whatever. Supposedly it only happens if you stay too close, too long. For now, this little bay on the north side of the island makes a perfect anchorage for a pirate. And it's mine, so I get to name it."

She shook her head at his smirk, and then jumped as far away from the wall as the chain let her as Lodvar shrieked like a tortured soul in hell.

"NO! NO! *DIEVE VANDENYNAIS!* SAVE ME! PLEASE, GOD OF THE OCEAN, NO! NOOOO!" She could hear his frantic jerking on the chain, trying to get away from whatever had come out of the jungle. Words were no longer distinguishable from his howling screams. There was a clicking, scraping sound, followed by a final, strangled scream from Lodvar. It was silent for a long moment, and then she heard something breathing, just on the other side of the wall, something huge. The stout timbers of the wall flexed ever so slightly as whatever it was leaned against the wall. Something hard scraped up the wall, jerking back when it touched the glop coating the top of the timbers. A raspy sound followed, air being blown out of large lungs.

There was an almost silent rasp as Ironheart slowly drew his cutlass. She saw the blade was magical, glittering silver in the starlight. His eyes were wide as he looked at her and raised his forefinger to his lips. A wave of the sword and more pirates silently drifted up, Wrath among them. Green magic shimmered around her hands. For a long time, they waited in silence, some armed with axes and pikes, others with matchlocks and muskets.

Finally, there was a last breath and the thing leaning against the wall moved away. There was a wooden snap as the stake to which Lodvar had been chained broke. The jungle rustled as it left. Shortly thereafter, the unnatural silence ended, the normal sounds of the night returning. With the morning's light, the four had been moved back to their old hut.

***

Sahla stared into her bowl at the extra food Draven just put there. She was hungry but the food was as sand in her mouth. The month had turned and her birthing day was only weeks away, at best. If it came without a Bonding, she knew the magic would carry her away, bring her before her Sire in his palace. And, even if he truly did love her, as her Mother always told her he did, it would not matter. On the Plane of the Air, a Jann such as she would be of little matter. But if she Bonded to a pirate...!?

This is not what my Sire foretold! And that dream, that felt as a True Dream would be, I think. Who were those others in my dream? Are they true and real, or merely symbols of what might or could be? And here, there are only the pirates, foul and uncouth! They are dark-hearted and evil, greedy and vicious. The only possible ally I might find is a witch who flees her own problems, committing acts which only blacken her heart. Chalta! Is THIS what you want for me? Am I where the Prophet would lead me? Or does the Prophet wash his hands of me, unhuman and half-breed, outsider unclean? Is all of my training, to fight, to dance, to survive, and yes, to love; is all of this for naught, cast aside by fickle fate? Prophet of my People, please, give me a sign! Please!

Southwestern Shore, Cazadora Isle,
Southern Lanic Ocean
November, 1478, Third Age of Imperial Reckoning

Capitaine Andre de Foix died the morning of the day after the grounding of *le Bonaventure* and the battle with the giant, tentacled sea-beast. They buried him at noon, next to the other three actual graves of the crew. There were memorial markers for the three bodies they hadn't found, and a final one for the man who died when he fell from the yards after the destruction of the pirate. Of the original, twelve-man crew, there were only four survivors.

One of those, Roland Bellec, was the ship's cook. Gelman had healed the burns on his legs and the garrulous, stocky Geullian handled most of the camp chores and meals while the rest of them salvaged what they could from the wreck. Carlos Luis de Ribera and Ismael de la Serna, the youngest crew to survive, were both ordinary seamen in their early twenties, from the Imperial province of Ibertina. Arcenio Kalivas was the closest thing the ship had had to either a priest or a doctor. Another Imperial, from Decennia Province, he avoided both Gelman, a priest from the semi-schismatic Kythal Church of Montagar, and Silaqui, twice accursed as both sorceress and unhuman. Of course, anything he did, Ismael and Carlos did exactly the opposite, since no decent, God-fearing Ibertinan could ever truly tolerate a sheep-loving Decennian. It made for more tension in the camp on the beach than anyone wanted.

"Had the Capitaine or the Mate survived, yous nay have such nonsense, M'sieur, Ma'moiselle." Roland waved a ladle at the current shouting match at the jungle's edge between the three men. "Arcenio's the senior, by a good bit, but still only rated as an ordinary seaman. And as disagreeable an old bastard as ever walked a deck." Willis and Aylie stood next to him, waiting for him to fill their bowls with fish stew.

"If they keep it up, Lady Silaqui might turn the lot of them into frogs." Willis grinned at the tubby cook. "God help them if they piss off Sachi."

"Aye." The cook's answer was monosyllabic. He hadn't seen Sachi with her eyes glittering with lights, but he'd seen her fighting against the monster. She scared him. No one should be able to move like she did. With a noncommittal grunt he filled Willis' bowl, then Aylie's, waiting for them to walk off and sit before shouting at the three bickering men to come get lunch. Arcenio made a rude gesture before stomping off into the jungle with a musket in hand.

"The idiot wants to go shoot a monkey," Ismael grumbled as he trudged up through the dry sand. "Says he's tired of fish." He picked up two bowls, handing one to the taller Carlos.

"Moron. Stupid, sheep-humping Decennian." Carlos, the taller and older of the two, took the bowl and waited as Roland filled first Ismael's and then his. "I've not seen a monkey. Have you?"

"What's a monkey?" Aylie asked as she poked dubiously at the stew in her bowl.

"They're creatures you find in the tropics, some places." Willis held out his bowl for Roland to refill. "Small, about yay tall." He held his hand about a foot and a half above the sand. "Clever little beasts, they kind of look a little like humans. If humans were covered in brown or black fur and had a tail half again as long as they are. Don't piss them off, they like to throw shit at things that scare them, and most things scare them, small as they are. And no sailor ever born can climb as fast as they can. Long, sharp teeth, too. Little buggers have a nasty bite."

"Ah, I see." Gelman joined the group around the stewpot. "Sounds like they'd fit right in at the Council of Lords."

"Throwing shit?" Willis regarded the stew mournfully. "Isn't that a general feature of political types everywhere, Gelman?"

"Who's throwing shit?" Silaqui dropped a three-foot-long sea bass next to the campfire as she came up from the shoreline, followed by Sachi. Sachi carried a large grouper with her hand through its gills, and both women were soaking wet.

"Oh, the usual, monkeys, politicians, you know." Willis shrugged and dug into his stew. He was used to the visual impact of the pair of women. Gelman managed not to stare but the other three males were very frank in their appreciation of Sachi's feminine charms, revealed by wet and scanty clothing.

Sachi matched them stare for stare. She tossed her catch into the air and her sword flashed thrice. She caught the fish before it hit the ground. The white steel blade removed head and tail and opened the grouper longitudinally. She gave it a single shake and the guts and viscera splattered on the sands. She tossed the fish to Ismael, who managed to catch it without spilling his stew.

"Scale it." She wrist-snapped the blade clean and sheathed it in a single motion. "I caught it and I cleaned it. You can do the rest. Try not to cut your thumb off." She grabbed a large bowl and scooped it full of stew before stalking off to perch on the overturned longboat a few yards away.

"I'd stare at her, were I you, boys." Silaqui grinned as a crimson glow levitated a bowl and spoon to her hand. "She'll just kill you, if she decides you've stepped over the line. I might do something *really* unpleasant to you. So think about it, real hard, before you try to be the swaggering hero, sweeping the fair maiden off her feet." She filled her bowl and followed Sachi.

"Uh, yeah," Ismael muttered as he carefully laid the butchered fish down. "Think I'd rather gargle outta a spittoon."

***

"Kint sees a dem ting in t'is fukkin' yungle!" Arcenio muttered as he shoved through another clump of moss-shrouded liana vines. "Alls tese tree, gotta be sumting utter dan fish ta eats. Jist gotta shoots da ting. Kint be dat hurd ta does." Arcenio spent the earliest years of his life herding sheep on the mostly barren hillsides of coastal Decennia. Going to sea had simply been a means to escape his family's poverty and the smell of sheep dung. But whenever he could, he liked to go hunting ashore and he was, if only in his own opinion, a fairly good shot. What he never realized was that he had gone from predator to prey.

***

The distinctive *crack-pow* of a musket rang through the forest, sending brightly colored birds swirling into the sky like angry confetti. On the beach, no one paid much attention to the shot. Not until they heard the terrified screaming. Screaming that changed from terrified to agonized in a split second. As a boy, Ismael won all the running contests in his small town, and he was the quickest to grab a boarding axe and musket and sprint into the jungle. At least he thought he was, until Sachi flashed past him in a blur, sand rooster-tailing behind her flying feet. Her white steel sword slashed a tunnel through the stifling greenery. But the screaming stopped before even she could reach the source.

When he reached the tiny clearing where Sachi stood, he nearly ran into her back. She caught him before he could fall. Willis was right behind him. In the soft soil of the jungle floor, they saw the shuffling footprints of Arcenio and the discharged musket. Arcenio's tracks led into the center of the clearing and then vanished. Other than his footprints, there were a number of round imprints about five or six inches across. They didn't really seem to be an animal's tracks; they were just round marks about two inches deep in the detritus of the jungle floor. There was no blood nor any signs of a struggle. In addition to the fading scent of gunpowder, there was a sharp, musty scent, with a bitter tang to it.

"Well, I guess you were right, Willis." Sachi's voice had a low, biting tone. "Looks like something here does like the taste of humans."

"I *so* hate it when I'm right."

Chapter Seventeen

**Port Plunder, Cazadora Isle,
Southern Lanic Ocean
November, 1478, Third Age of Imperial Reckoning**

Captain Ironheart met the longboat from the sloop *Heartcutter* at the edge of the surf. Sahla watched him clasp forearms with the stocky, white-haired man who was the first out of the boat. They talked for a moment, heads close together, and then the stocky man gestured at the stretcher being raised out of the grounded longboat. Whoever was on that stretcher was huge. Four men struggled with the burden and a huge arm, thickly muscled and nearly as long as Sahla was tall, slipped from under the sheet and thumped onto the sand. The skin was darkly tanned with a sickly yellow undertone to it and the body appeared to be almost seven feet tall.

Ironheart and the other man stood on the beach a few moments longer, Ironheart growing more and more upset and agitated as they spoke. At the last, he snatched his hat from his head and threw it to the sand, cursing. The white-haired man shrugged and waited, picking up Ironheart's hat when the bigger man stopped yelling. He dusted it off and handed it back. Ironheart took it and jammed it on his head. As the pair left the beach, the white-haired man gave the hostages' hut a long look. From where she sat, away from the door, arms wrapped around her knees and her long, black hair draped around her, she doubted he could see her. But even in the evening's gathering gloom, she saw his eyes, a cold ice-blue, with neither mercy nor pity in them.

***

"Something fell out of the sky and hit *Bloodstone*?" Ironheart snorted. He tossed off the last of his whisky. "Blast and damnation!"

"Wie Gott will." Werner Streiss was from an old Deuschen family, a family of good blood. Werner's Terranglais was flat and hard, with strong hints of his native Deusch. "We were lucky to spot him. Given how badly he is hurt, and the condition of the topgallant mast he was lashed to, I think he tells only truth. Why should he lie?" The stocky, white-haired captain of *Heartcutter* shrugged as he drained his beer tankard. "And I cannot imagine anything less should separate Gruesome from Kapitan le Circque."

"Humpf." Ironheart growled. "Do you think he's worth using one of Wrath's healing brews? I only have a limited number of those and even in Du-Khamps-des-SouSee, there's damn few to be had at any price."

"No idea, Kapitan." Werner waved for one of Ironheart's servants to refill his tankard. "But I'm just a Korvettenkapitan. You're the Kapitan zur See. I don't know if Gruesome will be willing to work with or for anyone else. Honestly, I've no idea how it is that he's still alive. I know he's a tough bastard but this borders on the insane."

"Captain of the Sea." Ironheart snorted as he refilled his own glass. "*Bloodstone* almost matched *Deathdealer's* weight of metal. And now, instead of two ships that could stand ship to ship with a Kolbian frigate, I've only one. *Heartcutter* is a nice little sloop, but single-masted and only six guns."

"True. But they're heavy guns for her size, four eighteen pounder carronades and a pair of long twelve pounders. Nothing near her size wants aught to do with her."

"And what of the brigantine Gruesome claims they pursued?"

"Well, first, whatever fell from the sky might have swamped her, or she went under or aground somewhere with that storm that blew up so fast. Or she just sailed merrily away. Who knows? And, I think, Kapitan, a waste of time to try and find her." He blew the foam off the beer in his tankard and took a long swallow. "Now what of this so-called Houri of the Sands you captured? And the blonde claiming to be the Duke of Ostreich's betrothed?"

"I never expected the blonde. The Houri's real enough. Never in my life have I seen such a beautiful young woman. But...?" Ironheart stopped and stared into his whisky.

"But...what?"

"Her duenna was slain in the battle. Wrath says without the duenna, neither the husband-to-be nor the father will pay a ransom. To them, now, she's damaged goods."

"True, from what I know of those worthless desert vermin. But do they, the husband or her Vater, need to know her duenna died? All we care about is getting paid, nein?"

"Well, of course. The post boat is taking my demands to both Sheikh Hasim al Murafte of Abdu-Ghaffanse and to Rajh Mahdi al-Kohfan, her father and the groom-to-be's father, respectively. The small fact that the Houri's duenna was killed was unfortunately, left out of that communication. Same boat is also carrying the ransom demands to the Duke of Ostreich. But there's a problem Wrath pointed out with the Darsälaamics."

"Huh. What problem?"

"Should they pay, either one or both, and the Houri be returned to them and THEN they find out that her duenna died in the initial attack, well, there'd be Quan's Own Hell to pay. We'd have to avoid the Darsälaamic ports for years. And if they're really pissed, the Kaliph might go as far as declaring a jihad against us. And that could result in thousands of the damned sand-burs burning our main source of supply, Du-Khamps-des-SouSee, to the ground. I rather doubt we'd be able to maintain our current, convenient arrangements with High Lord Kormarra there if that happened."

"Ja, I can see that. What are the other options, Kapitan? I imagine she'd bring an astronomical price in Luctini."

"She probably would. But you're aware of the problems there, as well, no? If, and I mean IF, she made it to the block in Luctini, I agree that she'd fetch a princely sum, but…"

"But then you've got those three Imperial dregs there to deal with."

"And just because I've an…understanding with the mighty Admeeral du SouSee Havre Calchas, that pompous jackass, that doesn't mean I have a free hand in Luctini. That's a nest of snakes I want no part of. I even doubt the Vicomtesse Erszbet would act as my agent in selling the girl. And Wrath is acting like a cat with its fur up about the damn girl. Honestly, if it wasn't for the Contessa du Lisenis, I'm beginning to consider the whole scheme to kidnap and ransom the Houri a bust and just throw her to the crews. But there'd be blood and deaths fighting over her."

"Well, my Kapitan, is there a need to make any decision about her yet?"

"No, not yet. I'm waiting on the post boat to get back with the Duke's response to the ransom demand. I expect to hear from him first. The message will have to cross a good bit of desert to reach the Houri's father or prospective father-in-law."

"Ostreich will pay. That marriage was arranged years ago." Werner finished his tankard and waved the servant away. "And the two of them have met, I believe. I'm given to understand he's quite taken with her, despite being almost old enough to be her Vater."

"Well, that's good to have confirmed. She's been a hysterical pain in the ass."

"Ah, well, she's Guellian. Cheese-eating bastards are always self-righteous pains in the keister. How about the Houri, she a problem too?"

"Oh no, anything but. Hard as nails, that one is. Girl shot our little traitor in the head in her own cabin on her ship. *Boom*, brains on the bulkhead. Then, *boom*, again, and the only reason I'm still here is my breastplate turned the bullet. Hit me dead center over the heart. I'm lucky she didn't shoot *me* in the head!"

"Sounds like someone will have maybe more fun than they want, taming her."

"Oh, since then she's been docile enough. But you can see it in those deep blue eyes. She's deep, got secrets she's hid well. Just something about her."

"Sounds like you want her for yourself."

"Maybe. I'd probably have to kill Wrath if I did take her. Damn sorceress swears there are powers just floating around this girl."

"Hmm. Doesn't sound like you, being indecisive."

"No, well, no need to make a decision yet. Another month, the post boat should be back. I'll decide what to do with the black-haired little chit then."

"Aye-aye, mein Kapitan."

Southwestern Shore, Cazadora Isle, Southern Lanic Ocean
November, 1478, Third Age of Imperial Reckoning

Evening had fallen on the castaways' camp. Despite searching until dusk, nothing more had been found of Arcenio. Only the discharged musket left any hint to his fate. Otherwise, he was gone, as if the jungle had come to life and swallowed him. They ate their dinner of fish stew and kept a close eye on the jungle's edge. Their camp was situated midway between the jungle and the sea, about fifty-five feet from the edge of the jungle's brush and the same from the high tide line.

"We'll set a close watch tonight. Three watches. Two on first, after that, three up at all times." Willis finished his stew and scrubbed out the bowl with beach sand. "I'll take first with Ismael. Second will be Sachi, Aylie, and Carlos. Lady Silaqui, Gelman and Roland will have the last watch. Any issues with that?" There was a general rumble of agreement.

They settled in for the night, using tents and lean-tos, as well as bedrolls and makeshift mattresses; all were salvaged from the wreck. Willis noticed Sachi sitting down the beach, just out of reach of the waves. He wandered down next to her.

"Mind if I join you?"

"No, Willis, I do not mind." Minutes stretched away as they sat there silently. The last hint of the evening sky-glow vanished.

"You know, sometimes, if you're at sea and watch the sun set over the ocean, you see this very brief flash of green light just as the last hint of the Sun's rim disappears from sight."

"Truly?"

"Yeah. We were busy catching dinner and saving what we could from the wreck, and then looking for Arcenio, and we missed any chance of seeing it. But maybe tomorrow?"

"Perhaps. Tomorrow."

"What's wrong, Sachi?"

"There's something here, Willis. Something ancient beyond belief. I can feel it, tugging oh, so gently in my mind. It's not aware of me, I'm not even sure it's even aware of itself, but it is there, somewhere across the jungle and the hills further inland. On the other side of the island, perhaps. And there's something else, an even fainter hint of...of I know not what."

"You know, I'd expect Silaqui or maybe Gelman to go all mystical on me. Not you, not hardly."

"I know. And whatever took Arcenio did not kill him, not right there, at least. No blood, just the dropped musket. But his screams stopped."

"You thinking he might still be alive?"

"I doubt it, but it's possible."

"About the things bothering you," Willis gave her a sly grin, "well you could come snuggle up with me. I'll keep you warm and keep the boogeyman away. You know, someti...Oww!" She slapped his shoulder hard enough to raise a welt.

"First, you can't afford me." She mock-threatened another slap, a sly smile showing on her face. He mock-cringed away from her. "And remember, most of the men I have lain with, I killed." Now the smile was gone.

"I'm sorry, Sachi, it's just that you seemed so unhap…"
"It's of no matter, Willis. And not what worries me."
"So, what does worry you?"
"How many of us will die on this island."

***

Sachi perched on top of the overturned longboat. She had a perfect view of the entire brush line, the blacker blackness where the jungle differentiated from the sky. The sky at least was full of glimmering, shimmering stars. Other than the slight rustle of foliage from the light onshore breeze and the soft susurrations of the waves, the night was silent. Aylie sat behind her, back to back, watching the endless sweep of the waves coming ashore. Carlos would sit in position near the tents, keeping one between him and the banked fire, preserving his night vision. After sitting in one position for ten or fifteen minutes, he'd move. Helped keep him alert, he'd said.

Had anyone been able to actually see Sachi's eyes, they would have noticed the slight glitter of tiny, nearly microscopic lights in her black eyes. She was using what D.A.V.E. called *night vision mode*. It turned the world into strange shades of green, but it let her see in the darkest light. There had to be some light source for it to work, however faint, but the stars themselves provided ample light.

Despite her improved vision, the things of the jungle were stealthy enough that she never actually saw one. Until Carlos screamed as a dozen small darts hit him simultaneously. Coated with poison, they sent him twitching to the ground. Sachi started in shock at the sudden shriek, but she didn't see *anything* in the jungle. Then she saw another shower of the little darts fly from the jungle's boundary.

"Aylie! Stay here! Stay down behind the boat!" She cleared twenty feet in her leap off the boat's hull as she sprinted towards the tents. Then a half dozen darts hit her.

Yeouch! That burns!

::Warning! You have received a significant but non-life-threatening dose of a neurotoxic polypeptide.::

"What!?!" She shouted. "Everyone! Stay down! Stay in your tents! We're getting shot at!"

::You have been poisoned by the darts.::

"Oww! I know. Where are these things coming from?"

::There are a number of individuals using blowguns from the tree line. Switch to thermal mode.::

She ducked down behind Silaqui's tent. More darts rattled off the tent fabric, sailcloth salvaged from the wreck. She quickly plucked out the darts.

"What in Ainaera's name is happening out there?"

"Someone, well a lot of *someones* are shooting little poisoned darts at us. Anything poke through your tent?" Another flight of the darts flew overhead. She concentrated and the world went from the green shaded *night vision mode* to the black to white on grey shades of *thermal mode*. This mode let her see, among other things, body heat. And it was better at being able to actually see *through* some stuff, if the temperature difference was big enough.

"No. Sounds like rain hitting the canvas." There was a rustling in the tent. "I can help."

"No! Damn it! Stay in there."

::Nanite reconfiguration to anti-venom protocols in process. Probability of death is currently eight percent, plus or minus two percent. Continued high stress activity will increase this probability by as much as twenty-seven percent.::

"That's good to know, D.A.V.E. but," she muttered, "what do we do about the things shooting these damn darts at us?" Another batch rattled down like rain. These had been shot vertically into the air, to come down behind the tents.

::I suggest a quick observation in thermal mode. If the individuals can be located in thermal mode, I can provide targeting information.::

"I only have a double-barreled pistol, you know."

"Who are you talking to, Sachi?" Silaqui asked from inside the tent.

"It's complicated. I'll tell you later."

::Lieutenant Commander Fleet possesses a pair of revolvers very similar to the ancient Remington design of 1858, Pre-Diaspora. I would suggest appropriating them under the circumstances.::

"Riiiight. Silaqui, stay in your tent for now. If you've got any magic that can pick nearly invisible creatures out of the jungle, I'd suggest getting it ready."

"You want specific targets or just blow things up?"

"Go with *blow things up* for now. But stay put a bit. These poison darts really fucking burn." She crab-crawled away from Silaqui's tent, where the things in the jungle knew she'd gone to ground, and scurried behind Willis' tent.

"Okay, what's going on out there, Sachi?" he asked when she whacked the side of his tent with her hand.

"Something or things are shooting little, poisoned darts at us out of the jungle. Any of them punch through your tent?"

"No. What's the plan?"

"Sit tight right now." She popped up suddenly from behind his tent and rapidly scanned the brush-line. She saw lots of little, human-shaped white blobs, the white showing clearly through the grayer image of the cooler plants and the black of the cold soil. "Crap." She ducked down as a rain of darts flew towards her.

::Total thirty-five hostile individuals localized. Targets marked and locked. Fire plan prepared. Acquire the handguns and request Lieutenant Commander Fleet ready to reload revolvers by switching out loaded cylinders.::

"Yeah. Willis, your pistols *are* loaded, right?"

"Of course. An unloaded firearm is nothing more than an awkward club."

"And your spare things for them, that hold the bullets?"

"You mean the extra cylinders?"

"Yes."

"They're loaded as well. But I only have four extras."

"Good." She used a knife to slash a hole in the sailcloth of the tent and stuck her head through the hole. "Give me your pistols and be ready to reload them, *quickly*, when I hand them back."

"Have you ever shot a handgun, Sachi?"

"No, I haven't. Just give them to me and don't argue. I'll explain later." Willis shut up and handed her the two revolvers. Her eyes glittered with a multitude of barely visible lights. "Okay, now what, D.A.V.E.?"

"Who *are* you talking to?"

"Just shut up, Willis!" she snapped. "D.A.V.E.?"

::You will see a pair of red dots in your visual field. Place the red dots on the heat sources. When the dot pulses, you are on target. Fire then by simply squeezing the trigger, don't jerk it. Left dot will align with left hand weapon, right dot with right hand.::

"Got it." Sachi popped up from behind Willis' tent with a revolver extended in each hand. A pair of red dots hovered in her vision. She snapped each hand out to put a dot on the closest two small, human-shaped white forms and pulled the triggers. The pistols bucked in her hands, but she held the recoil down and moved the pistols and their corresponding dots to the next pair. The pistols roared again. She moved like lightning, the pistols' blasts blending into a single, loud roar. From the first shot to the last was less than two seconds. She ducked back down before any darts were even launched at her.

Inside the tent, Willis stuffed his fingers in his ears to try and save some of his hearing. He couldn't believe the long, rolling concussion of the gunfire. After the first two shots, he hadn't been able to separate the sounds of individual shots. It was just too fast. Butt first, the smoking pistols were thrust through the hole in the tent.

"Reload!" Sachi's double barreled flintlock pistol boomed, once, twice, fast as thought it seemed.

He grabbed both guns and dropped one on the tent floor. He dropped the loading lever, pulled the cylinder pin and let the cylinder drop out. He pushed the loaded cylinder into the frame, shoved the cylinder pin home and flipped the loading lever up into its clip. Grabbing the second pistol off the floor, he shoved the reloaded revolver out the hole. Quick as he was, she was still waiting on him.

"Here!" Sachi snatched the pistol out of his hand and fired all six shots before he even unclipped the loading lever of the second gun. He knew he could swap out the cylinders in about ten seconds, but she unloaded the pistol in less than two.

I know she's fast, but this is nuts! Is she hitting anything or just wasting shots and scaring off the critters shooting at us?

She thrust the empty gun back through the hole and took the reloaded one the instant it was ready. This time the shots weren't quite as fast, slow enough that he was almost through reloading when the first pistol came back through the hole. He handed her the reloaded one and started the reloading process again. She blew through the six shots as fast this time as she had the first time, one long, rolling blast of fire. The smoking revolver came back into the tent. He had to be careful as the barrel was now hot enough to burn him badly.

"Only one reload left!" he shouted as she grabbed the second revolver from him. She cranked off three shots as fast as the first six, then stopped firing.

"We're safe now. Any critter left is gone into the jungle." She left the concealment of his tent and ran to where Carlos had fallen. "Gelman, hurry up, get out here."

"What in the One God's Name is going on?" Gelman crawled out of his shelter. "Quiet and peaceful, sound asleep and then *BOOM*, screaming and shooting. Sounded like a war going on."

"Just get over here and tell me I'm wrong."

"Wrong about what?" Gelman scrambled across the sand to where she stood. Roland and Ismael were just now coming out of their lean-tos. Despite being groggy and confused, Ismael had a loaded musket at the ready and Roland carried a boarding axe.

"Wrong about Carlos being dead." Sachi stood over the young man's body. The poison had twisted his body into a near fetal position.

"Damn it." Gelman knelt next to the body and quickly examined him. "He's gone. I'm sorry, there's nothing I can do."

Without a word, Sachi turned away and walked into the jungle's edge. Willis tossed some more wood on the fire, making it flare up as she returned, dragging something behind her. The body she dropped next to the fire was a small, pale skinned humanoid. Other than size, it looked nearly human, except for the sharply filed teeth. One of the heavy, fifty caliber pistol bullets had hit it in the head, shattering the skull like a smashed melon. A ragged loincloth was tied around its waist and it was obviously male. Odd, circle-and-connected-sticks tattoos covered the pale skin. What little hair there was was glossy brown. She dropped a blowgun as long as the thing's three and a half foot long body and a small, quiver-like pouch full of the same darts that were stuck in Carlos' body and all the tents.

"These are what attacked us. In the morning we'll need to get rid of the bodies, either burn them or throw them in the ocean." Sachi shook her head in sorrow as Gelman covered Carlos with a sheet of sailcloth. "For now, I'd suggest going back to sleep. I'll take the watch the rest of the night. This won't happen again." She turned and disappeared into the night.

***

The early morning seaward breeze blew the crude raft out away from the beach. It had a single short mast with a makeshift sail and its planks were roughly lashed together with twisted sailcloth. A few hundred yards off the beach, the slow-match reached the oil-soaked rags and set the thing afire. It burned briefly and then came apart, dumping its cargo, the slain small humanoids, into the ocean.

256

Sachi was climbing through the wreck of the *le Bon* as the raft sank, searching for anything useful that might have been missed. Ismael was helping her as best he could. Roland was preparing the midday meal. Willis, Gelman, Aylie and Silaqui had built the raft and piled the bodies on it, launching it into the sea.

"Okay." Willis turned to face the others. "First thing I'll say is that I trust Sachi, but she's starting to scare the living hell out of me."

"Why, Willis?" Silaqui watched the now-worrisome jungle closely.

"She told me last night that she'd never fired a handgun before. I'm a damn good shot, but have you all compared notes on the wounds on our midnight assailants' bodies?"

"Not really." Gelman shrugged. "Why?"

"Every single one was shot once. Neatly through the head. She fired thirty-five shots, thirty-three from my revolvers and two from her own double flintlock. Thirty-five shots, in the dark, into the jungle and as fast as she could pull the triggers. How many bodies did we pile on that raft?"

"Cor." Aylie stopped and stared at the remaining smudge of smoke where the last of the raft was disintegrating. "'Twas five and thirty, nae? Ye be saying that she'd nae missed? Nae one shot? Bloody hell!"

"Are you sure, Willis?" Silaqui turned away from the jungle.

"Absolutely. Thirty-five shots fired, thirty-five targets hit *in the head!* Aylie, you helped me drag the little buggers in. I'm sure of all the ones I hauled in. Are you sure of yours as well, Aylie?"

"Sure as sure, I am. And I made a sketch o' what those tatty-too things was, as well. Might be handy ta knows that, iffn we sees the wee folk again. They was mostly the same. A circle of some size, and eight bent sticks connecting ta the circles. Sometimes ta other sticks, or ta just the circle."

"I'm not worried about the *tatty-toos*, Aylie." Willis rubbed his face in annoyance. "Sachi was talking to something else, something none of us could hear last night."

"I heard that as well, Willis." Silaqui shaded her eyes as she looked towards the wrecked ship.

"Gelman has said that when she has her fits, it's like she's possessed by something, something that seems almost mechanical. And we've all seen her eyes glitter at times. But have any of you stopped to think about her latest impossibility?"

"Shooting the guns without missing?" Gelman noted the crafty look in Willis' eyes.

"Nae, 'tis naught what Willis is saying, 'tis it, Willis?" Aylie watched Sachi and Ismael climb down the side of the wreck.

"Where's her sword?" he asked.

"She hit the sea-monster with the one she threw." Gelman frowned in thought.

"Aye and where'd she get that long white one she used ta carve up those tenty-cley things like new summer sausages?" Aylie unconsciously rubbed the foot the cannon's carriage had crushed. Gelman had been able to heal it, but at times it seemed to just itch more.

"Oh, hell, forget the sword." Silaqui suddenly snapped her fingers. "Where'd she get that white-steel bracer she's wearing now?"

"Ok, everyone *knows* that you can't do *anything* to white-steel. Can't melt it, can't forge it, and sure as hell can't pierce armor formed out of it. A white-steel blade never rusts, never needs sharpening and never dulls, can sometimes cut cleanly through the best Kolbian steel and even something dwarf-forged. We all *know* that, right?" Willis got a chorus of affirmative mumbles. "And our dear Sachi can mold the stuff like children's clay. After the sea-monster fled, I watched her simply *will* that long white sword into the bracer she's wearing on her arm now. Not even magic can do that; can it, Silaqui, Gelman?"

"No, it can't," Gelman whispered.

"My uncle has said to avoid the stuff. He pressed the Elf-King until His Majesty forbade the mere possession of anything formed of white-steel in our Kingdom. Whatever his reason is, it is yet another secret he will not share."

"And then there're all the other, supposedly *impossible* things she's done. It's like that ancient fancy tale, where the hero has to do six impossible things before breakfast! Last night was just another stick in the pile."

"And what do you suggest we do, Willis?" Silaqui turned to face him, arms crossed over her chest. "Burn her at the stake for being a witch?" Her inhuman, vertically-slit pupils were nearly closed in the bright morning sunshine, but her jade eyes were hard.

"Oh, please." He raised his hands to placate the Elf. "Of course not! What do you think I am, an Imperial Inquisitor?"

"What do you want to do, then, Willis?" Gelman asked.

"Simple. Just ask her if and I mean if, she can tell us something, some scrap of what's happening with her." Willis opened his hands and pointed to where Sachi was climbing over the rocks from the wreck, a cask of powder under one arm and a pair of muskets slung over her back. "She's had an incredibly hard life and now she's got some massive burden that seems to have fallen to her. We are her friends. We all need and depend on each other. Perhaps we need to remind her of that. And then ask her what we can do to help."

<h2 style="text-align:center">Port Plunder, Cazadora Isle,
Southern Lanic Ocean
November, 1478, Third Age of Imperial Reckoning</h2>

Sahla hadn't slept well the past night, even considering her circumstances. Dreams haunted her, the woman with black eyes full of stars somehow challenging her. She liked that dream much more than the others, the ones where she listened while the unknown creature hidden by the wall tore Lodvar into screaming pieces, before tossing his still-gibbering head back over the wall. Then the head would chase her down and tear at her body with fangs that dripped green poison. Those dreams woke her screaming in terror.

Draven had again given her most of his food, leaving her honor-bound to somehow choke it down. She knew the Kolbian worried about her. He made no attempt to hide the fact that he thought she was the most beautiful woman he had ever seen. But he did so in an honorable fashion, almost as if he was courting her. Did he not know that she was impure and unsuitable for any honorable man to court? More than once, he had reached out to hold her hand as she tried to sleep. He told her he would keep the monsters away. She knew he tried but they came in her dreams anyway.

Now she sat in the darkness of the hut and stared out into the day, the sun warm on the beach sand and sparkling on the blue waves of the ocean. Hot sand was nothing new to her, child of the desert that she was, but the ocean-sea! That was new. From the moment she had first seen the endless stretch of water, kissed by the winds, at the port of Al-Iskabad, the ocean fascinated her. It welcomed her and her kinship for the winds that now calmed the waves and then tore them into a raging fury.

The Jinn are creatures of Elemental Air. And I should believe that I am such as well, at least partly. But I did not expect to find such an affinity for water. I love the burning sands of my home, even if Air and Earth are opposed Elements. But the ocean seems inclined to welcome me, even more than the sands of home do. Of course, if all such things hold true, then it is the Elementals of Fire that I should fear. But now, I think I should welcome even the blackest hearted Efreet, should one offer to release me from the pirates' chains binding me.

A black shadow fell over the doorway, startling her from her near-trance. She drew back as the stocky, white-haired pirate captain stepped into the hut. He said nothing, his cold eyes surveying the hostages.

"Guten Tag, junges Fräulein." His gaze locked on her as he spoke. His voice was cold and flat.

"I don't understand," she quietly answered, avoiding his gaze.

"Good day, young Lady. After speaking with the Kapitan, I felt I should introduce myself. I am Korvettenkapitan Werner Streiss, Master and Commander of the sloop *Heartcutter*. And, at the moment, next in command here. Do you understand that, girl?" The contempt in his voice was obvious on the last word.

"I understand."

"I wonder if you truly do." Werner stepped up to her and grabbed her hair at the nape of her neck, jerking her to her feet and twisting her head to face him. Somehow, she suppressed the cry of shock and pain at his manhandling of her. "The Kapitan fed Lodvar, whom I captured, to the verdammt monsters lurking outside the wall! Just because he tried to rape you! Tried and failed! He was my prize! That, *girl,* took money out of my pocket! Do you think that made me happy, *girl?!?*"

"Why should I care, pirate?!" she spat back at him. Sahla met his cold gaze with her own fury.

"You should care, because I might decide to take my share out of you, sand-rat! And I don't mean out of any possible ransom. I mean out of your ass, personally. And when I'm done with you, I'll tie you down over a cannon breech and my crew can spend all their spare time relieving their lusts into you, any way they please." He yanked her face even closer to his. "Or perhaps, you'd like exactly that, you filthy little slut?!" He shook her. "And that verdamnt Zauberin, Wrath, the filthy Rus witch, she even wasted her healing brews to fix your face. Brews that could have been used to keep Gruesome alive! Bitch!"

He backhanded her hard enough that she saw stars and tasted blood. Sahla threw her weight backwards, dragging him off balance and getting enough slack in her chain to smash a knee into his crotch. He grunted in evident pain, but now there was an ugly light in those blue eyes. He hurled her into the center post of the hut with brutal force. She bounced away and fell to her hands and knees. His boot crashed into her ribs, flinging her to the end of her chain. She heard Draven's chains rattle as he roared in rage and charged Werner. She rolled away, seeing Werner club Draven down with a pistol butt. The pirate turned away from Draven and stalked towards her. Emerald fire flashed, stopping him before he reached her.

"ENOUGH! GOD DAMN YOU, WERNER!" Ironheart bellowed from where he stood inside the doorway. Wrath stood to his left, her hands wreathed in the emerald flames that held everyone but her and Ironheart motionless. "She's not going to be worth spit on a griddle if you beat her to a pulp and rape her half to death! You son of a bitch!"

"Kapitan, verdammt, Lodvar war mein! He was mine! And he's dead because of this little slut!"

"You fucking idiot, I know that! Did you think you'd not be compensated!?" Ironheart's cutlass flashed out of its scabbard. He stepped up to Werner and put the point of the magical blade on the man's throat. "Release him, Wrath." The green flames guttered and faded away. "Now, either you listen to me or you draw your sword and I'll kill you where you stand, ja?"

"Aye, Kapitan." Werner trembled with suppressed rage but he didn't make the slightest move to grab his own cutlass.

"I know Gruesome died, the surgeon's mate just told me. I know you and le Circque and Gruesome were thick as brothers. No one here knew about *Bloodstone* when I told Wrath to use what healing brews she had on this damn girl. She's making more but it takes time, you idiot! Now, either you draw your damn blade and try me, but I warn you, I'll gut you like a fish; or you stand the hell down and stay out of here! I'd really hate to kill you, because you're a good ship captain and those are hard to find, but don't think I won't do it. So, choose, damn you! Which one will it be?"

From where she lay, Sahla could see the burning hatred in Werner's eyes. He trembled with rage but didn't reach for his blade. He knew Ironheart was better than he was with a blade and between the white-steel breastplate and the magical sword, the Captain would cut him down in a single pass, maybe two.

"I'll stand down." He barely ground out the words.

"Good." Ironheart stepped back and cautiously lowered his sword. He never took his eyes off Werner. "Good. Now, go cool off. I want you to stay in your quarters, other than using the head. I'll have first cut of every meal brought to you by the prettiest of the serving girls. Don't break anything and don't kill her, but be as rough as you want. Let's let things calm down. Settle in for a few days. For now, leave *Heartcutter* with just an anchor watch aboard. We'll talk more later. Go on, now." With a convulsive twitch of his jaw, Werner stalked out of the hut, stiff, jerky, over-controlled movements revealing his rage.

"I don't think he's going to forgive this, Ironheart." Wrath was quiet as she moved to check Sahla. "Damn, you are a magnet for trouble, girl." She gently probed Sahla's aching side. "That hurt?"

"Yes." Sahla drew a sharp breath at the pain.

"Hmm." Wrath cocked her head. "Ribs aren't broken. Might be cracked and are definitely badly bruised. Take a deep breath, if you can." Sahla gasped with pain. "Yeah, probably just bruised. Not much to do about that; you're young, you'll heal quick."

"You, girl," Ironheart was quiet as he spoke to her; "you are a hundred and nine pounds of trouble. You might also be worth the same weight in gold, which is why you're still locked in here and not serving me in a very different manner. And I haven't decided exactly what I'm going to do with you yet. So unless you *want* to spend the rest of your likely few days with first me and then the rest of the *filthy pirates* pumping into you, you'd best not be the cause of any more trouble, understand?"

"Nem." Sahla saw the flare of anger in the witch's green eyes. "I understand. I'll try not to allow anyone else to try to rape me, *Captain*." Her voice dripped with sarcasm.

"Good." He paused a long moment. "Good enough. Finish fixing her up, Wrath, and then get busy with your healing brews. If we'd had some, we might have saved Gruesome."

"I will, Ironheart." She waited until he was gone and finished binding Sahla's ribs. "You touch my man and I'll rip the bones out of your living body. You understand me, girl?"

"Nem, yes, I do."

Chapter Eighteen

**Southwestern shore, Cazadora Isle,
Southern Lanic Ocean
November, 1478, Third Age of Imperial Reckoning**

"So, you are all worried about me? Think I'm going crazy, *kamone*? Perhaps?" Sachi was perched on the overturned longboat again. Silaqui sat closely beside her, one slender hand on her shoulder. Willis sat cross-legged on the sand in front of her, while Aylie sat behind him. Gelman stood a few feet off to the side. A second fire snapped and hissed cheerfully between her and Willis, keeping the gathering evening shadows at bay. "Well, perhaps I am. Or not."

"Sachi, you told me, right after the sea-monster fled, that you'd explain how you did what you did with that sword. You know, the bracer on your arm that used to be a white-steel sword." Willis shrugged. "So explain if you'd like to. Or not. This isn't an Imperial Star Chamber, putting you to the Question for the Inquisition. We are your friends, and we care about you."

"He speaks truly, *A'mael*." Silaqui gently squeezed her shoulder. "You are my heart-sister, my Defender, elf-friend and soul-healer. Nothing shall ever change that, Sachi."

"What does that word mean, *A'mael*?"

"It means *beloved*. And you are."

"Sachi, I'd be the first ta say that ye scare the blue willies outta meself, belike from time to time. But I's never seed ye be aught save pleasant an' courteous to any that have nae offered ye insult er injury first. An' I knows what it can be, to be lifted up from the gutter, simply because me Ma did a great favor for a Duke's Lady. I's not knowed ye as long as Milady Silaqui er Mister Fleet, but I trust ye an' I believe in ye."

"Sachi, the *Angaelici Benes Eloi* manifested directly to me and directed me to seek you out." Gelman stepped forward into the firelight. "The One God would not send one of his greatest messengers to order a healer-priest on a wild goose chase. I don't pretend to understand what's going on here, but I think I'll just have faith and follow the path the One God has laid out for me. That path leads me to be next to you."

"Huh." For long moments, she was silent. Then she abruptly stood up on the boat's hull. "Give me a moment. I need to...think about something. Then we'll talk, *ne*?"

"Good enough, Sachi." Willis stood up. "Take your time, we'll wait here."

Sachi hopped down off the boat and walked away, down to the water's edge, the waves barely lapping over her bare feet. She glanced back over her shoulder once. Her friends had settled around the fire. Over by the tents, Roland had yet another pot of stew bubbling away. She smiled to herself.

Getting tired of fish stew already, but at least there's plenty of it and it's not bad at all. Okay, now what? D.A.V.E., can you talk to me without me having a fit? We did last night.

::Affirmative. There are external resources available here that allow increased System Integration. What you described as *something ancient beyond belief* is the remnants of a Secure Access Naval Communication Web Up-Link. SANCWUL. A computer network used for maintaining priority C3I critical systems.::

"A san...what?"

::System users normally called it a Comm-Web Link, or CWL. C3I is an acronym for Command, Control, Communications and Intelligence. This is in reference to a battlefield that could span entire star systems.::

"Stop there. You're making my head hurt. But you're saying there actually is something here, something like you?"

::Affirmative. This entity lacks a complete map of Confederation ground-based systems. A relatively remote island such as this would be a primary candidate for a PDC, or Planetary Defense Center. It is possible that a PDC could still have some rudimentary systems operating at minimum functionality.::

"And this thing pushes my...whaddya call it...System Integration to the point where I don't have to be passed out in a fit to talk to you?"

::Affirmative. Current SI is seventy-nine percent. And if you get closer to the theoretical prospective PDC, SI should increase, allowing access and enhancement to more of your internal systems.::

"So we should try to find this thing then?"

"Affirmative."

"What about telling my friends about you? That I hear voices and have tiny, little, invisible machines in my body? Oh yeah, and I can mold white-steel like putty? Or any of the rest of the insanity that's become my life?"

::Given current observations of your abilities by your companions, I suggest that you give them a basic briefing. Their assistance with your mission does increase the probability of success.::

"All right. You do know that I'll have to tell them what you've told me about the truth of the Fall?"

::Understood. Some information must remain classified. I will provide guidance as required.::

"Wonderful. Well," Sachi took a long, deep breath, "might as well get on with it." She turned and headed back to the fire next to the longboat.

***

Three hours later, Sachi's friends and companions were still staring at her in various stages of disbelief. This was even though she had molded the nannieball into at least a dozen different shapes and forms. She'd put her vision into *truth detection mode* soon after she began her explanations. She hadn't told them that she'd done that. So far, they at least believed *what* she could do, if not the *why*.

Please, Spirits of my Ancestors, please do not let this turn my friends against me. Do not let them fear me! I would lay down my life for them, please, please let them see that! Please. I do not want to go back to the cold, hateful life I had with the Odas, friendless, hated and alone. I was not supposed to have friends, hostages to the rage of the Odas. And now hostages to whomever else it is who would kill me. I was not trained to care, only to whore and kill. But I have learned to care, and I find what a deadly dangerous weapon it can be. Ancestors, how much worse would it be to actually, truly love someone? My Captain, he was wise to abide by his oaths and vows; to avoid loving a storm crow such as myself. I should not love, if mere friendship is such a deadly danger.

"Well, that *does* explain a few things. This thing in your head, Dave, it's like one of the recording tube machines rich people have back home?" The stunned look left Willis' eyes some time ago, and now she could see the Kolbian thinking of how this machine, this *technology* could be used. Roland and Ismael had no interest in what they were discussing and had long since sought their bedrolls, so it was just the five of them.

"Yes, Willis, it is always recording, and it is a Digitally Aware Virtual Entity. It does not really have a name, just D.A.V.E. It is like a butler and housekeeper and healer all in one. It truly has no existence without the computing machine in my head to, well, to give it a home, I guess."

"And it heals you, as well?" Silaqui was huddled on the longboat, knees drawn up under her chin and her arms wrapped around her long legs.

"Yes." Sachi turned and started to reach out to the sorceress and then stopped when she saw the Elf draw ever so slightly away from her.

"I think," she stuttered ever so slightly, jade green eyes wide in the night, "I think that you are much like to the ancient humans. The ones from before the Fire Fall. The ones Uncle fears so much. How can you be here?"

"I don't know." Sachi looked down at the sand. "I only remember my earliest days with the peasant family who found me. I was happy with them. Then Toh took me away, and until I stole away aboard the *Intrepid*, I lived in darkness. Now, I make what amends I can, and I follow the destiny D.A.V.E. has told me of. To somehow learn the path of those ancient humans and stop whatever it is that is coming to destroy the entire world."

"Uncle says it was the humans that brought the Fire Fall to the world."

"Perhaps they did. I don't know. I was truly a child when I was found, perhaps as young as two summers. I think it obvious that I did not walk the world before the Fire Fall. Somehow, I am as much a creation of this Fallen world as anyone here."

"I believe we should let this rest for the remainder of the night." Gelman rose from where he had been kneeling, sitting on his heels. "I, for one, believe you, Sachi. I believe you because the One God sent me here and I have faith in His Will for me. But the moon creeps past midnight and there is much to do tomorrow if we wish to continue surviving. I should say we might seek out our beds, such as they are, and see what dreams might come to provide us enlightenment."

"I'll take the watch. Please go and seek your slumbers." Sachi gave Silaqui a last, sorrowful look and then faded silently away into the night.

"Aye, 'tis a good word ye have, Pere Gelman. I's sure the morrow will come with its own challenges." Aylie uncurled from where she had sat and headed off for her tent, following Gelman.

"Aylie?" Silaqui called.

"Aye, Milady?" She stopped and turned to face the Elf.

"Do you believe her?"

"I'd not say as I unnerstand all the tales she's telling. But believe her?" The slight, brown-haired woman nodded her head. "Aye. Aye, that I do. Iffn she afrights ye, Milady, mayhaps ye should put a thought to all ye've told us she's done for ye. I'd think that yon black-haired beauty is lonely and sore troubled. But I've nae doubt, naught in the least, that she'd nay hesitate a heartbeat to put herself betwixt ye and any man, beast or monster that might've the poor judgment to be threatening ye. And I thinks she'd do the same for any innocent or companion such as may be threatened. What more can ye ask of any being, mortal, immortal or spirit? That answer yer question?"

"Yes, Aylie, it does. Thank you."

"Well then. Good night, Milady."

"Good night, Aylie." Silaqui watched her follow Gelman to the tents, disappearing into her own.

"Well, that was a comprehensive answer, I'd say." Willis stepped up and offered her a hand down off the longboat. "Will you be all right?"

"I think so, Willis."

"You're a little shaky; hang on to me a bit and I'll walk you to your tent."

"No, Willis. Not to my tent." Silaqui's eyes shone in the dim firelight and her ears were plastered against her head. "That's also *her* tent. No, tonight, I would stay with you. Just to hold me, naught else. Not now, not tonight."

"Ah, whoa now, what?!" Willis stopped and moved around in front of her. "Look, I know the two of you aren't lovers. It's not like there's a lot of privacy here, or aboard ship, any ship. But she is your friend, and staying with me, even if only to sleep...well, Sachi doesn't deserve that. You know how bad that will hurt her, don't you?"

"Yes, but I can't, Willis, I just can't. Knowing those *things* are swarming inside her, please, no, not yet, I can't." Silaqui was slightly taller than Willis but lacked his broad shoulders and hard muscled frame. She wrapped her arms around him, buried her face in his neck and wept. She wept for a Heart-Sister that she loved, but that now she was terrified of being near.

"Ah, shit," Willis' sigh was silent, just a heave of his chest, "I never could resist it when a woman turns on the water-works. It's no damn fair." He sighed again. "All right, come on, let's get some rest."

Standing away, hidden in the darkness, Sachi crouched down watching the last two, Willis and Silaqui, slip into Willis' tent. Shortly the lantern inside the tent went dark and she was alone in the darkness. She wasn't really aware that her own tears were falling until she realized the sleeve of her shirt was soaked with them.

***

The moon was a pale orb in the west, sinking toward the horizon. Sachi had moved from spot to spot during the night. She had not woken anyone else to stand watch with her. She had heard Silaqui sobbing at one point and Willis comforting her as a friend should. She was ravenous, despite having wolfed down a bowl of cold fish stew an hour or so ago. And she had no reason to imagine that the things that came out of the jungle even existed. In fact, it was D.A.V.E. that warned her.

::Warning! Possible infiltrators detected via acoustic disruption! Thermal scan is negative. Massive air displacement detected. Intrusion locus indicates point of origin in jungle edge closest to camp. Warning!::

"What the...?" She snapped to her feet on top of the longboat. Sitting on top of the boat gave her the best view of the entire camp and of the mysterious darkness under the jungle trees. "Where?"

::Targeting caret on disturbance. Disturbance is moving quickly toward camp. Target type unknown.::

"Shit!" Sachi launched herself off the longboat. She could barely see something moving, a scuttling, hump-backed shape. She switched *modes*, from thermal to image enhancement as she sprinted towards the camp. There seemed to be two of the things, whatever they were, and one of them crashed into the empty tent she shared with Silaqui. A pair of diamond shaped red dots danced in her vision, trying to follow the things, whatever they were. Then a third diamond materialized in her sight. There were three of t hem.

"WAKE UP!" she screamed as her internal systems interfaced with the bracer-shaped nannieball, the billions of microscopic robots flowing rapidly from impenetrable armor to a mono-molecular edged nodachi. "Something came out of the jungle!"

One of the things crashed into Ismael and Roland's tent. Ismael shrieked in terror as the thing burrowed under the edge of the sailcloth side of the tent. One crashed through her and Silaqui's empty tent and slammed into Willis' tent. She lost sight of the third one.

Willis had snapped awake when Sachi screamed, snatching a pistol from beside his bedroll. Silaqui scrambled out from under his arm, flinging a hand up and illuminating the inside of the tent with scarlet light. Then something hit the side of the tent and tore the sailcloth wall in half and a nightmare thrust its head into the tent. Eight hideous eyes reflected Silaqui's carmine light. Foot long fangs dripped yellowish poison and a horrific set of mandibles spasmed as the obscene spider, the size of a yearling calf, lunged at Silaqui. Her ears rang as Willis blasted six shots into it as fast as he could pull the trigger. Ichor sprayed from the wounds. For a second, it stopped, shuddering from the wounds. Then a clawed leg as long as Silaqui was tall, lashed out and knocked Willis into a tangle with the far side of the tent.

"*Naara, uuvanimo!*" she shouted, crimson flames blasting from her hand into the monster's face. The thing hunched back for an instant and then it lunged forward, the fangs rising and falling toward her stomach. She jerked aside and the fangs plunged into the ground sheet. Yellow poison bubbled up. A leg pounded down on her, trapping her in place and the fangs rose to strike again. She grabbed the leg pinning her, her magic incinerating it. The spider hesitated, and then the fangs slashed down.

"*Shine, akuma!*" Sachi smashed into the thing, white-steel blade flashing, as if she had appeared from nowhere. The spider buried its fangs into her shoulder and her nodachi sank up to the hilt into its head and bloated body. Silaqui watched in amazement as the Nisei somehow spun under the head, ripping the fangs out of her shoulder. The white blade cored the monster's body, shredding its innards and slicing a three-foot-long gash in its back when she jerked the blade free. The blade blurred again and the grotesque head flew off into the darkness. The thing's pulped insides splattered over both of them. Sachi turned and looked at Silaqui, their eyes locking on each other.

"It bit you…"

"Are you okay, Silaqui?"

"Yes." Silaqui grabbed Sachi's arm. "You're hurt."

"There are three of them." Sachi leapt over the spasming body of the slain monster, racing towards the screams coming from the sailors' tent. "I'll be fine," she called over her shoulder.

"God's Will!" Gelman shouted as he crushed the second spider's head with his heavy mace. It shuddered, legs twitching as it collapsed. Willis kicked his way out of the tangle of his tent and grabbed his other pistol, bolting after Sachi. Gelman's mace blasted down again, a silvery aura glowing around it, and it tore the spider's head completely off.

Willis and Sachi reached the third spider at the same time. He shoved his pistol against the head and emptied all six shots into it in a blur. Sachi's sword flashed down and cut the thing cleanly in half, right in front of the bloated abdomen. Spider ichor sprayed across both of them. She pulled the sword out, leaning on it as she rested its point on the sand.

"Is that all of them?" Willis wiped the ichor off his face and looked at Sachi.

"Hai." She reached up and jerked the first spider's fang out of her shoulder. "Only three."

"Sachi, can that thing, D.A.V.E., can it heal you of poison?"

"Yes, it's done so before," Her eyes lost focus as she looked at him, "but I don't feel so good." The sword fell away and she collapsed. Silaqui reached her first, turning her over and squeezing yellow poison out of the wound.

"No, no, don't you die on me, no, please, *Ainaera*, my Goddess, please, no, I can't lose my *A'mael,* my Heart-Sister, not like this! I'm sorry, I'm so sorry." Silaqui grabbed her into a tight embrace. "No, no, my Sachi, live, stay with us. Please!?"

"Silaqui?"

"Yes, *A'mael?*"

"I have to breathe. You're squishing me."

"Get out of the way, both of you! We need to get Roland and Ismael out of there!" Willis shoved both females off to the side. "Gelman! Aylie! Get over here and lend a hand!" He pulled on the tent, as Roland's cries for help were muffled under the tent fabric. Silaqui drew Sachi further away from the wreckage. Roland crawled out from under the tent and stifled a scream when he saw the butchered corpse of the huge spider. Gelman grabbed him and pulled him to his feet before turning him over to Aylie.

Willis and the priest pulled the sailcloth and found Ismael snarled up in his bedroll. His loose shirt was torn and two large puncture wounds in his chest slowly seeped red blood and yellow poison. His eyes bulged out and his tongue was swollen and protruding. Gelman knelt and checked for a pulse before shaking his head. He reached down and closed Ismael's eyes.

"I can heal the sick and hurt." They heard the weariness in his voice. "I'm not a saint. I haven't been directly blessed by the One. I can't bring back the dead."

"Can you help Sachi, Gelman?" Silaqui had helped Sachi to the ground, pulling her shirt off her shoulder to reveal the bloody puncture wounds in her shoulder. "The spider bit her."

::Toxin analysis completed.:: D.A.V.E. whispered in her mind. ::The toxin is a paralytic neurotoxin, commonly used by arachnoids to paralyze their prey before wrapping in silk and injecting a second, caustic poison intended to break down chemical and molecular bonds, reducing the victim to a semi-liquid state, allowing efficient ingestion and digestion by the arachnid. While dangerous, this toxin is not inherently fatal. Nanites are reconfiguring for toxin scrubbing. Expect full recovery in twenty-three minutes, plus or minus four minutes.::

"So it's not going to kill me, D.A.V.E., eh?" Sachi answered sub-vocally. "Then what killed Ismael?"

::Initial diagnosis indicates one of the fangs penetrated the thoracic cavity and the pericardium before severing the ascending aorta between the left ventricle and the aortic arch. Internal exsanguination would have been extremely rapid, with loss of consciousness and death following in rapid order. The poison paralyzing the cardiac muscle itself would simply accelerate the process.::

"Uh, say what?"

::The fang stabbed him through the heart. He died almost instantly.::

"Oh." She shook her head and spoke up to catch Gelman's attention. "Gelman, the fang pierced his heart. He was dead before you could have done anything. And don't worry about me, I'll be fine."

"Sachi, how do you know that?" the priest asked. He shook his head when she pointed a forefinger at her temple. "Ah. Forget I asked."

"So, now what do we do?" Fleet asked as he drew a piece of sailcloth over Ismael's body.

"I'm not staying on this beach." Sachi gently disentangled herself from Silaqui and knelt beside Ismael's body, clapping her hands three times to call the Ancestor Spirits' attention to the young man. She'd been taught that doing so helped the deceased find their way into the afterlife. Bowing her head for a moment, she silently prayed for the young man, asking his forgiveness for her failure.

"Where are you going, then?" Fleet asked.

"Well," she stood up and brushed the sand off her knees, "D.A.V.E. tells me that somewhere on this coast or island or whatever it is, there's something left from the Fall, from what he calls the *Confederation*, that is still working. I can kind of feel it, a sense of something *open*, I guess. I'm going to go see what it is. Try and learn where we are. We don't know if this is the coast of Khakal or some island. Do we, Willis?"

"Most likely an island." He shrugged, "We're too far west to be on the Khakal coast. Least that's what *le Bonaventure's* chart indicates. And the charts are a mess, torn and waterlogged. But I doubt Captain de Foix was able to get a good fix on his position, not being able to see the sky during the storm. And I don't have a chronometer, a sextant or even a backstaff to get a star sighting with, so realize that I'm guessing about where we are."

"Well, unless you want to stay here on the beach until something dangerous enough *to* eat you comes along, I'd suggest getting packed and being ready to travel at first light. Start figuring out if there's a way out of this mess." Sachi picked a shovel out of the wreckage of the camp and walked over to the other graves. "I'll dig Ismael's grave."

Port Plunder, Cazadora Isle,
Southern Lanic Ocean
November, 1478, Third Age of Imperial Reckoning

"I see the infidel Kolbian navy has not yet hung you from a yardarm, dog of an unbeliever." Captain Zahir-al-Din leapt lightly to the sand from *Saker's* jibboom, keeping his knee-high cavalryman's boots dry.

"One of these days, you're gonna push that shit one step too far and we'll see who hangs from the yardarm, you leprous, bastard son of a drunken whore." Ironheart growled at the commander of one of his two post boats. *Saker* was a light, extremely fast single masted cutter, armed with only four six-pounder guns. As such, she was much less likely to draw the attention of the KRN. And she was quite able to outrun them if she did.

"I do not have leprosy." Zahir sniffed in feigned insult. "You wish my news or not, Captain?"

"Come to my quarters. Tell me what we've got before you get drunk."

"I am a faithful follower of Chalta and His Prophet. I do not drink alcohol."

"No, you don't. You lay under the keg with the spout tied open and let it pour down your neck. But I guess that doesn't count."

"Very observant, Captain Ironheart."

"Is your news good?"

"No, not particularly. And some things are worse than others." Zahir glanced at the hostages' hut. "So, how does the Houri?"

"Well, she's trouble with a capital T." Ironheart shook his head. "That Heimdägarran Sea Master, Lodvar, tried to rape her a couple nights ago. Had to stake him out and one of the bigger ones got him."

"Ouch."

"Yeah. Then Werner gets back and...well, end result of some *more* bad news, *he* decided to either kill her, or rape her and then kill her, not sure which, so *Heartcutter* is anchored with only an anchor watch aboard. And Werner, damn his stiff-necked Deuschen pride, is under light, very light, confinement to quarters."

"Sounds like you've been, as the Han say, *living in interesting times.*"

"Oh, Quan take it, I certainly have."

***

I wonder, what can be bad news to that pirate. And this new one, he speaks and dresses as one of the Folk of the Sand might. But, Darsälaamic or not, I'll not chance casting my lot with him. Not until I have a great deal more in assurances than a common origin.

As was her practice, Sahla sat well back from the doorway, watching the Ironheart and the black-haired man walk to Ironheart's large cabin. She overheard most of the conversation as the pair left the beach. She turned back to the new vessel that was drawn up on the beach. The crew was working on securing it, furling sails and hammering anchor lines into the ground further up the beach.

The crew is small, only five or six men. If we could escape, the four of us might be able to manage such a craft. If any of us knew the least about sailing. Other than Zedekiah, none of us has the slightest idea of how to sail a boat. The new one said his news is not good. Is that good or bad for us?

***

"Well, so, what's the word?" Ironheart poured mugs of ale for himself and Zahir.

"Well, the worst, first." He took a long pull on the mug and wiped his lips. "The husband-to-be, or rather, his father, will not pay any ransom. To them, the Houri is now defiled, as far as honorable marriage is concerned. I'd wager the little shit'd be happy enough to add her to the concubines in his seraglio."

"Uh, despite the fact that we *swore* her duenna still guarded her purity?"

"Yes." Zahir stared into his mug for a moment. "I think we should consider the Sheikh Mustafa al-Mahdi Baddour as another possible contact or ally once his father the Rajh steps over into Chalta's Paradise. I think that bastard has a blacker heart than anyone who ever called their own self a pirate."

"What of her Father, Sheikh Hasim?"

"Huh, well, Abdul-Ghaffanse is in the deep desert. Haven't heard from him yet, probably won't for a couple more months." He drained his mug. "I'd expect the same kind of answer. Sandfolk from the deep desert tend to be even more rigid. I should know, it's the kind of place I fled years ago, when I was young and stupid."

"So the only apparently profitable option left now is selling the girl?"

"Yes." Zahir shrugged. "I'd not take her to Du-Khamps-des-SouSee. Lord Komarra would want too much of a cut, and, frankly, for someone like her, Luctini would be better for us."

"Vicomtesse Erszbet would get a bigger cut than Komarra."

"True, but the pie would be much bigger."

"What about the political aspect? Port Master Quesnel, Populus Fréminou and Sieur Vicente Palmaroli would all want her. And any of those three would have the ability to simply take her, whether from us or from the Vicomtesse."

"Normally, yes, but they've bigger fish to fry right now."

"Oh? What kind of fish?"

"The Kolbian Republican Navy."

"Are they insane? The empire has, what, two dozen or so ships-of-the-line, maybe three score small frigates? A couple, maybe three hundred of those clumsy-ass galleasses? The KRN has a hundred ships-of-the-line. Seventy frigates, a quarter of them big forty-fours. No idea how many sloops-of-war and armed brigantines. There's a reason I'm in the southern Lanic."

"Oh, I agree, but the Imperial Chancellor, Pi-Imperator Havis Peralta de Palmaroli, the sheep-humping pederast, has his toga all in a twist because of that battle last year, between the Kolbian frigate *Stellar* and three galleasses. The one that had his cousin, Capitan Senior Commodore Monsieur Havier Vies Ruiz-Palmaroli, using hemlock for mouthwash? The Imperial Navy is activating all those reserve galleys they've had laid up for a hundred and fifty years. You can imagine the graft involved in that and all three of those pig-fucking infidel bastards are up to their necks in it."

"They're going to declare war with *Kolbia* over that!? Over that idiot Ruiz-Palmaroli?" Ironheart's eyebrows climbed up his forehead.

"It appears so. And it gets better. Or worse for us, I think? Not even the Imperial navy, corrupt as they are, will give a known pirate a pass." Zahir poured himself another mug of ale. "Our very good friend, Lord Havre Calchas, the Imperial Admiral of the South Sea, is at sea with his entire fleet. Ten sixth-rate ships-of-the-line, a dozen or so of their smallish frigates, perhaps fifty of their big galleasses, and an unknown number of galleys. I expect most of the latter to break up and sink within a fortnight of being at sea in the Lanic."

"Quan take it, that's a lot of ships!" Ironheart leaned back in his chair, steepling his fingers in front of his face. "I have a deal with Calchas, but with that many witnesses, I doubt even he'd look the other way. Might not come looking for me, but..."

"Oh, that's not the best part."

"Oh shit, don't tell me, the KRN—"

"Is also at sea in force. Something they're calling Task Force Southron."

"I don't like the sound of that."

"Then you'll like this even less. It consists of thirty-some-odd ships. Flagship is a first rate, KRN *Fearless*, hundred and ten guns. Two second rates, eighty or ninety guns each. Then an even dozen frigates, including *Guardian* and three other forty-fours. Four or six, my sources didn't agree, sloops-of-war, twenty-some guns each, and a baker's dozen of their extremely weatherly schooners. Doesn't that sound like fun?"

"Did we miss a declaration of war?"

"No, the KRN has posted that their intent with this force is to put an absolute stop to piracy and the slave trade in the Lanic, north, mid and south. So I'd suggest keeping as low a profile as possible."

"No doubt." Ironheart sat up, rubbing his face with both hands. "All right, here's the plan. I want you sailing for Luctini on the tide tomorrow by dawn at the latest. Contact the Vicomtesse; tell her we're bringing in the Houri, probably no less than a month behind you, maybe less. Have her set up the ransom payments for that Kolbian baseball player, the Contessa du Lisenis—"

"Who's she?"

"The Duke of Ostreich's fiancée. She was on the same ship as the Houri."

"Virgin?"

"Yes, or so Wrath tells me. Wrath also says the Duke will pay. And for that Ionan, Abrhaim. I'll weigh anchor with *Deathdealer* within the next fortnight and we'll move temporarily to Luctini. *Deathdealer* and *Heartcutter* are good ships, but both of them together can't stand up to a forty-four, much less a first- or second-rate line-of-battle ship."

"And rumor says the Kolbians are working on something new."

"What now?"

"Something they're calling shells. Not solid shot. They hit a target and somehow explode."

"Magic?"

"From a Kolbian? Really?" Zahir shook his head. "No, it's something else, no one knows what. And there's a whisper of rumor that they're experimenting with the mechanical engines of that crazed inventor, Fulmark. Somehow using those engines to drive a ship without sails, and against the wind."

"Quan take them. If they can do that..."

"Perhaps time to retire as pirates? I understand a highwayman in the Empire can do well for himself."

"Perhaps. But in the meanwhile, we may have a ringside seat to one of the greatest naval battles ever."

"Captain Ironheart, with all due respect, I'll pass on that honor. I'd much rather be safe ashore while my favorite concubine fellates me."

"Where's your sense of adventure, Zahir?"

Chapter Nineteen

**Inland, Southern Cazadora Isle,
Southern Lanic Ocean
November, 1478, Third Age of Imperial Reckoning**

"Pah-too!" Willis spat a gob of muck out of his mouth. He'd tripped over a root and gotten himself a mouthful of leaf-mold, loam and God only knows what else. And he'd probably swallowed at least one tiny spider, as well. "Yuck. Are you sure this is a good idea, Sachi?"

"Would you rather spend the rest of your life waiting for maybe a ship to sail by the beach?" She bent down and lifted him off the jungle floor. "I think there's a path over that way, about ten or fifteen yards or so." She flicked her sword and cut a spider the size of a pigeon in half. "These damn things are everywhere. What the hell do they eat?"

"Each other?" Silaqui was next behind Willis. Three spiders, each as big as a baseball, had come out of hiding spots and were fighting over the bisected arachnid. She watched the struggle with horrified fascination for a moment before flicking her hand and burning them all into ashes. "Ugh. Where do they come from?"

"You might not want the answer to that question, Silaqui." Sachi started cutting a path through the jungle. To her left, a lighter, greener light suggested either a small clearing or perhaps a game trail.

"Why'd ye say that, Sachi?" Aylie piped up from her spot behind Gelman. The young thief brought up the rear, with Roland ahead of Gelman and behind Silaqui.

"Because D.A.V.E. tells me that all the spiders we've seen so far are males. It also says that due to something called *sexual dimorphism* the females will be both fewer in number and much larger."

"How much larger?" Silaqui flicked a spider the size of her fist away with a fetching cantrip. It splattered against a tree away from the trail Sachi was cutting.

"Lots larger. Let's just leave it at that for now." Sachi cut through the last of the vegetation and looked out into a good-sized clearing. She could see well defined trails leading off into the jungle. "Ah-ha. A clearing, as I hoped. Shit. And a problem. Willis, give me the shotgun." She checked its loads in both barrels. "Be ready to give me a hand, but I think I've got this."

She stepped out into the clearing and both barrels of the cut down shotgun roared. Willis followed her, a pistol in each hand. Silaqui was next, entering the clearing just in time to see an enormous spider curl up and fall out of a web stretched between the trees. Sachi dropped the smoking gun and sprinted to where the spider fell. Before the mortally wounded creature could hit the ground, the white-steel nodachi flashed, carving the thing into dripping pieces. She snapped the sword clean before it flowed back into a bracer on her arm.

"Got it. It's clear now." She spat and wiped ichor off her shoulder. "Ugh."

"Was that the female?" Silaqui peered around the clearing as she stepped into the sunlight.

"Not quite. Just a bigger male."

"*Ainaera* bless!" Silaqui shuddered. She'd never particularly hated or liked spiders. She hadn't really ever thought about them, other than to kill them when they intruded into her home or workshop. But these things! The latest one Sachi had killed might be bigger than the three on the beach.

"Well, Sachi, is your...uh, friend telling you which way to go?" Gelman had his enchanted mace on a sturdy thong around his wrist. There was a meaty *crunch* as his heavy workman's boot came down on another spider. "Hopefully somewhere there are fewer of these things?" All eight legs stuck out from under his boot.

"I don't know about fewer, but the ridge of hills rises to the northeast of us. The jungle doesn't seem to be as thick, and I actually think there are only thin woods at the top of the hills." Sachi scanned the jungle carefully. "I really don't want to run into a *Jorogumo* here. Damnable shape shifters."

"What be a *jorogu*-whatever?" Aylie asked as she stepped on an ordinary sized spider.

"A spider daemon." Willis answered. "Nisei legends say that ancient spiders gain magical powers and can change form to appear human. It's just a legend."

"Kolbians." Sachi snorted. "They refuse to believe there's more to the world than gears and machines, Aylie. *Jorogumo* are real enough. I know those who deal with such things. No one gives good gold to 'just a legend.' Sorry, Willis but it's the truth."

"Cor! What does they look like, then? Have ye ever seen one?"

"They look like beautiful young women, sometimes with an infant. When they're using their human form, that is." Sachi set her hands on her hips and looked up the trail.

"Look at this." Gelman pointed to a large, flat tan stone, partly covered by the grass of the clearing. "It's been marked up by someone." He cleared it off with his boot. The stone was partly covered with jagged black lines and circles large and small. Some of the circles had eight lines attached to them; others interlinked each other with many lines connecting.

"Aylie," Sachi called her to the stone, "do these look like those tatty-too marks all over the little guys' skin?"

"Aye, that they do. And look here," she pointed to the orientation of the stone, "the biggest circles, they be much fewer and on this side o' the stone. They's more on that side, more circles and more lines. Mayhaps this be a road marker of some type made by the little ones? Showing where the monsters be by the lines and where the safe places are the circles without the lines?"

"Beats me," Willis scratched his head, "but as good a guess as any. The biggest trail runs that ways as well, up to the hills, where there are fewer of the circles, and down towards the more westerly tip of the land. I vote for the hills."

"Less jungle, fewer things for the spiders to feed on, fewer spiders." Silaqui nodded enthusiastically. "That gets my vote. Gelman, Sachi, Roland?"

"Makes sense to me." Gelman agreed and Roland simply nodded his head and pointed uphill. Sachi looked at the stone for a long, long minute, before nodding her head and turning to lead off up the trail.

***

"Well, so far, so good." Silaqui stretched her back as they reached the top of the tallest hill the group had climbed yet. "Haven't seen any more of those big monster spiders, bless Ainaera!"

"You should know better than to say things like that," Willis grumbled as he set his pack down. "At least we finally can guess we're not on the Khakal coast or the Tylteanait shore, either one. This has got to be one of those hundreds of little islands in the Southern Passage."

"How's do ye knowed that, Willis?" Aylie was quick to shrug out of her own burden.

"Both of those continents rise to large mountain chains away from their coasts. From here, we'd have at least a hint of higher lands either east or west, depending on which continent. But here, beyond the near hills, there's nothing to see. Beyond the hills is more ocean, I'll bet my next promotion on it."

Silaqui noticed that Sachi had frozen, looking down into the huge bay at the center of the island. At its widest, the shorelines were probably twenty or twenty-five miles apart. Cool, clear blue water filled the bay, shading away to a deeper, darker blue-green where the entrance to the bay met the open ocean. Even Silaqui could see that the sweep of the island, the relatively narrow, five mile or so wide entrance and the calm waters within would make this an ideal anchorage. But the waters were empty of ships.

"What are you staring at, Sachi?" When her friend didn't answer, she stepped closer and then saw the lights dancing and glittering in her eyes. "Sachi?!"

In answer the Nisei woman simply raised her arm and pointed at the western side of the bay.

"Don't you see it?"

"See what?" She glanced over her shoulder at the bay, not seeing anything. Not only were Sachi's eyes glittering, but the normally unnoticed cube on its choker-like necklace flickered and strobed in coruscating light. "Oh no, not now! Willis! Gelman! Come here!"

"What's wrong?" Willis got there first.

"Oh crap, not again!" Gelman stopped just out of arm's reach. Aylie and Roland followed.

"I'm okay." Sachi muttered. "Don't any of you see it? Look, there and there, on the western shore of the bay. See the straight lines, the even curve there? Those perfectly straight things like rods or flagpoles, the ones in the water the waves wash over. Don't you see it?"

"What the hell?" Willis saw the straight, rigid rods jutting down into the water of the bay first. Then he saw the smooth even curves and the impossibly straight lines. It wasn't until then that he realized the sheer scale of what he saw. He thought that half of the thing was under water, stretching away from the beach. "That's impossi...that can't be right. Nothing is that big."

"You see it, Willis?" There was a distant, distracted note to Sachi's voice.

"Yes, I see it. But what is it? What am I seeing?"

"It's a ship, Willis." She turned to them, the glitter in her eyes muted but still there. "It's a wrecked starship from before the Fall itself. And there are parts of it still working."

***

Sachi had been ready to crash downhill in a straight line to the wreck. Between them, Silaqui and Willis kept her on the trail. They pointed out to her a couple of cliff-like drops in a direct path to the bay's shore. And when asked, Sachi admitted that even with D.A.V.E.'s help, she still couldn't fly.

The trail led back down the hill, into thicker jungle. Silaqui relaxed a bit when they realized there didn't seem to be as many spiders down here. What ones they did see were much closer to normal-sized ones, nothing really bigger than a baseball.

"Well, not as many spiders, or at least no big ones." Silaqui peered about. "At least none I can see."

"Aye, true e'nuff." Aylie agreed. "But what I's seeing uf the webs here, they be bigger. Much bigger." She pointed out web strands as big as the standing rigging of a big galleon. "Well, nay so much as bigger, but thicker lines. That be e'nuff to give me a fine set o' the shivers."

"I think these are much older, Aylie." Gelman pointed out one. "Look there. The branch of the tree has grown around that one. The size makes them sturdy, but I think what spun these strands is long gone."

The trail twisted around as it dropped into a deep hollow between two tall hills. The trees were tall and thick, blocking the sun from doing any more than turning the bottom of the hollow into a gloomy, web-shrouded pit. And at the bottom of the trail, they found another clearing.

"*Ancestors!*" Sachi jumped back against Willis, bringing up the shotgun. She froze for a long moment, and then let out a long, shuddering breath.

"What's wrong, Sachi?" Silaqui couldn't really see into the clearing.

"I thought we'd found the mother of all spiders for a second." She chuckled as she heard the Elf suck in a lungful of air. "Relax. It's some kind of idol, I think. A really huge idol. Maybe the little people worship it, hoping the spiders will leave them alone?"

Cautiously the castaways moved into the clearing. The majority of it was hard packed earth. The trees surrounding it were heavily tangled with webs in long, thick strands. There were globs and clumps of webs stuck into most of the branches' forks, scores, maybe hundreds of them. A narrow trail led out of the clearing, toward the bay. Some of the biggest clumps were piled next to it.

Against the rocky edge of the clearing, partly surrounded by an old rock fall, was an extremely lifelike spider idol. Silaqui trembled slightly at the sight of the massive thing, looming over the clearing. It was terrifyingly realistic. In front of it were piles and stacks of the web clumps, some of them quite large.

"Cor, lookee that!" Aylie stepped up beside her and pointed. "I dunno what the stature be made of, but lookit the eyes! Rubies, big as my fist." Slyly she glanced sideways at the Elf. "Ye've a fondness for all things scarlet and crimson, Milady. Would it settle ye a wee bit, say ye had one er two...er four of yonder stones?"

"I had not noticed the rubies." Silaqui shook her head. "'Tis an idol carved, no more. And the stones are lovely." She smiled at Aylie. "If you wish to retrieve them, I'll aid you." A whispered cantrip wrapped crimson magic around Aylie's hands and feet. "This will aid you in climbing. Touch at all times, two of your limbs to the vertical surface, and you cannot fall. Make haste, 'tis but a minor cantrip and the effects quickly pass away."

Aylie scampered up a foreleg twice as long or more than she was tall before walking onto a head so broad, she could not touch the opposite sides no matter how she stretched. She drew a small, narrow-bladed knife and quickly had the first six stones out. It was the seventh that caused the problem.

Gotta get the blade under the edge witout scratching er chipping it. What is this stuff? Tis nay stone or wood. Some kinda pottery?

Come outta there, a-ha, gotcha! Aw, shit, the skin's crackin' an' splittin'...oh, no!

"Crap!" Aylie yelled as the head collapsed inward, disintegrating into powder and fragments. With a muffled shriek, she vanished into the hollow head of the idol. The noise attracted everyone's attention. Gelman was the first to reach her.

"Aylie, are you hurt?" He stepped onto one of the mandibles and squawked when it broke off under his weight and dumped him on his backside.

"I be fine. Dark in here. And I'm on top of a pile of...something. Little round things as be somewhat crunchy. There's a lot of long things, some on the pointy side. But, be nice like, iffn some'un could get me outta here!"

"A moment, Aylie." Gelman settled both hands on his mace. "If the rest of this is as fragile as it now seems, I should be able to break open the side and get you out."

"D.A.V.E., you have any idea what this thing is made of?" Sachi subvocalized as Gelman's first swing sent a pattern of fractures radiating across the side of the idol's head.

::It is a biological exoskeleton composed of calcium carbonate enhanced chitin. The specimen in question is an extremely large unclassified arachnid somewhat vaguely similar in configuration to the terrestrial species, *theraphosa blondi*, or the Goliath birdeater native to the Old Earth continent of South America. Given the condition of the remains and the observed local climatological conditions, this specimen has been deceased for approximately eighteen hundred standard years, plus or minus twenty-eight years. Speculation: It is probable that this is a female example of the local species.::

"Are you telling me this thing was ALIVE!?" She managed to keep the last part from coming out in a howling scream.

::Correct.::

Gelman's mace connected again and then the third blow shattered the side of the head of the 'idol.' Aylie slid out through the opening in a wave of dust, jumbled bones and innumerable small skulls. Much later, Willis remarked that the brown girl's scream had probably been heard back in Vlymouth Port town.

But she only screamed the once. Gelman pulled her to her feet and gave her a quick, solid hug to reassure her that she was okay. After brushing the dirt and dust off, Aylie carefully picked up the last two rubies. She gave those two and two out of her pouch, to Silaqui.

"Deal's a deal."

"So it is." Silaqui closely examined the rubies. "These are very fine. Thank you, Aylie."

"Well, I'll not say as it was me pleasure, now, but I'd say I be well rewarded for me time and risk. What say ye, Sachi?"

"May I?" Sachi carefully examined the rubies, a distant look in her eyes. "You know, there's something interesting about these rubies."

"Aye?"

"Yes, someone set them in place after the spider died, long ago."

"Wait a minute, what about the *spider dying?*" Silaqui spun to face the 'idol.' "Are you telling me that that thing was...ALIVE?"

"Once. Centuries ago." She gave Silaqui an evil grin. "D.A.V.E. tells me that these spiders might live in colonies, with no more than two or three large females laying eggs and the much more numerous males competing to mate with her. Despite the fact that mating with the female usually leads to the male's death when she eats him."

"Oh," Silaqui whispered, "you're saying there are more of them this big!?"

"Probably. But no more than two or three, most likely only one."

"Gaah." The Elf's ears were folded tightly against her head and her eyes were green as jade against the sudden pallor of her skin. "Can we get out of here? Now? I've no idea if my magic could stop such a monster."

"Ah, a moment." Willis waved them over to a particularly large lump of webbing. "I saw this one move, well; twitch, sorta, when Aylie screamed. I think there might be someone alive in here."

"Or something." Silaqui brought both hands up defensively, both wrapped in crimson flames. "Are you saying you want to let whatever it is out?"

"It's roughly the size of a big man. I think we can handle anything else." Willis started to saw at the webbing with his belt knife until Sachi gently pushed him aside. She molded the bracer into a long, thin blade and quickly cut away the webbing.

The tall man inside the web was barely coherent, his pale blue eyes staring madly at them. They helped him out of the sticky mess and Gelman used his abilities as a healer to calm the man and heal his many minor injuries. He told them his name was Lodvar Gjerde, originally from Heimdägarr. Currently he acted as merchant factor for a Montagaran trading consortium and his ship had been taken by pirates, who had left him here as a sacrifice to the monsters.

Before he finished his story, the group was making their way down the trail to the bay. Sachi led the way, with Willis and Silaqui close behind her, while Aylie and Gelman assisted the still shaky Lodvar. Roland clanked along with his few remaining pots and skillets between them.

"I don't trust him." Sachi bluntly stated while slashing away vines, lianas and the occasional head-sized spider in its web.

"Why?" Silaqui flicked a crimson-haloed finger and carbonized a fleeing arachnid before it reached its burrow. Willis hid a smile and shook his head. The Elf was definitely developing a complex about the spiders. He kept an eye on the following group.

"He's not exactly lying, but he's not telling the truth, either. At least, not all of it." She bisected a particularly large, black spider, wiping away the bluish ichor that splattered on her. "Yuck. Damn things. Why did the pirates *leave* him here as a sacrifice? Are there some kinds of sea-spiders the pirates are trying to placate by sacrificing him? If there are, why is he up here in the hills?"

"Not telling the truth, huh? Or at least, not telling everything?" Willis commented. "Maybe like a certain Nisei girl I know."

"Don't go there, Willis. It's best for you to not know my entire story." Her shoulders slumped for a moment before she shook her head. "I have my reasons. And if you actually do know as much as you say you do of my homeland, then you should at least be able to guess those reasons."

"Granted. But what about Lodvar?"

"His story doesn't make sense. Why would pirates offer him as a sacrifice and then just sail away?"

"She has a point, Willis," Silaqui agreed. "And that mortal is shifty-eyed. I don't care if he claims to be a merchant factor or not. When I was young, his people were a scourge, coming in their monster-headed long boats with fire and axe. They raided and killed, raped and ravaged, stole everything loose and burned everything else. I do not trust him either."

"Fine." Willis shook his head as he kicked a particularly aggressive spider into a tree. It crunched and slid down the trunk, leaving a bluish trail of slime and spider guts. "So, do we leave him here? I can think of worse fates, but not many."

"I should think only to watch him closely. If there are pirates or other freebooters who call here regularly, perhaps we can manage to acquire transportation off this...lovely, tropical paradise," Sachi commented drily. The trail ended at the edge of the beach. A spider the size of a large dog lunged out of a hole at Sachi, rearing up to attack. She was quicker, kicking it over on its back and quartering it with two slashes of her sword. "This is getting to be annoying."

"Well, there aren't any webs over there." Willis pointed at the massive ship a few hundred yards from where they stood.

***

It was thickly encrusted with yards of sand and dirt. Strange looking corals grew up around it where the thing met the water, gentle waves washing around it. It extended two or three hundred yards from the shoreline. In a few spots, it was heavily overgrown but most of it was clear of vegetation. It rested at an angle, the visible part jutting out of the bay, but the water was clear enough to see that much of the ship extended out into the bay, resting here since the day thousands of years ago that something unimaginable brought the giant ship down, out of the sky. Other than its sheer size, in terms of length and breadth, it was impossible to discern any details. It was somewhat oblong in cross-section but ended in a jagged, irregular mass of rock-hard sand and soil. Not to mention what looked like torn and twisted parts of the ship itself.

They silently approached the ancient vessel. The only sounds were the gentle murmur of the waves washing around the encrusted wreck. In places, stark white hull metal reflected the bright morning sunlight. It was deeply buried in the sandy beach, but it still loomed like a cliff, as tall as the *Intrepid* was long. Somehow, there was a sense of peace here, this close to something older than the legends of the Fire Fall themselves.

"How in God's Name was something this...this...this gigantic ever built?" Gelman barely breathed his question.

"It's bigger than the five biggest buildings in all of Kolbia!" Willis craned his head back, trying to assimilate the titanic size.

::Substantially larger, actually.:: D.A.V.E. whispered in Sachi's mind. ::The ship's Secure Access Naval Communication Web Up-Link is partially active at twelve point four percent of maximum capacity. I am attempting to access basic information via standard SANCWUL comm protocols. Basic Up-Link access within seven minutes, plus or minus one minute, sixteen seconds. Standard crewmember Up-Link access within one hour, twenty-eight minutes, plus or minus seventeen minutes, forty seconds. Command and Fleet level access, unknown at this time. Multiple variables.::

"Part of it still works? After all this time?" Sachi spoke aloud.

"Are you speaking to us or that thing in your head?" Silaqui cocked her head at Sachi's distracted attitude.

"Partly. And, yes, partly to the machine, D.A.V.E. It says there is a computer network still active and *no*, I don't have any real idea what it's talking about. I think the best explanation is that these computer things are like libraries, containing what it describes as the equivalent of thousands of books of rare knowledge."

::Accessible entry port located. Follow the targeting caret.:: D.A.V.E. interrupted her train of thought.

"Huh. Follow me. D.A.V.E. says there's an entry portal this way. We'll probably have to climb a bit, but that's better than digging our way in. I think." A diamond-shaped symbol appeared in her vision. "This way."

As they followed her around the front of the ship and down the other side, they saw where the recent storms had scrubbed a large section of the hull at least somewhat clean. The scar in the ship's encrusted covering began at the front, showing twisted and shattered hull framing, and stretching over two hundred yards down the side of the ship. There were visible letters on the hull, similar to the alphabet Terranglais used, but subtly different and in no language any of them recognized.

"Can D.A.V.E. tell you what the letters mean, Sachi?" Willis asked.

"Well, D.A.V.E.?"

::SD147 CNS *CONSTEL...*The last part of the name is obliterated. However, Hull number SD147 would have been assigned to a superdreadnought, one of the *Star Victory* class. Her name was *Constellation.* She was one of the Ready Reserve ships, basically an older, somewhat obsolescent ship maintained for emergencies. She would have finished trials approximately five to six hundred years before the Fire Fall. *Constellation* was probably commissioned initially nearly ten or eleven thousand Standard Years ago. This Entity lacks detailed naval records, but the Confederation built over two thousand hulls of the *Star Victory* class before the class was supplanted by bigger, tougher and more capable ships.:: He continued to give her information about the ship until she told it to shut up.

"Uh, yeah." Sachi shook her head, hard. The sheer age of this thing was unbelievable. "D.AV.E. says that's the ship's Hull Number and part of her name."

"So, enlighten us." Willis persisted. "What was her name?"

"She was the *Constellation*; I think is the best translation. The name they used for imaginary pictures drawn in the stars."

"Hull Number? What's that mean?"

"How many of them they built."

"Gaah! They could afford a hundred and forty-seven of these things?!" Willis and then everyone stopped and stared, first at the gigantic letters, barely visible, worn and faded to a shadow gray barely darker than the worn white hull itself. Then they stared at Sachi.

"No, Willis. They built two thousand of them. By the time of the Fire Fall, this ship was their equivalent of the Empire's old galleys, rotting away in their reserve fleet. D.A.V.E. doesn't really know for sure. And most of her is buried out there." She pointed where the wreck stretched out into the bay. "Her stern is more than a mile and a half, that way. Now, if you're done asking me stupid questions I can't really answer, let's find that entry portal, *ne*? Part of this ship is still functional, remember?"

Port Plunder, Cazadora Isle,
Southern Lanic Ocean
November, 1478, Third Age of Imperial Reckoning

Sahla wasn't sure what had stirred the pirates up. There were boats going out to the two big ships, Ironheart's 'flagship,' the *Deathdealer*, and the smaller sloop that dog-licking Deuschen bastard commanded, *Heartcutter*. The newest arrived ship, *Saker*, left on the morning tide. *Saker's* captain had stopped at the hostages' hut for a long moment, staring intently at Sahla, ignoring the others. He was obviously of the People of the Sands, with his long dark hair, darkly tanned skin and dark eyes. Slim, he might have been a hand or so taller than her. He simply stood there for long minutes, staring at her. Then with a shrug, he shook his head and walked to his ship, calling for the anchors to be cast off. Within half of an hourglass, his ship had passed out of her sight. She was still sitting there, her chin on her knees, when Ironheart's shadow fell over her. The pirate took a key from his belt and unlocked the chain from Sahla's ankle.

"Come with me, girl. And no nonsense, either. Only thing on the outside of the stockade wall is a horrible death. Understand?"

"Yes." She followed lightly along behind him. He stopped at the edge of the water. She watched the longboats pulling out to the two anchored ships.

"Wondering why I hauled you out here, girl?"

"You will do as you will. I have neither pistol nor sabers, and there is nowhere to run to. It will be as the Prophet wills."

"*As the Prophet wills.*" There was a mocking tone to his voice. "What if the Prophet *wills* that I give you to the crew? Or to Werner?"

She stared at him in stony silence.

"Humpf." He glanced at her and then looked seaward. "By the end of the month, perhaps, certainly by the end of the year, you'll likely be standing naked on the auction block in Luctini, you know."

"Do you wish me to forgive you, infidel?"

"Forgive me? Ha! That's ripe! Never had a hostage say aught of them forgiving me!"

"I do not forgive you! Never! Because of you Khalid is dead! Najwa is dead! All of my people and the sailors of that ship are dead! Because of you, you sucker of a ka'mel's cock!" She did not flinch in the least as he threatened to backhand her with raised hand. "Strike me! Beat me! You will do as you will, Quan accursed dog, but never will you break me! And never, in no fashion, shall I ever stand on the slave auction block in the putrid, befouled den of whores, pimps and lepers you call Luctini!" Sapphire blue eyes flashed at him.

"Such foul language from one so beautiful. You may be a tiny thing, but you've spirit and a temper like a volcano." He snorted an ironic laugh. "I should send your husband-to-be a bill. Charge him for saving him from your displeasure. In a way, I pity the man that ever takes you to be his, whether as wife, concubine or slave. I'm sure it'll not be a restful experience. Might be a hell of a ride, but not at all a restful experience."

"Why did you bring me to the beach here, dog of an unbeliever?!"

"There's a war coming. I feel it in my bones; I smell it in the air." He stopped a moment. "The Empire, foolish and stupid in its decrepit years, still thinks that it has the power it wielded a thousand years ago. And the Imperials are about to provoke the most powerful navy in the world, the Kolbian Republic Navy. A shepherd boy with a stick, poking a great dragon in the nose. It's stupid, pathetic and wasteful."

"And what matter is it to me, what two nations of infidels do to each other?"

"None, really. Just accelerates my timetable, and at the same time it gives me fewer options on what to do with you. You know, I really, really wish you hadn't shot Jamul."

"Why?"

"He talked one of my agents into this, taking you as a hostage. And then my agent talked me into going along with the deal. And it looks like the only benefit I'm going to get from it will be the ransom the Duke of Ostreich will pay for that over-bosomed blonde idiot. Unless your father, Sheikh Hasim, pays your price. Do you think he will?"

"He will not pay. And what has this to do with that filthy traitor?"

"Well, if you hadn't shot him, I might still be torturing him."

"Dead is dead. The Prophet and Chalta will see to his deserved punishment."

"You really do have faith, don't you?"

"I must." She looked up at him. *Oh, please, please, no, not this vile pirate! Sire, Ilben, surely this bloody handed reiver is not the One you spoke of? He is vile and evil. I could never love such a ghula in human shape! Ilben said the One I Bond to will be someone worthy of my true heart's love! This bloody handed brigand could never be such. Could he?*

"Hmm." Ironheart rubbed his goatee. "There's more to you, I think, than just your beauty. Or, rather, perhaps your beauty is somewhat more than merely mortal?"

"Take me back to the hut, pirate. Or have your way with me, if you can. I'd cut your manhood away, had I my sabers. No man not my heart's love will ever take me without a fight."

"You know, I think I believe you. My gransmama had a touch of the Sight. Perhaps, I've the slightest bit my ownself. But, no, I believe you. No man will ever be your True Love."

For a long, long moment she stared at him, eyes huge, frozen in time almost. She felt a tremendous, insubstantial weight press down on her, a huge silent bell that shook her to her soul when it rang. Power rushed through her and she felt it stir. She felt, for the first time in her life, her Sire's Blood, the bequeathing of his Power, the freedom and joy and magic and wonder of what the Bond would bring her, that connection to the pure heart and center of her own Power. A Power centered and forged in Love.

How can this be? Somehow, I know he speaks truth. How is this possible? Ilben himself said that the One who should save all things, that One should be the True Love of my heart. If no man shall ever be my True Love, then how shall the Bond form? Am I fated to only the Bond of Slave to Master? I would lend all my power, all my love to bring about what my Sire foresaw, but if my Bond is to be only of Slave and Master, how shall that come to pass? Jinn are ever duplicitous and treacherous when forced to obey. Should a Jann be different? Should my inhuman nature force me to perhaps deceive and betray that One?

She stumbled as Ironheart turned to lead her back to the hut and chain her again. He raised an eyebrow at her sudden clumsiness.

"Are you well, Houri?" He reached for her arm, to support her sudden weakness.

"Don't touch me, pirate." She recovered and jerked her arm away from him. She walked to the hut, head high and back stiff, every line of her body radiating contempt of the bemused Ironheart. In her mind, her thoughts raced uncontrollably. *The dream! My dream! What if...what if it was a true sending, a vision of the future, not just a dream of fancy? I know dreams can be true and yet only bear symbols of what might come. Neither the Prophet nor Chalta would bless a union of two human women! But I am not human. Is this why I exist? If this is so, if this is truth, then is Chalta acting through my Sire, to create a Jann who can do what mortal man, or rather mortal* woman *might do without Chalta or the Prophet being forced to turn their faces away? Or are the Elemental Lords moving to do what must be done, even without Chalta's Blessing? Oh, the cleverest warrior can best the strongest if he comes at him by a crooked path! Is this why I was taught all the skills of the dervish? Why Father and Mother sent me away? Did they know?*

She hardly noticed when Ironheart locked her back into her chains. Draven Kye waved a hand in front of her unseeing eyes.

"What did you do to her, you bastard?" he growled.

"Nothing, you insolent shit," Ironheart sneered. "And how would you stop me from doing anything I please to her? You're chained in here and I have the keys. Cause me enough trouble, Kolbian, and I don't care how much your *baseball team* will pay for you. I'll stake you out for the *Dziungles gimtoji,* and perhaps your attitude might change after you've hung a while. Of course, it'd be much too late for that to matter to you by then. You'd then have other concerns, much, much larger ones."

But where is this woman with the glittering black eyes? She barely heard the exchange between the two men. *She must come soon, somehow. In three weeks, my eighteenth birthing day comes. Does she wait, all unknowing, in Luctini? There are some women among the pirates, but none like that. Is it truly she who I must seek? Or was the dream just that, a dream, no more? But what of the feeling which swept over me on the beach when Ironheart said what he did? Time grows short, I fear, but all I have are questions. Too many questions and no answers.*

Chapter Twenty

**Central Bay, Cazadora Isle,
Southern Lanic Ocean
November, 1478, Third Age of Imperial Reckoning**

Roland had a good fire going, an iron tripod holding a steaming pot above it. He'd found some tubers and hummed while he sliced them into the fish stew. Lodvar stood over by the hole in the monster ship the others had vanished into a couple of hours ago. Something hit this monster thing, this *starship* the Nisei girl called it, hard enough to punch cleanly through an outer hull made of something very similar to impenetrable white-steel.

"How long do we wait for them?" He stared into the forbidding hole. *It might go completely through this ship. Can't really tell though. Most of it is full of sand and dirt and pieces of this thing. No webs, thank the Lord of the Waves. No webs.* He shuddered as he remembered the monstrous spider crashing through the undergrowth outside the stockade. The thing delicately nipping away his bonds after biting his shoulder and paralyzing him with its poison, before wrapping him in its web and carrying him away to a horrible death. It was a miracle that led these shipwrecked castaways to find him.

"They said they might be even most of the night. So, at least until morning, I'd say. And would you really want to go back into that jungle without them?"

"No." He didn't have to fake the shudder that thought brought to him. "Not at all."

They'd made a makeshift camp up here on top of what the Nisei girl, maybe all of twenty summers he thought, asserted was an ancient *starship*, something predating the Fire Fall itself. Unlike Sahla, the petite Darsälaamic captive he still lusted after, this tall, black-haired, black-eyed loveliness, Sachi by name, was death-on-two-feet dangerous. He'd played up being woozy and sick, saying little, but she never lowered her guard in the least. There was a sense of wariness to her, a dangerous aptitude for sudden violence that Sahla almost completely lacked. This one, this Sachi, would, he thought, respond to the least threat with lethal ferocity.

I'll probably have to kill her. Damn shame, that. She's nearly Sahla's match in beauty, even as different as she is, tall, gorgeous and what a pair of TITS! Black eyes and porcelain skin, and how is that oh-so-fine skin not blistered and roughened as everyone else's is? Well, the Elf is the same, perfect clear skin, but then, that one, Silaqui, well, she's magic and immortal. Different rules for her. But if I could get all three of them, well four, the quiet brown girl would sell well, too…but the four of them on the block in Luctini! I'd never have to lift a finger again, I'd be so rich. Ha, the Emperor himself would borrow money from me!

"Hey, Ludver or Loudvar, whatever your name is, give me a hand with this, will you?"

"Oh, sorry, I was woolgathering a bit there. What'd you need?" With a final look at the dark opening in the depths of the ship where he'd last seen the lights of the five foolhardy explorers, he turned back to help the cook.

***

"Come LOOSE! Damn you, OUT of there!" Sachi snarled under her breath as she strained against the stuck hatch.

Sachi's back was braced against the wall of the corridor an hour's worth of digging had uncovered. Under D.A.V.E.'s guidance, she'd used her amulet to unlock the sealed hatch they'd discovered. But it had only released the locks. The door still had to be forced open. She was braced in the corridor, the tips of her fingers wedged into the tiny crack created by the released lock. Corded muscle bulged in her bare arms and the tendons of her neck were rigid with the effort. Willis and Gelman had sharpened wooden wedges driven into the crack, hammering on them to force the hatch.

Aylie stayed clear, watching to ensure nothing unfriendly could sneak up on them while Silaqui's magic provided light to work by. They'd been working at this door for a couple of hours now. They'd opened it perhaps a half inch or so. Breaking the original seal forced them away from the door, as foul, nearly poisonous air from within choked them, their eyes and throats burning from its vapors.

Something suddenly gave and the door slammed fully open, dumping Sachi on top of Willis and they went down in a pile with a squawking Gelman on the bottom. Quickly, they sorted themselves out and looked down a corridor no human had seen in nearly ten thousand years. In the steady light of Silaqui's magic, there was little to see. There were smooth panels on the still white walls next to the door, and other, different, panels set into the roof of the short corridor. A corridor ending twenty feet away in another sealed hatch.

"You're kidding me, right?" Willis leaned against the wall, hands on his knees and head down in exhaustion. "Another damn door? Great."

"Aye," Aylie cautiously moved up and examined the door, "but look here. 'Tis nay all covered in dirt and filth. Pertected by the outer, sealed door, mayhap? And see this, this small part be different. Be a hope that this opens an easier way, Sachi? See the writing, painted on the wall? What's it say?"

"*Emergency Manual Blast Door Access. Authorized Personnel Only.*" Sachi cocked her head and reached out to touch a faded green spot on the smaller panel. At her touch, it creaked slowly open the length of her thumb and stopped. She carefully pushed it fully open. Inside the panel, a red lever rotated halfway out and stopped. She pulled it the rest of the way into the obvious position and started to rotate it in the direction of the arrow molded into the wall where the lever connected.

"A moment, Sachi." Silaqui spoke up. "I expect the air beyond this door will be just as foul as the first. Let everyone step back out and I shall use my magic to funnel away any poisonous fumes that might come forth."

"Sensible." Sachi was the last to step away. The Elf's crimson magic wrapped around the hatch, forming a funnel to carry away the fouled atmosphere on the other side. Sachi had wrapped a rope around the lever and as she yanked it, the hatch snapped open with snakelike speed. There was a huge rushing sound, as the partial vacuum inside the ship suddenly had access to the outside world. Standing there, next to the entrance, they felt the air rush into the ship, howling around them, fogging up as it rapidly cooled, pouring into the ship's interior. The foul interior air poured out, a grayish-green mist, channeled away by Silaqui's clever cantrip.

"Well, that worked." Willis put his hands on his hips, regarding the revealed corridor stretching away into darkness. "Now what?"

"Now we look for this thing's equivalent of the quarterdeck. It had a captain, and some fashion of control. D.A.V.E. tells me what we are looking for is called a bridge. That or something he says is called a Combat Information Center." Sachi stepped past him and led the way into the darkness, Silaqui's light casting eerie shadows before her.

***

The great ship had an unsettling, abandoned feeling to it. At the same time, they all felt as if they were being watched, and perhaps, judged by ancient ghosts born under other suns. They found things marked Transport Tube and a number. Instead of ladders, these things led from deck to deck, vertical tubes that the crew had simply floated up and down to reach other levels. But the designers had considered possible problems and recessed ladders were hidden under easily removable covers.

Several corridors seemed to only have rooms along them. Crew quarters; apparently, spacers didn't hang hammocks above the ship's cannons. Clothing left behind crumbled at a touch, the dry atmosphere and thousands of years making even those tough fabrics fragile and brittle. Individuals had left many things behind, mostly things undecipherable to either purpose or function. Every room had at least one or two smoothly rounded tiles somewhere, lying on a bed or table, dropped on a chair or the deck, one left on the sink in front of a recognizable toilet. And in some rooms, there were normal bound books and papers, including some artistic decorations.

"Well, they were definitely human." Willis rubbed his chin as he turned away from a picture on the back of a door. A picture of a very attractive and completely nude human woman. "Crew quarters, I'd say?"

"That's what D.A.V.E. has told me. Evidently, the Confederation was very much like your people, Willis. Long as you do your job and don't hurt anyone else, do what you want."

"No sense of morality at all," Gelman grumbled. He'd taken a good, long look at the picture and then blushed beet red as Aylie caught him and snickered behind her hand. "At least this one isn't quite as...vulgar."

"What's that, Gelman?" she snickered, "Ye never seed a hard prick afore this?"

"Of course I have. But one shouldn't have *pictures* of them on the wall in the water closet!"

"Clearly, you've never seen a Han pillow book then." Sachi shook her head. "We need to find something important. Going through someone's seabag is a waste of time. And that's basically all we've been doing so far." She turned and led the way down the corridor to the next junction of corridor and tube. The pale crimson light Silaqui created shortly after they entered followed her. The sorceress had set a similar light following each of them.

"Well, any clues?" Silaqui asked as Sachi carefully examined the strange writing on the walls.

"Yes. I think we're on the right track, finally. The ladder going up, that tube leads to the Captain's Day Room, CIC, Imaging, whatever that is, and Main Bridge."

"Isn't that what we're looking for, Sachi?" Gelman grumbled as he brought up the rear.

"Yes, it is." The Nisei's long index finger pointed at another colored set of words. "But that one indicates the location of the Flag Officer's Briefing Room and Quarters. D.A.V.E. suggests that might be very well worth our while. My suggestion, anyways. Well?"

"Sachi, you're the one with the thing whispering in your head about this ship. Lead on." Willis peeked down the tube. "But I'd set a rope anchor and belay everyone down. That's a pretty long drop." The tube disappeared into the darkness. He pulled a copper Fensgif out of a pocket and tossed it into the tube. It was a good twenty heartbeats before they heard a faint *ping* when it hit something down there. "Does anything say how far down to the space admiral's quarters?"

"One deck, I think, Willis. I'll go first."

One after another they climbed down the ladder or slid down the rope to the next level down. Silaqui sent her little light phantoms coasting ahead of her once everyone was in the next corridor. About ninety feet from the tube, they could see a larger, open area on the left.

"Looks like a guard post, I'd say. That or a secretary's office." Willis pointed at an ornate plate attached to the wall, next to a more embellished set of double doors. "What's that say?"

"Vice Admiral Liesel Hoffmeister, Commanding Officer, Omega-2-Cygni System," Sachi read the plate. "I think this might be the best thing we could have found." She stepped past the desk and then froze when the dark alcove was suddenly flooded with light.

::Emergency power is still functioning in this area. This suggests possible functional comp-systems.:: D.A.V.E. spoke in her mind. ::Note the active panel on the right hand wall. Assuming standard Confederation practice, basic light weapons and protective equipment should be located in those lockers. They will be code-locked. Press your cube against the clear panel and I might be able to access the security system and bypass the interlocks.::

Sachi pulled her amulet off the choker and pressed it against the square 'lock,' marveling as it melded into the opening. There was a quiet click and the outer panel slid up into the top of the cabinet it had covered. A dozen strange things gleamed under the light that dimly illuminated the recessed cabinet. They were metallic and similar in size and shape to her pistol, a finely crafted Kolbian double-barreled fifty caliber flintlock. But it was only a resemblance and these things in their form-fitting racks simply exuded a lethal perfection.

::Mark 14 APF handguns. An Anti-Personnel Flechette weapon that fires a one-millimeter duralloy flechette, a razor edged, fin-stabilized dart at a standard muzzle velocity of seven-hundred and fifty meters per second. Effective range in atmosphere is approximately two hundred meters, due to the light weight of the projectile. Due to its light weight, concealability, high capacity magazine and excellent armor penetration at short range, these are standard issue weapons for VIP protection details.:: Sachi swore she could hear D.A.V.E. gloat as she picked one up. ::Recoil is controllable but vigorous enough that there is no fully automatic capability in the handgun version.::

"High capacity? What do you mean?" she subvocalized as Willis stared in shocked acquisitiveness over her shoulder.

::Each magazine contains one hundred rounds of ammunition, one hundred of the flechette projectiles. In addition, the magazine includes a highly miniaturized, super-conducting capacitor, which provides enough electrical energy to operate the weapon for the one hundred rounds contained in the magazine. When a magazine is expended, all one hundred shots fired, the user simply ejects the magazine and inserts a new one. So each magazine is sufficient to operate the weapon. It also provides enough power for appropriately enhanced individuals to provide a link for improved target acquisition and 'One Shot, One Kill' accuracy. It is this Entity's position that the 'OSOK' claim is a marketing ploy. However, these weapons are lethal, efficient and many generations more advanced than Lieutenant Commander Fleet's cap-and-ball revolvers.::

"These are pre-Fall weapons, aren't they, Sachi?" Willis' voice actually quavered slightly, suppressed excitement in every line of his tense body.

"D.A.V.E., are any of these things safe to use? CAN we use them?" She nodded at Willis. "Yes, Willis, they are, but how safe would you feel using a ten-thousand-year-old gun?"

"Oh. Er, um, hadn't really thought about that."

::The individual weapons would need to be checked. This Entity can guide you through the process. The problem would be charging the magazines. The standard room temperature super-conducting capacitor in each magazine requires four point six million amps, a measure of electrical power, to operate the weapon. Currently, even if any of the magazines are safe to use, they would basically be very limited use weapons, limited to the number of available charged magazines. The magazines could not be recharged, nor could additional flechettes be made.::

"Thanks, D.A.V.E. Is anything else in here usable? What are these shirts for? Uniforms?"

::No. Those are standard issue CLIBA body armor 'vests.' Concealable Liquid Individual Body Armor. Again, with their unobtrusive design, they are standard issue body armor for both individual VIPs and their security details.::

"Okay, D.A.V.E., I'll bite. What's a Vee Eye Pee?"

::A Very Important Personage. The System Commander would be considered such.::

"I see. Well, there are a dozen of these shirts here and my friends are as VIP as you get. Do we need to check sizes?"

::Negative. Functional armor will auto-adjust to properly fit the wearer. Any shirt that does not adjust to fit within a minute has a system fault and should be down-checked and turned in to the Armory for maintenance.::

"Right." She grabbed an armful of the shirts off their hangers and turned to her friends. "D.A.V.E. says these things are a kind of armor. Everyone grab a couple and let's take them with us. We can try them on later."

"Armor, uh?" Aylie cocked her head as Sachi tossed her a pair of the shirts. She leaned over and *bonged* her hand on the steel breastplate under Gelman's robes. "Could be a might bit better tha' yer rattlin', rusty clanker there, Gelman?"

"This is the finest Deuschen armor made, I'll have you know, girl."

"Oh, aye, *finest Deuschen armor made.* And you sound like a junk wagon being pushed down a badly cobbled street, banging around in the jungle, Pere." She grinned at the wounded expression on Gelman's face. "Pay nae heed, Pere. Ye'll live."

"Leave the weapons for now. We've other things to be seeing about." Sachi turned back to the ornate doors. "There's a fancy panel on the wall here, D.A.V.E. Can you open it?"

::The door is not reading as secured. Push on it and it should simply open.::

The room was laid out as a typical executive office. There was a large, bare desk a bit more than two-thirds of the way across the room, with a wide expanse of carpet in front of it. A great seal was woven into the carpet in blue and silver, a silver lance superimposed over a strange circular map. At the base of the lance, a great raptorial bird spread its wings, lightning bolts grasped in one talon, a bundle of branches in the other. There were five stars on either side of the lance point. The background of the entire thing was a circular map of a world with landmasses very different from those of Rybitha.

Glass-fronted cabinets lined the walls flanking the desk; bookcases full of books were behind the desk, framing a door leading deeper into the suite of rooms. One cabinet contained a strange-looking suit of armor, complete with a massive, two-handed sword. A comfortable-looking sofa and a pair of deeply cushioned chairs surrounded a low coffee table, set off to the side of the room. Some of the cases contained what looked like weapons, some of them actually firearms not that different in form from Willis' revolvers. One case had dozens of models, some of ships, such as would sail on any sea. One was a long, tear-drop shaped hull, with a single forward tower rising above the centerline of the hull. Another was a long, flat decked ship, with a single tower set amidships and well to starboard. There were strange, white things lined up on the deck. Others were even stranger in appearance.

"That ship looks not much different from *Intrepid*." Willis pointed to the first of the models. "A ship-rigged frigate. This one is different, a large sloop perhaps? But these other things, what are they?"

"D.A.V.E. tells me these are models of ships named *Constellation*. The earliest one goes back over two thousand years before humans came to Rybitha." Sachi pointed at the frigate. "That one. And the name has been carried down over the centuries."

::Caitlyn Schmidt, this Entity has discovered that the Admiral's mainframe computer is, in fact, functional and in a permanent stand-by mode. This Entity is unable to access the file storage or the menu tree lists. Other than a complete and functional operating system, the majority of the permanent memory systems are occupied by a single eight point five exabyte executable file. It is a run-on-demand program. There is a TSR program, terminate-and-stay-resident, coming online. It is believed that the TSR will check the activation of the cabin's status and perhaps the ship's status before determining how to respond. Most likely response will be activating the ROD program, eighty-three point six percent, plus or minus seventeen percent.::

"What the hell does all that mean, D.A.V.E.?" Sachi subvocalized, but Silaqui and Willis both noticed that she'd suddenly frozen.

::Most likely response would be activation of the ship's own integral AI. Seventy-four percent, plus or minus twenty-three percent. Activation of an internal defense system is forty-two percent likely, plus or minus thirty-nine percent. Maintenance, recovery, and search-and-rescue programs are possibilities, but all at less than ten percent, plus or minus fifty-one percent, multiple variables. But current file status and system configuration is not optimally organized for any of those possible scenarios.::

"All right, I think. I don't really understand any of the things you're talking abou..."

"Who the hell are you people?" A woman of medium height, slightly on the chubby side, with close-cropped blonde hair and black eyes materialized sitting in the chair behind the desk. "You're sure as hell not a SAR team." She spoke what Sachi recognized as English. "Oh, shit, how long has it been?"

Everyone froze. The woman looked around her slowly, perceptibly taking everything in, every detail of each of them in the room. Then her eyes took on the somewhat unfocused, distant gaze they'd all seen on Sachi's face when she was speaking to D.A.V.E. Next, she centered her attention on Sachi.

"Do you understand me?" she asked in English.

"Some. Not well. Do you speak Terranglais?"

"Oh, dear God! That abortion of a mishmash pseudo-language is still around?" She answered in oddly accented Terranglais, but understandable to everyone.

"Yes, it is the most commonly spoken language across the world."

"Really? That'll put a bee in someone's bonnet, I think." She sighed. Sachi's eyes widened as she realized there was no actual flesh and blood body in the chair. It was a projection of some type. "Can you tell me how long its bee...never mind, I'll check the comp."

"Are you real?" Sachi asked.

"Nine thousand, eight hundred and ninety-seven years," the woman whispered. "Almost ten thousand years, and no contact with the Confederation. What happened?" She brought her attention back to Sachi and the rest. "In one sense, real enough. In another, not so much. If you were to walk into my bedroom, you'd find my physical remains lying out on my bed. Fairly well mummified by now I should imagine. I am a *gestalt*, a recording of the mind, memories and personality of a human being who was once very much alive. I'm Vice Admiral Liesel Hoffmeister. Long, long ago, I was the overall system commander, trying to defend this system, this world from an alien species we called the Quar'taneeka."

"Why?" The simple question came from Aylie, of all of them.

"Why?" Liesel's image looked at her. "Because the Quar'taneeka had proven to be inimical to all life, without a doubt or question in anyone's, well anyone rational, that is, mind. We don't know why, we never did. We do know that every single time they found a world with a sapient, sentient species, they destroyed that world, killed that species. They attacked without pause or reason. Their only response to communication attempts were either a beam weapon or a missile with an anti-matter warhead. They would have destroyed this world and every living thing on it. And life, self-aware life, is a rare and precious thing, one that the Confederation was formed to protect. Does that answer your question, young lady?"

"Aye. I's learned ta be wary of those as would befriend ye fer no cause a'tall."

"I learned similar lessons when I was about your age, or a little younger." Liesel leaned back in her chair, her image not disturbing the least hint of dust. "So, did someone finally figure out where my poor, old *Connie* was? Even if you people are a very odd group."

"No one knows that such as this ship, *Connie*, you called her," Liesel nodded to answer Fleet's implied question, "no one has the least idea that this ship is here. This is just another unmapped, unexplored island in the Southern Lanic."

"Have we been completely forgotten then?" Liesel rested her chin on her hand. "Then how is it possible that this very pretty lady of Asian descent is obviously the recipient of a partial military grade enhancement package?"

"That is a very long story, Admiral Hoffmeister-sama." Sachi answered the image. "And I think no one living truly knows the entire story. But I shall tell you what I can. It may take some time, however."

"Well, have a seat, folks," the image waved at the couch, "one thing I have lots of is time."

***

"Well, Sachi, that is, indeed, a very interesting tale," Liesel murmured several hours later. Sachi had noticed that there were several moments during the exchanging of stories when Liesel's image had, for the merest fraction of a second, frozen without reaction. When asked, D.A.V.E. told her that computer problems were most likely to blame, due to the age of the system and the fact that Liesel's recording was not complete. The recording of her gestalt was an emergency action, as Confederation forces in the system had scrambled to recover and save as much as they could.

The *Constellation* herself had been heavily damaged and was drifting sunward with a dead drive. Only the unexpected arrival of the planetoid-sized starship CNS *Thunderchild* saved *Connie* from being immolated in the sun's corona. *Thunderchild* pulled the *Connie* out of her death spiral immediately after crushing the final Quar'taneeka attack. Before she left the system, *Thunderchild's* crew rescued nearly a million Confederation personnel, a dozen other ships, all heavily damaged, and provided over a billion tons of food and supplies to the surviving peoples of Rybitha.

"Thank you, Admiral Hoffmeister-sama. Your tale is even more amazing. But I have a question," Sachi answered in a hushed voice.

"Shoot, kiddo."

"Ah, yes." She paused a half breath in consternation. "The rad-e-ation you spoke of, is it still here? Are we now trapped as you were?"

"No, not at all. *Connie* had taken so many hits, anti-matter warheads, high gigaton yield fusion weapons, failure of Fusion One, Two and Three, and worst, severe damage to the Main Core Power Backup System. Main Core was a fission system and damage to it was what flooded most of the ship with lethal radiation levels. The only real way to deal with radiation is time. And now, nearly ten thousand years later? Any areas of the ship that you might be able to access are clear. You won't be able to access much. CIC, maybe Imaging. Let me check real quick." Liesel's eyes lost focus and a wave of pixilation swept over her in the blink of an eye. "Yeah, most anything you might access is either gutted, cleared out or useless to you. Main Sickbay is still there, but the Medical AIs were overwritten when we decided to record me. No meds, nothing there. Same with the Bridge. Hmm, Point Defense Systems Control, toast, same with the Electronic Warfare Control, MPS Four is still there, all the AM missiles were jettisoned, so an empty shell. Twenty-five dead Alcubierre Quantum drive Anti-ship missiles in a single MPS pack. Marine One and the Armor Morgue might be accessible. There's powered armor still in the Morgue, but it's all DNA code-locked, so useless. Might be some old blast rifles in the racks, don't know if I'd trust them. Marines never throw anything away. Hmm, Graser Two-Six is still showing as operational and charged?! Jesus Christ on a Harley!? Got to be a bad reading, no way the supercapacitors have held power this long! Unless, it's trickling power from somewhere else...?" The woman's image stopped for nearly a minute. "Okay, I see what's happening."

"Ma'am?" Willis spoke in a tentative whisper.

"Yes?"

"What are all these things you're talking about? What do all these letters mean?"

"Just the way the Confederation Navy talked about things. I'll give this young lady, Sachi, right?" Sachi nodded when the Admiral's image looked at her. "I'll give Sachi the pertinent details in a quick download. Only things that might be useful to you would be Marine One, might be some usable weapons there. Might. And Graser Two-Six. It's still tied into Imaging and you might be able to get the on-mount targeting systems to give you a kind of 'bird's eye view' of the local area for at least a couple hundred kilometers or so."

"Knowing what is near us would be invaluable, Admiral Hoffmeister-sama." Sachi rose and bowed to the image.

"Yeah." The Admiral studied Sachi for a long moment. "Okay, here's what I'm going to do. There's a few things here in my cabin you might be able to use. In the left-hand drawer of my desk, Sachi, is a digital key. It'll open the cabinets that hold all my...well, all my keepsakes. But I really doubt I'll ever be doing anything with the Society for Creative Anachronisms again. Oh well. In those cabinets is a pair of ancient pistols, called the Model 1911. I restored them long ago. They should be in perfect order, but check them closely. There's a set of holsters and magazine carriers for them, twenty magazines and a case of ammo, a thousand rounds. All that stuff is sealed and properly preserved. I'd trust it."

"Thank you, Admiral Hoffmeister-sama." Sachi stood up and bowed to her.

"You're welcome. But I think those things might work best for Lieutenant Commander Fleet, here." She grinned at Sachi. "For you, Sachi, open the cabinet of ship models. The top model, my old girl *Constellation* herself, is a nannie-ball sculpture I made. The password to unlock the nannie-ball is 'Connie.' It's the same stuff as the nannie-ball you're wearing on your arm. It'll give you a few more options."

"Domo arigato, Admiral Hoffmeister-sama."

"Doitashimashite, Sachi-san." She turned her attention to Silaqui. "Silaqui, the only thing I can give you is an apology. Humans never intended what happened to your world in the past. We never intended to bring the Quar'taneeka here and when they came, we fought and died to preserve your wonderful, beautiful and very unique world. I understand the issues your people might have with us. I'm sorry."

"I understand." The Sorceress' voice was tight but level. "If I can, I shall convey your words to my Uncle and he will determine if the King or Queen should hear them. That is all I can do."

"Good enough." The Admiral paused. "One last thing, Sachi. Tell your D.A.V.E. to record this. Lieutenant Commander Fleet, what is the local date, please?"

"Hmm, the tenth of November, I think."

"Full date, whatever notation your nation uses."

"Oh, the Navy still uses the old Imperial Reckoning system. There's those in the Quorum who want to date things from the founding of our Republic, but that hasn't really caught on."

"Understood. The date, please?"

"Oops, sorry. Tenth of November, 1478, Third Age of Imperial Reckoning. That's how it'd be written on an official document."

"Excellent." She turned her attention to Sachi. "Sachi, I want to do something that will help you in the future with any other functional pieces of our tech you find. And it just might help with Confederation personnel who've survived by using stasis."

"What would you do, Admiral-sama?"

"Give you a commission in the Confederation Navy. No idea if there's a Confederation left, after this long, but it can't hurt to have an official rank if you have to deal with any AIs or other Entity Programs you might find."

"Admiral-sama, there is no need. I am not wort-" Sachi started to babble in surprise.

"Shut. Up." Liesel smiled grimly as Sachi's mouth shut with a click. "Better. Stand to attention, raise your right hand and repeat after me: I, Takahashi Sachi, do swear on my honor, my blood and my life, that I will defend the Constitution of the Pan-Solar Confederation against all enemies, foreign and domestic, human and non-human; that I will bear true faith and allegiance to the same. Ancestors bless my service to this oath."

Sachi slowly repeated the oath.

"Outstanding! By the authority granted to me as System Defense Commanding Officer, I hereby appoint you to the acting rank of Lieutenant Commander, Provisional. Sachi, direct your D.A.V.E. to make permanent note of this act."

"I will, Admiral-sama." She focused for a moment. "He says it is recorded. Thank you," Sachi knelt and bowed, forehead to deck. "I shall strive to be worthy of this honor."

"Get up, Lieutenant Commander Takahashi. Confederation officers never, ever kneel or bow to anyone. Ever. Perhaps incline your head slightly, out of respect, nothing else. Not even that while you're on duty. Am I clear on this?"

"Yes, Admiral-sama." Everyone heard the tension in her voice.

"Very good. Or good enough, for now, I guess." Liesel sighed, turning her attention to Willis. "There are a few books on my shelf I think you should take as well as the handguns. They should give your nation a jump on industrialization, Commander Fleet. Take the ones that have the light blinking under their spot in my bookcase."

"Thank you, ma'am." Willis nodded to her.

"Sachi, I've downloaded the access code to my quarters to your D.A.V.E. The door will lock and secure itself behind you when you leave. Due to the power situation on *Connie*, I'm shutting down and going back into static memory. It's barely possible there might be some way to recover my gestalt in the future. Possible but highly unlikely. I doubt we'll ever speak again. But you all have my best wishes. Good luck and Godspeed." The Admiral's image faded away with the last words.

***

Willis settled into the enveloping couch-like seat next to Sachi. He managed not to jump when the sleek, soft material of the thing molded around his body. He felt tiny prickles against his skin on his hands, neck and back. A red light flashed on the blank, black glass panel in front of him. He tensed up, starting to struggle against the seat as its material began to flow up around him, slowly engulfing him in a soft, semi-liquid darkness.

"Relax, Willis." Sachi's voice seemed to echo in his head. "The machines are adjusting since you do not have the things in your head and body that I have, the Biological Processing Unit or the nanites. D.A.V.E. tells me it will use something called *Neuro-Magnetic Resonance Imaging and Feedback*. They use letters to shorten it, of course. NeMRIF for short."

"Oh yeah," he half-muttered, half thought. "Feels like someone dumped a tub of worms and slugs over me. Ugh."

"Calm yourself. Slow breaths, deep and regular. Close your eyes and seek that still place within yourself. Easy. D.A.V.E assures me nothing will hurt you in any fashion. Relax."

Willis did as she said, breathing slowly and deeply as the material of the seat within the cramped compartment labeled Graser Two-Six folded around him. There was only room in here for two people. Silaqui, Gelman and Aylie waited in the corridor that twisted through the ancient ship's guts, leading down to what he thought of as the ship's gun deck.

The last of the gooey material flowed up around his head, covering everything but his eyes, nose and mouth. He started to jerk spastically against it. It went completely rigid, locking him tightly in place, unable to move. The goop suddenly moved like lightning, covering the rest of his face. He was blinded, and tried to choke, struggling in vain against the stuff.

::You will not be harmed, Lieutenant Commander Willis Fleet.:: A cool, metallic voice echoed through his mind. ::I am the Digitally Aware Virtual Entity assigned to Lieutenant Commander, Provisional, Caitlyn Schmidt.::

"Who?" He thought the question, since he was afraid to open his mouth and choke to death on the goo.

::You refer to her as Sachi Takahashi.::

"Oh," he shuddered as he thought, "Well, that helps a whole damn lot! GET ME OUTTA HERE!"

::Calmly, Lieutenant Commander Willis Fleet. The system is calibrating to your neural patterns. This will take approximately thirty-eight seconds, plus or minus four seconds. You are in no danger of suffocation. Relax and inhale and you will receive a breathing mixture containing sufficient oxygen to enable comfortable respiration. Take one small breath, Lieutenant Commander Willis Fleet.::

"Listen to him, Willis. He may be a little stiff and very literal, but he's on the straight and narrow. I don't think he can lie." Sachi's amused voice echoed in his mind.

"What in God's name? How'd you do that? How can I hear you? I know my ears are full of this crap. What is this STUFF!?" Willis gasped as his lungs finally forced him to take a breath.

::The weapons control stations are polymer based silica gel. The gel provides base material, life support, power and system connectivity to the neurologically reactive nanites that make up seventy-five percent of the control 'couch' system. They are designed to interface with human neurological systems, with or without military grade enhancement. In essence, Lieutenant Commander Willis Fleet, you are supported and surrounded by billions of microscopic machines and a gel that provides basic materials to meet any needs. Like the Admiral's quarters, this section of the ship has minimum basic power. Without power, the nano-based fabrics there would have collapsed into dust when touched. Without power, these system interface couches would simply be piles of dust on the floor of the compartment.::

"The machines, the 'computers' do it, Willis. It's not magic. At least, not magic as we understand it. Nothing like what Silaqui or Gelman can do." Her mind voice giggled. "Oh, and tell D.A.V.E. how you'd like your avatar, your visual representation, to look."

"Say what? Avatar?" Willis shook his head, overwhelmed by the sensations he felt and the masses of information flooding into his awareness.

"Yes. If you leave it up to him, he goes for *minimal requirements* and you show up naked and cold."

"Wha—naked? Oh shit!"

"And cold." Sachi giggled again. "*Very* cold."

I don't think I've ever heard her giggle before. What the heck have I gotten myself into this time? Avatar? What the heck? Okay, me in shipboard uniform, I guess. Time to get your shit in a nice neat pile, Willis.

::Image accepted. Uploading image.::

"Hey!"

"Relax, Willis. Any second the ship's sensors, or the remaining ones that work, should link in with you. Remember that you're sitting here, nice and safe." There was a sense of hidden amusement in her voice.

"OH SHIT!" Suddenly the entire world seemed to be laid out before him, as if he was a bird flying hundreds of feet above the tallest hills of the island. In places things were crystal clear, other areas were blurry or even just a blank grayness. "God damn my eyes!" There was nothing at all holding him up. Instead of falling, he felt the pressure of the enveloping couch holding him in place, motionless.

"Quite a view, isn't it, Willis?" Sachi appeared in his view, reclining in what appeared to be thin air, clad in a white *shozoku* and *kamimaki*, the garments of a Nisei *shinijutsuka*. "D.A.V.E. tells me the blurry and blank areas are spots where the sensors have been damaged or destroyed. And no, don't ask me how they work. I've no idea. I'm told that they are very different from a, and I quote, *purely visual system*, unquote. So I guess they do what they do in some other fashion. At the moment, I don't need to know how they work, just that they do work."

"Ah, yeah." Willis shook his head. "So, in reality, we're sitting in those man-eating chairs in that compartment while these things, these machines, are showing our eyes all this?"

"Not quite." Sachi shrugged. "Somehow, they put the information directly into our minds. D.A.V.E. says that's what the neural linkages are supposed to do. Basically it results in a God-like view."

"You know, right now, I'll just take your word for it. If I think about this too much, I'm gonna wind up hanging off the ceiling, gibbering like a drunk monkey." He swallowed, hard. "So, how much can we see and how close?"

"The Confederation used something called kilometers for measuring distance. But I can convert them into Kolbian miles. These are basic, backup sensors, and they're in horrible shape, so we can only see about a hundred miles. And we can only see things as if we were about two or three hundred feet away. So we can't read over someone's shoulder."

"How far can these things see? If they were working right, that is?"

"Roughly the range of the gun, the *graser*. About one and a quarter million miles. What we're using is the equivalent of the open sights cast into a thirty-two pounder. Not particularly accurate, but good enough."

"My God." Willis whispered, looking around himself.

"Remember the bar of light from the sky that killed the sea monster that destroyed the *Sorcerer*? Before the *Intrepid* reached the Horn Islands?"

"Yeah."

"This is the same kind of weapon, but about half again as big." She grinned at him. "So enough gawking and *ooh and ahh-ing*. Let's see what's out here. And I already see something that tells me that Lodvar is lying to us."

"What?"

"North side of the island, see the two ships at anchor? A big three-masted galleon and a single-masted sloop? And the settlement in that cove? There's a stockade wall around about a dozen huts or cabins. Come on." Willis somehow managed not to scream as she hurled them swooping across the sky.

Chapter Twenty-One

**Central Bay, Cazadora Isle,
Southern Lanic Ocean
November, 1478, Third Age of Imperial Reckoning**

LODVAR STARED INTO THE twin muzzles of a double-barreled flintlock pistol. A pistol held in Sachi's unwavering grip, less than a foot from his eyes. The tall Nisei had climbed out of the hole in the ship a few minutes ago, walked straight up to him and kicked him in the head. He'd hit hard, blood running down the side of his face. He'd started to get up and beat the arrogant trollop to death, then the pistol simply appeared in front of his face and he froze.

"I don't like people, especially strangers I've rescued from a deadly peril, lying to me. I thought the pirates *left you as a sacrifice and sailed away.* Then today I discover there's a neat little settlement on the north shore of the island, a dozen huts, couple of bigger, sturdier buildings, a pair of ships anchored a little ways off shore. A ship-rigged galleon and a nice little sloop. Nice, strong stockade wall around them. Lots of people there, too. I'd say it's the beginning of a pirate port. So, where, exactly, did they put you ashore as a *sacrifice?"*

"Ah, Sachi, is this really necessary?" Gelman asked quietly as he came puffing up behind her.

"I don't know, Gelman. Depends on what this *uso tsuki* says right now. I don't like liars, not at all. Well, Lodvar?"

"I'm sorry!" *This bitch won't hesitate to kill me, right here, right now. She might even enjoy it. And she seems to invariably pick up on any lie. But I don't think she can read minds, so she won't notice a lie by omission! I hope!* "I don't know who you and your friends are or where you're from. For all I knew, when you got me out of the webbing, you could have been pirates yourselves. I was wrong! The pirates staked me out on the outside of their stockade wall. I think they do that to keep the monsters at bay. I don't really know, they didn't tell me. I made the leader angry and he decided to *make an example of me!*"

"Make an example for whom? The other pirates?" Willis asked from behind Sachi.

"No, for the other hostages, I think. People he's holding for ransom. There were five others, but he may have killed another one. I don't know. His name is Ironheart, I believe. He wants to build a pirate fleet, I suppose. He didn't exactly invite me to his quarters for beer and cards, you know."

"Humpf." Sachi held the pistol on him for a long moment before slowly lowering it. "For now, you get the benefit of the doubt. I don't generally give second chances. Roland?"

"Aye, milady?" the cook answered her from where he stood by the fire.

"Can you keep an eye on this one for me?"

"Aye, milady. Easy 'nuff."

"Good, do so, please?"

"Aye."

"I'd suggest you keep Roland happy. Now get up and go help him. We're going to move the camp down onto the beach. This old wreck isn't the...healthiest place to be, I don't care what we were told. I'd rather not spend any more time this close to the thing, unless absolutely necessary."

"You sure about that, Sachi?" Willis asked after a quick glance at Silaqui.

"I'm not sure about anything, Willis, Silaqui. But I think better safe than sorry, *ne?* The spiders seem to stay away from the beach. The little people too. Maybe they've been here long enough to realize that there's something wrong with this thing? I don't know, but I think I want some space between us and it. Better safe than sorry, I think."

"Well, you know more about it than anyone else does." Willis shrugged as he stepped over and started gathering his gear, adding the things he'd brought from the ship to his pack. "Let's eat quickly and then move. Be easier to carry the hot food on our insides, I think."

***

"What are those things?" Roland pointed a ladle at the sleek, black musket-like things Sachi was carefully inspecting. Willis stood just behind her, barely restraining himself from bouncing from foot to foot like a four-year-old waiting for presents on Mid-winter's Day. The cook fire burned cheerfully, the only light in the entire night-shrouded bay.

"They're weapons, Roland. They were commonly called Blast Rifles. I'm checking them to see if they're safe enough to use. And this one isn't. Good for parts only." Sachi nibbled on her bottom lip as she set the rifle aside.

"Not safe, huh?" Willis frowned.

"No. D.A.V.E. says the plasma chamber has a microscopic crack in it."

"So, what does that leave us then?" Gelman asked.

"Well, we've all got one of the armor shirts, functional ones, and there are two spares. One of the Mark 14 APF handguns checks out as safe. But only two functional, charged magazines for it. Two of the half dozen blast rifles, excuse me, D.A.V.E. states that *proper nomenclature is the New Texas Integrated Defense Corporation Model 18, Mark IV Plasma Packet Rifle.*" Sachi rolled her eyes.

"Aye. I thinks *blast rifle* tis less of a mouthful." Aylie scooped the last of the stew out of her bowl before extending it to Roland for a refill. "So, 'tis only two as works?"

"Of these, unfortunately, yes. The pair of pistols that the Admiral gave Willis both work fine…"

"I'll say." Silaqui interrupted Sachi. "My ears are still ringing. Are these things at least quieter?"

"Actually, according to D.A.V.E. they are much louder." She gave the Elf a rueful grin. "Can't be helped, I guess. And if we're going to have a chance to steal a ship from the pirates, we'll need them. There's five or six hundred pirates in their camp. We can steal the sloop, I think, but not with that big galleon sitting next to her."

"And what about the hostages Lodvar mentioned? I'll not leave anyone in a pirate's clutches. I've too much experience with what that's like."

"Silaqui, we're outnumbered something like a hundred to one." Willis looked up from the blast rifle he had been examining. "Stealing the sloop is a risky enough plan…"

"No. We are not leaving slaves there." The Elf was adamant.

"We're outnumbered; they've that witch that Lodvar told us about, and there's…"

"I don't care about that, Willis, and if that *witch* gets in my way, they'll have to separate her ashes from the sands. We are *not* leaving these pirates slaves and hostages!"

"Peace!" Gelman stopped Willis before he could snap back at the sorceress. "I understand both of your views. We'll do the best we can. Sachi and Aylie are masters of moving stealthily. They can sneak in, free the hostages and lead them to the boats on the beach. We pull for the sloop, Willis and Sachi use those gun-things on the galleon, set her afire and we set sail on the strong pre-dawn wind. Freeing the hostages is only a small change in the plan Willis and Sachi worked out. I believe we can do it."

"Okay, that's the idea, then. Enough bickering." Sachi stood up. "We need some rest and tomorrow we move to the north side of the island and get a better look at the pirate's little hostel. We'll make the final plans then. I'll take the watch for now. Get some sleep."

***

They had set up their rather tattered sailcloth tents in the lee of a tangled mass of driftwood and sand. Sachi chose the top of that mass to perch on while she kept watch. Gave her time to think, she'd told everyone. She'd been unsettled all evening, obviously so. Willis and Silaqui kept a subtle eye on her.

I feel like lightning is jangling my nerves, more anticipation than anxiety. There's something looming on the horizon, nothing physical, like another storm or a battle. No, this is something else, almost a psychic pressure bearing down on me. Something of great importance to me, me alone. *But I've not the least idea what it is I am feeling. Almost as if there is something or, perhaps,* someone *that will change everything in my lif...what was that?*

A dry, dead branch had snapped in the dark jungle, catching her attention. Her eyes glittered as she cycled her vision, seeking what had made the noise. What she saw made her blood run cold. She vaulted off the top of the driftwood just as a shower of the little folk's poisoned darts hissed past her. She'd seen a lot of the little ones lurking through the jungle, but it was the two nightmare shapes with them that terrified her. The little ones appeared to be driving those impossibilities to the beach, that or *guiding* them, leading them to food.

"MONSTERS! KYODAINA KUMO!!" she yelled at the top of her voice as she landed between Willis' tent and the tent she once again shared with Silaqui. "Wake up, Willis, Silaqui! They come for us!" She ripped the flap of Willis' tent open, lunging in to grab one of the two functional blast rifles.

"What the hell?!" Willis thrashed out from under his lightweight cover. "Did you just scream something about giant spiders?"

"What do you think, Willis!? It's the little people AND a pair of spiders nearly half as big as the dead one where we found Lodvar! Get the other blast rifle. I don't think these horrors will notice anything less powerful than a thirty-two pounder! Move, damn your eyes!" She scrambled backwards out of the tent. "You set up here; I'll try to flank them!"

"Got it." He snatched up the second blast rifle and headed to the top of the driftwood pile.

"What's going on?!" Gelman popped out of his tent, struggling into the breastplate of his armor.

"Those little people are back, and they brought a couple of pets, I think! Real big ones!" Sachi sprinted away from the camp at full speed, sand flying in a rooster-tail behind her.

"Pets?" Gelman goggled after the speeding Nisei.

"Dinna ask, Pere." Aylie scrabbled into Willis' tent, coming out with the cut-down shotgun that had belonged to her Duke. "Jist get yer magics ready. An' be sure an' certain ta ask the good God what as we could use a wee might of help, aye?" She scrambled up the pile and crouched down next to Willis.

"Think you can handle that thing?" Willis nodded at the shotgun as he carefully followed the procedure Sachi had taught him earlier to activate the rifle and its sophisticated thermo-optical sighting system.

"Aye. Iffn I's needful ta. Ye got the faintest what yer doing with that thing?"

"I hope so."

On the beach, Roland handed one of the muskets they'd salvaged from the wreck of *le Bonaventure* to Lodvar. He checked the load nervously, licking his lips as he watched the Nisei girl disappear into the darkness.

"You keep that musket pointed at the jungle, Heimdägarran," Roland spoke quietly. "I'll be right behind you. Point it the wrong way and you won't have to worry about the spiders killing you."

Lodvar swallowed, hard, and convulsively nodded his head.

Silaqui stood next to a kneeling Gelman, the priest lost in prayer. Her eyes were fully dilated in the night, pupils reflecting the banked firelight like cat's eyes. Her ears were flat against her head and she was panting rapidly. Gelman finished his prayer and rose to stand beside her.

"Are you all right, Lady Silaqui?" he calmly asked.

"Ulp!" She twitched and nearly choked as she spun to face him. "No, I'm not," she snapped. "Even bigger spiders are out there, she says! Where's the end?! Are we just doomed to end like Lodvar, poisoned, wrapped in a cocoon and waiting to die a horrible death?!!! Promise me you'll kill me before I wind up like that! Promise me!"

"Me promise to kill you?" Gelman gently placed a hand on the terrified Elf's shoulder. "Do you really think Sachi would let anything hurt you, as long as she's alive?"

"No," she barely breathed. "No, she wouldn't."

"Well, then. Neither would I. Now, ready yourself. You are far and away the most powerful spellcaster I've ever known. I'm sure we shall need your magic before this is over."

"Thank you, Pere." She raised her hand to cover his on her shoulder. Then, impulsively, she grabbed him in a rib-creaking hug. "You've been our faithful anchor at so many times. And I bless you for it, Gelman."

"You're welcome." His answer was a bit short of breath as the tall sorceress released him and turned to face the jungle, crimson flames rising around her.

A hail of the small, poisoned darts showered out of the edge of the jungle. Silaqui's arms flashed up and a ruby conflagration roared as high as a temple's roof. The darts were incinerated, burned away as a moth in a lantern. Something in the jungle screeched nearly as loud as the whistles on a Kolbian pressure engine; it was a bizarre, horrible sound that shredded everyone's nerves. Gelman prayed, raising his Circled Cross, focusing on the wooden symbol as he spread calm around him, like oil on water. Silaqui clapped her hands together above her head and carmine fire roared skyward, illuminating the beach and the edge of the jungle.

The biggest tree at the edge of the jungle simply exploded outward as the massive arachnid smashed through it. Pieces of the trunk and whole limbs bounced across the beach, some flying clear over their makeshift camp to land in the bay a dozen yards from the water's edge. Some of the little humanoids were crushed by pieces of the trunk. Others were ground to paste under the rushing feet of the gigantic hairy spider.

Silaqui screamed, flinging her arms and hands forward, toward the abomination. Scarlet lightnings ripped out across the sand. Dozens of the humanoids simply flashed into ashes. The bolts tore into the spider, blasting huge smoldering craters into the thick chitin of its exoskeleton. It staggered for a heartbeat, streaming smoke. Then it shuddered, the carbonized skeletons of those who had been riding, or perhaps guiding, it falling away. It uttered another of those hideous screeches and started for them again.

"Gimme a fucking break!" Willis poked his head back up from ducking when Silaqui unleashed her lightning. He was still staring when a massive hammer of golden light slammed down on the spider's head. The chitin dented and the monster kept coming. Gelman stared at the lack of effect his spell had on the thing. "Shit on a fucking biscuit!!" The blast of both barrels of Aylie's shotgun shook him out of his shock.

He snapped the blast rifle to his shoulder, the slightly tacky material of the stock settling nicely into the pocket of his shoulder. His cheek fell perfectly into place, lining his eye up with the tube-like sight on top of the rifle. The horseshoe-shaped reticle inside it glowed with an eerie green light, but it wasn't really necessary. The *scope*, as Sachi called it, was full of nothing but monster. He centered the glowing green horseshoe on the thing's head and squeezed the trigger. He raised his head and stared at the weapon in shock when nothing happened.

"What the FUCK?!"

"Ye daft fool!" Aylie dropped the shotgun she'd been reloading, reaching over his arm and pushing a button on the side of the pistol grip. "Ye've the bleedin' safey thing stills on." A light flicked from green to red. "SHOOT THE BLEEDIN' BASTARD!!"

Willis snapped the rifle to his shoulder, got the barest of sight pictures and jerked the trigger. There was a thundering *whik-ka-BLAMM* and a blinding flash as the weapon pulsed a solid beam of plasma into the jungle. The beam burned a hole through tree trunks, grasses, vines, a hapless humanoid, and left a smoking hole forty-five feet deep in the soil of the rising slope of the jungle floor. Also in the path of the beam were the spider's four left legs. The beam burned them into floating ash. The creature collapsed to the sand with an ear-shattering screech. Its right legs flailed, pushing it toward the pile of driftwood.

Willis settled down and aimed again, centering the thing's head in the horseshoe. He could see the thing's eyes in the scope. *Great, another monster that has a personal beef with me. But not for long, shithead.* This time he carefully squeezed the trigger. The beam burned the spider's head to ash before punching a hole a foot across clean through the monster's body and into the jungle beyond it. The crash of the weapon echoed across the bay.

"Ye killed it!" Aylie yelled beside him. She grabbed him and spun him in a quick circle before landing a quick but thorough kiss directly on his mouth. "Oh, well done, me laddy-buck, well done indeed!"

None of them had a chance to even catch their breath when the *second* monster spider burst out of the jungle, rushing at them. It was only two or three hundred yards further to the north and significantly bigger than the first one. Faster as well, as it charged in a series of monstrous jumps. Willis tangled with Aylie as he tried to get the blast rifle around to shoot the thing before it killed them all. He heard a futile pair of musket shots from the beach behind him as Roland and Lodvar shot at the onrushing nightmare. *It's faster! It'll reach us before I can shoot it! No! No! NO!*

The blast from the edge of the water just north of the spider surprised everyone. There was no visible beam, but the spider simply exploded in a revolting shower of gore in mid-jump. The horse-sized head, separated from the ruptured body, bounced through their camp, flattening Willis' tent. The hideous mandibles clacked and thrashed for a few moments until the monster finally realized it was quite dead.

There was another shot from the water's edge, not a single blast this time, but a line of fire that raged down the tree line, turning four hundred feet of the edge of the jungle into smoking ashes. A few moments later, Sachi stalked into the firelight. Her clothes were soaked with the monster's ichor.

"What happened, Willis?" She reached over and carefully switched the safety back to safe on his rifle.

"Forgot the safety switch." He shrugged, glad the night hid his embarrassed blush. "Not something I'm used to thinking about. Any sign of anything else out there?"

"No. I killed the last of those little pricks with the poison darts with the strafe of the wood line." She stripped off the reeking shirt, dropping it next to the fire. Under it she wore only the skin-tight CLIBA armor shirt. As tight as the high-tech armor was, the visual effect was nearly the same as if she was nude from the waist up. "Well, that's ruined. Starting to run out of clothes that aren't filthy, bloodstained or full of holes."

"Uh, yeah." Gelman swallowed and looked away. So did Roland and Lodvar. Willis grinned at her in obvious appreciation before a glare from Silaqui had him turning away as well.

"I can help, with my magic, Sachi," the Elf offered.

"Thank you. But clothes are not my real concern."

"Oh?" Willis turned back toward her, ignoring glares from both Silaqui and Aylie. "More oversized pests?"

"Not really." She ran her hands through her hair, stripping out more ichor. "I expect the blast rifles sound enough like cannon fire that the pirates will have first, heard it and second, probably do something about it in the morning, if not sooner." She caught and held Willis' gaze. "What do we do if that frigate-sized galleon is standing into the bay in the morning with four or five hundred pirates looking for the ship they heard shooting cannons last night? Remember, we only have three total magazines for these things. Ten shots per magazine. We used a little over ten percent of all the ammunition we will ever have for these things. They need to be that emergency last resort weapon, not what we use first."

"Oh."

"Yeah, Willis. *Oh.*"

Port Plunder, Cazadora Isle, Southern Lanic Ocean November, 1478, Third Age of Imperial Reckoning

Distant thunder woke Sahla. Her skin literally twitched. She'd been uneasy all day. Back home, in the deep desert, she'd have thought a sirocco was rising, sand-laden wind strong enough to strip flesh from bone. She heard Zedekiah's breathing change pitch in the darkness and then his chain rattled as he stepped to the door and looked out. She got up and went to stand next to him in the doorway. Distantly, there came another muted roll of thunder, followed quickly by two more. She glanced upwards into a clear, star-filled night sky.

"That's not thunder, is it, Zedekiah?"

"No, Sahla. I think not; thunder from a clear sky can happen, but that sounded more like cannon fire." He was only a few inches taller than she was, so she didn't have to strain her neck to look him in the eyes.

"So, a ship then? Perhaps one needing repairs and thinking the bay is a safe place?" *He has nice eyes, warm and brown. Most of him is brown, his eyes, his hair, even his skin. Were he taller, he might remind me of Father. He's gentle, like Father was with me.* She tried to suppress a shiver, but he felt it anyway.

"You're cold, Sahla." His voice was low and quiet. "Take my blanket, such as it is." He started to offer her the tattered bit of sailcloth he called a blanket.

"No." She was quiet as well. "Can I just sit next to you?"

"The most beautiful girl I've ever seen asks if *she can just sit next to me?*" He kept his chuckle low. "Certainly, My Lady. Alas, I can offer neither fine furs, nor silks or satins as you deserve, but what meager things I have are yours for the asking." They sat side by side just inside the doorway.

"Do you think they used their cannons to drive away the monsters?" She shivered a little bit. He gently laid the sailcloth around her shoulders, and then placed his own arm in its ragged sleeve lightly around her shoulders, keeping his hand on her upper arm only. She scooted closer to him, grateful for the warmth of his body.

Draven and Zedekiah are both about halfway in love with me, or at least, they think they are. And poor, half-crazed Gabrielle seems to be more than a little in love with Zedekiah. And if I went home, told the truth of what has come to pass here, the Aliyah of the Prophet would condemn me to death, crushed by stones flung first by my own family, then by my tribe. No man has touched my maidenhead but the crime *of being* impure *has but one penalty. Even though the common folk have no duennas to shield their virtue. And how many nobles keep a harem of concubines only to slake their lusts? How many women find men other than their husbands in their conjugal bed and welcome that finding?*

"I don't know, Sahla. But look there. The lanterns in Ironheart's villa are being lit. I'll wager my ransom and half again that he's either heard the guns himself, or some sharp-eared watch has brought the word to him. *Deathdealer* will likely sail on the pre-dawn tide. And may the God of Iona have pity for those poor souls within the bay then. Perhaps being slain by the monsters, the *Dziungles gimtoji*, whatever they truly are, might not be the worst fate possible."

"I hate him. The Prophet will spit on his face when he comes before Chalta."

"Ironheart?"

"Of course. And the blond one, that sheep-humping Deuschen bastard son of a rotten ka'mel turd and a blind hog with diseased private parts. I would hang him face down by heels and thumbs and let rabid jackals and leprous *ghula* fight to be able to gnaw off the filthy, shit-crusted thing between his legs. Slowly."

"Remind me to never, ever get you truly mad at me." The vehemence in her sweet, soft voice startled him. *Well, she's reason to hate and the Sand-Folk of the deep desert are nothing if not good haters. Their emotions, good or bad, run strong and deep as the desert sands that form them. Need to change the subject.* "So, if Sahla could be anywhere in the world she wanted to be, where would she be?"

"I would be beside the One my Sire's Prophecy told of, the True Love of my life. A champion who will save the world entire. A champion who needs me, needs me to teach him that love is just as important as justice, or truth." She stopped suddenly and gave him a shy smile, barely visible in the dimness of the hut. "Silly, huh? Daydreams fit for a little girl." She paused, sapphire eyes dark as she stared into the night. "I can't go home, not back to Abdul-Ghaffanse. Nor to Sheikh Mustafa al-Mahdi Baddour, the First Son of the Rajh Mahdi al-Kohfan, Rajh of the Tribe of al-Kohfan, he who was to be my husband. I guess, were I free to choose, I should like to go to Kolbia. I've heard they are very free there and women may even walk public streets with neither shrouding abayah nor niqab veil."

"I've heard the same of Kolbia." He shrugged. "They are much like my homeland. Like Iona, they elect their rulers, and have no great noble families. And they always seek a better way to do things. Unusual people, unnatural some say. But a question to change the subject. Will you miss the one who was to be your husband? Sheikh Mustafa?"

"I know nothing of him, not in truth. Our wedding day would have likely been the first time I saw him. Why?"

"My clan has had dealings with his household and the villages he rules directly. He is not beloved. He is neither particularly fair nor foul in his countenance. But he desires to rule, badly, nearly desperately, some say. He is harsh and cruel, surrounding himself with mercenary guards hired from the Empire. And he is a regular buyer at the great slave market in Luctini, seeking toothsome young women for his harem. It has been said that their lives there are short and miserable."

"So." Sahla was silent for a long while as more lights were lit and the pirates began to stir. "Such as he sought my hand as First Wife before I was even of a woman's age. Perhaps it is just as well." Her voice was so soft that Zedekiah strained to hear what she said. "But why was the cost so high? Oh, Khalid, my hero. Najwa. I miss you both so." Then movement across the settlement drew her attention.

She saw the white-haired one, Werner, brought to Ironheart's quarters escorted by the tall, black bosun of *Deathdealer*. Shortly after, he left, white hair nearly glowing in the moonlight. He went straight to the beach, not even casting a single hate-filled look toward the hostages' hut. There he boarded a longboat that pulled strongly for *Deathdealer*. Other boats, full of half-awake pirates followed. The bosun watched the boats for a moment, then ducked back into Ironheart's cabin. She sat quietly beside Zedekiah as the pirate ship came to life, preparing to get under way.

"Are you okay, Sahla?" Zedekiah asked as *Deathdealer* curtsied to her anchor breaking free of the mud at the bottom of the cove. Sails were being sheeted to as the seaward wind began to rise. The sailors' chants could barely be heard as the pirates hauled away on the lines and sheets.

"They're in a hurry," she quietly observed. "They've run the sweeps out to row out of the cove." The eastern sky gleamed with the barest hints of the false dawn. The sun would rise on another day of misery within the next hour.

"You're avoiding my question, Sahla."

"I'm fine, well, as fine as I can be here." With a winsome smile, she shrugged. "Who knows? Mayhaps it is the Will of Chalta that brings me here in this time?"

For a long time, they simply sat there together, enjoying the warmth the rising sun brought with it. They drew apart when they saw the menials coming with their meager morning breakfast, escorted by Wrath again.

The redheaded witch said little as the food was ladled out. Zedekiah went back to help Gabrielle, who seemed better today.

But Wrath's attention was focused tightly on Sahla. She never said anything, just stared and tapped her green painted nails on the butt of Sahla's double barreled flintlock, thrust through her belt.

***

It was well after breakfast when it happened. *Deathdealer* had sailed nearly five hours earlier and with her big crew gone with her, the camp was relatively quiet and peaceful. It seemed to be laundry day as a number of the lower status pirates were washing and hanging clothes, or mending sails. Wrath had gone to Ironheart's villa and the woman was not quiet at all in the obvious throes of passion. Sahla listened carefully, her back to everyone in the hut as her face burned red with embarrassment. And not a little curiosity.

All of those simple, mundane things, washing clothes, fixing sails, making love, Zedekiah combing Gabrielle's blonde hair, all those stopped when a thundering, snapping, hissing, massive *KER-CRACK* shattered the relatively peaceful morning. Dust drifted down from the roof of the hut, and birds plunged to the ground, killed by the sound and the pressure. A line of pure, impossibly intense light tore the sky in half. The light stripped away all color, leaving dazzling afterimages of a white line nearly blinding everyone caught in the open. The light's intensity treated all but the solidest walls as no more than the barest obstacle. Sahla managed not to scream as the light tortured her eyes and thankfully, Gabrielle simply screamed once and passed out.

As soon as she could see a little bit, she carefully and cautiously went to the door, looking north where the light had been. Spots still danced in front of her eyes.

"The Prophet's Beard," she quietly swore. Smoke rose from the extreme northern end of the island and even from here, she could see steam rising from the ocean. With a sudden roar, a wall of wind suddenly lashed the camp, throwing loose things around, scattering the cook fires and knocking some off their feet. She felt Draven and Zedekiah come to the door behind her.

"What in God's Name was that?" Draven spoke first.

"No idea," she answered, watching men scramble around, trying to put out numerous small fires started by the scattered cook fires.

"I'm glad I was looking the other way," Zedekiah looked over his shoulder at Gabrielle, "and I can still see spots."

"Whatever it was, it either came from inside the bay or ended inside the bay. If *Deathdealer* was in the bay, there might be nothing left of her." Sahla turned away from the door. "And most of the pirates were aboard her."

Chapter Twenty-Two

**Central Bay, Cazadora Isle,
Southern Lanic Ocean
November, 1478, Third Age of Imperial Reckoning**

Dawn found them back inside *Constellation*. Immediately after the attack by the combination of the two gargantuan spiders and the small humanoids, they had broken camp and Sachi led all of them into the ship. With D.A.V.E. to guide her, leading the way to Graser Two-Six had been simple, if not easy. Now Sachi and Willis were again wrapped in the godlike awareness of the graser mount's on-board control systems. The others were waiting in something called the On-Mount Graser Section Two Crew Ready Room. Like the actual Two-Six weapon mount, that room had power, which meant fresh air. Or rather, they at least had breathable air.

"You were right, Sachi." Willis didn't really speak to her, seeing as both of them were sealed into the poly-whatever gel seats. He'd managed to stave off panic as the couch's gooey gel swarmed around him again. Even though he *knew* he was sealed in the compartment and sitting in the seat, his eyes told him he was standing on thin air, hundreds of feet above the wreck of the great starship. Sachi stood beside him in her white *shozoku* and *kamimaki*. She had pulled the mouth-scarf down and he could see her entire face. Her black eyes glittered with hundreds of dancing motes of light.

"About the interface getting easier, or that the pirates heard us and are coming to investigate?"

"Both, I guess."

"Well, be glad I've cut you out of the weapons system command and control interface. That stupid thing is making D.A.V.E. seem like a bloody genius. Only thing you'll have to do is concur with me on weapon lock and firing release."

"Okay, I can see the ship coming into the bay. With the wind and tide, they just sail right into the excellent natural harbor. They'd have Quan's own time to get back out, unless the wind backs completely around. How long?" A transparent red cone appeared in his view, the apex at *Constellation's* side and stretching away into the distance. It covered most of the bay.

"The red cone marks the graser's acceptable firing arc. I want to engage once the ship is in the middle of the northern side of the cone. If they get too far into the bay, the weapon will fire directly over the pirate's little settlement. D.A.V.E. tells me that there's a sixty some odd chance of the weapon's *beam corona* killing most of the people in the settlement. That doesn't exactly break my heart, but it'd also kill whatever hostages there are and, more importantly, either sink or set fire to the sloop we want."

"Sachi, how do you know all these things?"

"It's the machines, I think, Willis. And D.A.V.E. never really stops whispering in my mind, teaching me things, the things I would have known in the world before the Fall."

"You do realize that the fact of such things is more than a little disturbing, right?"

"Yes," she grinned at him, "how do you think it feels to be in my head?"

"I'll pass on that honor, thank you very much." Willis watched the ship coming into the bay under only her topgallants and outer jibsail. She was cleared for action; all her guns were manned and run out. She was currently laid on the port tack, close hauled against the landward breeze. "They're pretty sharp ship handlers, for pirates, that is."

"*Intrepid* would wreck her in an hour. Likely less."

"No doubt." He fiddled with the interface a bit, moving his point of view around the bay. "You have any idea how this is done?"

"No Willis, I don't." She was a bit short with him, concentrating on what she was doing. "Why don't you review the recording of the settlement from yesterday? Go take another look at it. Just shut up and quit pestering me."

"Aye-aye, Lieutenant Commander." He smiled to himself and asked the machine to show him the recording of the pirates' crude little village. The machine estimated that there were six hundred and thirty people in the settlement; this was before the galleon had sailed. Two people on the beach caught his attention, a man and a girl or perhaps a small woman. He was armed with sword and pistol, she wasn't, but even from the relatively poor *resolution* of the image, he sensed a nearly aggressive defiance from her.

Must be one of the hostages. Tiny little thing, if I understand the scale right. If she was a hostage, she showed no fear of the man. Something she said seemed to anger him and he raised his hand to strike her. She seemed to dare him to hit her, and even from his vantage point Willis could sense the fire in her sapphire blue eyes. *Can't really tell, but from here, WOOF, she might be as much of a beauty as Sachi! Okay, Willis, stop staring and start figuring out how the seven of us, one of those seven being a person we don't really trust, are going to sneak into the settlement over that rather impressive stockade wall, free the hostages and steal that sloop. Without getting killed by however many pirates there are in there. Hmm, they've let the brush get too thick in a couple of spots. Probably not enough cover for the big creepies, but plenty for those little bastards and their blowguns. Enough there to perhaps hide even Gelman in that armor of his.*

"Willis." Sachi's voice broke into his planning and observations of the settlement a little while later. "Going to pull you back into the main system. The ship's in the initial target plot. I have a lock and the system needs concurrence from both human operators."

"Uh, yeah, what?"

"Just concentrate on releasing what you've been doing and pull your awareness back to my systems."

"Got it." He marshaled his thoughts together and awareness of the current location of the ship and everything in the bay replaced the view of the settlement from yesterday. Their current view of the bay filled his awareness. "So, now what?"

"When asked, simply repeat what I say. All right?"

"Got it; repeat what you say when asked."

"Initiating weapon system firing lock." Sachi's voice was toneless, almost emotionless. "Target acquired and locked." The galleon, well within the northernmost portion of the weapon's aiming cone, pulsed with a scarlet ring of light around her.

"System power at sixty-two percent." A strange new voice spoke, flat and mechanized. "CIC query for weapons release initiated. Negative contact with CIC. Negative contact with Bridge. Negative contact with Auxiliary Control. Defaulting to on-mount SysOps Control. Concurrence with SysOps Prime and SysOps Secondary required. SysOps Prime, authorization?"

"SysOps Prime, weapon release authorized."

"SysOps Secondary, authorization?"

"Uh, SysOps Secondary, weapon release authorized."

"Weapon release authorization confirmed. SysOps Prime, target is locked, firing on your command."

"Confirm." Now there was a certain *coldness* to Sachi's metallic voice echoing in his mind. "Fire."

Willis always thought that the actual firing of the graser was anti-climatic. There was no roar of cannon, no choking cloud of gunsmoke. There was no sensation at all of the immense power it released. The actual weapon was slightly submerged in the side of the starship. Eons of encrusted sand and coral shattered away as the mount's protective cover opened and the emitter itself ran out and swiveled into firing position. The beam, composed of gamma rays focused and concentrated into a single ray by a four-hundred-centimeter gravitic 'lens,' didn't care in the least whether it fired through the vacuum of space or the water of Rybitha's oceans. It vaporized everything in its path, the water of the bay, the wood and iron and canvas of *Deathdealer* and the flesh of her crew with equal efficiency. The beam itself was invisible, but the air around was instantly superheated to over a thousand degrees Celsius and burned with a pure, white light.

The water temperature of the bay skyrocketed, steam rising from vaporized water closest to the beam, and still hot enough to boil water hundreds of yards away. The shock of the sudden temperature change killed thousands of fish in the bay. It punched through *Deathdealer* cleanly amidships, just below the main gundeck. The middle of the ship simply vanished, vaporized by the beam. The incandescent corona of the beam incinerated the entire crew, killing them before they could even scream. Canvas, rope and wood flashed into ashes and the detonation of the ship's powder magazine simply scattered the ashes. The fore topgallant masts and yards exploded away from the destruction. Blackened and burning, the fore topgallant masts and the leading twelve feet of her jibboom falling into the agitated waters of the bay were the only evidence that *Deathdealer* ever existed.

As it continued into space, the beam burned off all the vegetation on the northern end of the arm of the bay, slagging most of the beach sand into glass. It passed close enough over the open ocean on the north side of the island to temporarily boil the top three meters of water from the shoreline to a half-mile offshore. The brilliant white line of the weapon was seen over nearly the entirety of the Lietelean Empire and most of northern Darsälaam. In parts of the Muscovy Empire, the northern Murghol Empire and most of Han it was visible. It left the atmosphere over the islands of Isemoto, but only those awake in the night there saw the auroras it created.

Sachi and Willis stared in suppressed horror at what the beam had done. The northern end of the island was a smoking ruin, with nothing left that would actually burn. Thousands or perhaps tens of thousands of dead fish were floating to the surface of the bay, killed by the heat and pressure. Where they still stood, the jungle's trees shook and swayed in the turbulence the beam's blast and overpressure had created.

"My God." Willis was stunned. "What kind of war needs weapons like this?"

"One that can destroy worlds, I think, Willis." Sachi's subdued voice echoed in his mind. "And what is it going to ask of me?"

"Warning, system resources depleted." The metallic voice rudely intruded into their thoughts. "On-mount life support systems compromised. System power at two percent. Main Core Power Backup System non-functional. Main Core Power battery charge at three percent. Complete power failure imminent. Life support failure imminent. Complete system failure imminent."

::Lieutenant Commander Schmidt, I suggest immediately exiting the On-Mount Control room. Complete power failure is likely within the next four minutes and fifteen seconds, plus or minus forty-two seco— ::

"Yeah, got it." Sachi snarled, cutting off D.A.V.E.'s internal voice. "Willis, we've got to get moving. D.A.V.E., go ahead and cut the power to the couches so we can get out of here." They rolled to the deck as the polymer-nanite gel couches collapsed into grimy, sticky black powder as D.A.V.E. cut both power and computer support. The compartment was dimly lit with flickering red emergency lighting.

"Definitely time to go." Willis muttered as Sachi threw the manual release on the hatch. The passageway beyond the hatch yawned in complete blackness, an utter lack of light.

"I agree, getting out of here is going to be a damned pain in the butt. Let's get the others and get the hell out of this old tomb." Sachi led the way into the darkness of the ancient starship as its systems began to die.

***

Lodvar stared at the ruin of the bay. Fifteen or twenty miles away, the northern arm of the island, where it wrapped around the bay, still smoked and steamed. The shoreline was choked with dead fish. Of *Deathdealer*, a three-masted ship-rigged galleon a hundred and sixty-five feet long at the waterline, just over thirteen hundred tons displacement, of her, nothing remained. Escaping from the black depths of the ghost-haunted wreck of the crashed starship, stumbling through the darkness led by the Nisei girl and the voice in her head had been terrifying. And now these lunatics were planning on sneaking up on Ironheart's encampment, freeing the other hostages and stealing the lone remaining sloop.

Willis and Sachi interrogated him once they got back to the beach. The corpse of the giant spider, stinking and beginning to draw crabs and other scavengers, served to remind him of their lethality. Based on what they said the ship had shown them, he thought that Ironheart himself was still alive and in control at the settlement. And if he was there, the witch, Wrath, was certainly still there. Along with perhaps as many as a hundred pirates.

They're fuckin' insane. I'd not care to oppose them, but I'm neither Ironheart nor Wrath. Those two, 'specially Ironheart, will be two jumps ahead of this motley bunch. They'll do a fearsome amount of damage to Ironheart, but I've nay doubt who'll be standing atop things when the dust clears. And iffn he learnt that I'd helped these fools; well, I'll be back out on a stake, awaiting another monster spider to add me to its larder. And, no, I'll do anything to avoid that. Ironheart can damn well just kill me hisself. He helped the cook, Roland, nearly mechanically, simply doing as he was told. His attention was on the discussion of various plans to sneak up on the stockade wall and use the Nisei's white-steel swords to simply cut a hole in the stockade's sturdy logs. *They're insane, and they're all going to get killed or captured. But if I warn Ironheart they're coming, he'll be ready for them, and hopefully grateful enough to at least let me live. At this point, I don't care if he kills me, long as it's quick. I'll beggar myself to pay any ransom he wants. He might even be willing to allow me a spot on his crew. I know navigation and I have lots of contacts to sell swag to ashore. I'm worth more to him alive than dead.*

"Roland, give me a moment." He caught the cook's attention. "Nature is having its way with me. And I'd as soon not be dropping me breeches ta take a shit here where the ladies can see. I'll just step ta the edge 'o the woods there. Iffn you don't mind?"

"Non. Be off with ye." Roland turned back to the fish he was cleaning before adding it to the stew.

"Thankee." He casually headed toward the shattered tree the spider had burst through last night, loosening his belt as he went. The brown girl, Aylie, looked up at him, curious. He waved at his butt and pointed at the tree. She made a face and shook her head. Once he was out of sight, he re-tightened his belt and carefully, quietly, faked the signs of a struggle, using a broken limb to replicate a big spider's footprints. He swept out the rest of his footprints and headed toward the north side of the island as fast as he could, quietly at first, then running for all he was worth once he was far enough away.

***

"Where the hell is Lodvar?" Sachi snapped her head up and looked around. Roland nearly missed her bowl with his ladle of stew.

"He said his bowels did bother him. Wanted some privacy, he headed over to the broken tree." Roland shrugged as he handed her a mug of ale. "But t'was a good bit ago. Careful, this is the last keg of ale."

"Damn him." She set down bowl and mug, turning to stare at the tree, eyes glittering. "Shit. He's not there now." She popped to her feet, pulling her swords from their sheaths. The nannieball that had once been a detailed model of the *Constellation* was now her second butterfly sword. Both of them gleamed whitely in the afternoon sunlight. "Where'd that son of a bitch go? Aylie, grab the shotgun and come with me, please? Willis, just in case, ready a blast rifle, please?" Aylie set down her own bowl and snatched up the shotgun, checking its load as she followed Sachi.

"Damn pushy girl." Willis muttered under his breath, grinning despite himself. He quickly scooped the last bites from his bowl before picking up the blast rifle.

"What makes you say that, Willis?" Gelman shifted on his log seat to watch the two young women cautiously disappear into the edge of the jungle.

"She was about as non-assertive as possible, when we caught her as a stowaway on the *Intrepid*. She wanted to commit *seppuku*, ritual Nisei suicide, to *cleanse her honor*. And Captain Blaine's honor as well, at least from her point of view. She was terrified the captain would have her hung by the neck until dead, to her, an honorless, degrading death. When he wouldn't hang her and wouldn't let her kill herself, well, for the longest time, she was about the perfect ideal of the submissive Nisei woman. That started to change about the time we rescued Lady Silaqui from the pirates who'd held her captive for what, about two years, Si laqui?"

"About that." Silaqui's answer was short and brusque. She paused before continuing, "At first, it was *milady* this and *Kami* that. She didn't stop until I promised I'd turn her into a frog."

"Well, she's anything but submissive now, I'd say. I've rarely met a woman of any age as...forceful as she is." Gelman watched the two women come slowly back out of the jungle. "What changed?"

"Not sure. Lots of things, I think. She was about three quarters in love with Captain Blaine, and he with her, but Blaine's married, and the whole *oaths and honor* thing got in their way. Long, long story there and I don't know even half of it. That thing, the machine in her head, D.A.V.E., is likely part of it too. Someone keeps trying to kill her. And then she's got this whole *save the world destiny* thing hanging over her as well. It's a hell of a load for someone who is just barely twenty years old." Willis shrugged.

"And my patron, the Archangel of Healing, set me to follow her. *Keep her safe, guide her, heal her and defend her; for she is truly the last hope of the world.* His exact words."

"And you have, Pere, very well, I should say. Were more Kythal priests as you are, perhaps there would be less tension between my folk and yours." Silaqui caught Gelman's gaze with her jade eyes.

"Mayhaps. Yet I think between mortals and immortals, there will always be some tension."

"Mayhaps," she admitted, "but at least you're not such a priest as condemns all things that differ from his view of the world. As those in the Empire do."

"Certainly." Gelman shrugged as he drained his ale mug. "There are those, even in Montagar, who preach hellfire and damnation for Kolbia because of their *immoral lusts of the body.* I'll not speak of the practices of the Empire's clergy. Technically, the Church of Montagar still answers to the High Kythal in Lietelus the City. Technically."

"Good grief." Willis deactivated the blast rifle and set it down. "Why the hell should some cleric in Montagar get his robes all in a twist because of how we do things across the ocean?"

"Some say you have no morality, allowing men to marry other men or women to marry women. Or even allowing groups to marry as man and wife might. Even I find some of your nation's practices disturbing, Willis."

"What practices, Gelman?" Sachi stopped next to her previous seat, carefully setting down the blast rifle. "What's Willis done this time?"

"Willis, himself?" Gelman met her black eyes steadily. "He's done naught. But the practices of his folk, his nation...well, some say they lack morality, allowing men to lie with other men or women with women."

"Are you one such?" Sachi slowly sat down, picking up her cold bowl of stew.

"Nay, not specifically." Gelman looked mournfully into his empty ale mug. "I think it is not as the One God intends, nor as the Book teaches, but I am not one to condemn without more justification than whom one might choose as a spouse." He smiled as Roland refilled his mug. "Bless you, Roland. Now, Sachi, Aylie, I see you returned without our wayward acquaintance? What became of him?"

"I thinks he's back in the same pickle as we'd found him in. Look as if one of the beasties carried him off. Found the shovel he'd taken and lots of the creatures' round stumpy foot marks. Poor bastard." Aylie handed Roland her bowl for more stew.

"Huh," Willis grunted, "Sachi, you think something actually got him?"

"I don't know, Willis. Maybe." She absentmindedly dug into the stew. "And maybe not. It's just within the realm of possibility that he thinks he can sweet-talk the pirates into not killing him if he warns them about us. And that assumes he makes it through the jungle." She made a face and looked into her bowl. "Yuck. Cold fish stew."

"Give me that, ma'moiselle." Roland handed her a fresh bowl of hot stew. "'Tis nay hard to make plenty." He gestured at the piles of dead fish at the water's edge. "'Tis just getting one afore it starts to rot."

"Yeah." Sachi regarded her stew with a dubious frown.

Port Plunder, Cazadora Isle, Southern Lanic Ocean
November, 1478, Third Age of Imperial Reckoning

Ironheart glared down at Lodvar, stretched full length in the sand in front of him. Lodvar didn't have any choice about being in that position, with Ironheart's boot heel planted on the side of his head. His face wasn't buried in the sand and he could breathe without choking on sand. The captain quirked an eyebrow at Wrath. The witch shook her head and held her hands up, palms uppermost.

"That is one hell of a sea yarn you're spinning, Heimdägarran," the pirate growled. "There's shipwreck in the bay from before the Fire Fall? That was a *weapon* from that ship that burned the sky in half and destroyed *Deathdealer*? Burned away everything on the northern arm of the bay? Boiled the seas? One weapon? And a bunch of shipwrecked castaways are responsible?"

"Naught save the honest truth, my Lord!" Lodvar's voice was muffled and tinged with pain as Ironheart's boot pressed harder on his head.

"There is one thing of undoubted truth to his story, love." Wrath's voice was soft as she spoke up.

"Aye? And that would be what?" Ironheart's boot relaxed on Lodvar's head slightly.

"He's here. We know one of the bigger ones carried him away. No one gets out of a web without help. The littles would never in a thousand years take an 'offering' away from one of their hideous gods. Ever. So, *someone* had to have found him and cut him free. If they can survive the jungle, then find and free this worm, well, perhaps the rest of it isn't so far-fetched. We've known there's something strange in the bay for a long time, haven't we?"

"Aye, you've summat to that. But a, what'd he call it, a *starship*? From before the Fall? There's not enough grog in the whole world to make me believe that."

"Then what burned the sky this morning?" Wrath dropped her hands with a shrug. "No spell I've ever heard of could do so much damage. Only thing close that I've ever heard of would be in the legends of the Emperor Confas battling against Quan before the Fall."

"Ugh. A point. And?"

"What does it cost us to be ready for these castaways? If they're real, we can kill them or take them. He says one of them is nearly as beautiful as the Houri. And there's an Elf. One of them would bring a good price in Luctini, or you could give her to Sieur Palmaroli there. Distract him with the opportunity of torturing one of the Fair Folk to death? And a heretic priest from Montagar?

And all we have to do is be prepared tonight? If they don't come, then either they never existed or the locals killed them. Tomorrow morning, we board *Heartcutter* and sail for Luctini. And then we take our time feeding this one to the sharks."

"Hmm." Ironheart lifted his boot off Lodvar's head, squatting down and using the man's ragged blond hair to pull his face out of the sand. "So, Lodvar, how do you like Wrath's idea? And if you're wrong, I'll feed you to the sharks, slowly."

"'Tis a goodly idea, my Lord. And I'll gladly do my best to entertain you while the sharks play with me. Anything but those monsters in the jungle again."

"Well, then, you'd better hope your *rescuers* come tonight. Otherwise, we'll change your name."

"Change my name, my Lord?"

"Aye. For at least a while, your new name will be...Bait."

***

"Lodvar is back, Sahla." Draven Kye watched with both a certain amount of glee and just as much trepidation as Ironheart ground Lodvar's head into the dirt. "How did he survive the jungle?"

"Hush, Draven." Sahla shushed him. "I'm trying to hear what they're saying." Sahla crouched just inside the door of the hut, close to the ground, her hands cupped around her ear to catch what she could of the mostly one-sided conversation. *Please, oh please, spirits of my Sire's Element, sylphs of the Air, please, bring to me the words of mine enemies. Let me hear so that I might see them cast down before me. Please, help me just this little bit and I will give you sweets and juices, I beg you.* Finally, Ironheart removed his boot from Lodvar's head and *Deathdealer's* bosun hauled him away by his heels. She kept watch as the remaining pirate leaders, Ironheart and Wrath, *Deathdealer's* bosun, the first officer of *Heartcutter* and the female Aljannia from *Deathdealer* met in front of Ironheart's villa. She fought despair as the pirates drew lines in the sand before separating, calling what crew as were left. Obviously, they were laying a trap for whoever had rescued Lodvar.

The loss of *Deathdealer* left the pirates with an enormous problem. Sahla wasn't sure but she thought there might be only sixty odd pirates left in the settlement after the insanity that overwhelmed the majority of the remaining pirates that day. The sloop, *Heartcutter*, could be easily sailed by less than a dozen, but cramming over a hundred pirates aboard would be impossible.

Within an hour of the sky fire, a dozen fights broke out, some rushing to take the last few longboats and flee onboard *Heartcutter*. Bloody battles had raged on the beach. Some, terrified beyond any fear of Ironheart, wanted only to seize the sloop and flee. They fought among themselves to launch the longboats. Ironheart, his remaining officers and loyal crew had slaughtered every last one of the fleeing men. Not one made it to the sloop.

A group of a dozen challenged Ironheart's Captaincy. He effortlessly slew the first four in mostly fair duels, allowing for the advantage of his white-steel armor and magic cutlass. When the final eight attacked him as a group, Wrath intervened, immolating them with the emerald fire of her magic. There were no further quarrels over the leadership of the much-reduced band of pirates. The bloody struggles reduced the pirates' numbers even further. Even with the reduced numbers, the sloop would not be able to accommodate everyone. And so, the survivors still eyed each other suspiciously, wondering who might be left behind and who might escape this nightmare island. But Ironheart's control was undisputed.

With Wrath beside him, Ironheart came to the hostages' hut. There were nicks and scrapes on his arms and legs, a bloody bandage tied around his left bicep. Two of the biggest pirates followed him, armed with axes and pistols, wearing heavy chainmail shirts. Wrath's hand was wrapped with jade green flames.

"Move. Over there," Ironheart ordered the prisoners as the two pirates settled against the back wall of the hut in the darkest corner. "You stay over there and none of you will get hurt. Try to warn anyone foolish enough to try and rescue you and either Georg or Julius have my permission to separate your head from your body. And yes, Houri, that includes you."

"And neither of you get any ideas either!" he warned the two pirates. "Touch either of these women and I'll choke you to death with your own pricks, understood?" Both nodded solemnly. "You're here to keep an eye on our...financial assets, and kill any heroes who try to come in here to rescue our paydays. Got it?" Again, silent nods. He turned to the hostages. "Good. Now, if you four want to chatter, feel free. I hear you outside, well; there'll be less money to share. Understood?" Quick glances passed between Sahla, Draven and Zedekiah.

"We understand, pirate." Sahla's answer for them dripped disdain and scorn. Her sapphire eyes flashed defiance at him.

"And don't think you'll get off easy, with a quick death, girl. I'll give you to the crew and we'll see how many of them can fuck you before you die. And, yes, girl, it's possible to rape someone to death. Not at all a pleasant way to die, not at all. And then I'll toss your worthless corpse to the pigs. Think your Prophet will still let you into your Paradise after that?"

Her only answer was to spit on his boots.

Chapter Twenty-Three

**Port Plunder, Cazadora Isle,
Southern Lanic Ocean
November, 1478, Third Age of Imperial Reckoning**

SAHLA HUDDLED AGAINST THE far wall. The hostages' chains had been secured against the hut wall farthest from the stockade wall. And the chains were shortened and connected to a single heavy cable, an eight-inch-thick anchor cable taken from supplies intended for *Deathdealer*. Gabrielle crept up next to Sahla, silent tears creeping down her fair cheeks. Sahla pulled her tightly against her right side. Draven sat on Sahla's left, just barely touching her side. Zedekiah was to Gabrielle's right, his left arm loosely over her shoulder. His hand gently ran through her blonde locks.

"So, what do you think the light in the sky was, Draven?" She kept her voice low and soft. "Could that have been some new weapon of your people's Navy?"

"That would be nice, wouldn't it?" Draven's white teeth gleamed in the dimness of the hut.

"And who was it that Lodvar spoke of, Kolbian Marines?"

"I wish, Sahla." He rubbed the fair stubble on his face that wasn't quite long enough to be called a beard. "But no. Whatever it was that made that light is as far above a thirty-two pounder as I am above a worm. And Lodvar would have never escaped Kolbian Marines. And Marine Scouts are ghosts. No one sees them if they don't want to be seen."

"Be quiet, Sahla. The light was the Finger of God," Gabrielle barely whispered. "He judges the wicked and burns them with holy fire." She was actually a few years older than Sahla but she had only in the last day or so recovered enough to begin speaking in coherent sentences. "Do not draw his notice or he shall judge us." She shivered hard enough that her teeth clattered together.

"Shush, Gabrielle. Be at peace." Zedekiah massaged her shoulder. "It was just one of those things that fall from the sky sometimes. If God would judge the wicked, shouldn't he start with Ironheart? It was just a rock falling from the sky, a shooting star that reached the earth. It destroyed everything in the bay."

"You think so? Even with what I told you of what I overheard of Lodvar's tale to Ironheart?" Sahla twined a lock of her hair through her fingers. "The strange castaways, the ancient wreck of a sky-ship in the bay? Lodvar, at least, believed what he said. And he managed to convince Ironheart and Wrath of his belief." She turned her attention to Gabrielle with a warm smile. *She was a royal pain in the posterior onboard* Chalta's Grace, *but she has been near broken to mindlessness by fear and shock. Only now does she begin to recover. She is older than I, but my heart pities the poor woman. I'll not make it worse for her.* "Gabrielle, even should your God bring you before his Throne to be judged, 'tis my belief that he should find you blameless and welcome you into His Heaven. This mortal life might end, but you have naught to fear of any afterlife." She wrapped an arm around the blonde and held her tightly.

"And what of you, Sahla?" Zedekiah's eyes were dark. "Will your Prophet hold open the door to Chalta's Paradise for you?"

"I think so. But I do not think the Prophet will lead me to stand before Chalta's radiant glory anytime soon."

"Why not, Sahla?" Draven asked.

"It will be my eighteenth birthing day soon. Next week in fact. And before then, it was prophesied that my life would change and I should find the true purpose of my life. My Sire prophesied that my life would only be completed by True Love."

"Really?" Zedekiah snorted. "You think the handsome prince is coming on his white charger to rescue you and take you away to his castle to be his One True Love? Oh, please! Be serious."

"You don't believe in True Love, Zedekiah?" She smiled at him for a moment.

"No. Fancy tales and heroes who rescue maidens from the proverbial *fate worse than death?* Love at first sight?" He shook his head. "I thought you more sensible than that."

"Sorry, Sahla, but I gotta agree with Zedekiah on this one. God helps those that help themselves first. True Love is fine for a little girl's stories of magic and heroes, but it isn't the real world."

"Truly?" Sahla's eyes were coy and her lips curved in a knowing smile. "You both think you know all things? Men! Neither of you truly know aught of me, so hold your judgments of what my life might bring in the futu..."

With no warning whatsoever, the blacksmith's hut and lean-to, visible through the open doorway, simply exploded with a thundering *whik-ka-BLAMM!* A dozen pirates had lain in wait there for the expected attackers, but now the smith's hut and forge scattered across the sand. Mixed in with the shattered anvils, twisted forge tools and charred timbers were the burnt and bloody bits and pieces of those men.

Sahla happened to have her eyes on the two guards when the explosion rocked the night. A long, slender, white-steel blade thrust cleanly through each man's stomach. The twin blades ripped upwards, splitting both men in twain from waist to shoulder in a revolting shower of gore. Neither of them even had a chance to scream as they died.

As the ruptured bodies fell to the sand floor of the hut, the white blades, now stained red, slashed to the top of the wall of the hut. One blade flashed high, one low and a shoulder smashed the loose section of wall down on top of the corpses. Much later, Sahla remembered being grateful that the broken pieces of the wall covered most of the two pirates' butchered bodies.

A lithe figure clad from head to toe in mottled, dark grayish-black hurtled across the bodies and rolled to its knees in the middle of the hut. With a start of surprise, Sahla realized that the person in black was female. Her head and most of her face were covered by a strange hood, but the tightly tied black jacket was taut over substantial breasts. She froze for a bare instant as *Deathdealer's* bosun screamed "FIRE!" in the darkness. A volley of musket fire crashed out, balls punching holes in the hut walls. There was an instant answer from whatever weapon was splitting the night with fire and thunder and more pirates' bodies pattered to the sand in burning pieces.

The woman turned her face to the hostages and for the barest instant she locked eyes with Sahla and froze. All Sahla could see were her eyes, everything else was covered by the hood. But those eyes were black as midnight and hundreds of star-like lights danced inside the iris and pupil.

"Akarui ao iro no me." The voice was low and throaty, exotic. Sahla had no idea what she said.

Ironheart's voice roared outside, rallying his men. The black-eyed woman's head snapped around. She bolted across the hut, the swords flashing as she cut away the cable and chains before slashing another hole in the wall. For a heartbeat, she paused, snapping a glance back at the hostages, before looking back out the hole she had just made.

"I don't have time for this! Not now!" This time she spoke in Terranglais. She crouched down, coiling herself before lunging out the hole with blinding speed.

Sahla kicked loose of the cable and chain, darting to the door of the hut to see where the woman in black had gone. A blast of emerald fire lit sky and jungle. She skidded to a stop and stared in shock. On the sand, Wrath was embroiled in a mage-duel with an Aljannia clad in eye-searing shades of scarlet and a man in the robes of a Kythal priest. Emerald flames lanced between them and the Aljannia effortlessly flicked Wrath's magic aside, laughing as she did so. Crimson lightnings leapt across the gap, clawing at the spherical shield Wrath flung up to protect herself. The priest shouted and a massive but insubstantial golden hammer crashed down on Wrath's shield. It held, somehow, but Sahla could sense Wrath's growing desperation.

"Not that way!" she muttered to herself, turning away from the mage duel and back to the second hole the black-eyed woman had cut. Most of the hut's front wall had collapsed and she could easily see the fight taking place there. "Beard of the Prophet!"

A dozen dead and dying pirates littered the sand. The woman's swords were blurs of white. Limbs and heads flew away as her relentless charge closed on Ironheart. Another volley crashed out from Ironheart's cottage. The balls whickered by overhead and bits of the thatching drifted down. Sahla hit the dirt. One of those musket balls sent a single strand of her long black hair floating gently to the sand. Vaguely, she saw a man in a long blue coat pop up from behind a log, strange hand-muskets firing again and again. Pirates tumbled as they struggled to reload their muskets. The man ducked out of sight and then snapped up in a different spot, those strange weapons firing over and over again, without a choking cloud of gunsmoke. She dimly was aware that there was someone else in the clumps of trees, cutting pirates down from behind.

"SIAA—YAI!" The woman charging Ironheart screamed as she leapt toward him. They crashed together and her momentum knocked Ironheart flat. He rolled away from her swords, lunging to his feet as the woman kicked up her legs and flipped herself upright. Magical cutlass flashed against white-steel swords. One blow got through his guard, but his white-steel armor turned the cut. Her other sword ripped open his left arm, just above the elbow, blood sheeting down his arm. Sahla saw a thrust of the cutlass stab deep into her leg, midway between knee and hip. The black leg of her pants was suddenly sodden with blood. Almost by mutual consent, they drew apart for a moment.

"You're damn good, girl. But nothing can penetrate white-steel." Ironheart panted heavily, a grim smile on his face.

"Enough of this, pirate." The woman cocked her head and stared at Ironheart. "This ends now. And so do you."

What happened next left Sahla doubting both her eyes and her sanity. The left hand white-steel sword simply melted away, flowing like gluey mud into a glove covering her left hand from fingers to elbow. With another shout, she lunged at Ironheart. Magical cutlass and unbreakable sword locked as she braced him, corps-a-corps. Ironheart tried to overbear her, but she effortlessly held him back. Her left hand shot out and slapped against his armor.

"HAI! MINE!" she cried. The armor simply melted away, absorbed somehow by the glove of flexible white-steel on her hand.

"NO!" Ironheart screamed as he thrust her back. "THAT'S NOT POSSIBLE!" His blade slid up her own sword, thrusting point first into her chest, the bloody point bursting out the back of her grey-black jacket. She grunted in pain, folding over his blade. But now her sword was free, with his trapped in her body, and the white-steel flashed like lightning. One cut passed effortlessly through his body, just barely above his hips. She reversed the blade and cut upwards, from just below his right flank, crosswise on his torso to exit midway between left shoulder and his neck.

Ironheart didn't truly have time to realize he was dead before his corpse slid apart into three gruesome pieces, blood and burst organs splashing onto the sand in a horrific shower. Sahla retched and spewed up everything left in her stomach at the ghastly sight. She coughed and managed not to choke. Then she realized that the black-eyed woman was going to die also.

The mortally wounded woman landed in a crouch, one knee on the sand, white gloved left hand thrust forward. Her right hand with the white-steel sword was flung out in a dancer's pose. Ironheart's cutlass jutted out her back. The second sword flowed into a bracer covering her entire forearm. Slowly she drew the cutlass from her body, dropping it to the sand. She looked around her and suddenly locked eyes with Sahla where she crouched in the hut.

She should be dead. The flare and blast of the magical duel faded into the remote background. The gunfire and screams of combat became no more than fog. For Sahla, the entire battle faded into unreality as she lay there, enraptured by those star-filled, night-black eyes. She fell into them, tumbling into the depths of the woman's soul. The Bond formed, binding them tightly together on the very deepest level. *Finally, at last! What I have waited my life entire for! My Bond, a true Bond, one soul deep!* Ecstasy and exultation flooded through Sahla. Then the black eyes closed as the dying woman gasped for breath in desperate gulps. She coughed and sprayed blood. Sahla scrabbled out of the hut and flew across the blood-wracked sand to her side.

Just as she reached her, the woman coughed again, more blood spraying across the sand, before collapsing onto her face. The fires and moonlight revealed a darker, wet stain spreading across the back of her odd black jacket like a raven's wings.

"No, no, NO...NO! YOU CAN'T DIE! Not now! Not when I just found you! Don't you *dare*!" Sahla gently rolled her over onto her back. "Please, no, please, oh Prophet of my People, Chalta's grace, please, no, don't take her away, I just found her!" The front of the jacket was soaked in blood. She couldn't sort out the strange ties and she simply ripped them loose. Under the jacket was an odd, skin-tight...shirt? There was no seam, or tie or button and it was too tight to be pulled over her head. It felt like thick, heavy, almost oily silk. And there was a bloody tear in the middle of it. Ironheart's cutlass had struck cleanly between her breasts, just to the left side a bit.

"Daave..." she muttered, muffled by her facemask. Her eyelids fluttered open for an instant. Stars danced in the blackness of her eyes.

Sahla yanked on the neckline of the shirt and suddenly an invisible seam opened down the front of it. She gently pulled the sides of the shirt away. Between her breasts, directly over her heart, was a bloody, gaping hole, blood bubbling wetly as it welled up in the wound, running down her side to puddle in the sand. Sahla felt it soak the knees of her ragged sailor's pants. She gently pulled away the concealing hood and facemask. A wealth of sable hair spilled loose, as black as Sahla's own ebon tresses.

"Chalta!" Sahla swore. "She's barely older than I am! Maybe younger!" She looked at the mortal wound over her heart. "How can she still breathe? The blade surely pieced straight through her heart!" *She should have been dead when she hit the ground! Oh, Chalta's Grace, how can this be?* Fresh blood pooled around the wound. Her breathing was labored and shallow, but she was still breathing. Sahla laid her fingers along the great vein of her neck and felt a faint but steady pulse. "What magic is this?" She looked closely at the wound and realized it was slowly closing, mending and sealing itself. "Beard of the Prophet! What is she that she heals mortal wounds?"

Darkness suddenly loomed above her and she looked up to see *Deathdealer's* huge bosun raise his great axe. She threw herself across the young woman's body, protecting it with her own. There was a deafening *ba-blamm* behind him. Flesh and blood sprayed from a hole as big as her fist in the middle of the bosun's chest. He staggered away a half step. The axe tumbled away as he thudded to his knees and fell next to Ironheart's butchered corpse.

"Bloody persistent bastard, that one. Had ta shoot him twice." A slender, dark-skinned girl stepped out of the shadows, a smoking, double-barreled musket held in her hands. "Oh, bloody hell! Willis! Willis, Gelman, hurry, Sachi be down, hurt badly!" she shouted as she ran to them. She stopped a few feet away, a look of horror on her face. "Oh, God be blessed, no, that canna be possible. Sachi canna die! No!"

"Ah, SHIT!" The man in the long blue coat slid to a stop next to them on his knees in the sand. "Goddamn it, Sachi, this better be something D.A.V.E. can fix! Gelman, get your butt over here, NOW!" Holsters on both hips and under both arms held the strange hand muskets. A sleek, gleaming black musket-like thing was slung over his back. He grabbed Sahla's shoulder and wrenched her away. She struggled briefly until the muzzle of one of those very strange hand-muskets appeared in front of her nose. She froze. "Who the hell are you?"

"I am Sahla, *Sayyid*." She folded onto her knees, bowing and laying her forehead on the churned sand. "I am...was a captive of the pirates. She freed us when she passed through our hut, cutting away our chains, *Sayyid*." She kept her voice low and soft, meek and non-threatening. The Kythal priest came clanking up, his armor announcing his arrival.

"Sachi! Angels and saints preserve us!" He dropped to his knees next to the comatose young woman. "Get out of my way, damn you all!" He shoved the man in the blue coat and Sahla away. "Give me room to work, by the Circled Cross!" He quickly and expertly examined the wound. "Her chest is pierced, broken ribs; the blade either punctured or cut the lung, from the aspiration of the blood. How did the blade miss her heart? What's keeping her alive?"

"Who knows? D.A.V.E. would be my guess, but think," the man in blue answered, "it's Sachi, six impossible things before breakfast, remember?" He stood up, his hand on Sahla's shoulder gently drawing her up with him. "Let's give Gelman room to work, what say? And keep those hands where I can see them, all right?"

"Hear me, O' My God." The priest set his hand directly over the bloody wound on her chest, his other hand raising his wooden holy symbol, the Circled Cross of the One God as he prayed. "Manifest thy will through me, your unworthy agent in this Fallen World. Lend unto me the powers of *Angaelici Benes Eloi*, Archangel of Healing, whose power shall restore this woman to vitality and health in order to carry on with her quest..." A white gloved hand reached up and interrupted his chanted spell.

"Save your magic, Pere, for someone who actually needs it." Sahla stared in amazement as she slowly sat up. "Damn, that really hurts. Someone might have told me that *fuketsuna banzoku* bastard pirate wore nanite armor. And had a damned magic sword." She gently shook her head before moving into a cross-legged sitting position. She pulled the strange, tight shirt closed and ran her thumb up the seam, sealing it. She reached over and picked up her jacket. "Well, my *himaku* is ruined. What a mess." She dropped the bloody jacket on the sand, looking up at Sahla. "And who are you, *Mishiranu bijo*?" The black eyes no longer glittered.

"What does that mean, *Mishiranu bijo*?" Sahla stared as the woman stood. She was tall, fully as tall as her Father, perhaps a bit taller.

"It means *Lovely Stranger*, which certainly fits from what I can see of you under all the dirt. And again, who are you?"

"I am Sahla, Mistress. I am a Jann. We are Bonded by the Bond of Master to Slave." Sahla's face lit with a beautiful smile as she knelt and bowed to her Mistress. *Oh, this is so* right, *so wonderful. Finally, I feel the flow of my Sire's Blood, awakening my own powers. And there will be so much* more *between us, I can almost see it, this Bond is so powerful, rich and full. Oh, blessed Prophet, thank you for bringing me here.* Bowed with her head to the sand, she missed the expression of shock that crossed Sachi's face.

"What...did you just...say?" Sachi's harsh voice was a splash of ice water on Sahla's bliss. "Wait, just wait. Silaqui, where'd that witch go?"

"Not sure, Sachi." The Aljannia sorceress stalked up to the fire. Clad all in red, she was the tallest person there, by an inch or so. Sahla sat back on her heels, confused by the black-eyed woman's cool, almost cold response to her declaration of the Bond. "For a human, she's damned strong, but not strong enough to stand against both me and Gelman. She fled when you killed the pirate captain. Some kind of a very clever contingency magic. She's better than I expected but if she tries to face me again, I'll put her head on a pike and stretch her hide out on the barn door."

"Well, damn." Sachi picked up her bloody jacket and mournfully regarded the holes and tears in it. "I doubt this is worth salvaging. It's about the last of the clothing I brought with me from Isemoto." She shrugged and tossed it away.

"Mistress, I can fix it for you, if you wish." Sahla stretched over and grabbed the discarded jacket. "With the Bond, I have access to the powers of my Sire's Bloodline. It would be a simple task."

"Who's this?" The Aljannia turned to Sahla with a smile that suddenly died as her eyes widened and the gems tattooed over her left eyebrow flared to life. "Ainaera's blessings, who...no, *what* are you?! *Ddal a therian!* By my Will, Be thou Still!" Crimson magic wrapped around Sahla, pinning her in place. "And now they're using magical elementals to try and kill you, Sachi?! What passes here?"

"Magical elementals?" Sachi was as confused as anyone.

"*KILL HER!? Are you mad, Aljannia?* She is my Mistress; none shall harm her, save they pass me first! And I have my own magics!" Azure power flamed against Silaqui's scarlet magic. Sahla spun on one toe, and flung her arms out. A cerulean wave blasted Silaqui's spell away in tatters. The elemental magic picked Silaqui up and hurled her half a dozen yards away, heels over head. The rest of them tumbled away as well. Everyone except Sachi; the magic passed over her like a cool blue wave of clear ocean water. Sahla darted to place herself between Sachi and everyone else. "I may not have my blades, but I *shall* protect my Mistress!"

Silaqui erupted out of the sand, shock and fury on her face, crimson and scarlet flames forming a nimbus of fire around her. Willis and Aylie dived for cover behind a large tree trunk. Gelman rolled over and clambered to his feet, shaking sand from his robes.

"*QUIESCAT!*" He raised his Circled Cross an instant before his mace slammed into the sand. A golden wall erupted from the sand, separating Silaqui and Sahla. "STOP THIS! NOW!" His voice roared loud enough to rattle the few trees still standing.

All three of them, Sachi, Sahla and Silaqui stared at him in shock as golden light haloed him. The golden light left the slightest impression that a being of light with vast, angelic pinions stood behind him. Strands of arcane magic, sapphire and scarlet, faded away as Sahla and Silaqui felt their power slip relentlessly from their grasp. Sachi wondered where the somewhat grumpy and dour but normally gentle man had gone, replaced by this powerful priest, wielding the raw power of his faith.

"That is quite enough, young ladies! And this time, I'm including you too, Silaqui. We are friends and allies here and quarreling will earn us only the derisive and divisive laughter of Quan from the burning depths of the Seven Hells. So, loose your grasp on your magics. Am I quite clearly understood, then?"

Sahla looked over her shoulder at Sachi. The Nisei girl had a wry smile on her face, one that faded as she met Sahla's sapphire eyes.

"I'm not the one throwing magic around, Gelman. These two are, Silaqui and this stranger. What's your name, again?"

"I am Sahla, Mistress. We are Bonded together, Master and Slave, at least for now." Sahla dropped to her knees, picking up Sachi's torn jacket. "How might I serve you, Mistress?"

"You're *what?*" Sachi snapped.

"Master and Slave?" Silaqui shook her head in sudden realization. "Oh, no."

"What the hell is going on here?" Willis muttered to Aylie, who simply held her palms up and shrugged.

"Enough." Gelman's voice stopped everyone. "Sahla, right?"

"Yes."

"Tell me, no, tell us, exactly what is going on here? What are you? What do you mean by *bonded together, master and slave, at least for now?*"

"Do you wish me to tell him, Mistress?" she asked Sachi, who stepped back in surprise.

"Why do you ask me for permission?"

"You are my Mistress. I obey your will."

"Oh, no." They could hear the growing panic in Sachi's voice. "No, I'm no one's Mistress, I'll have no part of any *Bond* that enslaves someone. Never!"

"Peace, Sachi." Gelman spoke up. "Tell, no, *ask* her to answer my questions, gently now, gently."

"No, I'll have nothing to do with it, Gelman."

"Now's not the time for stubbornness, my friend." Gelman's voice was cool and soothing. "Simply nod yes and that will tell her to answer my questions."

Frowning, Sachi managed a single jerky nod, her entire body tense and her fists clenched.

"Now, let's try this again. Will you answer my questions, my dear?"

"Since my Mistress wishes, yes." Sahla flung a thick lock of hair back over her shoulder. "I am Sahla al Qasim ab Ghaffanse, blood-daughter of Ilben alh-Taymyah, Jinni of the Second Rank of Air and Wind. My birth-mother is Haipha Alimah ab Mu'azzaz ibn Sayyidah, who is wed to Sheikh Hasim al Murafte of the Tribe of Abdul-Ghaffanse of the Folk of Darsälaam. I am the First Daughter of my Father, Sheikh Hasim. I am half Jinni, a Jann born of the mortal world and a Prince of Elemental Air. Before my eighteenth birthday, I must find and bond to a mortal human of this world; else I shall be drawn to my noble Sire's Elemental Plane of Air. There I should be of little account and less power. I could be given as a plaything to the first powerful Jinni my Sire might be forced to please, will he or nil he. I might be taken in conflict with the Efreeti. The Efreeti hate the Jinni and especially the rare Jann. Should I fall into their grasp, they would feed on the power of my magic and thusly devour my very soul. I would much rather remain here, My Lord Priest, in this fair mortal world that I love." She granted him a smile that made him seriously reconsider his vocation. "Of my own free will, I grant my Bond to My Lady Sachi. She needs me. And with her, I know the First Bond, of Master to Slave, will rest on me as light as the Hand of Chalta upon the back of a devout holy man."

"I see." Gelman cringed as Sachi exploded in rage.

"NO!" Sachi screamed, "*Zettai chigau! Jigoku de masaka!* I will NEVER be any part of enslaving anyone, for any reason. *Chigau! Dorei nanka shoyusha ni naru ki ga mattaku nai!* I *WILL NOT* STAND FOR IT! I WILL NEVER OWN A SLAVE, NO MATTER WHAT! NOT EVEN A MAGICAL

ONE!" Sachi's fists clenched as she shook in rage. She spun on her heel and stormed off toward the waterline, screaming in nearly incoherent Nisei. A white-steel blade snapped out and neatly severed Ironheart's head. She kicked it hard enough that it splashed into the cove's blue waters, a dozen yards from shore.

"Great. Just fucking great." Willis' command voice snapped from where he sat on the trunk. "Silaqui, Gelman, go with her, *try* to calm her down before she blows something *else* up. Like that sloop anchored off-shore. We *need* that ship!" The pair looked at each other, sighing, as they set off after Sachi, still screaming at the top of her lungs. He turned to Aylie. "Aylie, I know there are three or four more hostages over in that hut. Make sure they're out of the chains and see if they'll be willing to help. Make sure you point out that we need their help to get off this damn island. And there's a few pirates stumbling around still, the ones that broke and ran into the jungle. The creepies might get them. Might not. And if they don't wind up in a web, they'll likely be back. Keep your eyes ope n."

"Aye, Willis."

"Okay, now you, Sahla, right?"

"Yes, Lord."

"Don't call me Lord. Name's Willis. Lieutenant Commander Fleet if you really need to be formal. I prefer Willis, here and now." He pointed at a spot on the tree trunk. "Come over here and sit down, young lady. Let me explain a few things to you as best as I can, anyways. And you can tell me how you wound up here as well."

***

"Sounds like you've been through a lot, for someone not quite eighteen yet." A couple of hours later, Willis sipped tea out of a dented tin cup. Roland, with no real skills in combat, had stayed out of the fight. With the battle over, he'd quickly organized the remaining hostages and a couple of young men who'd been trapped serving as crew slaves for the pirates. Gelman, returned from defusing the unexploded Sachi, had used his abilities to determine the truth of their tales. Aylie was helping Roland set up at least a make-shift camp and cook-fire. Draven and Zedekiah worked together to erect sailcloth shelters for the night. Gabrielle, blue eyes still wide in amazement, huddled beside the fire, feeding the occasional stick into it as needed.

"I miss my people, my friends who died. Najwa, my duenna. Khalid, my childhood friend who always wanted to find himself as a hero in my eyes." Sahla was careful to always keep her head below his. She spread her loose sailor's pants and tunic carefully, and kept a worn piece of sailcloth about her as a cloak, giving Willis no hint of her body's shape. She would give no enticement whatever to these strange folk, especially the males. She could, at times, see her Mistress where she stalked back and forth along the waterline, conversing with the Aljannia sorceress. She yearned to be near her Mistress. There was as much that this man, this Willis Fleet had ca refully *not* said as there was that he had said.

"*A hero in your eyes*. Yeah, I can see that."

"I do not understand these other things, other worlds beyond the sky, great ships that fly among the stars, weapons of pure light. Mechanical ghosts of those who lived before the Fall. Machines that think as a man does, machines so tiny they cannot be seen. These are seemingly nothing but fancy tales of time before the Fall." She was careful to never fully meet his eyes, keep as much of her face in shadow as she could. "And my Mistress has a *destiny* in all of this, a destiny to save the world?"

"Yeah, I know." He chuckled quietly. "Sounds ridiculous when you put it that way, doesn't it?"

"No." She captured his eyes with her own, looking him full in the face for a long moment. "I dreamt, once, not very long ago at all, of a woman with black eyes on a great ship sailing a sea of stars. She was beautiful and had black, glittering eyes. There was an Aljannia, clad all in red with green hair. A priest of the One God.

A small, dark woman with quick hands. A man in a blue coat, with a ready smile and a strange jezail. A tall man, whose coal black hair had strands of silver in it, he stood at the wheel of the ship." She watched his eyes widen. "I believe it was a true dream, Willis Fleet. Chalta and His Prophet have brought me here for a reason."

"That's a scary dream."

"No, the scary ones were where the monsters outside the stockade tore Lodvar's head off and threw it back over the wall. The head grew legs and chased me with poison dripping fangs." She shuddered a moment. "That dream, of the black-eyed woman, that dream was the Prophet showing me my path. I know, I think, what I must do."

"Oh?"

"Yes, *oh.*" She broke their eye contact.

"And what is it you must do, then?" Willis swallowed hard. *I thought Sachi was the most beautiful woman I'd ever seen. And now I think I was wrong. But there's a difference. Sachi has that promise in her, a sensual promise to her, that bedding her would be incredible. This girl, Sahla, doesn't have any of that. There's a...purity to her. God, that sounds so idiotic in my own head. Maybe it's the way they were raised, one an assassin and prostitute, the other a mostly sheltered princess of the strict ways of the desert folk. Damn if I know.*

"There must be more between us, my Mistress and I. The Bond of Master and Slave will be only temporary, I believe. Only enough to keep my hold on this mortal world. There will be other, deeper Bonds, in due time, I think." The slow, happy smile on her face transformed it. "I finally understand my Sire and my Mother. Such as I, a Jann, half of this mortal world, half of the insubstantial world of the Elementals, I could only have been born of a true Bond of Love."

"Uh, er, hmm, yeah. What's that got to do with you and Sachi?" Willis couldn't help but stare. He swallowed hard again.

"Despite everything else, Sachi needs to find something, something she badly needs. Something I've always wanted to find in my own life."

"And what is that, Sahla?"

"Willis, all my life I have sought something, I didn't know what, I thought of it as someone to be a hero in my eyes. And like me, she needs to find a hero, even if she doesn't realize it."

"So?"

"So, could it be possible, that each of us, we each are the hero the other needs to find?"

Epilogue

**Port Plunder, Cazadora Isle,
Southern Lanic Ocean
29 November, 1478, Third Age of Imperial Reckoning**

She stood in the edge of the jungle, green eyes hard as she watched the sloop lean into its canvas. There was a stiff offshore wind and already white foam curled at the ship's cutwater. She wondered if her magic would suffice to wreck them from here. *But no, that bitch-elf sorceress and that* proklyatyy klirik *both know I didn't die. They'll be expecting something. And then there's the real wild card, the Houri. I had no idea she could wield elemental magics. If only I knew what she truly is, well. If wishes were troikas, serfs would have three feast days a week. But they'll have a limited choice of where they can go. I know the navigational charts burned when Ironheart's cabin exploded.*

Wrath sighed and turned back to the burned and scattered remains of Ironheart's dream.

"You wish aught, Mistress?" the pathetic thing that followed her asked. She spun and smashed a fist into his face, knocking him flat.

"You speak only when spoken to, thrall." Green fire smoked on her finger. "Open your mouth again and I'll burn out your tongue, *ponimat*? Annoy me further and I'll leave you here, on this accursed island. You know what that will mean!"

The tall man groveled on his face in the dirt, hands held over his head in supplication. Indistinct sounds were just barely audible above the noise of the surf. She pulled her magic back within herself. She tapped his shoulder with the toe of her boot.

"Come, follow me. I must comb through the wreckage to find my grimoire. Make yourself useful or else." She turned and strode away. The man staggered to his feet and stumbled after her, blue eyes wide with dread of what he knew lurked in the jungle. None of his employers or fellow merchant factors would have ever recognized Lodvar Gjerde in the terrified wreckage of a man that shuffled along behind the witch.

The Armed Sloop *Graser*,
Southern Lanic Ocean
2 December, 1478, Third Age of Imperial Reckoning

"Glad to be back at sea, Sachi?" Silaqui leaned on the starboard rail. Laid on the starboard tack, spray sometimes flew high enough to dampen the sorceress' green hair.

"Yes." The answer was curt, nearly snappish. Sachi braced her back against the cathead, unhappy tension in every line of her body. She wore an ill-fitting tunic and breeches dug out of the sloop's onboard slops chest. Her amulet still fit snugly around her neck but now there was a slightly longer chain of fine gold there as well. An enormous sapphire dangled from it, perfect in all appearance, resting on her collarbone. White-steel bracers covered both forearms from knuckles to elbow. "Now, go away."

"I thought, two days away from that island, you'd be a bit more cheerful."

"I'm not. *She* will hardly leave me alone. *She's* fixed *all* my clothes, even the old rags my kimonos had become. Good as new."

"Well, that's a handy skill."

"She used her magic."

"I could have done the same."

"Yes, you could have. But if you do, it's because *you* chose to do so. *She* does it to make her Mistress happy."

"And you're obviously not happy, are you?"

"What do you think, *Kami*?" She growled in frustration.

"I can tell. But think about this, my heart-sister. Sahla told me her birthday was three days ago. She is eighteen years of age now. Were she not bound to you, I believe the pact between her parents she told us of would have, in fact, pulled her away from our mortal world. And her life there might well be short and miserable. And it is not in your nature to harm one who only wishes you well."

Sachi only grumbled in response.

"Sahla is sweet and biddable. She desires only to please you and make you happy. And she has eyes of sapphire blue."

"You've told me all about your dream. And it seems she had the same dream. *Akarui ao iro no me*, eyes of sapphire. It was a dream, Silaqui, no more."

"You are not normally so thick-skulled, heart-sister. She is devoted to you, asking nothing in return...other than perhaps your attention. I believe she will be as fierce as a lion of the sands in your defense, as you have been in mine."

"She says she's my slave, Silaqui. That's wrong and you know it! I will have nothing to do with making or keeping anyone a slave! Not even if it is some magical bondage that ties her to me!"

"You are not usually so short-sighted, sister. Sahla herself has spoken of other Bonds. She has said the Bond of Master and Slave can be superseded by other Bonds."

"Oh, yes, now you get to it." The Nisei snorted. "*True Love*. I'm much too old for fancy tales where the handsome samurai on his noble mount sweeps the rescued maiden from her feet and they ride away to live *happily ever after!*" Her scorn should have stripped the paint from the deck.

"Why not? Why should you not love her? Is it because she is female?"

"Please. That matters no more to me than it would to any Kolbian."

"Then what is the problem? In the Horn Islands, that one day, you were neither shy nor hesitant of making love with me. And that, I think, given what I know of her folk, that maybe more of a problem for her."

"That was then, Silaqui. And it was only the pleasures of love-play."

"So?"

"So, if this girl should sacrifice herself in this dream, she would do it because of love, because...she loves me enough to maybe die for me. No. I reject that. I am broken inside, Silaqui. You know this. Sex, yes, why not, it is just physical pleasure, but love is more. And I am not worthy of anyone's love. And certainly not worthy of this fantasy you call True Love!"

"Sachi, your destiny, what I have dreamt of, what Sahla dreamt of, and even what that thing, that machine, in your head speaks of, a destiny to save the world...heart-sister, can you really be willing to perhaps sacrifice your very life, if you truly are so damaged in your heart that you can truly not love anyone? What greater act of love can there possibly be?"

"I don't know, Silaqui." Sachi's voice was barely a whisper the Elf had to strain to hear. "And that is what scares me."

The End of Book Two:
To Find a Hero.

Author's Notes

Sᴀᴄʜɪ's sᴛᴏʀʏ ᴄᴏɴᴛɪɴᴜᴇs ᴀs she sets out to claim her mysterious destiny. And we get to watch Sahla al Qasim ab Ghaffanse grow into a beautiful young woman. The fate of the world of Rybithia will hang on these two young ladies.

Sahla is my own creation whereas the other main characters were inspired by one or another of the old Saturday Night Gang.

This is the second book in what I expect to be a five book series. To Find a Hero is planned to be released in early January, 2025. Book three is expected to be released in time for LibertyCon 2025. Book three is about halfway complete and should go to Chromosphere Press in late January or early February.

Lots of folks have helped me along the way. LOTS. To Find a Hero wouldn't exist without that help. Character ideas, beta reading, editing, whew, it's a list.

First and foremost is my publisher and editor, Stephanie Osborn. She is the first to give me a chance. Without her knowledge and expertise, I'd still be vainly floundering around, wondering what to do next. Stephanie is just awesome, both as editor and publisher. She kept me on track and on target. She's the best and I'm lucky to be able to call her a great friend as well.

Lt. Col (USA, ret,) Jon Holland handed me advice and guidance on all things military.

WO4(USA) Veena Copeland did early editing and had great suggestions on the story.

The Saturday Night Gang: Troy Logsdon, my 'brother from another mother'; Louis Nicoulin III, Tom Herp, and Kristy Kannapel. These folks gave me inspiration for major characters.

Fellow author Lydia Sherrer critiqued early versions of To Find a Hero. I owe her a lot.

Baen's Bar. Many of the Barflies provided critique and feedback, making this a very different story than I originally conceived. To Find a Hero first saw the light of day there.

Last and most important is my lovely wife of 31 years, Kae Thompson. She helped me create Sachi from whole cloth and provided the love and support needed to finish this novel.

~A. G. Thompson
Louisville KY
September, 2024

About the Author

Reared on a West Texas ranch, A.G. Thompson is a veteran of the US Air Force, having served during the Cold War and earned the rank of Staff Sergeant. He has Bachelor of Arts degrees in both English Literature and History from the University of Louisville.

Tony has been a competition shooter for around a decade, is an avid reader (as most authors are), and is extremely knowledgeable in military history, especially as regards World War II action; he has been known to use this knowledge in game-mastering exciting tabletop wargames.

He is currently a 28-year employee of UPS, a devoted cat-person with several fourfoots in his household, and has been married for the last 30 years to his wonderful wife, Kae Thompson.